RAISED IN CAPTIVITY

A novel by

Marty Thompson Arnold

Illustrations by Marty Thompson Arnold

Cover art and book design by Paul Arnold

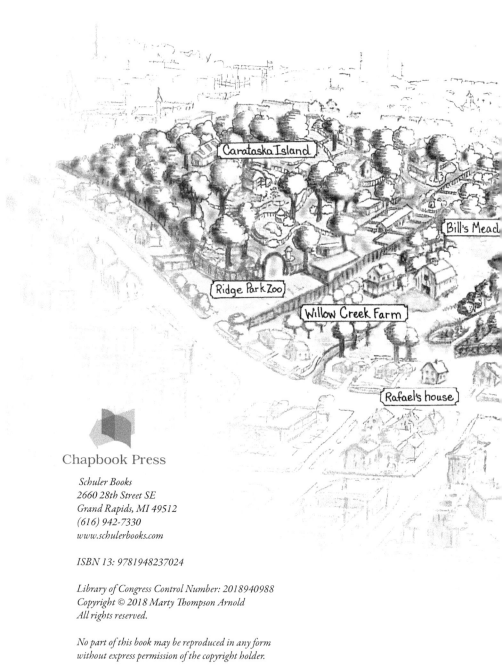

Chapbook Press

Schuler Books
2660 28th Street SE
Grand Rapids, MI 49512
(616) 942-7330
www.schulerbooks.com

ISBN 13: 9781948237024

Library of Congress Control Number: 2018940988
Copyright © 2018 Marty Thompson Arnold
All rights reserved.

No part of this book may be reproduced in any form
without express permission of the copyright holder.

Printed in the United States by Chapbook Press.

Saskawan, Michigan

Overlook

Stoddard Gypsum

for Paul, my matching piece

PROLOGUE

When people from Saskawan, Michigan explain where they're from, they raise their right hand, palm out.

"Right here," they say, pointing to a spot just below the knuckle of their ring finger.

Not everyone gets this.

"*You* know—" they prompt, "Michigan's shaped like a *mitten*?"

Michiganders, in fact, pity those from amorphously shaped states like Maryland and Hawaii without a handy visual aide.

Like many American towns, the name Saskawan has both Native American and French origins. In 1810, a French-Canadian named Etienne St. Pierre paddled up a river from the east shore of Lake Michigan with a canoe full of goods to trade for fur pelts. Several days in, a half mile cascade obstructed his way. Etienne decided this natural portage would make an excellent spot for a trading post. So, he set up camp and began selling birch bark, pine gum, muskets, blankets, hatchets, needles, kettles, mirrors, linen shirts and tobacco to anyone who came his way.

Wondering what to name his enterprise, Monsieur St. Pierre asked an Ojibwa hunting party the name of the place. Pointing at the ground, he grunted in rudimentary Ojibwa, "What name this?" Thinking he meant the ankle-deep mud, they answered, "*A-zhash-kii-wan*" or, "It is mud."

Etienne liked the ring of this and painted Asasquewan Trading Post over his cabin door, giving the spelling a French twist. Only a few years passed before settlers from New England shortened it to "Saskawan."

This tri-lingual game of telephone resulted in dozens of barely pronounceable Michigan place names: Kalamazoo (boiling pot), Mackinac (big turtle), Ishpeming (on high) and Saugatuck (place by the river). The Upper Peninsula town of Ontonagon is said to mean, "There goes my dish!" after an ill-fated washing incident at the riverbank.

To this day, the Ojibwa citizens of Saskawan are split over whether to be offended or amused by their town's name. Some say white folks butchered the Mother Tongue as surely as they butchered the buffalo and the passenger pigeon. Others just enjoy sweet revenge at the Saskawan Casino—which some Indians still call "the Mudville Club."

1
SILENCE

Wednesday, June 8

Something watched her as she stood barefoot at the open upstairs window. Before she could find her glasses on the nightstand it darted into the barn. It was there now, somewhere in the dark interior.

Iris was used to an audience. Chickadees flitted overhead as she filled the feeder with sunflower seed. The woodchuck watched her from under the woodpile as she tossed kitchen scraps on the compost heap. But on this morning, someone or something new was out there. She could feel it in the silence.

She wasn't sure what had awakened her—the absence of sound or the shattering of it when the crows voiced their outrage. The house wren had stopped chattering beside his little cedar house in the dogwood. The blue jays were not declaring their general superiority as they did every other morning. Even the fierce little red squirrel had retreated into her knothole in the maple. Everyone seemed to have left the yard to the crows—and whatever was lurking in the barn.

Curious, Iris thought.

Listening was the first task of her day. The soothing sounds of a warm June morning, as familiar as her own breath, were daily affirmations that the planet had made another successful turn on its axis, and that she, Iris Walker VanWingen of Willow Creek Farm in Saskawan, Michigan, had been carried along with it.

At eighty-four, this was a blessing.

She pressed her forehead to the glass to get a better look at the crows' tangled nest in the white pine. Perhaps a feral cat or an owl had made off with one of their hatchlings.

With eyes fixed on the barn, she slipped off her nightgown and reached for her clothes on the back of the rocker. She hooked her bra in front, twisted it around and lifted the straps onto her broad shoulders.

One of the crows was on the barn roof now, cocking its head to peer with one eye, then the other, into a hole in the shingles.

"The roof's rotted through," she announced to the dog standing in the bedroom doorway. "Bill'd be surprised it lasted this long." Zelda, her black Labrador of questionable pedigree, whined a morning greeting, glad to finally be noticed.

Iris slipped into a faded denim skirt and one of Bill's button-up plaid shirts. She ran her fingers through her thick silver hair, twisting it into a loose bun and securing it with hairpins from the china dish on the dresser.

This morning ritual was performed with the inattention of a woman used to being alone and giving no thought to how others might judge her appearance or find it wanting. When people admired her abundant hair, she only sighed, "Yes, well, I have more than my share." She would have dismissed, too, any idea that her chin was strong, that her arched brows were striking or that her steel-blue eyes possessed special powers that made two generations of high school students squirm in their seats.

The door of the weathered barn stood wide open, its sliding mechanism rusted in place long ago. The crows were taking turns now, swooping down for a look and looping upward to land with quick hop-hops on the mossy shingles.

"If they stomp any harder they'll cave it in," she said to Zelda, who was now on the second and third steps of the stairway.

Downstairs in the kitchen, Iris opened the back door and watched Zelda charge down the porch steps and cross the driveway to squat in the tall grass. Under the apple tree by the garden gate, the bird feeder lay in pieces. Iris clucked in annoyance.

A less rational mind might suspect that the farm was possessed lately, or perhaps cursed. Two weeks ago, her watering can disappeared then materialized a few days later on the porch *right* where she'd left it. (Unless, of course, she'd walked by it a dozen times without seeing it, which meant it was *she*, not the farm, that was possessed.) Something was making her tomato plants turn a sickly yellow, too. And there was that ridiculous incident with the car. She was certain she had at least half a tank in the station wagon that day in the grocery parking lot. The bag boy who drove her to the gas station treated her like a doddering old fool. That was a bother and a humiliation she didn't want repeated.

Effects without apparent causes? There were always explanations for unexplained phenomena if you used your head. For pity sakes, watering cans don't just sprout legs and wander off.

And now, something was in the barn. *Strange doings,* she thought. Between sips of coffee and bites of a hard-boiled egg at the open screen door, she continued her surveillance of the yard.

Zelda had finished her business and stood on the gravel drive tipping her muzzle up once, twice, three times like a compass point. Then she dropped her nose to the ground to follow a scent in circles around the yard. Iris noted this piece of data.

She stepped into a pair of flattened moccasins by the kitchen door and opened the screen door, nearly losing her footing on slurry of coffee grounds, eggs shells and cantaloupe pulp.

"Damn!" she said, catching herself on the door jamb. The compost bucket lay on its side against the porch railing. This was the second time this week.

One of the crows let out a high-pitched, *Aw-Aw.* At the top of the porch steps she cupped her eyes to look up. "What's in the barn, Junior?"

She was quite certain this individual was one of last year's fledglings. A few years ago, this crow family set up housekeeping in the white pine behind the house. Junior was the spitting image of his parents now, but his excitability betrayed his youth. This summer he was being tutored in the finer points of parenting at his parents' nest—an admirable familial arrangement in Iris' opinion. His assignment this morning was, apparently, to guard the nest from whatever was now in the barn. And by the looks of it, he was taking his work very seriously.

Zelda circled around the station wagon parked in the gravel, but stopped dead at the barn door. Then she returned to the porch with an impressive neck-to-tail mohawk.

"What's in there, girl?"

Several of Iris' newly potted geraniums and tomatoes were knocked off the barn windowsills and lay scattered on the ground. She sighed irritably. "Must be that boy," she sputtered. A dark haired boy of nine or so had been skulking around all week. When she called out to him, he had bounded into the woods like a scared rabbit.

"He's a strange one," she said. *Probably eating a fistful of my strawberries in the hayloft right now,* she thought. Although that didn't explain the crows' agitation, Zelda's mohawk or the fact that her strawberries were still green. *Scrap that hypothesis.*

She took the corn broom from its place by the kitchen door and went into the yard. Zelda sat down on the top step of the porch and whined.

"Some watchdog *you* are," Iris sniffed as she started across the yard. Above her, the crow family was perched wing-to-wing in the walnut tree. They too had gone silent. She knew they were gathering for a family confab. Today's topic: whatever had slipped, slithered or darted into her barn.

She turned to address her audience. "You're a bunch of cowards. Every last one of you."

She leaned into the open doorway.

"Who's in there?" she demanded of the darkness.

Silence.

Sunlight sliced through the cracks in the siding, making swirling constellations of the dust motes. She made out a rake lying tines-up on the dirt floor, an overturned apple crate and a trail of half-eaten watermelon rinds leading to the hayloft ladder.

Herbivore or omnivore, Iris thought, feeling some relief. Then, aiming the business end of her broom into darkness, she announced to the silent multitude, "Wish me luck. I'm goin' in!"

2

REMNANTS

1865-2014

When the tractor died, the chicken coop collapsed and the cottonwood toppled into the garden, Iris' husband Bill began calling the old place "Wither Crank Fart."

Willow Creek Farm wasn't even a farm really—just a remnant of the hundred and fifty acres the Walker family had worked for generations. The "Walker girls," Iris and her sister Lillian, toiled right alongside their parents, selling fruit, maple syrup, jams and pies at a stand at the end of the long driveway. Between customers, they cut paper dolls and read *Nancy Drew*.

After dinner, they'd lie on their pink and white chenille bedspreads and look at *Life Magazine* photos of bread lines, bombed out cities or GIs charging up Omaha Beach. These troubles seemed to exist on another planet—far from Saskawan, Michigan.

Her parents, of course, knew better. They bought war bonds and saved scrap metal to be made into airplanes and tanks. And they worked the farm. Everything—new school clothes, Girl Scout dues and democracy itself—depended on the harvest. Crates of Empire, Russet and Jonathan apples and Red Haven and Garnet Beauty peaches were shipped all over the Midwest from August right through to October. Some were shipped overseas to feed the troops.

"Just think, Iris," Lillian said, contemplating a plump red and yellow Jonathan, "this apple might be eaten in a foxhole."

"Not with that bite out of it," Iris said, giving one of Lillian's thick, honey-blond braids a yank. She was proud of her family's part in building America's great arsenal of democracy.

At the New Netherlands Christian Reformed Church, when they were supposed to be praying for the orphaned German and Japanese children, Iris crossed her fingers so God wouldn't get confused about which side He should be on. Each night at dinner, when their mother thanked God and Jesus for "This, Thy bounty," Iris suspected her father was thanking the farm's rich soil, prime location and their own hard labor, but on matters of religion he was generally silent.

Willow Creek Farm was situated on the buckle of Michigan's legendary fruit belt which stretched up the western coast of the state. Iris' great-grandparents, Marita and Thomas Walker, had discovered this through trial and error. In 1865, they left Connecticut for Wisconsin with a wagon load of hope and milk cans full of apple saplings. But after years of failed harvests, they conceded that the lush green hills of Wisconsin were better suited to fur-covered dairy cows than apple trees.

On a trip to the general store in Madison, Marita saw crates of apples marked "Fruitport, Michigan." She ordered a Michigan map at the post office and she and Thomas studied it for weeks. Even the place names, Fruit Ridge, Peach Ridge and Paw Paw, seemed to advertise a fruit-growing Promised Land. The Walkers sold their farm, and with their savings sewn into the hem of Marita's petticoats, they headed east around the bottom of Lake Michigan.

It was spring and the hills around Benton Harbor were a haze of pink peach blossoms as far as the eye could see. They pulled up at a big, square farmhouse and asked how far it was to the best apple-growing land. The tall farmer with a singsong Dutch accent laid their map on the porch floor and circled a spot with his finger.

"I tink if ya wan'ta grow gut apples, dare's da spot." He tapped three times on a place fifty miles further north. "Da *Ridge*. Ya. Dat's wot day call it up dare."

The Ridge, an area eight miles wide and twenty miles from top to bottom, pushed up like a potbelly a hundred feet above Lake Michigan and twenty miles inland. This location protected fruit trees from nature's lethal one-two punch of an early spring thaw followed by a late killing frost. The lake's warm breezes brought ample summer rain and stretched the apple harvest well into October.

Marita and Thomas Walker found land for sale on the eastern edge of the Ridge, just three miles west of the riverfront village of Saskawan. The town had a Methodist church and a schoolhouse not a mile down the road. Marita declared it perfect.

They set about building a one-room cabin with a lean-to for their ox team, Nip and Tuck. All winter, Thomas cleared timber from the hills. In the spring, his logs floated downriver to be milled and shipped to Chicago where the Great Fire of 1871 had created an insatiable market for Michigan timber.

Nip and Tuck pulled stumps and were rewarded with a two-story barn with real stalls, room for a milk cow and plenty of storage for fruit crates. The tall hip roof would hold enough hay to feed the livestock through the long, snowy West Michigan winters.

Early in the second spring, the Walkers planted ten acres of apple and peach saplings and two parallel rows of sugar maples on each side of their long driveway.

With lumber he'd set aside, Thomas started work on a three-bedroom house which he and Marita would eventually fill with two sons and three daughters. Years later, for their twenty-fifth anniversary, Thomas built a deep, wrap-around porch trimmed in lacy white gingerbread.

The Walkers worked the farm well into their sixties. Their daughters married and moved away. Their younger son went north to grow cherries. The eldest, Thomas Junior, began seeing a pretty, blue-eyed Dutch girl named Hermine. Her Old World accent and strict Calvinist views worried the elder Walkers, but their son was smitten. Hermine would make Tom an efficient, hard-working wife, despite being exceedingly God-fearing and humorless. The couple's only son, Joseph, married another Dutch beauty, Peitrenella or "Nella" (Iris' mother) in 1929. She turned out to be her mother-in-law's equal in every respect.

Three generations of Walkers tended the orchards and cut back the forest until the family had seventy-five acres in fruit production. Each generation experimented with new varieties that promised to ripen earlier, keep longer or be more resistant to disease. Willow Creek Farm survived apple rust, peach fire blight, the heat wave of 1936, the Great Depression and two world wars. But when real trouble came, no one recognized it until it was too late.

After the war, when Iris was in high school, the city of Saskawan annexed Ridge Township around the farm. The city offered Joe and Nella a shocking sum for twenty acres, including their west meadow with its small spring-fed pond for a city park. (The sudden windfall sent Nella into a guilt-induced depression that didn't let up until she made a large donation to the building fund of the New Netherlands Christian Reformed Church.)

Next came the developers. In 1948, they offered the Walkers more money than they could have made in a lifetime of fruit growing for a strip of land along Russet Ridge Drive and forty acres north of Willow Creek. When the dust settled, the farm had shrunk to just twenty acres with a narrow panhandle connecting it to the street.

Iris and Lillian protested bitterly, but their parents said simply, "We have debts," and left it at that.

Iris dreamed of studying agriculture at Michigan State University in East Lansing, but at her father's urging, she switched to biology. After graduation, she taught science at Saskawan Central High School where she met a young English teacher named Bill VanWingen. They were married the following year.

Joe and Nella gave Iris and Bill the farmhouse as a wedding gift and moved into one of the modern tract houses at the end of the driveway. Iris and Bill had two daughters, Annie and Cindy, the fifth generation to grow up on the farm.

Iris stayed at Central High for forty-four years, determined to inject some basic understanding of the universe into her students and, in time, her students' children. On field trips to the farm, her sophomores tramped over the hills collecting leaves. Her AP Science students identified trillium, hepatica and marsh marigold in her ravine. Two of her former students became botanists. One became a marine biologist who supervised the cleanup of the Gulf oil spill of 2010. Another was making nature documentaries for the BBC. A few sent Christmas cards or stopped by when they were in town.

Bill was promoted to principal, then assistant superintendent. During the summer Iris raised produce for her own daughters to sell at the fruit stand. Sometimes she hired her students to pick fruit, but each year the trees produced less and less and there was no money to prune them. Despite this, working the land fed something in Iris. Bill always said he could gauge her mood by the amount of dirt under her nails.

He, on the other hand, tolerated farm chores only if he had his Walkman to listen to. He promised to make the farm a higher priority when he retired. This turned out to be the only promise he'd ever broken. Just before his seventy-fifth birthday, he collapsed in the barn. In the hospital three days later, his heart just stopped.

Bill had been right—the farm was withering away. But Iris was unable to think of it as anything less than an ailing family member in need of care. This land had raised her as much as her parents had. Now, with Bill gone and the family scattered, the land had no one but her.

During a recent phone call with her daughter Annie, Iris complained about her neighbors.

"They think my ravine is a dump. They throw grass clippings, old Christmas trees and dead plants over the fences. It's unbelievable!"

"It'll rot eventually." She could hear Annie's shrug all the way from North Carolina.

"But they leave *tinsel* on the trees and some of the plants are still in their plastic pots! First the developers flattened my hills, filled in my valleys, cut the trees and made a real mess of things, now the homeowners smother everything with sod and fertilizer and put up fences to keep out—I don't *know* what—the *woods*, I guess. The other day I heard a mother scream at her daughter, 'Come out of that woods now, Tiffany! And don't touch *anything*, it might be poison!'"

Annie laughed. "Cindy and I practically *lived* in that ravine."

"Kids around here don't even climb trees anymore. They have plastic 'play spaces' that protect them from every imaginable injury."

Annie laughed again. "You'd be shocked by some of the stuff Cin and I did."

Iris sniffed. "Try me."

"Um, okay. I'll tell you the *third* worst thing we did. Cin's going to kill me. Okay. You know that chain link fence around the mine? Well, there was a gap where the creek ran under it. I made Cindy crawl under it and touch one of the big trees. I was sure she'd fall in a sinkhole and get buried alive, but it was *so* worth the thrill."

Any child who grew up in the Ridge neighborhood of Saskawan feared the property over the Stoddard Gypsum Mine. The forested hills that bordered Willow Creek Farm to the east were rumored to hide sinkholes capable of swallowing naughty children. Between the barbed wire and chain link fence and plenty of warning signs, everybody—with the apparent exception of Iris' own daughters—pretty much stayed away.

Iris frowned. "Why on *earth*—?"

"Blackmail. I threatened to tell you and Dad that she drove the tractor when you were at school. Oops, I just told you the second worst thing."

"Your Aunt Lillian and I almost ran away with the circus," Iris said, with a touch of one-upmanship.

"You did not. You just sneaked out to watch it."

"Your Grandma Nella was sure the circus was the work of Lucifer himself."

Annie sighed and laughed in the same breath. "So, I still haven't succeeded in shocking you? I feel like such a *failure*, Mother."

"I was always more concerned about what that mine was dumping into Willow Creek. But, if it'll make you feel better, you're officially grounded—until menopause."

"Ha! Too late."

"It's sad though, really," Iris said absently.

"What's sad?"

"House-bound children who never get to do anything daring like you did."

"Mm," Annie said in agreement. "They probably don't even know what a double-dog dare *is*."

"Exactly! They inhabit a world with no sharp objects."

"You're right, Mom," said Annie, sounding suddenly tired. "You're right. It's a sorry state of affairs."

Iris smiled into the phone. Getting others to share her indignation always boosted her spirits.

"But you're never going to change your neighbors, you know. I wish you could just relax and enjoy what you have."

Iris stifled the "humph" that wanted to come out. Last Christmas the girls had sent her *Knitting for Dummies* with three balls of red yarn and a set of needles—a gift that would go down in her book as the most ill-conceived *ever*. And recently, her daughters' calls were more frequent, which made her suspect she was being checked-up on. It was maddening.

"You're lucky to still have twenty acres right in town, you know," Annie pointed out.

There it was again, Annie's unsinkable optimism, which she got from her father. It was like a rubber band snapping back into place. Her daughter's pep talk hadn't helped.

"It isn't just my *human* neighbors, you know," Iris said. "I have to put up with all that pitiful bellowing and carrying on at that zoo. The place stinks, too. To think people *pay* to see wild animals pace back and forth in their own excrement!"

"We went to the zoo in Asheboro last year. They don't keep animals in cages anymore."

"So lions roam the streets of Asheboro, do they?"

Annie sighed again. "Of course not, but—"

"Then, I *still* don't think much of zoos."

For some, Willow Creek Farm was a curiosity. Dog walkers and bikers wandered up the long, gravel driveway and finding her in the yard, would say, "I always wondered what was up here." Or, "Great old barn. Did this used to be a farm?"

But recently there were others—men with briefcases driving shiny red pickups—who figured they'd take the farm off an old lady's hands. For decades, developers ignored the deep ravine behind the house. But nowadays, they saw its potential for "upscale wooded home sites."

"Let me quote you a price," they'd say. "You could retire some place real nice if you sell while the market is up." Eventually, they'd drive off, judging the elderly farm widow to be senile, hard-of-hearing or both.

"Have there been any firm offers, Mom?" Cindy, her other daughter, had asked when it was her turn to call.

"Who cares? I'm *not* selling."

"You could get an appraisal at least," Cindy suggested. "Just to see." She had also suggested, more than once, that Iris move to a retirement community near her in Austin. "Good developers are respectful of the land these days. They won't just level everything."

Iris caught the inevitability of "won't." She sighed. "They think I'm just waiting for a free ride to the nursing home. I told them, 'Over my dead body!' Funny, huh, at my age?" She didn't mention that a pair of them had come back three times and been so persistent and slimy that she finally put up a No Trespassing sign at the end of the driveway.

"Look, Mom," Cindy breathed into the phone. "I love the farm. You know I do. But you're almost eighty-five. What if you fell down the stairs or got hurt in the barn? What about one of those pendants with a call button?"

"Cynthia Joan!"

"Okay, okay. But please, Mom, just think about the future."

But that was the problem. She *was* thinking about it. The vultures were circling. Before her ashes were cold, they'd bulldoze the house, the barn, the orchard, the meadow and her garden—and she couldn't think of one way to stop them.

3
VELOCITY

Wednesday, June 8

Caroline Finch hit the brakes halfway into her parking space and just a hair short of the chrome-plated exhaust pipe of Kirby's Harley-Davidson. She backed up and tried again, slower this time. She was as wound up as an overachiever on report card day.

She killed the engine and gave herself a three-breath timeout. *One*, she exhaled slowly. The adrenaline needed to pull off her first fundraiser was still pumping through her veins—and the twelve-ounce café Americano she was working on wasn't helping. *Twoooo*. She needed to go for a run after work. It had been over a week. *Threeee*. She should do some yoga, too. She rolled her head to the right and heard a crack. *Ow!*

She inspected her chestnut ponytail in the rear-view mirror and threaded it through her dark-green baseball cap with its black and white zebra logo. She smoothed the collar of her matching green zoo polo shirt. Then she stepped out into the employee parking lot of Ridge Park Zoo in Saskawan, Michigan.

Peter, the staff veterinarian, waved from across the lot.

"Hey, Peter," Caroline called out. She set her travel mug on the car roof and opened the rear door.

"Nice event last night," he said, stopping to wait for her. With his full, white beard and ruddy complexion, he looked like Santa's kid brother and had the personality to match.

"Thanks! I thought it went rather well," she said, gathering her laptop case, purse and sweater from the back seat.

"There were a lot of new faces," he said. "That has to be a good sign."

"Hope so. And by the way, thanks for mingling with the guests, Peter." Not everyone on the staff was so comfortable talking to donors. "So you *really* think it went well?" She had one knee on the back seat and was struggling to unwedge a box of campaign flyers from the floor.

"Here. Let me," Peter said. His rapport with animals extended to anxious, newbie co-workers in need of assistance. He bent over the heavy box and came up grinning. "Actually, I was just lobbying for a few million for my new clinic."

She rolled her eyes. "Funny."

Peter knew perfectly well that last night's event—besides being the grand opening of the zoo's new monkey exhibit—was a fundraiser for the referendum campaign. Come November, the voters of Saskawan would decide whether Ridge Park Zoo would move to one hundred gloriously vacant acres in the suburbs, or have to stay in their cramped urban park. Everything depended on getting supporters to the polls—and that took money.

Caroline clicked her key fob and the car chirped back. Peter walked ahead and waited at the door of the administration building. He called out, "Don't forget your coffee."

She grabbed her mug off the roof and caught up with him.

"It would be a shame if it fell off and dented Kirby's Harley. I mean, *two* close calls in one morning." He gave a low whistle.

"I guess I'm still a bit keyed up," she said, sheepishly. "You won't mention that bumper incident to Kirby, will you?"

Inside, Peter began pulling mail out of his mailbox, grinning. "So, *when* did you say I'd get my new clinic?"

Caroline laughed. "Would noon be soon enough?" She pushed her own mail into the side pocket of her laptop case and took the box from him. "So, did your wife have anything to say about the party?"

"Let's see," he said. "I think she said it was cunning."

"Stunning?"

"No. I'm pretty sure she said 'cunning.'"

"Really? How so?"

"Inviting donors to see the new monkey exhibit, plying them with free food and beer, then giving them the big pitch for the Zoo on the Moov campaign."

Caroline cocked her head and thought. "Cunning, huh? Not, clever, creative or a work of genius?"

"Ah! She said the *banana splits* were genius—with the monkey theme and all."

Caroline elbowed open her office door and dumped everything on her putty-gray desk with its putty-gray file drawers. She sat down, and wedged her foot against her desk and yanked the bottom drawer open with a screech that could shatter glass. Then she pushed her purse into the space behind the hanging files and frowned.

Six months ago that drawer was empty. Now, folders threatened to crowd out her personal belongings, which, when she thought about it, was a metaphor for her current work/life balance—or lack thereof.

Her new office was a cubbyhole compared to her spacious "ergonomic work environment" at MidWest Energy. But, with the possible exception of the riverfront view, the expense account and—*okay*—the decent *salary*, she hardly missed her old job at all.

For nearly eight years she had been "Sunny" Finch, the face and voice of the regional electric company. When West Michigan's weather wreaked havoc with power lines, viewers looked to Sunny, bundled in her MidWest parka in front of man-eating snowdrifts or sparking wires, to assure them their power would soon be restored.

Between "weather events" she promoted energy conservation and represented the utility at galas, walkathons and golf outings for dozens of charities.

It was a good job. She had paid off her husband Rob's medical school loans and more, but after their divorce a year ago, she wanted a change.

When Engelsma Construction announced it had offered one hundred acres for a new zoo, the story was all over the news for weeks. Caroline followed it with only mild curiosity until she read they were looking for someone to head up their multi-million dollar capital campaign. Caroline thought for weeks about applying, but as the deadline loomed, she hadn't even updated her resume.

It was her best friend, workout partner, neighbor and former roommate, Isabelle, a.k.a. "Bella" Canelli, who hounded her into applying.

"But I don't know anything about fundraising, *or* zoos," Caroline had pointed out. They were having coffee at The Third Base, Last Stop Before Home Café near their apartment building.

"What's that mountain of books on your coffee table then?" Bella asked.

Caroline had practically cleaned out Barnes and Noble of any title having to do with zoos or fundraising.

"Ffft!" Bella said, wiping foam from her upper lip. "What did you know about power outages when you applied at MidWest? Jeez girl, you could sweet talk a tiger out of a hunk of meat, and besides, you know where the money is in this town! I say go for it!" (This, from someone who gave about as much thought to her career choices as she did to what brand of laundry soap to buy.)

In regards to decision-making—and just about everything else—Bella and Caroline were opposites. Caroline was Macy's-L.L. Bean-white wine-Sunday crosswords, while Bella was more Goodwill-Goth-Jell-O shots-Oblivion video games. If Caroline didn't watch every mouthful, she'd look like a pile of inner tubes, while Bella—at barely five feet and one-ten—burned off calories chewing potato chips and cheese dogs.

She knew Bella was right. She *was* qualified. So what was this self-doubt that nagged at her? Her confidence had once been legendary. When she was seven, she bragged to the camp lifeguard that she could swim to the raft. As he pulled her from the lake bottom, she sputtered, "I wasn't finished!" In fifth grade a boy she liked dared her to jump off the garage roof. Earning the nickname "Superwoman" was worth a few weeks on crutches.

During her freshman year at U-W Madison, she persuaded her advisor to let her take advanced chemistry. This had two regrettable consequences. First, it knocked her out of the running for med school and Doctors Without Borders. Second, it allowed Robert Ingram Finch—her chemistry tutor and eventual husband—to trespass onto her life. Their ten-year marriage was the biggest fiasco, bar none, of her thirty-six years.

She was different now. Being questionably qualified for a job wouldn't have stopped pre-divorce Caroline. But post-divorce Caroline was a completely different animal.

"I feel like a con artist," she told Bella the day she got called for an interview.

"Eh, you'll figure it out. Mr. and Mrs. Bigbucks'll go ape-shit for a new zoo. Just sell 'em a brick with their name on it. How hard could it be, eh?"

As it turned out, a lot harder than either of them imagined.

The light on Caroline's desk phone blinked urgently. She punched in her password and listened to her messages.

"Morning, Caroline. It's Chappy." It was the voice of the zoo's senior keeper. "I found a set of car keys by the island. I assume they belong to a party guest. I'll bring them by later."

She would save him the trouble and take a walk to Caratasca Island where Chappy would be getting the monkey troop ready for their first day on public view. Caroline looked for excuses to get out of her office and talk to keepers as they worked. She still had a lot to learn about zoos, and her tiny office wasn't where that was going to happen.

Just yesterday, she watched Mr. and Mrs. Otter floating on their backs, sound asleep and holding hands. Later, she watched Peter give three baby capybaras their first checkup. Her salary might be a joke, but this job had its perks.

She hit the message button again.

"Hey, Caroline. What's the haps?" It was Kirby, reptile keeper and proud owner of one shiny, still unscathed Harley. "One of my caimans hatched. Big eyes. Little up-turned nose. Way cute. I have cigars. Come take pictures any time. Okay. Just doin' my bit for the team."

She opened her laptop, typed "Caiman, Wikipedia" and read, " . . . *alligatorid crocodylians* . . . inhabits Central and South America . . . smaller than other alligators, but more aggressive." Nowhere did it say "cute."

In the looks department, Kirby himself fell somewhere between Abe Lincoln and a whooping crane. With a nasty scar above his right eye, courtesy of a cranky monitor lizard, thinning shoulder-length hair and a few bristles that didn't quite qualify as a beard, the man was as eccentric as his animals. Anything that repelled or frightened normal folks, such as snakes, spiders, poison frogs or giant, chrome-clad motorcycles, fascinated The Kirb.

And yet, it was she, Caroline Scott Finch, a good ol' garden-variety English major —vanilla-flavored in the great Baskin-Robbins of life— who was treated like an alien species by her co-workers. The irony was baffling.

Kirby's birth announcement was a response to her most recent plea for more information from the keepers. "Visitors won't come to see the new baby porcupine if they don't know about it," she'd said at a recent staff meeting. "And I can't tell *them* if you don't tell *me*."

"Did that sound bitchy?" she asked Bella later.

"Yeah, they'll probably slash your tires."

"*Seriously.*"

"Geez, Caro, I have no idea! As Grandmama Canelli would say, 'They're big people.'"

At least Kirby had gotten the message. Caroline would visit the newborn caiman later in the day. The blessed event merited a mention in her zoo blog. She'd pass on the cigar.

She blew out a long breath. This job was more than a career change; it was a life-reclamation project. She thought she'd have a couple of kids by now and a real house with her grandmother's purple irises growing in the yard. But instead, she was single again. Mid-life was turning out to be vague and featureless. All the reassuring milestones—graduation, first apartment, first job, marriage—were behind her now. The way ahead seemed hazy and uncharted.

It had been a full year, but she wasn't over it. "It" being the divorce. How could anyone get over being de-loved by the one person who promised to love you forever? The old buoyancy she thought was congenital was gone. *Poof!* That selfish bastard, jerk-wad, asshole of an ex got it in the divorce settlement, and she wanted it back!

At MidWest, she had taken on new projects without a glance over her shoulder. Now, she endlessly enumerated the twenty-seven ways she could fail. She was a seasoned communications professional, so *why* did she feel like such a rookie?

The distant squawks of a pair of cockatoos snapped her out of her latest pity party. All this pestering self-doubt *had* to stop.

She listened to a sales call from a print company and deleted it.

Even more than change, she needed velocity. Last fall, she told Bella that if she didn't get the zoo job, she might do something crazy—like get a boob job, join an ashram or hike the Appalachian Trail.

"You? You've never done anything *remotely* unconventional," Bella said.

Bella had practically *dared* her to take the zoo job, and most days it was just what Caroline needed—unconventional, risky and fun. There were wondrous moments—like the day Peter returned from Alaska with Sitka, an orphaned moose calf. The whole staff watched as she picked daintily at a fresh willow branch in her pen. If convincing the good citizens of Saskawan to get behind a new home for beautiful wild creatures wasn't as easy as she thought it would be, it was at least a cause worth fighting for.

Next message. "Caroline? Victor." (Zoo Director Victor Torres, nicknamed "Silverback" for his alpha-male command of things and his thick black and silver mane.) The sound of his voice sent a pang of anxiety through her solar plexus. "Thank you for your efforts last night," he said. *Efforts? Like, I-know-you-really-tried, but...* "Let's meet at 9:30 to debrief. My office. Just senior staff."

Last message. "Caroline. Tom here." (Tom Engelsma, board president, über-donor of one hundred acres in Nord Haven.) "I have a few more pledge cards from last night. I'll put them in the mail. The party last night was terrific. My friends thought so, too. Thanks."

Most board members headed for the hills when it was time to raise money, but Tom was a fundraising machine, and his friends were making the biggest donations. Even better, they were donors who had never supported the zoo before.

Caroline exited the admin building and walked briskly toward Caratasca Island to see sixteen white-faced capuchin monkeys about to make their big debut.

She could hear Chappy, their keeper, whistling from the monkeys' sleeping quarters hidden inside a cement cliff. He had already let the troop onto the island and was cleaning up and prepping their breakfast.

Caroline watched the island's tiny inhabitants explore their new home. These South American monkeys were no bigger than human newborns with tails as long as their bodies. Their serious pink faces, large eyes and brown fur had reminded Spanish explorers of brown-hooded Capuchin monks who also lent their name to the coffee drink.

Several monkeys were turning over the leaf litter and searching the rock crevices for whatever they might have missed the evening before, but for a full breakfast, they'd have to wait.

Caroline looked down at the water-filled moat fifteen feet below. This was all that separated monkeys from visitors. The island itself was crisscrossed with a maze of rope hammocks, ladders and climbing platforms that looked like the set of *Swiss Family Robinson*. In a rocky valley, a mist machine created a cool, private place away from the prying eyes of zoo visitors.

Last evening, Victor, Tom and other major donors had posed with over-sized scissors behind a wide, red ribbon as cameras clicked. Victor asked for silence as Chappy opened the hidden door in the cliff and sixteen monkeys tumbled onto their new island paradise. Last night's event was Caroline's first big test, but it wouldn't count for much if the referendum didn't pass in November.

Below her, the monkeys looked as keyed up as she was. They were chasing each other along the ropes and calling back and forth. Two females had discovered a cache of nuts. They turned their backs to the others to conceal their find, but a large male ran them off and claimed the prize.

"Hey! That wasn't nice," Caroline said.

"Who's not nice?" Chappy asked. He was coming up the walk with the uneven gait of a man who had left youth behind. He wore khaki shorts, a dark-green zoo polo shirt and heavy work boots. A walkie-talkie, a water bottle and a trash bag hung from his belt. Hats were optional for staff, and the only part of the uniform that reflected the personality of the wearer. Chappy's was a Detroit Tigers baseball cap.

Caroline pointed an accusing finger at the male monkey. "He stole their food."

"That's Big Daddy, the alpha male. He's just lettin' them know who's boss. The guy's got a tough job."

Caroline frowned. "Well, I don't feel sorry for him."

Chappy's face revealed deep crow's feet, laugh lines and straight, white teeth—a face made for smiling. He picked a gum wrapper out of a bush inside the railing. "Someone called about the car keys. I took them to the front gate. Sorry you had to come up here."

"No problem. I wanted to see the island and ask what you thought of the event last night anyway," she said. "I was stuck behind the information table most of the night."

Chappy looked thoughtful. "The guests had a lot of good questions—though a few were pretty loaded by the end of the evening," he said, shaking his head. "I hope everyone got home safe."

At the sound of their keeper's voice, several monkeys began whirling in circles, chattering up at him. A female bounded into the moat up to her knees and called, "*Arrawh-arrawh!*" She paced back and forth looking up at Chappy.

"She doesn't look happy," Caroline said.

"She has a son just a little over a year old. This island is big enough for him to hide from her. She's not used to that."

The female ran to the top of a swinging rope bridge and sat down, gripping the rope with her hands, feet and tail.

"What I wouldn't give to have four hands and a tail," Caroline said. "I could talk on my phone, type and drink coffee all at once. Awesome!" She pantomimed this, making Chappy laugh.

"You'd think with all those appendages they could get their *own* breakfast," he said. "I better get to it."

"See you at the staff meeting in a few minutes. And by the way, good luck today."

"Thanks," he said, surveying the island. "I mean it, Caroline. This exhibit would never have opened without you. I owe you one." He gave a sharp whistle and walked back toward the sleeping quarters. The whole troop chortled back.

Chappy was right—Caratasca Island almost hadn't happened.

When Tom first offered land to the zoo last August, the media was all over the story. Film crews tramped over the fallow cornfield in suburban Nord Haven as Victor described his vision for a zoo five times the size of the current one. Tom soon joined the board and recommended they hire a fundraising professional.

Enter Caroline.

At first, it seemed a new zoo had universal support. Caroline created appeals, web pages and posters showing plans for the proposed zoo and its lush "natural habitats." She and Tom called on foundation directors and corporate leaders for major gifts. Caroline plunged headlong into her new job with growing confidence.

But it turned out to be a short-lived honeymoon. By mid-winter, opposition began hitting them from all sides. One group wanted the zoo to remain an amenity for city residents. Nord Haven residents worried about traffic, zoo smells, noise and the influx of "outsiders" into their upscale enclave. Animal advocates opposed *any* zoo on moral grounds, and a few preservationists even argued that the old iron cages were quaintly "historic."

After two months of packed meetings, the city and county commissioners decided to put the question to a public vote. Come November, the question of whether Ridge Park Zoo should move would appear on a countywide ballot.

Caroline, who barely knew an annual gift from a charitable annuity or an ibex from an oryx, found herself heading up a bitter referendum campaign. Her face broke out, her fingernails disappeared and her nightmares featured mobs with pitchforks.

Her boss Victor didn't take this turn of events well, either. Caratasca Island had been under construction for almost a year, but fearing the public would view a new exhibit as a waste of money, he abruptly canceled the project. For Chappy, who had been making regular visits to the troop in Ohio, this was a personal and professional embarrassment.

After several tense weeks of watching and listening, Caroline knocked on her boss' door.

"What if we used Caratasca Island as a model exhibit?" she suggested. "We could open it this summer so visitors could see what they'd be getting if they vote for the new zoo."

Victor folded his arms, leaned *way* back in his chair and scowled.

"If we start now," she continued, "we could combine the grand opening with a kick-off for the referendum campaign."

Victor let out a guttural growl and scratched his head.

She maintained eye contact with difficulty while he decided whether to give credence to this greenhorn's brazen suggestion.

Finally, he stood up to look out the window overlooking the zoo entrance and sighed. "Make your case to the board next week."

And that was it. Within two weeks, the project was fast-tracked for an early June opening.

It had been a risky move. She wasn't sure she was right or if Victor's confidence in her was deserved. She had acted on the flimsiest of instincts, but last night—as donors clapped and pointed appreciatively at the monkey troop—she had dared to feel something approaching vindication.

Victor had told the guests, "Exhibits like this are the wave of the future for first class zoos everywhere. And with your support, Ridge Park will *be* first-class—on a hundred acres in Nord Haven."

The opening of Caratasca Island was an auspicious start.

4
FAT CATS

Mist rose over the cat exhibits where Donna, the large mammal keeper, was hosing down the lion enclosure from the rocky overhang. Caroline watched from behind the railing. Donna's muscles rippled beneath her tanned skin. Her thick, reddish-blond hair was streaked with gray and hung thick and loose at her shoulders.

Like all zookeepers, Donna possessed an eclectic set of skills. She had the strength of a longshoreman, the agility of a rock climber and the reflexes of a cop. Chappy, Kirby and Donna were fearless risk-takers. A few generations earlier, they would probably have sailed the high seas, prospected for gold in Alaska or ridden the Texas range. But zookeepers also had to be astute observers and meticulous collectors of data. A change in appetite or behavior in one of their charges could mean circulatory problems. Pacing, rocking and excessive grooming, known as "cage stereotypy," were signs of stress or boredom.

Donna pulled a plastic shaker from her pocket.

"What's that?" Caroline asked, shading her eyes from the morning sun.

"Hey, Caroline." She backed up and held out the jar. "Take a whiff."

Caroline held the container to her nose. "Curry?"

"Cumin. Cats love the stuff. I'm hoping it will calm Kenya's nerves."

The smaller of two lionesses sat alone at the lowest point of the enclosure. Goldwyn, the big male, and his consort Daisy were sunbathing together at the top of the enclosure. Kenya had arrived from another zoo just a month before.

"Daisy won't let her near Goldwyn," Donna said. "Now Kenya's licking the fur off her paw, see? She's pretty stressed."

Caroline leaned forward to get a better look at the spot of exposed, pink flesh on the young lioness' front paw. "Poor thing. Come on, Daisy, don't be so hard on the newbie."

Donna aimed the hose at a fresh pile of scat and smiled.

Caroline said, "So, cumin, huh? Is it like catnip—or Valium?"

"A little of both. Need some?"

Donna had a keen stress-detector, Caroline thought. "I'm meeting with Victor in a few minutes to talk about last night. So, yeah, maybe later."

"I wouldn't worry. I mean there were tons of new people there. Were they your friends?"

"Tom Engelsma's, mostly."

Donna began coiling the hose on a hook concealed behind a bush. "So, that little fat dude with the girl, was he one of Tom's friends?"

"Yup. That's Patrick Malone. He owns the Uncle Paddy's Pizza chain."

Donna nodded. "I thought I recognized him from his goofy ads. Anyway, he told me he's really into big cats. He said he's going to Africa pretty soon."

"Interesting," Caroline said. "He made a big pledge for the referendum and Tom thinks he'll give a lot more if it passes. Maybe you can help me talk him into building the Patrick Malone African Savannah?"

"No, thanks—I like *big* cats, not *fat* cats." Donna vaulted the railing and landed on the pavement. "Good luck with Victor. I'll save you some cumin, just in case."

Back at the admin building, Caroline headed to the stuffy, windowless break room known as the Bat Cave. Boxes of party supplies dropped off by the maintenance crew only added to the usual chaos. The tables were typically covered with someone's research project or a mailing-in-progress that had to be pushed aside at lunchtime. This early in the day, the room was empty except for Peter and his young, redheaded veterinary assistant, Julie. They had finished their rounds and were taking a break.

They were a complementary team. Peter, who was generally soft-spoken, seemed perpetually amused by Julie—the source and purveyor of all zoo gossip.

"Hey, Caroline," Julie sang out. "Helluva party last night."

"Thanks," Caroline said, opening the first box.

"What are the chances of this thing passing anyway?" Julie asked.

"The referendum? Excellent," Caroline said with more confidence than she felt. She began sorting through zoo maps, tee shirts, souvenir cups and logo pens. "Our big selling points are larger enclosures and new animals."

"And my big new clinic," Peter reminded her, wiggling his bushy white eyebrows.

"And my paycheck." Julie winked at Peter.

Caroline raised her hands. "Hey, if it were up to me, you'd both get bags of gold."

Salaries were a sore subject at Ridge Park Zoo. Most of the staff—from curators to keepers to maintenance workers—could have made more money in any commercial enterprise, but they had taken what Peter called the "zoo vow of poverty." He should know. He could be earning six figures in private veterinary practice, but he had followed his heart into zoo work.

"Careful, Pete," Julie said in a stage whisper, "Caroline's in PR, she'll tell ya anything ya wanna hear."

Caroline shot back, "And I can get a rumor started quicker than you can down that coffee sludge."

"Oooh, I *love* a good rumor!" Julie said. "Make one up about me'n that adorable new grad assistant." She twisted in her chair to face Caroline. "Hey, who was that paunchy old letch with the bimbo last night? They were *wasted*."

Apparently Uncle Paddy Malone and a girl half his age who clung to him all night had made a big impression on the staff. Judging by her sequined tube top, mini skirt and four-inch platform heels—and it was hard not to judge—she was probably *not* Paddy's assistant. However, given the size of his campaign pledge, Caroline felt protective.

"He's made a *very* generous pledge," she said.

"He owns the Uncle Paddy's Pizza chain, right?" Peter asked.

"Well, no wonder his girlfriend was so cheesy!" Julie said with a snort.

Peter gave her a reproving look.

"Well, did you *see* them?" Julie protested. "He practically had to *carry* her. 'Assistant' my ass!" Julie grabbed Peter's forearm. "I saw 'em admiring Goldwyn's, er, manhood. The bimbo was laughing so hard she had to run to the bathroom."

Caroline refolded a tee shirt. "Paddy's pledge is going to help us get a *lot* of yes votes this fall. We should give the guy a break."

Peter frowned, looking apologetic at his inability to rein in his assistant.

"So, where was *your* date last night, Caroline?" Julie asked.

Caroline frowned. "Sadly, he had to plant a flag on Mt. Everest. No, no. That was *last* week. He was opening a new restaurant in Paris, then had to fly back to argue a Supreme Court case." She sighed heavily. "So, so, so busy."

Julie whispered to Peter again. "Caroline has an imaginary boyfriend. Hey! Let's fix her up, Pete." She twisted to face Caroline again. "No one can stay single in Saskawan for long. We Calvinists are suspicious of single women. And besides, Dutch men make great daddies, as long as they aren't *too* churchy."

Caroline tried to appear absorbed in tee shirt folding.

"What about Kirby?" Julie said. "He's single. Some women find snake guys very sexy."

There were footsteps in the hall. Caroline looked at the clock. It was almost time for the senior staff meeting with Victor.

Peter put a finger to his white mustache and got up. "You can finish up those charts while I'm gone, Jules. Keep an eye on that meerkat. This meeting shouldn't last more than an hour."

Caroline flattened three empty boxes, poured herself a cup of coffee and followed Peter into Victor's office.

Victor Torres was sitting at his desk reading something on his laptop as Caroline and Peter took seats by the window. Gwen, the zoo's curator, rushed in like the White Rabbit, checking and rechecking her watch. She was a petite powerhouse with a straight pageboy and bangs cut an inch too short. A pair of comical, round reading glasses hung from a cord around her neck. She gave Caroline a perfunctory nod and settled into her chair. Chappy followed her in and sat near the door.

Victor was wearing the same blue oxford dress shirt he'd worn to the party. It was rumpled and the sleeves were rolled tightly against his beefy forearms. He had apparently worked through the night. Lately, he was like a caged beast, unable to relax or, it appeared, to sleep.

The Torres family had lived in east Texas for many generations. On the far side of six feet and 230 pounds, he looked like he could wrangle a steer and come out the winner, but the row of framed biology and business degrees on the shelf behind him suggested he could do a whole lot more.

A photo of his three children, now grown, was propped on the credenza behind him. Next to it were three lines of graceful calligraphy in a gold frame that read: *In the end, we will conserve only what we love; we will love only what we understand; and we will understand only what we are taught. – Baba Dioum.*

During her second interview last fall, Caroline had asked Victor about it. The quote was taken from a 1968 address by a Senegalese environmentalist to the International Union for Conservation of Nature. The calligraphy was a gift from Victor's daughter. At that moment, Caroline decided that if the job were offered, she would take it.

"Okay, people," Victor said, scanning the group over his bifocals. "Gwen has some news."

The curator moved to the edge of her chair. "Yesterday I got a call from Louisville. We have final approval on two breeding pairs of black-footed ferrets."

"Outstanding!" Peter said, slapping his knee. "When?"

"As soon as we have an exhibit to put them in," Gwen said.

"Meaning after the move—three or four years," Victor added. "The important thing here is that we have a firm commitment." He looked at Caroline. "The black-footed ferret is one of the most endangered mammals in North America."

Caroline tapped her phone and found an image of a kitten-sized animal with Mickey Mouse ears, a black bandit mask and stunning sable and black markings. "*Adorable*," she said. "I didn't know ferrets were endangered."

"Not all ferrets," Victor said, "but these guys prey on prairie dogs out West and move into their burrows. When ranchers went to war on prairie dogs, ferrets died with them. By the 1970s, everybody thought they were extinct. But then in—when was it?"

"1981," Gwen said. "A dog in Wyoming killed one and brought it home. His owner took it to be stuffed. The taxidermist about fainted."

"It would be like finding a freshly killed passenger pigeon," Peter added.

Gwen nodded. "Turns out there was one last colony of about a hundred seventy individuals near there, but they were in bad shape."

"Why?" Caroline asked.

"Ferrets get a couple of nasty diseases," Peter said, "including distemper."

"So how did they survive?" Caroline asked.

"The Fish and Wildlife folks captured twenty-four," Gwen said. "Several died almost immediately, so they were left with—" Gwen checked her notes. "–eighteen. That's about as bad as it gets."

"Eventually, they asked zoos for help," Victor said. "The Louisville Zoo and several others started a breeding program that we'll be part of now. But the best part is the reintroduction program. Zoos have been releasing ferrets back into their native habitats out West and in Mexico. How many are in the wild now, Gwen?"

"Over a thousand," Gwen said. "And most are wild-born descendants of captive bred ferrets."

Caroline was taking notes and wondering if anybody made black-footed ferret plush toys.

Victor drummed his desktop excitedly. "Well, folks, the stakes for this referendum just got even higher. We need a new zoo, ASAP. No room for ferrets here."

"If we make a splashy announcement just before the election, it will be another incentive for voters," Caroline said.

Victor nodded. "And speaking of splashy, let's talk about last night."

Caroline reported on attendance, number of checks and pledges received—all good news. "Our biggest pledge was from Paddy Malone, the pizza restaurateur. He told Donna he has a passion for big cats."

"I hope he hasn't forgotten his pledge," Gwen sniffed, making her disapproval clear. "I bet he and his companion are a tad hung over this morning."

"I'll camp out on his doorstep if I have to," Caroline said, tiring of the gossip.

"And let me remind you all," Victor said, "that the money raised last night is earmarked for getting out the yes vote in November, not zoo improvements. Those will have to wait."

Gwen took off her glasses and scowled. "Well, I don't see why this referendum has to cost so much." As one of those people who mistook rudeness for candor, her question implied that fundraising—and possibly Caroline herself—were unfortunate distractions from the *real* work of zoos.

Caroline felt everyone's eyes on her.

"Well," she said. "We need air time, ad space, print literature and yard signs. I'll put yard signs by the mailboxes for you all to take home and give out to friends, neighbors and family. We *all* need to be *active* supporters."

Gwen lifted her arms and let them drop into her lap. "I don't get these opposition people. Why in God's name would *anyone* want us to turn down free land?"

Caroline was considering her response when Chappy, who rarely spoke at meetings, took a breath to speak, then seemed to lose his nerve.

Vic lifted an eyebrow. "Chap?"

He cleared his throat. "It's just that—. There are people who—." He looked out the window, away from Gwen's fierce glare. "A lot of people love this zoo for what it *is*."

Gwen rolled her eyes. "And what pray tell is *that*? An overcrowded, outdated municipal zoo?"

"Okay, Gwen," said Victor, raising a hand.

The phone on Victor's desk rang. He jabbed at the mute button and scowled. Julie was supposed to intercept all calls on the clinic phone during senior staff meetings. One had apparently slipped by her.

Victor gave Chappy another nod. "Say more."

Chappy wore a pained look that made Caroline want to pat his hand. "Well, I just feel—. I mean, our big trees—."

The door flew open and Julie rushed in waving a square of pink paper. "Sorry, Vic. I tried to call."

Victor shot her a withering look. "Take a message."

"I *did*," Julie said, waving the paper again.

"Can't this wait?"

"No!" Julie pulled at a tight red curl, took a deep breath and blurted excitedly, "Aladyfounda*monkey*!"

All heads snapped in her direction.

"A lady found a monkey—in her barn," Julie repeated more slowly.

"Have her call Animal Control," Victor said, scowling.

"But, she lives *there*." Julie pointed in the direction of the employee parking lot, the zoo's perimeter fence and Willow Creek Farm. "It's that lady who owns that farm next door, Mrs. Iris VanWingen." She read from the slip, "She said, 'If you want your monkey, come get it *now*.' Oh, and it busted up her bird feeder. She sounds pissed."

5

MONKEY BUSINESS

Victor, Peter, Chappy and Gwen leaped from their seats, firing questions at Julie.

"Is it injured?"

"Just one?"

"Are we sure it's ours?"

"Is it still loose?"

Someone moaned.

Julie looked ready to laugh, until she saw Victor rise from his chair. She read solemnly from the pink slip again. "She has it in some sort of crate. I said we'd be over right away."

"Gwen!" Victor barked, "Call Donna. Have her do a count at the island and stay there. Pete and Chappy, get the E.R.T. equipment and get over to the farm, now! We're Code Yellow. Julie, call Kirby. He and I are going to walk the perimeter fence. Go! Everybody! *Go!*"

Gwen already had Donna on the radio as she and Peter stampeded down the hallway. "Donna, one of the capuchins got out . . . No, I'm not joking! At that farm next door. Get over to the island and get a count . . ." Her voice was drowned out in the noise of shouted orders.

Caroline watched her mild-mannered co-workers morph into a commando SWAT team. If she remembered the policy manual correctly, E.R.T. stood for Emergency Response Team. Keepers had trained with law enforcement in the use of tranquilizer guns, catch poles, nets and even firearms to handle escapes and other emergencies. Code Yellow was used for non-lethal animals posing little danger to the public. Of course, even an eight-pound monkey could deliver a nasty bite or cause an accident on Russet Ridge Drive—not to mention sully the reputation of an overcrowded, outdated municipal zoo, and tarnish the career of a thirty-six-year-old divorcée in serious need of a paycheck.

Caroline walked the few steps to her office and stood with her hand on her forehead wondering what her own Code Yellow should be. At her window she watched Peter and Chappy speed out of the lot in the zoo's zebra-striped van.

She sat down to think. This was the zoo's equivalent of a tornado ripping through power lines. *No. It wasn't like that at all.*

The phone rang, and "WSAS-TV" lit up the caller ID. *Probably a coincidence.* She counted to three, picked up the phone and said calmly, professionally, "Hello. Caroline Finch."

"Sunny!" said a familiar voice. "Derrick Wolcott."

"Hello, Derrick."

"Wow! You're at the zoo now, huh? We haven't talked since that big thunderboomer, what, about a year ago? I wondered where you went. How's the new job?"

"Love it." Her mind raced. "How can I help you, Derrick?"

His voice dropped an octave, "Well, Miss Finch. We got da monkey, see? Bring twenty grand in unmarked bills and come alone." Then he laughed.

"I'm not laughing," she said, smiling to herself.

"Ok. I've got my crew here at—" he paused, reading, "—Willow Creek Farm, just a hop, skip and a swing over your fence, as it happens." He laughed again. "You guys wouldn't happen to be one monkey shy of a barrel, would you?"

"Our keeper and vet are on their way over."

"Ah! They're just pulling in now. So, what's my lead? 'Visitors love new monkey island. Monkeys vote with their feet.'?"

"Hold on. For all we know, it's someone's pet."

"Seriously? Is that your statement?"

"Of course not, but obviously, it's too soon to speculate."

"Well, I'd like to do an interview with your director."

She pictured Victor's purple face and rumpled shirt drenched from a jog around the perimeter.

"He's rather busy at the moment, but I'll talk to you." She said this with a tone that implied that dealing with animal escapes was routine, but then realized that was the wrong message. "I'll come over," she added.

"Great," he said. "I'm just about to interview the lady who found him, a Mrs. Iris VanWingen. There's a kid, too, who helped her catch the monkey. Nice set up for a story. I'll see you in a few minutes."

She knew Derrick from her MidWest days, when she was skilled at answering his questions about storm damage, utility rates and power outages. But an AWOL monkey? What was the right message there?

Caroline walked briskly to her car as she dialed Peter. "I'm coming over... If the TV reporter asks, just tell him we don't know anything yet. You won't use a tranquillizer gun, will you? *Lots* of people will see this... Okay, good. Where is this farm?"

She slipped between a mail truck and a minivan, then braked almost immediately at a boulder the size of a major appliance that marked the gravel driveway Peter had described. In all the months she'd driven by it, she'd never noticed this two-track. She drove through a tunnel of maple trees and passed a No Trespassing sign. A hundred yards back, the drive widened into a turnaround between a weathered white farmhouse and a dilapidated barn. A sign over its open doors read Willow Creek Farm, Est. 1875. The zebra van was backed into the doorway.

She parked next to the WSAS-TV van, its white radar dish beaming news of an escaped monkey all over West Michigan. A dog barked from somewhere nearby. She got out of the car and wiped a bead of sweat from her forehead. She could use a good roll in a cloud of cumin right about now.

In front of the barn windows, Derrick was holding a microphone toward a tall woman with a Gibson-girl knot of silvery white hair. She wore a red plaid shirt that was several sizes too big, a denim skirt that had seen better days and a pair of moccasins. She pointed a broom toward the barn as the cameraman panned the scene. She was not smiling.

Caroline walked into the scene and whispered to Peter. "Everything okay?"

"Looks like it," Peter said. "I'll check him over when we get back." His cell phone rang. "It's Vic." He walked past her into the yard.

Chappy stepped forward. "He's not hungry, that's for sure," he said. He pointed toward watermelon rinds littering the barn floor. Sweat had turned the front of his green polo shirt black. The safety of this monkey was his responsibility and he was feeling the heat.

If Donna with her years of post-graduate work in zoology was the "new breed of zookeeper," Chappy was strictly old guard. He was highly experienced and respected, but had no formal training. In the 1970s he was the city maintenance worker assigned to the zoo. He began filling in for keepers on vacation until he could do just about anyone's job. Eventually, he rose through the ranks to become senior keeper. No one who worked with Chappy questioned his ability, but there was always pressure on zoos to hire credentialed staff. In a profession where more than eighty percent of keepers held advanced degrees, Chappy often called himself an endangered species. If he was found negligent, Victor might be forced to replace him.

Peter came back into the barn. "Vic says the other animals are accounted for and nothing seems out of place at the island. Pretty weird."

Caroline nodded. "So how did he get out?"

Peter shook his head. "No idea."

Caroline looked at Derrick and the woman he was interviewing and whispered, "I'll need to tell the media something. What do we know about her?"

Peter nodded toward the woman. "Her name's VanWingen. I heard her tell the reporter that her birds were acting strange this morning. She found the boy feeding the monkey watermelon in the hayloft. They lured it down by baiting that apple crate." He pointed to a wooden box about a yard square with Willow Creek Farm stenciled on the side. "She threw a tarp over the top and called us. The monkey's one of the young males, by the way, about fourteen months old."

Caroline turned to Chappy, "So, that female who was so upset this morning—was she the mother?"

He nodded slowly. "I thought he was just hiding from her. Guess I should've been more suspicious." He scratched his head. "I don't know. He pretty much trashed her yard, too." Chappy looked toward Mrs. VanWingen, who was scowling at Derrick. He left the barn and began righting several pots of geraniums that the monkey had apparently pushed off the barn's windowsills.

Peter began picking watermelon rinds off the dirt floor and tossing them into the back of the van. A spot of sunshine lit up the barn floor. Caroline followed it upward to a hole in the roof where two crows seemed to be watching them.

Chappy came back in. "The little stinker turned over her garbage pail, broke her bird feeder and tore into her strawberry patch," he said.

Peter looked into the yard with his hands on his hips. "Man, this place is a fossil. A farm completely surrounded by city. I hear she's got twenty acres. This barn is a relic, too. All the big fruit operations have metal pole barns now. The land the zoo sits on used to be part of this farm, years ago."

"Really," Caroline said, trying to picture this. The house was old all right, with a deep, wrap-around porch trimmed with graying gingerbread trim. Baskets of peach and white impatiens hung from the porch ceiling. The gravel turn-around was ringed with peonies heavy with pink pompoms. "With a new coat of paint, this could be a showplace."

Chappy moved toward the van. "Let's get going, Pete. I can't take much more excitement."

"Wait," Caroline said. "I need to know what to tell the media. Do you think the monkey was out all night?"

Chappy shook his head. "Sixteen went in last night. Sixteen came out this morning. He must have taken off just before you got there this morning."

She shuddered to think of the tiny primate dangling over Goldwyn's enclosure.

"We can't be sure, though," Peter said.

"I'm sorry to ask this, Chappy, but could you have miscounted?"

Chappy wiped his forehead with the back of his hand. "I don't know. With three little males the same size jumping every which-a-way and the whole troop pretty hyper over the move *and* the late night, maybe I miscounted—but I don't think so."

"But we don't even have theory about how he got out?"

Peter shrugged. "Sorry. But you can say that the island was designed by reputable zoo architects. There are similar exhibits in zoos all over the world."

"Okay, good." She walked out of the barn, past Derrick and Mrs. VanWingen to the side of the barn closest to the zoo. There were rows of gnarled apple trees as far as she could see with grass growing knee-deep between them. The zoo was probably just a couple hundred yards away, with the employee parking lot, the admin building and the clinic just over the fence.

She came back into the barn. "So, the monkey came through the orchard?"

"Apparently," Peter said. "Anyway, it wouldn't take a monkey long to get here. Fences wouldn't slow him down one bit."

"Okay," Caroline said, "keep me in the loop—good news or bad. If the public smells a cover-up, things will get ugly."

Chappy nodded solemnly. Peter lifted his thumb. "We got it. No Monkeygate for Ridge Park."

A chirp came from the carrier.

She leaned over the small carrier. "May I see the little fugitive?"

Chappy folded back the blanket. The monkey looked up with round childlike eyes and chirped again. He was even smaller than he looked from a distance. He was nibbling the last of the watermelon, smacking his lips and chattering at them between bites. Then, he pushed a piece through the mesh toward Chappy.

Peter laughed. "A peace offering."

Chappy turned his back and folded his arms, "No way, Mister. You can't bribe me!"

Caroline peered into the carrier. "So, what do you have to say for yourself, little monkey man? Such a ruckus you've caused!" She tapped the wire with her finger and whispered, "If you promise to stay on that nice island we made for you, I'll bring you more watermelon. What d'ya say?"

Five doll-sized fingers reached through the wire and closed around her index finger. She gasped and held still. The tiny, cool fingers, the morning sun on her back, a flowery fragrance carried in on the breeze made something flutter beneath her breastbone.

"Can I say goodbye?" a small voice asked.

She jumped, tumbling back from wherever she had been. A dark-eyed boy of nine or ten was standing next to her. He wore a red baseball cap, a blue Detroit Lions football jersey and blue shorts. He had his eye on the wire carrier.

"Can I see him?" he asked.

"Oh!" she said, standing up. "Of course."

Chappy put a hand on the boy's shoulder. "This is Rafael, Mrs. VanWingen's neighbor. He helped her get the monkey into the crate."

The boy's face was deeply tanned and fringed with thick, black bangs that nearly covered his thick, black lashes.

Caroline noticed that the cameraman had his lens trained on them now. She extended her hand. "Nice to meet you, Rafael. Thank you for keeping our monkey safe until we could come get him."

"He might still be hungry," said the boy, running to a bucket and returning with several melon chunks.

"Where did you find the melon?" Peter asked.

"My house," the boy whispered, perhaps expecting a reprimand.

"Pretty quick thinking," Peter said. "How'd you know he'd like it?"

"My uncle used to have a monkey like him."

"Where?" Chappy looked concerned. Capuchins make difficult house pets.

"At home. In El Salvador." The boy pointed down the drive, as if Central America was just across Russet Ridge Drive.

Chappy started to close the back of the van as Peter climbed into the driver's seat. The boy's face fell. "Where are you *taking* him? He doesn't like it in that cage."

"Don't worry," Chappy said. "Dr. Pete is an animal doctor. He's going to make sure the monkey isn't hurt. Then we'll take him back to his mom. He lives with his whole family on a little island."

"An island?" Rafael looked up sharply, not buying this.

"At the zoo," Chappy said. "Right next door."

Rafael still looked unconvinced.

"You've visited the zoo, haven't you?"

Rafael looked down at the dirt floor.

"Well, how about you come see your friend real soon?" Chappy looked up at Caroline. "We can arrange that, right?"

Caroline nodded. "Of course."

Derrick was walking toward them.

"Good luck," Chappy said, looking worried. He climbed in and the van rolled slowly down the driveway.

The old woman was making her way toward the house carrying her broom.

Caroline called out, "Hello! Mrs. VanWingen?" But she had already reached the house and let the door slam behind her. Caroline stopped at the bottom of the porch steps feeling foolish. The woman was either hard of hearing or extremely rude. A black dog barked menacingly at her through the screen door.

Derrick asked, "Are you ready for your close up, Sunny?"

She turned, wearing her on-air smile. "Any time you are."

He motioned for her to stand with the barn as a backdrop. She instantly regretted her lack of makeup and ponytail-zoo cap coiffure, but it was too late. Viewers would say, "She kind of reminds me of Sunny, that MidWest girl, but a lot older and not as pretty."

She pinched her cheeks and bit her lip to bring some color to them.

When Derrick raised the microphone Caroline cupped her hand over the mesh tip and said, "By the way, Derrick, you'll hear from MidWest's legal department if you try to resurrect that 'Sunny' character." This was a complete lie, but it needed saying.

Derrick shook his head. "Too bad. I miss ol' Sunny."

Caroline stifled an eye roll in case the camera was rolling.

Derrick's questions covered public safety and the exhibit design. Caroline repeated what she knew and gave assurances that Goldwyn and Monty, the python, were safely inside their enclosures.

"Can you tell us more about the little runaway?"

"He's a white-faced capuchin monkey, sometimes known as an organ grinder monkey. He's a native of Central and South America where his wild cousins live in the forest canopy in colonies or troops. Capuchins are known for their intelligence. They can also get into a lot of mischief, as we've just seen demonstrated this morning."

"How did he escape?"

"We need more time to determine that, Derrick, but I *can* assure you that the design of our beautiful new Caratasca Island exhibit is not at issue." She hoped this was true.

"What will happen to him now?"

"After a check-up, he'll go back to the island where his mother is waiting anxiously for him."

"I suspect the little guy may be in a bit of trouble with her."

"I'm sure she won't let him out of her sight for a while." Caroline turned toward the camera. "I hope your viewers will come see him at Caratasca Island. The exhibit is open for the first time today." She hoped this was still true.

"Thank you Caroline Finch of Ridge Park Zoo. It looks like we have a bit of a mystery. Stay tuned for details as we learn more about this little Houdini's daring escape. Derrick Wolcott, WSAS News."

Derrick dropped the microphone to his side and beamed. "Thanks, Sunny."

"Houdini? Daring escape?" She shook her head, showing her deep disappointment.

"It just came to me," he said with a grin. "You can't script these things."

6

MENAGERIE

The staff was crowded into the Bat Cave to watch the midday news when Caroline came in. Victor and Gwen leaned against the back wall, looking moody and official. Donna and Chappy sat with Peter and Julie. Plastic dishes, yogurt cups and fast food bags were spread out in front of them, but no one was saying much. Chappy hadn't touched the sandwich in front of him. Kirby walked in with a bag from Mr. Burger and clapped Chappy on the shoulder in a gesture of solidarity. Chappy nodded, but kept silent. Everyone knew the pressure he was feeling.

The TV was playing a game show with the volume muted. Caroline sat down next to Peter, then got up for a cup of coffee she didn't want. She opened and closed the refrigerator, but had no appetite for the leftover bratwurst she'd saved from last night's party, which now seemed to have happened weeks ago. She opened one of the party boxes and stared into a jumble of name tags, zoo hats, paper plates and flyers. This morning she was cleaning up after a successful event. Now, she was neck-deep in a crisis she wasn't prepared for.

After leaving the farm, she'd Googled "crisis management," only to learn she'd already broken Rule #1: "Plan for a crisis." *Oops.*

Apparently, she should have trained her CEO, board president and the media in the proper response to an AWOL zoo monkey. Instead, she'd watched from the sidelines as her co-workers sprang into their well-rehearsed Code Yellow Response Mode. *Double oops.*

Fortunately, Rule #2 was "Act quickly." That, she could do. By eleven she'd posted a statement on the zoo website giving the facts of the escape and addressing the public's safety concerns. Then she added a darling picture of the monkey being hugged by his mother—a nice touch, she thought.

Julie was waving frantically at the TV, her mouth full of spaghetti. "News is on."

Caroline turned up the sound.

"Good afternoon, West Michigan. I'm Lauren DeHaan and it's High Noon in Saskawan. We have breaking news coming from the Ridge neighborhood where a young monkey was discovered in a barn near Ridge Park Zoo. We take you now to Derrick Wolcott."

Derrick stood in front of the barn. *"That's right, Lauren. I'm at Willow Creek Farm, right next to the zoo. Just after nine this morning, the owner of this barn was shocked to discover a small monkey in her hayloft. She was able to capture it, and I'm glad to report, the little guy is back at the zoo safe and sound."*

The camera panned the VanWingen yard, took a tight shot of the apple crate, then cut to shots taken the day before of monkeys cavorting on Caratasca Island.

"The five-pound male escaped from the zoo's newest exhibit called Caratasca Island. This is the first day that it was to be open for public viewing, Lauren."

"Can you tell us what happened?"

"Somehow, the little fellow found his way to the adjoining property of Mrs. Iris VanWingen just a couple hundred yards from the zoo."

There was a shot of the perimeter fence behind the employee parking lot.

"Mrs. VanWingen and her ten-year-old neighbor lured it into this crate." The camera showed the stenciled wood box again. *"I have here young Rafael Rojas who first discovered the monkey and assisted in the rescue."*

Derrick knelt next to the boy. *"Can you tell us what happened?"*

"I was just playing when I saw him in that tree. At first, I thought he was a cat, 'cause of his tail, but then I saw he was a monkey. When I tried to climb after him, he ran into the barn and up the ladder."

"What happened then?"

"I tried to close the barn door, but it was stuck, so I ran home and got some watermelon. Then the lady came out—"

"Mrs. VanWingen."

The camera cut to a shot of Iris pointing to the barn, looking dour.

"How did you catch him?"

"We put watermelon in that big box. When he went in, BAM! That lady threw a blanket over the top."

"Okay, thank you Rafael. You did a fine thing today." Derrick shook the boy's hand and looked at the camera. *"Now over here we have Mrs.*

Iris VanWingen, the owner of the barn." He tilted the microphone. "I guess it was quite a shock to find a monkey in your barn."

Iris looked icily at Derrick. "*What's shocking is keeping a wild animal that belongs in South America in a cage in Saskawan.*"

Donna dropped her carrot stick.

"Uh-oh—" Kirby said.

"Shhh!" Gwen hissed.

"*It's remarkable it wasn't killed in the street or mauled by a dog. When I called that pitiful menagerie over there, they hadn't even missed it.*"

"*Sounds like you're not a fan of zoos.*"

Mrs. VanWingen crossed her arms and gave him a menacing look, but didn't answer.

Julie threw down her fork. "Holy crap!"

Derrick continued. "*How would you respond to those who say that zoos educate the public about wild animals?*"

"*Zoos only teach us how animals behave behind bars. Bears don't live on cement and eat jellybeans and caramel corn all day. Wild animals belong in the wild.*"

The next shot showed Ridge Park's black bears in their concrete, fifties-era enclosure eating, what looked *exactly* like jelly beans.

"Those are mulberries!" Donna said, pushing back from that table. She looked ready to pounce on the television and knock it to the floor.

"*What about endangered animals?*" Derrick asked. "*Aren't zoos helping to save them?*"

The camera showed the zoo's river otters circling their undersized pool.

"*How many of those poor creatures are actually endangered? And those that are should be released to propagate their species naturally. Instead, we're destroying habitats and putting the survivors behind bars. Zoos are benefiting from worldwide habitat destruction. That has to stop.*"

The Bat Cave went silent.

"*The photogenic creatures get all the attention—pandas, apes and leopards. Meanwhile, Michigan's frogs and bats and turtles are disappearing right under our noses. Turtles have practically disappeared from my property because the zoo dumps its waste into my creek. Sometimes that place smells so bad, I have to close my windows.*"

Caroline saw Donna roll her napkin into a projectile.

Derrick turned to the camera. "*Let's make it clear to our viewers that Mrs. VanWingen's farm is immediately next door to the zoo,*" Derrick said, *"and Willow Creek flows directly out of the zoo."*

The camera panned the barn, cut to Willow Creek and zoomed in on a plastic cup caught in the vegetation. The zoo logo was as plain as day.

Chappy lowered his head. Julie groaned.

The next shot was of Peter and Chappy outside the zebra van, followed by a close-up of the monkey peering pitifully through the wire bars of the carrier—which could easily be mistaken for the monkey's "cage" at the "menagerie." There was a brief shot of Caroline mouthing words to Derrick's voice-over.

"Well, there you have it, thoughts on zoos from Iris VanWingen of Willow Creek Farm. And I should add, Lauren, that Mrs. VanWingen is a retired science teacher from Central High School. I think we've just had our lesson for today."

"Indeed, Derrick. Do we have a statement from the zoo?"

"Yes. They tell me the monkey is safely back in the exhibit and reunited with his mother. They don't know yet how he escaped, but as you can imagine, Lauren, monkeys are very smart and are known to be escape artists—I guess this guy is a regular little Houdini."

The anchor laughed. *"He sure earned that name today. Any thoughts on how this might affect the zoo referendum, Derrick?"*

"Interest in the zoo's future is running high since county voters will decide in November whether the zoo can rebuild in Nord Haven or have to stay where it is. We'll just have to see."

"Thanks for that report, Derrick." She turned to face the cameras. *"We have just learned that the zoo will delay opening until 1:00 p.m. today as a precaution."*

Julie turned off the TV and sat down. "That woman has no clue!" Others cleared their throats or looked down at their hands. Chappy hadn't moved a muscle.

"This is even worse than I thought," Gwen said, pinching the bridge of her nose.

"What an old witch!" Julie said.

"Okay, okay," Victor raised his hands. "If you can stay, let's talk about how to handle this. Caroline, what are your thoughts?"

She had discussed some crisis management strategies with Victor before lunch, but that was before she'd heard the broadcast. As she stood to face her colleagues, she wasn't sure what words might come out of her mouth.

"This is a setback, for sure," she began, choosing her words carefully. "Mrs. VanWingen is misinformed, but she's obviously not stupid, and she's not entirely wrong. You've all said this zoo isn't adequate, which, of course, is why we want to move. And our bears deserve better than a cement enclosure, even if they don't eat jellybeans. Am I right?"

There were a few murmurs of begrudging agreement.

She continued. "The referendum is five months away. I think she's given us an opportunity to make the case for a bigger, better zoo. We've got the public's attention now. They will be asking us about some of the half-truths we just heard. It's up to all of us to set the record straight." She paused and looked around the room, "So, what does the public need to know?" This was met with stony silence. "If we're not incarcerating animals for the public's entertainment, what *are* we doing?"

"A lot of our animals are rescues," Kirby offered. "Both our bald eagles are here because they have permanent wing injuries."

"And Xavier," Julie said, meaning the zoo's yellow cougar. "His owners declawed him as a cub. He could never survive in the wild."

Gwen stood at the back, looking like a pint-sized bouncer at a biker bar. "Hunters shot our black bears' mother in the Upper Peninsula. The Humane Society found them ofon chains in a farmer's backyard. They were a mess. Right, Pete?"

Peter nodded. "Full of worms and covered with abscesses."

"And Howl." Kirby said, referring to the zoo's barred owl. "Somebody found him half-starved. He had cataracts and couldn't hunt. Pete removed the cataracts, but he'll never see good enough."

Howl was a frequent visitor to schools and nursing homes as part of the Zoo Ambassadors Program. He also took dollar bills from people's hands at fundraising events.

Caroline smiled. "Good ol' Howl. He brought in ninety-two bucks last night."

Donna spoke up. "I don't get what Mrs. Van*Whatever* is smelling over there, but I can tell you, it's not this zoo. I bet our enclosures are cleaner than her kitchen."

Peter put down his coffee before speaking. "Mrs. VanWingen also said zoos only care about photogenic animals, like pandas. But I bet she doesn't know that Kirby implants tracking devices in massasauga rattlers for a team that's studying their habitat needs. They are becoming rare in Michigan."

"Go, Kirb!" Julie piped up.

Kirby beamed. "Thanks, but who says they're not photogenic?" Laughter rippled through the room, uncorking some of the tension.

Peter folded his arms. "If we had more room, we'd be able to do more conservation and research work. Grad students want to work with us on turtle breeding, but we don't have a place for them to work."

"Excellent point," Caroline said. "So building a new zoo isn't just about bigger, better enclosures for cute mammals, it's about research, rescue and release."

"Ooo! Three *R*s," Julie said. "Catchy."

Caroline looked pleased. "I know this seems obvious to all of you, but a lot of this is news to the community. Either *we* tell our story, or people like Mrs. VanWingen will tell their own version. What else?"

Donna's chair scraped against the floor as she pushed away from the table. "Okay. Another thing. Did that woman actually say zoos *benefit* from habitat destruction? Wow. That's rich. If she wants to blame somebody, let it be the private collectors and animal traders." She paused, struggling to maintain control. "Only a *tiny* percentage of captive tigers in the U.S. are in reputable zoos. Most of them live in people's apartments or basements. And people *keep* breeding them! Did you know that it's easier to get a hold of a tiger or a bear cub than it is to adopt a dog from the county shelter? And did you know that a *dead* tiger is worth more than a live one? There's a black market for just about *every* part of a dead tiger—the head, the gall bladder, pelt, even the testicles. Poaching in Asian parks is out of control. Shipping zoo tigers back to Asia would be a death sentence. It wouldn't *save* them." Donna looked down at her closed fists and whispered. "To be honest, I don't know what will."

Silence fell over the room while the staff wrestled with their own thoughts. Iris VanWingen had opened an old wound. Everyone in the room knew the contradiction inherent in zoo work. They devoted their lives to wild animal conservation, but they devoted their days to caring for animals who, with very few exceptions, would spend their entire lives in captivity.

Caroline caught Chappy's eye. "Anything to add?"

He looked down at his untouched sandwich. "I guess I take her comments personally. She all but accused me of negligence."

"No one here thinks that, Chap," Gwen said. "No one."

"We're all behind you," Donna said.

Kirby raised his hand in a high-five. "Yeah, dude."

The room gradually split into side conversations. Peter got up to refill his coffee, but no one made a move to leave. When Victor moved to the front of the room, everyone quieted down.

"Of course, we're all behind you, Chappy. But even if a mistake was made—by you, the architect, the designer, the contractor or *me*—we will deal with it openly. There will be no cover up—not publicly and not internally."

Caroline looked down at her hands and suppressed a tiny urge to smile. Her boss was paraphrasing the advice she'd given him just an hour ago. His tone left no room for debate. Victor's first instincts had been to circle the wagons and treat the escape as an internal matter. But he was a quick study and, above all, a pragmatist.

He continued. "Mrs. VanWingen is badly misinformed. But let's keep in mind that animal advocates like her aren't really mad at zoos. They're angry at the state of the planet. They're mad about global warming, over-population, habitat destruction, oil spills in the Kalamazoo River, Asian carp and zebra mussels invading Lake Michigan. It makes people feel helpless. They want to blame someone."

This was pure Victor. On the subject of animals, he needed no coaching. There were nods and murmurs of agreement around the room.

Victor rocked on his heels. "It's hard to find a bull's eye on the target these days. When the public hears there are more tigers in captivity than in the wild, there's a certain logic to blaming zoos. Our very best work—research, rescue and release, as Caroline just said—is more evidence of the horrors our species has visited on the earth.

"It's always tempting to look for simple solutions to complex problems, but there's nothing simple about what zoos are doing." He walked to the door and pushed it open before looking back. "Caroline will deal with the media. But she needs all our help keeping our visitors informed. I'm deputizing all of us as part of Caroline's PR team."

Julie crossed her arms and grinned. "Okay by me, but then Caroline has to shovel poop once in a while."

"Yeah!" Kirby said, instigating applause that lifted the gloom. Caroline felt some of the tension leave her. She knew much of what they had just said had been for *her* benefit—the fledgling in need of endless tutoring on the ins and outs of zoos.

"One last thing," Victor said. "Before any of us feel holier-that-thou, let's remember Judy." He left the Bat Cave and let the door close behind him. Kirby and Julie's smiles vanished. The room gradually cleared, leaving Caroline and Gwen alone.

Gwen was rummaging in the back of the refrigerator.

"Hey, Gwen," Caroline said. "Who's Judy?"

The curator set a brown lunch bag on the counter. "She was our Asian elephant. We got her in the mid-sixties, way before any of us worked here." She put a glass container in the microwave and leaned against the counter with her arms folded. "She lived in a cement yard tethered to a stake. She ate dry hay or whatever people threw at her."

"That's awful," Caroline said.

Gwen took off her glasses and polished them on her shirt. "She died when she was about twenty—young for an elephant. She had a lonely and miserable life, just like Mrs. VanWingen described. Vic's right, we have no right to be arrogant."

Caroline caught up with Victor at Caratasca Island a few minutes later. His hands were thrust deep into his pockets again. She was learning her boss' body language. Hands-in-pockets meant he was either fully relaxed or afraid he might punch somebody. She guessed the latter.

She looked down at the monkeys. "Which one's the runaway?"

He ignored the question. "*Honra y dinero se ganan despacio y se pierden ligero.*"

Caroline hesitated, translating. "Honor and money are—what?"

"Earned slowly and lost quickly." He squinted into the distance and bit his lip. "This could be the end."

"Of what?"

"Everything. The zoo. Our jobs," he said, looking around.

"What?" She wasn't expecting this.

"The media and the commission are going to use this escape to discredit us and turn the public against any sort of expansion. Then, it's a slow death." He looked away. "I won't stay and watch it happen."

"Wait a minute, Vic. Are you saying you'd *quit*? Or, close the zoo?"

He looked away. "I'd rather shut everything down than continue like this."

"I—I don't know what to say."

"This is just between you and me, Finch." He ran both hands through his hair. "If the zoo stays here, we can't grow, and if we can't grow—and give these animals the room they need—we'll lose our accreditation and our funding with it. I won't be the director of a 'pitiful menagerie.'"

"Vic," she said, choosing her words carefully. "I don't mean to downplay the seriousness of this escape, but *come on*, it's not like the snow leopard or the python got out and ate somebody's Chihuahua." She smiled, hoping to get one back.

He looked away, not seeing the humor.

She went on. "Most people will think this whole escape is . . . interesting, even amusing."

"Amusing?" He gripped the railing as if he might rip it from the cement.

"Look at it from the public's point of view," she pleaded.

"So, they'll get a laugh out of a runaway monkey, but who's going to vote to expand a zoo that can't keep track of its *goddamn animals*?" He looked around and lowered his voice. "What's to stop people from thinking the snow leopard or the python are next?"

"We'll manage that."

"Manage? Is that what you call it? How?" He glared at her.

"Well," she paused, waiting for her thoughts to catch up with her mouth. "First of all, the public needs to see business-as-usual around here. Rudy Giuliani on September 12."

She could see his jaw grinding.

"Like you said, I'll handle media and marketing. That's why you hired me, right?" She waited for a response. "Come on. It was just *one* naughty little monkey. And a cute little bugger at that."

They watched an adult female chase after one of the youngsters, possibly Little Houdini. She caught him by the tail and pulled him into her arms, inspecting his ears, arms and legs as he squirmed to free himself.

"Looks like Little Houdini's grounded," Caroline said. "By the way, I held his hand this morning. I guess I shouldn't have, but I couldn't help it."

A smile flickered across Victor's broad face. "My daughter wanted to be a primatologist until she found out they don't get to hold the baby chimpanzees."

"I get it. I figured furry animal petting would be part of my job. I'm kinda bummed about that."

The little monkey arched his back and screamed until his mother let him go. He scampered off to play with his mates with his mother at his heels.

Caroline faced Victor. "I may be new at this job still, and no expert on animals, but I know *people*. As long as all the carnivores stay put, this is just a fun zoo story."

"Hmm," Victor rumbled.

"By the way, I had a word with Daisy this morning about being nicer to Kenya."

"Did you hold her paw, too?" He flashed her a begrudging smile and backed up. "Okay, Finch. I'll stay out of your way." He looked at her once more, perhaps looking for a cape or magic wand. Then he sighed. "I hope you know what you're doing."

Those were Caroline's sentiments exactly.

Victor's walkie-talkie crackled on his belt. He unclipped it to speak. "Gwen? Are we good? . . . Okay, open the front gates." He turned to Caroline and shrugged. "All right, go spin or flack or whatever the hell it is you do."

By 2:00, Russet Ridge Drive was backed up for blocks outside Ridge Park Zoo in Saskawan, Michigan. By 2:30, the parking lot was full and cars began searching for parking on side streets. Volunteers and staff stopped waiting to be asked, and simply directed visitors to "Little Houdini" as soon as they entered the front gate.

7
SLEEPING QUARTERS

In the chaos of the day, Caroline had skipped lunch. Now, her temples were throbbing in sync with her left blinker. She was rushing home to record the six-o'clock news. Traffic cleared and she gunned her Fiesta onto Russet Ridge Drive.

That afternoon, she had mapped out a crisis strategy, which included a press release, several posts to the website and a media event scheduled for Tuesday. It was a solid plan, but it depended on discovering how the monkey escaped and proving that Ridge Park—or more specifically, Chappy—was not at fault. This was going to be tricky.

She had done several phone interviews. The questions were predictable. How did the monkey escape? If a monkey could escape, what about a lion/bear/python? How safe/old/reliable is the zoo's security system? Where was the staff during the escape? Was the exhibit design/zookeeper/weather/phase of the moon/international terrorism to blame? How will this affect the referendum? *Blah. Blah. Blah.*

She had escorted several photographers to Caratasca Island and pointed out "Little Houdini," though she wasn't sure which one he was. She answered questions and allegations until her vocal chords were as irritated as the rest of her.

But now she headed home, thinking only about a hot dinner and an even hotter soak in the tub.

Home was apartment 310 in a 19th-century warehouse along the river. It had creaky, polished plank floors, twelve-foot ceilings and tall, east-facing windows. More importantly, it was affordable on a non-profit, non-utility company salary. Her best friend Bella, to whom she owed everything, lived in 311.

Caroline had never lived alone, unless you counted sharing space with an absentee husband. But this time—*this* solitude—was of her own making. The hand-thrown pots she'd made in college, which had lost out to her husband's precious orchid collection in their old apartment, (not that she was bitter) were finally enjoying the light of day on her living room shelves. She had ditched the bloated leather couch Rob thought was "classic" and bought a rumpled camel-colored sofa with soft turquoise throw pillows.

At times, she questioned whether her contentment was real or just an excuse to avoid the work of a relationship. But for now, solitude seemed right.

For now. Because to be honest, her life wasn't where she wanted it to be. Caroline had schedules and she was clearly running behind at this point in her life. While she was performing CPR on a dead marriage, the universe had moved on without her. Until her divorce, her life had chugged along nicely—graduation from Evanston High School, a BA *cum laude* in English and drama from U-W Madison, marriage to a med student and a couple of great career moves. No jumping the tracks to Wild Oatsville. No drugs, tattoos or piercings below the ears for good old, reliable Caroline.

Her personal life had gone off the rails the moment she married Rob—someone whose mistress was medicine. Her mother had called him "Caroline's promising young doctor," which was prophetic, since he promised to be home by seven, promised to help her shop for Christmas, promised to take a vacation, meet her for lunch, take out the garbage, pay the bills, change the oil—promising, indeed!

In the early years when he studied all the time, it seemed selfish to complain, and besides, she was busy with her own job at an ad agency in Chicago. To be fair, they were both too busy and self-absorbed to work on their marriage.

She was happy when Rob took a residency in Saskawan, Michigan. Although it sounded like the backside of nowhere, it would be a second chance. Riding high on the notion that big city people were more *au courant* than locals, she was offered a job in MidWest Energy's marketing department.

She and Rob settled into a second-floor apartment in a charming Queen Anne mansion within walking distance of the hospital. She made a list of restaurants to try and bought season tickets to the local theater. Finally, they were going to have a *real* marriage.

But a medical residency, it turned out, was just another name for school-where-you-can-actually-kill-people-if-you-didn't-do-your-homework. Rob joined a study group, took extra night shifts and slept in the on-call room. They argued endlessly about his work schedule.

In retaliation, Caroline threw herself into her own career. Before she knew it, she was "Sunny" Finch with a solid schedule of public appearances at schools, nursing homes, Rotary lunches, charity board meetings, golf outings and fundraising events. Her performance reviews noted her "impressive work ethic." Having no reason to go home at night had its rewards.

The distraction of her job delayed the divorce by several years. At work, she put Rob out of her mind. At home, they fell into a marriage-by-sticky-note-proxy—yellow squares left on the fridge. "Could you water my orchids? ☺ -R." "Car's out of gas again! ☹ -R." "On-call this weekend. Go without me. Sorry. -R."

She wanted to blame Rob for letting his work hijack their marriage, but in truth, she could have been more assertive or insisted on counseling. Instead, she made excuses. Lots of married couples, she reasoned, lived back-to-back and got by. In many cultures, misery and lifelessness were insufficient grounds for dissolving a marriage. Children were the consolation prize for being shackled to someone by mutual disregard and reciprocal disgust—but she didn't even have that.

She joined a health club where she met Bella, a single woman about her age, which was a rarity in Saskawan. They began spending so much time together that one of the trainers called Bella her "partner." Caroline was beyond mortified when Bella slapped her on the butt and said, "Come on, muffin. Let's hit the showers and head home."

Bella was an unflinching realist, and a plainspoken critic—qualities Caroline admired, but could never emulate. She was a stranger to the hand wringing that plagued Caroline. This economical approach to emotions left her with boundless energy. She worked at a trendy jewelry boutique, had a small pet-walking business and did some nude modeling for the Saskawan State University art department.

Bella was a "Yooper," a native of Michigan's wild Upper Peninsula. Her people were descendants of scrappy French trappers and their tough Ojibwa wives, with a smattering of Italian, Finnish and Cornish genes mixed in. Yoopers lived on smoked white fish, venison and tasty little meat pies called pasties. They died in mine explosions, hunting mishaps, snowmobile accidents and shipwrecks. They voiced resentment of their more numerous Lower Peninsula neighbors by calling them trolls, "Because you guys live *under* the Mackinac Bridge," Bella explained.

It was Bella who first called Caroline's marriage into question. Over coffee and bagels at the Third Base, she asked if Caroline's wedding vows included celibacy.

"Very funny," she said, "Actually, we're going to try to get pregnant next year."

"Will you remember *how* by then, eh?"

Caroline refused to take the bait.

"How many times has he promised you that, eh?" Yoopers tended to end sentences with "eh," a habit Caroline found oddly contagious. Bella dropped her bagel on her plate. "I don't get it, Caro. You never even *see* the guy. Will next year be different?"

"He'll have more seniority, and he won't have to do the night shifts."

Bella lifted one pierced eyebrow. "You sure he isn't doing the night *nurses?*"

If her friend left her feeling defensive and bruised, Caroline knew *The Gospel According to Bella, the Unabridged Version* was what she needed to hear.

On the night of Rob's thirty-fifth birthday she waited for an hour at the Thai Garden. Once upon a time, she would have waited longer before texting him. And she would have forgiven him when he texted back, "Sorry! Called into surgery. Totally forgot."

She texted back, "I'm done."

"U ate w/o me?"

"Not what I meant."

"?"

"We're done. Don't come home."

She shut off her phone and drove to their Queen Anne apartment—the one she once loved—and posted a yellow sticky note on the apartment door, "Rob Finch doesn't live here anymore! ☹." Then, she slid the chain into the lock and crawled into bed.

In the gym locker room the next morning, she burst into angry tears when she saw Bella. They sat side-by-side on the locker room bench as the rest of the women tiptoed silently around them.

That afternoon, the doorbell rang in the downstairs hall. On the porch floor was a grocery store bouquet of carnations wrapped in wrinkled wax paper. The card read, "Free at last! Love, Bell." On the street, Bella was perched on the hood of her car wearing an over-sized sweatshirt, yoga pants and a fedora. "Get your stuff, Finch. You're coming to my place tonight. It'll be fun!"

Caroline slept on Bella's couch that night and for the next two months while the attorneys sifted through the wreckage of her life. Without savings, a house or kids, the divorce was simpler than breaking the lease on their apartment.

The day she signed the divorce papers, a blue-gray fog enveloped her. She felt suspended. She felt nothing. The act of divorcing Rob was like popping an under-inflated balloon. No great truths revealed themselves. Nowhere among the ruins did she find the fertile seeds of self-knowledge. She did not feel redeemed.

Bella tried to be supportive, but, "It's over. He's-a-jerk. Move on." pretty much summed up her position. By August, she was threatening an intervention if her friend didn't snap out of it.

When Caroline shuffled home from MidWest, ready for a night of television, Bella hounded her until she put on her running shoes. She dragged Caroline to festivals in Riverbend Park. On what would have been her eleventh wedding anniversary, Bella baked a sour cream, lemon upside-down cake. They soaked it in half a bottle of peach Schnapps and sang "You're So Vain" and "I Will Survive" on the balcony until the neighbors complained.

Caroline lost the twelve pounds she'd been carrying around since college, cut her hair chin-length and with Bella egging her on, got two new piercings in one ear.

Bella tried fixing Caroline up with old boyfriends, friends of old boyfriends and brothers of old boyfriends, but Caroline refused. If she had learned anything at all, it was to trust herself, and everyone else, a whole lot less.

When she showed Bella the job posting at Ridge Park Zoo, Bella had gasped, "Just what you need, girl! New surroundings, new friends, new challenges!"

Yes, Caroline owed her friend everything.

Now, a year after her divorce, ten months in her own apartment, six months into a new job and nine hours after a monkey escape, Caroline Finch was very, very glad to be heading home to apartment 310.

She trudged up the same stairs she had bounded down so eagerly that morning. Tonight she was returning with a new load of stress and self-doubt.

The hallway creaked under her feet as the door to 311 flew open.

"Caro!" Bella yelled, stepping into the corridor wrapped in a blue terrycloth bathrobe. Her short hair was wet and spiked. The color-of-the-month was, apparently, Orange Crush. "So, how was work at the menagerie?" she asked brightly.

Caroline groaned.

"That old witch really stuck it to you, eh? It's been all over the news," Bella said, stating the obvious.

"No kidding." Caroline patted her pockets for a bulge of keys and looked behind her to see if she'd dropped them in the hallway.

"Exciting day, eh?"

Caroline set her laptop case on the floor and rummaged in her purse. "You could say that."

"So, what'll happen now?"

Caroline sighed. "Dinner. A bath. Or, maybe dinner *in* a bath." Her purse slid off her shoulder and fell to the floor. A nickel rolled down the hall. Caroline slumped against the wall and whimpered. "Damn it, Bell! I pulled off an awesome fundraiser last night."

"Which is *still* awesome, eh?"

"And *record-breaking* attendance this afternoon."

"Also awesome."

"But in between A MONKEY GOT LOOSE AND I'VE LOST MY EF-ING KEYS!" She threw her head back and squeezed her eyes shut. "And I lost my nickel."

"Aw, not so awesome."

"So, I have *no* idea how I am. Tired... confused... keyless... *starving*. I know that." She shook her purse. "Crap! I *just* had them!"

"Let me." Bella rooted around and pulled out the keys.

"Thanks." Caroline exhaled dramatically. Suddenly, she didn't want to be alone. "Hey, wanna watch the news with me? You can pull me off the windowsill if I try to jump."

Bella nodded. "Might be fun."

"I made curried chicken soup last weekend and I'll toss us a salad. Bring some bread."

Dinner with her best friend. Just what she needed.

If Caroline sometimes felt like a cracked china doll, Bella was one of those inflatable, Bozo Bop Bags that rights itself after each punch. It was Bella's firm conviction that the world was a giant cesspool, so she was rarely disappointed. Guys didn't call, landlords were bloodsuckers, bosses were jerks and once in a while you got a speeding ticket. Suck it up and keep going.

On a Saturday morning after Caroline had moved across the hall, Bella was keeping her company while she cleaned the apartment. At noon Caroline went to pick up their mail and came back waving a green envelope.

"You got mail for an Isabella Farber. Must be a mistake."

Bella had wedged herself on the floor between Caroline's camel couch and her coffee table and was painting her nails in alternating shades of lavender and black.

"No, that's me," she said casually.

Bella explained that in her early twenties she had been married, *very* briefly, to someone named Paul Farber. Then she went back to painting her nails.

Caroline let her arms fall to her sides. "And *what*? You never thought to share that tiny *tidbit*?"

Bella blew on her pinky. "My divorce experience won't help you. We can't co...co-mis...er...able...ate—"

"Com*mis*erate."

"Whatever. I can't be miserable with you. Sorry."

"But it had to *hurt*. It *still* has to hurt!"

Bella stopped mid-stoke. "I broke my collarbone skating in seventh grade. It hurt then," she said, bending over her nail, "but not now."

Caroline shook her head. "You, Isabella Farber or Fibber or whoever you are, are a wonder to behold!" She began speed polishing the windowsills.

Bella laughed. "Yoopers are tough, eh? Plus, we drink a lot."

This response was completely unsatisfying. "And we... *trolls*... aren't?" Caroline's hands—one holding the Endust and the other a rag—were on her hips.

"You?" Bella scoffed as she admired one lavender nail.

"What are you saying?"

"I'm *saying*, you're always tidying and fixing and needing everything to be *perfect* and having everybody *like* you and *commiser*—, you know. *Agree* with you." She waved the nailbrush for emphasis.

"I'm not like that," Caroline protested, dusting the dining table for the second time. "Put a magazine under that before you spill, please."

"The trouble with you, Caro, is you're so—" She searched the ceiling for the right word. "You're so *likeable*."

"And what's wrong with that?"

Bella looked like she'd just sucked a lemon. "Waaaay, way too much work! You gotta take a little shit sometimes, and give it, too. We're all standing knee-deep in it anyway." Scatological references were Bella's favorite rhetorical device.

Caroline wanted to argue, but decided to let the critique stand as some sort of Bella-style therapy. She lifted a ceramic teapot off the glass shelf and polished its perfectly fitting lid. Cleaning cleared her head. When she was depressed, bored or stressed, she cleaned. It was her default setting. *What's wrong with that?*

"Girls like you," Bella said, starting in again, "think you can make *everyone* like you. Believe me, it's a losing proposition."

"Girls like me."

"Yeah, you *try* too hard." A drop of lavender polish was clinging to the end of the brush above the tabletop. "You get all weirded out the minute someone doesn't like you. I know the type."

"We—*I*—do not!" she protested, watching the elongating droplet, simultaneously knowing Bella was probably right, but thinking, *doesn't everyone want to be liked?*

"They also dust their dustless apartments every damn Saturday." She punctuated the air with her nailbrush, allowing the lavender glob to fall to the table and begin the immediate process of bonding to the finish. "Oops," Bella said, covering her mouth with three fingers.

Caroline bit her lip. Bella blew on her nails. It was a standoff.

Finally, Bella sighed and got up for a paper towel. "*Breathe*, poor baby," she said. "I'll clean it up."

"Never mind!" Caroline snapped. She deftly wiped the spot, then sprayed the whole table with Endust again and gave it a close inspection. She couldn't decide how annoyed to be.

Bella sat down to apply the black polish, spreading paper towel on the table. "Honestly, Caroline, sometimes you come across as—" she paused to find the right word. "–prim. A prim little kiss-ass."

Caroline huffed and went to the kitchen for the Windex.

"Now you're flouncing," Bella called after her. "I rest my case."

Caroline was heating soup when Bella arrived, still wearing her bathrobe.

"I found your nickel in the hallway." She lobbed a loaf of soft white bread at Caroline and began slamming drawers until she found a corkscrew.

"I figure you could use this," she said, opening a bottle of chilled chardonnay.

"I have work tomorrow. One glass." Caroline slumped against the counter and managed a weak laugh. "Make that two."

They took their plates to the sofa. Bella took her usual spot on the floor and helped herself to bread, left the salad and started fishing mushrooms and peas out of the broth.

"Vegetables are our friends, Bellie."

Caroline turned on the news and set it to record. WSAS-TV opened with a teaser about a monkey escape, spent five minutes on the weather, did another teaser showing the monkey, cut to commercial and finally repeated the noon broadcast, plus a few minutes of Caroline talking about capuchins.

Bella jeered and hissed at Mrs. VanWingen until Caroline threatened to send her home. Caroline turned off the TV and sighed.

Bella asked, "So, do you guys really dump animal crap in her creek?"

"Of course not. At least, I don't think so. I should check."

Caroline took their plates to the kitchen and poured more wine. Then she and Bella sat at opposite ends of the sofa with their feet entangled.

"Who were those two zoo guys on the news?" Bella asked, meaning Chappy and Peter. "They look a little too old for you."

"And a little too married. Don't start."

"Aren't there *any* single guys at that zoo of yours? Because, I don't know how else you'd ever meet anyone."

"I've told you, they're all married or they smell funny or they're the wrong species. If I were a lioness, oh man, Goldwyn would *definitely* be my type. Thick red mane, strong jaw." Caroline spread her arms to show the size of his massive head.

A half hour later—after Caroline had nudged Bella out the door—she was submerged in a hot tub, trying hard not to think about so, so many things.

8
MONKEY MECHANICS

Thursday Morning, June 9

Her first voicemail of the day began with throat clearing. "Caroline. Victor here. We had record weekday attendance yesterday." There was a long pause. "You know exactly nothing about zoos, but I have to say you know your people. Okay. That's all."

When she heard him come out of his office, she turned up the volume and hit "repeat" as he passed her doorway.

"You're welcome!" she called after him.

A few minutes later she left her office and headed to Caratasca Island to go over the exhibit's security system with Chappy. The sooner she had a plausible-but-boringly-technical explanation, the sooner Saskawanians would forget the incident and start focusing on the merits of a big, new zoo. But what if Chappy had just left a door open? It was hard to imagine a scenario that didn't involve some kind of mistake.

The sleeping quarters of the troop was concealed inside a cement cliff that reminded Caroline of the hideout of a Bond villain. Skylights let daylight into the interior, making it a comfortable space when the monkeys couldn't be outside.

When Chappy saw her approaching, he said, "Did you know they call capuchins 'monkey mechanics'? These guys love taking things apart." He rattled the heavy metal door and flipped the lock open and shut to demonstrate. "But there's *no way* they could pick this lock.

"So, any guesses?"

Chappy shook his head.

"Hunches? Plausible hypotheses? Wild theories? *Any*thing?"

He shook his head again.

"So, if he didn't get out through this door, he must have escaped from the island, right?"

"Look," he said, gesturing for her to follow him outside. "This may be a new exhibit, but the principles of confining animals—the moat and the negative angle and height of these walls—have been around for years. No monkey could get out of this enclosure on its own."

Caroline studied the sculpted, overhanging walls. "What if a raccoon got onto the island? Could a monkey get out if it was in a panic?"

"No. And if a raccoon got in, it wouldn't be able to get out either." Chappy shielded his eyes from the sun and surveyed the island. "A hawk or an owl could fly in and out with a small monkey, but Houdini wouldn't have survived that. He didn't have a scratch on him."

A young capuchin jumped from the rope hammock to his mother's back.

"Is that him?" Caroline asked.

"Sure is, the little trouble-maker."

She recalled the cool grasp of his miniature fingers.

"So, he must have gotten out yesterday morning. Right?"

"Well, you heard his mom. She started in with that *"arrawh-arrawh,"* which means 'I'm here. Where are you?' Sort of monkey sonar. Capuchins keep track of each other with more than a dozen different calls."

"So he was climbing around right over our heads." She looked up into the canopy of trees. "What time did you let them out?"

"About 8:00."

"I came by around 8:45, and Mrs. VanWingen called Julie about an hour later. So he'd have plenty of time to get to her barn." She pushed a lock of hair behind her ear and cleared her throat. "I have one more question and please don't be offended. A reporter asked me if, um, the keeper had any alcohol at the party on Tuesday night."

Chappy crossed his arms over his barrel chest and fixed his eyes on her. "You can tell that reporter, and anyone else, that 'the keeper' doesn't drink on the job. And just so you know, he doesn't drink *off* the job, either."

She touched his wrist. "I'm so sorry, Chappy. I'm just trying to clear this up as fast as I can."

He leaned heavily onto the railing and closed his eyes. "I know. If I can't give Vic an explanation soon, he's likely to put me back on maintenance, or worse."

"He's not going to do that," she said. She had no idea what their boss might do, but Chappy looked so miserable.

"He'd have no choice. We could lose our accreditation. My grandson starts college this fall, the first in the family. I promised I'd help. I can't lose my job now."

The look of fear and resignation on his face made Caroline feel ill.

"Hey," he said, remembering something, "you going to get that kid, Rafael, over here? Rafael Rojas. I promised him, you know."

"Sure. I'll work on it."

9

JUDY

After lunch, Victor came into Caroline's office with unsettling news. Two city commissioners had called, demanding an investigation of the zoo's security system, a move Victor called "politically motivated hysterics." They backed off when Victor said there would be a full investigation by the Association of Zoos and Aquariums—a professional organization of two hundred zoos—known as the AZA.

"Really? When did that happen?"

Victor grinned sheepishly. "About ten minutes after I hung up the phone. The AZA will send a team in thirty days if we need them. That buys us a little time. But there's more," Victor said, sinking into the chair across from her. "The city rescinded our budget increase next year. They say they want to 'see what the voters decide' about the new zoo."

He picked up her antique glass paperweight—a cherished gift from her father—and began turning it over as if he were warming up for a line drive. It was hard to focus.

"That's bad," she managed to say. "Really bad. Is there anything I can do?"

"Yeah. There is something. You can get that woman off my, *our*, backs."

"Mrs. VanWingen? Why?"

"She can do us a world of hurt with that column of hers."

"Column?"

"'Natural Curiosity?' She writes a column every Sunday for *The Evening Star*—environmental topics. Has for years."

"I thought she was a retired teacher. Derrick didn't mention it when he interviewed her."

He shrugged. "She uses the penname Iris Van. I also suspect that man can't read," he said, throwing up his hands. "Anyway, our neighbor is sort of a local icon. Some call her 'the Rachel Carson of Saskawan.' Half of this town had her for high school science. Back in the seventies, the city was planning to build flood walls along the river, a huge project costing millions, but she organized her students to oppose it. The kids did research and argued that a park would provide better flood protection, be cheaper to build and do less damage to the environment."

"Did they win?"

He laughed. "I keep forgetting you're not from around here. Ever hear of Riverbend Park?"

"I live right next to it. I *love* that park!" She pictured the bike trails, picnic tables and pedestrian bridges where she and Bella ran together.

"Apparently, when she and her students took the mayor and the commissioners on a canoe trip down the river, that cinched it."

"Does anyone read this column of hers?"

"You betcha. Her former students worship her, and fear her, too, from what I hear. She doesn't suffer fools. I've heard her speak a couple of times. She's smart and opinionated. I've been trying for years to involve her here, but she has always ignored us. I wasn't aware of her stance on zoos, but I suspected as much. So anyway, I need you to, you know, bring her over to our side." He gave a conspiratorial smile and wiggled his fingers in the air. "Work your charms."

Caroline didn't like the sound of this. Working one's charms sounded dangerously close to ass kissing. To buy time, she opened her laptop and waited for it to come to life.

Did she really have sycophantic tendencies? Her mind sped off in several directions. *Riverbend Park?* Saskawan had that prickly old woman to thank for that? Would she write about the escape in her column this Sunday?

She typed "VanWingen" into a new Word document.

"What's her first name?"

"Iris."

She added, *I-r-i-s.*

"If she makes the zoo one of her causes," Victor said, "she could mobilize the entire community against us."

Teachers have real influence, Caroline thought. Her own tenth-grade biology teacher had made her memorize the Latin names of fifty trees of Illinois. At the time, she thought it was ridiculous, but twenty years later she still knew a *quercus palustris* from a *populus tremuloides.*

"I—uh—" She had no idea where to begin.

There it was again—chronic second-guessing that clung to her like a sticky film. How nice it would be to spend the rest of the afternoon curled up under her desk.

Victor was waiting for her response.

She typed, "Kiss her ass," lifted her chin and forced a smile. "Sure, Vic. I'll go see her."

A satisfied smile crossed his face as he started to get up. "Okay, then."

"But wait, Vic. I have a question, if you've got another minute."

He looked at his watch. "I'm meeting Donna and Kirby up at the kitchen to talk about storage. Let's walk and talk."

They walked under gray skies toward the zoo kitchen. At the pond, a flamingo was inspecting a flamingo-sized visitor in a frilly pink dress, undecided as to her species.

"What's on your mind?" Victor asked.

"I want to know what happened to Judy, the elephant. Gwen said she died young."

He paused in front of the snow leopard enclosure. The big black and white cat, known as Dotty, had found a spot of afternoon shade under an overhanging hickory.

"Judy's enclosure was here, but it was just a flat cement yard back then with an iron fence around it. Her winter quarters were even smaller—a cage with barely room to turn around. Her keeper, a guy named Max, did his best and Judy considered him family. But when he retired in the late sixties, she became aggressive. They had to tether her to a stake."

"People brought their kids to see a chained elephant?" Caroline said. "Were we really so heartless back then?"

"No one knew how social elephants are—or how intelligent. Judy's death was a wake-up call, so her life wasn't entirely without meaning, I suppose. I'm sure Mrs. VanWingen knew about her, even if she didn't visit the zoo."

"How did Judy die?"

"She wouldn't let her new keepers near her. Eventually, her feet got infected from standing in her own excrement. A couple of times, they called Max out of retirement. He'd whisper in her ear and calm her down. The two of them had quite a connection. But finally she got so sick that the zoo had to euthanize her. On her last night, Max came to sit with her. She tried to get up for him, but couldn't. He stayed with her until the very end. Old Max died just a couple of months later."

"He must have been heartbroken," Caroline said.

"I wish I could say we've learned our lesson, but we still have enclosures that are terribly inadequate. Just about all the larger animals need more space, more grass, less concrete. Lack of resources is a bigger problem for zoos these days than outright cruelty—at least at reputable zoos—but the results can be just as devastating."

They left Dotty and threaded their way through a group of young adults in wheelchairs.

At Caratasca Island, the monkey troop was busy foraging in the tall grass.

"We used to feed monkeys bananas because they like them and they're cheap. We didn't know it was causing them to become diabetic. Now we let them forage for nuts and vegetables throughout the day, which is more work for Chappy, but better for them."

Two monkeys were grooming each other, half shrouded in the cooling mist.

"I haven't seen an elephant enclosure on the new site plan. Is that intentional?" Caroline asked.

"More and more zoo professionals believe elephants can't be accommodated in zoos. I'm one of them. As long as I'm director, Ridge Park won't have elephants."

"Not even in Nord Haven?"

Victor surveyed the little island below. "I'm proud of this exhibit. The monkeys interact and basically live like wild capuchins. They act like monkeys are supposed to act. But captive elephants can't live like wild ones. If a herd of wild elephants lived in Michigan, they'd roam the entire state in a year and interact with fifty of their relatives." He shook his head. "In Africa, they can't even keep wild elephant herds inside of *huge* game parks. An elephant just cannot be contained. God knows, they need protection, but zoos aren't the answer. The same could be said for polar bears, whales, probably dolphins. I agree with Mrs. VanWingen on that point. Some animals just don't belong in zoos."

Finally, some common ground, Caroline thought. It was a start.

They followed a man carrying a small boy on his shoulders past the otter pond, where the otters were floating on their backs in the water, holding hands again. "I *love* when they do that!" Caroline said.

"That's how they keep track of each other," Victor said.

Caroline sniffed. "I'd rather believe they're in love."

This seemed to amused Victor. "Could be. We have a lot to learn about animals." He paused before speaking again. "An aquarium kept finding apparently healthy fish dead in their tanks in the morning. Eventually they figured out that when they switched off the lights at night, the fish panicked and swam into the glass. A dimmer switch solved the problem. Another aquarium built a state-of-the-art pool for its dolphins with lots of great enrichments. But when they released the pod into it, the dolphins just raced in circles and refused to eat."

"Why?"

"No one knew. Finally they realized that the pool's filtration system emitted a high-pitched sound inaudible to humans, but was like fingernails on a blackboard to a dolphin."

Caroline covered her ears. "Enough. I get it. Humans are horrible and ignorant."

"Yes, but we're learning. The stakes are a lot higher these days. Not only do zoos need to keep individual animals healthy, in some cases, we need to save entire species. Zoos have been called modern arks."

"Arks? As in, Noah? Forty days and forty nights?"

"Let me show you." He led her past the otter pond to the steep hillside home of a pair of South American maned wolves. The ginger-colored canids looked more like foxes on stilts than wolves.

A visitor standing nearby said to his companion, "Do you smell pot, or is it just me?"

The woman nodded and looked around for the offending smoker and saw Victor in his uniform.

"Excuse me, but do I smell what I *think* I smell?"

"That's the wolves' scent markings," he said. "It has a chemical also found in marijuana. You're not the first to notice."

The woman swatted at the air. "Smells like a frat party in there." The couple walked on, laughing.

The leggie wolves stepped gracefully from ledge to ledge.

Victor said, "Traditional South American peoples considered these guys to be good luck. They hunted them for their tails and eyes. They're protected now, but they still get hit by cars and catch diseases from domestic dogs. AZA zoos are maintaining a healthy population as a genetic back-up for the species."

Caroline nodded. "Right. A Species Survival Plan."

Victor nodded. "That's why I can't agree with Mrs. VanWingen that every wild animal belongs in the wild. It's not always in their best interest."

Caroline made a mental note to share this.

"How many species have SSPs?"

"Over four hundred around the world. Captive breeding may be the last, best hope for tigers, snow leopards, several rhino species, Spix's macaws, California condors or Arabian oryx. Ridge Park participates in about a dozen programs. I'd like to do more."

"So, zoos are keeping animals safe until the waters recede and the dove appears with an olive branch. Nice."

"But this time around, it's human interference that's killing animals. It's an international geopolitical crisis that zoos can't solve alone."

Donna entered the back of the enclosure with a bucket of dead mice and began tossing them. The wolves rose to their hind legs to catch them or ran up the rocks like retrievers chasing a rubber ball.

"Have these guys been bred?" Caroline asked.

"We don't have room here. But we could send one of them to another zoo."

"I read that chimps and gorillas sometimes select prospective mates from photos."

"Animals know their own minds."

"Good for them," Caroline laughed. "Swinging female seeks alpha male. Must love grooming in the moonlight."

Two teenage girls stopped to take selfies with the wolves and moved on.

"All this extinction, Vic. How do you keep your spirits up?"

He shrugged. "It would be harder to sit on the sidelines."

A white-haired volunteer appeared with Howl perched on her gloved arm. A group of visitors formed a small circle as she began her talk. "This is Howl. He's a wild-born, native barred owl. He was rescued –."

Caroline turned to Victor. "I'll go see to Mrs. VanWingen tomorrow."

"Good. But remember, zoos can't claim moral superiority any more than she can claim that zoos are simply prisons for animals. There are good zoos and bad zoos, just like there are good and bad columnists, farmers and science teachers."

"You're welcome to come with me." Caroline flashed her most charming, kiss-ass smile. "Might be fun."

He checked his watch. "You'll be fine. Just silence that woman before she turns the whole county against us."

"How about cement shoes? Or, should I just make it look like an accident?"

He fought back a smile and disappeared through the crowd.

She turned back toward her office, thinking about her new assignment. Iris VanWingen might be a legend, but she'd behaved like an ill-informed, ornery old so-and-so yesterday. Caroline shuddered at the memory of the No Trespassing sign, the slamming screen door and those accusatory steel-blue eyes.

This wouldn't be easy. What Caroline needed first was an excuse to call on the zoo's next door neighbor.

10

BREAKING ICE

Friday, June 10

From where she knelt between the tomato rows, Iris VanWingen saw a black and white streak disappear around the far corner of the barn. Either a zebra had escaped that zoo, or that boy was back.

"Hey!" she shouted. *What was his name? Ruiz? Rodrigo?* She couldn't remember. She twisted to get a better look at the barn, and felt her *levator scapulae* spasm in her neck. "Boy!" she shouted again.

A hawk called out from somewhere in the ravine, a truck rumbled by on Russet Ridge drowning it out, but the boy wasn't answering.

She'd probably scared him off by yelling. He seemed a wild, untamed thing—all smiles and chatter when they were chasing that monkey, but now sneaking around again. He had been upset when those zoo people took the monkey, so she'd offered him lemonade and walked him home. He lived in one of those ticky-tacky boxes on Russet Ridge Drive over by the mine fence.

She wondered what had brought him to her barn this time, and decided to have a look. She needed tomato cages anyway. At her age, efficiency of movement was the key to getting things done. She couldn't be running to the barn every whipstitch.

Getting from knees to feet wasn't a graceful operation anymore and she wondered why grunting was so pleasantly satisfying. On bad days, like this one was turning out to be, she kept a shovel within reach. She steadied herself against it and cursed the grinding in her hip—the *acetabulofemoral* joint—to be exact.

She stepped over the runner beans, leeks, tomatoes and strawberries and closed the garden gate behind her out of habit.

The cool nights meant the whole garden was slow and now her tomatoes were turning yellow for some reason, but the lettuce was producing nicely and was still mild and tender. She'd thin the rows later and have enough for a supper salad. There would be strawberries coming soon. That monkey had helped himself to a few green ones and spit them right out, the little rascal. She smiled at the thought of a monkey sampling her garden and was sorry she hadn't seen it. She supposed the poor thing got only bananas and popcorn at that zoo.

Zelda got up from her nap on the porch and accompanied Iris to the barn.

"Now, what do you suppose that boy wanted in here this time?" she asked Zelda. They stopped in the doorway. Nothing was out of place that she could see.

There was the familiar shape of her grandmother's Eastlake dresser under a tarp—the one her daughter Cindy kept saying she wanted, but had never taken home. The John Deere was parked in its usual spot on the oil-stained dirt floor. There were bales of straw, several apple crates, a rusty Radio Flyer wagon and Annie's ancient three-speed Schwinn. But mostly, there was gardening equipment—bags of peat, stacks of pots of every size and tools—in the same disorder they'd been in for sixty years.

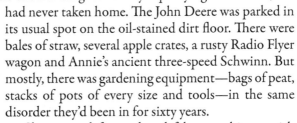

She stepped forward and felt something squish under her foot. A little piece of watermelon those zoo people had missed. But there was another . . . and another, dozens of small chunks strewn around the barn.

"Holy *smokes!*" Iris gasped, looking around for a monkey invasion. But everything was still. She let out a whoop of laughter, followed by an unexpected welling of tenderness. That poor child was hoping for the little monkey's return.

There was a time when Annie was six or seven that she'd found a newborn fawn curled up in the tall grass beyond the garden. Annie waited at the same spot for three days and worried when the little thing didn't return. Iris explained that the mother had found a new hiding place. But Bill, who was better at these things, took the box of sugar cubes from the shelf and handed their daughter two lumps. "Maybe you'll find him today, Annie. If not, you've got a treat for later."

Iris put her free hand on her hip. Now, what was it she'd come in here for? That boy was a distraction. She stood with the afternoon sun on her shoulders waiting for the thought to pop back into place.

"Tomato cages."

She rummaged among the shovels and rakes until she spotted them.

Through the dusty windowpane overlooking the meadow, she caught sight of that streak-of-a-boy. She rubbed the glass with her sleeve and saw him bound toward the creek, taking great leaps that gained more height than distance. Her mind went back to wild things. The trick was to live next to them and protect them without scaring them away.

Late that afternoon Caroline Finch walked up the gravel driveway of Willow Creek Farm. She passed sugar maples (*acer saccharum*, if memory served) and the No Trespassing sign, hoping she wouldn't find the homeowner looking down the barrel of a shotgun. But Victor's instructions were clear: "Get that woman off our backs!"

She emerged into a clearing where the house and barn baked in the afternoon sun. Purple iris and pink peonies bloomed along the L-shaped porch. Potted geraniums, looking nicely recovered from their spill, were once again waving their red pompoms from the barn windowsills. She was heading for the porch when she saw Mrs. VanWingen in the garden.

"Hello!" she called out. "Mrs. VanWingen?"

Iris turned, steadied herself on her shovel and fixed a pair of flinty blue-gray eyes on the intruder. "You could give somebody a coronary, sneaking up like that."

"Sorry. I didn't mean to startle you." Caroline smiled warmly, and walked into the garden. "I'm Caroline Finch. From the zoo?"

The old woman pushed a funnel-shaped cage over a plant. She was wearing the same worn denim skirt, another over-sized shirt—blue striped this time—moccasins and a wide-brimmed straw hat.

A rather large black dog with a crooked white blaze and black freckles barked twice and came forward from where it had been lying under the rhubarb leaves. Caroline froze, wary of the social skills of any dog belonging to this woman. It lowered its head and seemed to be waiting for a command to rip her limb from limb.

"I tried calling first," she said, letting the dog sniff her hand. "But when I didn't get you, I decided just to walk over. I can always use the exercise." The dog licked Caroline's hand. "What's your dog's name?"

"Zelda," she said, absently. She seemed more interested in a yellow leaf she had just plucked from a tomato plant.

"Nice to meet you, Zelda." Caroline said. The dog sat down and lifted her paw. "Aw! Such nice manners." She looked around the yard.

"Your garden is beautiful, Mrs. VanWingen. In fact, this whole place is amazing."

There was no response.

Caroline tried again. "It feels like you're out in the country."

Again, nothing. *Note to self: Flattery has no effect on this woman.* The compliment was sincere, though. The vegetable garden was huge, with something green and promising in every row.

Caroline was contemplating her next move, when Mrs. VanWingen turned to look at her, "No monkeys today."

"Uh. Excuse me?"

"If you're looking for your monkey, he's not here."

"I . . . um . . . I don't . . . What?"

She squinted at Caroline and laughed. "That was a joke."

Caroline smiled weakly. "Oh," she said. This was a very odd woman.

"But, you'll be glad to know we're ready for him if he decides to make a run for it again." She started toward the barn. When Caroline didn't follow she turned back. "Well? Come take a look."

In the cavernous doorway she pointed out pieces of watermelon scattered across the dirt floor.

"I don't understand."

"It's the boy. He's hoping for the monkey's return apparently."

"Oh, dear," Caroline said, laughing. "Well, I can assure you, that won't happen."

"Can you now?" She picked up a bucket from among the gardening equipment. "Well, he'll be mighty disappointed."

"It's nice to know you're ready, just in case."

"So, have you figured out how it got loose?"

"On or off the record?" Caroline said coyly.

Mrs. VanWingen turned to look at Caroline fully for the first time. "Do you read my column?" Those eyes definitely belonged to a teacher.

"Not so far, I'm embarrassed to say," Caroline said, "but I will this Sunday."

"And you've come to offer a bribe?"

Caroline recoiled before realizing she was being teased again.

Mrs. VanWingen pointed her shovel at a jagged hole above them and winked. "Could use a new roof."

Caroline laughed. "How about a new bird feeder, to replace the one that . . . um, got broken. What will that get us?" She looked up at the hole. "How many shingles for a public endorsement of the referendum?"

"Too late. I turned in my column yesterday."

Caroline stooped to pick up several melon pieces and dropped them into the bucket.

"So, how'd the little fella get out?" Iris asked.

"I wish I knew. We can't find anything wrong with the exhibit or security system. That's one of the reasons I came to see you. I'm planning a media event next week. I want to invite you and Rafael so we can thank you properly."

"I'll pass." Mrs. VanWingen left the barn carrying the bucket and walked beside the garden fence with the dog at her heels.

Caroline tagged behind, feeling foolish again. "But we'd like to thank you and Rafael for rescuing the monkey."

Mrs. VanWingen turned over a pile of leaves with a garden fork and buried the watermelon. "No thanks, but Rafael should go. He could use some attention, I think."

Caroline sighed. "All right. Do you have his phone number?"

"Nope, but he lives that way." She pointed toward an opening in the trees that started just off the driveway. "Follow the path 'til you get to the mine fence. His house is right there, at the fence corner. There's a picnic table in the backyard."

"Okay. I think I can find that. There's a mine there?"

"Sure. It borders my property on the other side. I'm wedged between a zoo and a mine. Imagine that."

"What kind of mine?"

"Gypsum."

Caroline looked blank.

"Plaster. I don't think they're in business any more, but they have a lot of nice property." Mrs. VanWingen started back toward the garden gate, still carrying her shovel. "Anyway, you'll find the house easy enough."

"I'd still like to have you over to the zoo sometime, Mrs. VanWingen—just to be neighborly. I could show you our new monkey island. That little monkey doesn't live in a cage, you know."

Mrs. VanWingen kept walking.

"We're doing some interesting turtle research, too."

She swung around to glare at Caroline. "Research? How to keep 'em alive in glass tanks?" She opened the gate and latched it behind her, shutting Caroline out. "You people have *no* idea."

Caroline stepped back. "We're going to breed them—Blandings turtles, I think—to repopulate the species. They're threatened in Michigan, you know."

"Maybe because you've got 'em all in your zoo. I wondered where all my Blandings went."

Caroline felt her face flush. "All our turtles have permanent injuries, or were raised as pets."

Mrs. VanWingen grunted skeptically.

"In fact, a lot of our North American animals are rescues," Caroline said. "Our black bears, our bobcat—."

Mrs. VanWingen turned away.

"Our eagle, too." Caroline sighed. "If you'd just come see for yourself... When was the last time you visited Ridge Park?"

"I took my students once." 1968 or '69, she figured. "That was *quite* enough."

"You might not know we breed endangered Puerto Rican crested toads and return tadpoles to the island for release. When—*if*—we move to Nord Haven, we'll be able to breed large animals, too, like snow leopards. We'll be able to give all our animals more space and freedom—like our capuchin monkeys have already."

Mrs. VanWingen's scowl softened into a triumphant grin. "Freedom, eh? So I can expect *more* zoo animals in my barn?"

Caroline cursed Victor for this assignment. This woman was proving to be immune to her very best ass-kissing.

Mrs. VanWingen was jabbing her shovel toward the path again. "Go on now. You might see him along the way. Seems like a nice boy, by the way. Not like the ones who chop down my trees and terrorize my frogs. They think I'm a witch, you know," she said with a wink. "And I don't tell 'em otherwise."

Caroline remembered an elderly woman in her Evanston neighborhood who screamed at the children, "Get off my grass! That isn't yours!" The older boys claimed her lawn was fertilized with the bones of the children she'd kidnapped. Caroline imagined there were plenty of stories about the witch of Willow Creek Farm.

"That boy, Rafael, is different," Mrs. VanWingen was saying. "Good with monkeys. How many kids can you say that about?" She chuckled to herself as she shooed Caroline toward the woods. "You'll find him."

⁘

The path to Rafael's house was worn clean of undergrowth, perhaps, Caroline thought, by deer or the dozen families whose yards were sandwiched between Russet Ridge Drive and Willow Creek Farm. Here and there yellowed grass clippings and the dried skeletons of rose bushes and Christmas trees marked the farm's boundary.

A German shepherd lunged at the fence as Caroline hurried by, then ambled off to lie in the shade of a rusted barbecue grill. A few doors down, a cat scratched inside a red plastic sandbox, then darted behind an above-ground pool when it saw Caroline.

Further along, the trail curved away from the backyards to follow the rim of a steep ravine overhung with lacy hemlocks. May apple umbrellas and trillium pink with age carpeted the forest floor. Somewhere a red-bellied woodpecker called, *"Chuck-chuck!"* A pair of cardinals chipped softly to each other from the branches of a nearby dogwood.

Caroline Finch of suburban Chicago couldn't put names to all these species, but she was as capable as Iris VanWingen of appreciating their beauty. She paused to watch the little creek, thirty feet below, tumble over rocks and under fallen trees. Its silvery waters seemed to have already forgotten its humble, gray-green origins under the flamingo pond. The wind rustled the leaves overhead, canceling the noise of traffic just yards away, but there was no sign of the boy Rafael.

The path ended at the corner of an eight-foot chain link fence with several strands of barbed wire strung along the top. Orange and black signs, rusty with age, hung at intervals. They read, DANGER! *PELAGRO!* Unstable Ground. KEEP OUT! or NO TRESPASSING. Violators Will Be Prosecuted To The Fullest Extent Of The Law. Stoddard Brothers Gypsum Mine.

Inside, the land rose up, hiding the interior from view. She reached out for the fence but jerked her hand back. Was it electrified? She stood on her tiptoes for a better look. *Unstable ground?* The trees inside the fence swayed above her, oblivious to the peril beneath their roots.

A dog barked, making Caroline jump. She swung around, expecting to see the German shepherd charging her from behind. But the bark came from inside the fence. An enormous golden retriever galloped toward her.

"Well, hello there! What are you doing in there?"

Giant paws rattled the chain links as the dog hoisted himself up to inspect her face-to-face. He panted, smiling at her, as only a golden can do.

"Are you lost?" Caroline offered the back of her hand and the dog reached his tongue through the openings. He had a red collar with jingling tags and certainly hadn't missed any meals. A man wearing running clothes appeared above her at the top of the hill. He bent over to catch his breath. He smiled and raised a hand in greeting.

"Come on, boy." He slapped his thigh. The dog looked longingly at Caroline, dropped to all fours and trotted back up the slope. The man disappeared into the vegetation.

The boy's house was like a thousand mass-produced tract homes in Saskawan, and a sad contrast to the vintage farmhouse of Willow Creek Farm. The deck was black with mold and had a picnic table covered with leaves and twigs. Two and a half pairs of boys' sneakers were dropped outside a sliding door.

She circled around the garage to the front of the house. The noise of late afternoon traffic on Russet Ridge Drive became deafening. She rang the bell. An open window allowed the strong aroma of cumin to escape. She pictured Kenya nosing around this sweet smelling house, then shuddered at the thought.

A petite, dark haired woman, a girl really, no more than five feet tall opened the door and smiled hesitantly. "Jes?"

"Mrs. Rojas? I'm Caroline Finch. I am from the zoo." She pointed down the street toward the zoo entrance.

The woman nodded and opened the door wider. "The monkey! Jes. I hear." She stepped back, grinning now. "Come. Come!"

"Is Rafael at home? *Es . . . Rafael . . . aquí?*" Two years of high school Spanish and a drama minor were coming in handy.

Mrs. Rojas pointed toward the backyard. "He come now." She sat down at one end of a long couch and gestured for Caroline to join her.

Caroline began, "We are having a big . . . thank you . . . uh . . . *grande gracias. Quiero . . .* uh *. . . decir gracias y . . .* uh *. . . fiesta.*" How does one say press briefing in Spanish? "Tuesday. *Martes.* Can you come?" Mrs. Rojas nodded, said something in Spanish and shook her head. They had reached the limits of bi-lingual charades.

The patio door slid open and slammed shut with a bang.

"*Rafa! Ven acá!*"

One shoe, then another, sailed through the air and tumbled across the living room carpet.

Mrs. Rojas rolled her eyes. *"Rafa! Por favor!"*

The boy leaped through the door and landed in a Spiderman crouch on the living room floor. When he saw Caroline, he rose slowly.

"Hi, Rafael. Do you remember me? I'm Caroline, from the zoo."

The boy climbed onto the arm of the sofa next to his mother. "You took the monkey," he said. His tone was accusatory.

"We took him home to his mother," she corrected him.

Rafael looked through the front window toward the driveway, perhaps hoping to see the zebra stripped van. "He could come here, sometimes. I could watch him and play with him. I wouldn't hurt him."

"How would you like to come see him at the zoo?" Caroline asked.

He looked at his mother. "My mom says it costs too much money."

Over the next ten minutes, with Rafael translating, Caroline arranged for Rafael to come to the zoo on Tuesday afternoon. Mrs. Rojas explained that she had started a new job at the Holiday Inn downtown, and was in training all week and couldn't join them.

Caroline arranged—quite cleverly, she thought—to meet Rafael at the farm, giving her one more reason to call on Mrs. VanWingen.

She walked along the sidewalk, back toward the zoo, marveling that a ten-year-old boy and an elderly science teacher living in the shadow of a zoo could know so little about it.

She wondered, too, why such an intelligent-looking man would jog on "unstable ground" inside a chain link fence posted all over with danger signs. She thought about this. *Of course! He couldn't see the warning signs from inside of the fence.* But why hadn't she warned him? She *should* have warned him. Now, if he and that beautiful dog of his fell into a mineshaft, it would be *her* fault.

She quickened her pace and tried to put the image out of her mind.

11

MISS CONGENIALITY

Saturday, June 11

So far on this Saturday morning, Caroline had changed her sheets, folded three loads of laundry, dusted, vacuumed, cleaned out the refrigerator and paid bills. Just as she was considering a second breakfast, Bella showed up, dropping her running shoes on the floor, and demanding like a cooped-up house dog to go for a run.

Yes, Bella was good for Caroline.

As they jogged along Riverbend Park, Caroline described her latest encounter with the ill-mannered Iris VanWingen.

"So, let me get this straight," Bella said. "You need to convince this grumpy old columnist that you're not incarcerating animals or letting them run wild in the streets of Saskawan, eh?"

"In a grossly-oversimplified way, yes. If she really loves animals—and I think she does—she'll eventually have to see the wisdom of building a better zoo—"

"I hate to say it, but you *are* incarcerating animals."

They slowed to get around two women pushing strollers the size of Volkswagens.

"We're *displaying* animals so people can learn about them. Plus, we're protecting them."

"Can't you do that in the places they come from, like the lady said?"

"It's more complicated than that. If it weren't for the work of zoos, a lot more animals would be extinct by now, like Przewalski's Mongolian horse, for example. Did you know that when they became extinct in the wild, zoos started a worldwide breeding program? Now there are hundreds running free."

"For real? I'd like to see one."

"We actually don't have any at Ridge Park."

"*What?* That's not going to impress the neighbor lady."

"I suppose not, but we do captive breeding with toads and turtles, too—"

"Hey!" Bella grabbed the back of Caroline's tee shirt. "Where's the fire? I can't keep up with you today." She stopped to take a sip from her water bottle.

Caroline laughed. "Sorry. This stuff gives me a rush—literally." She jogged in place and let Bella catch her breath. "I feel like I could run to Mongolia today."

"I think you've drunk the zoo Kool-Aid. Zool-Aid. Ha!"

"Funny," Caroline said.

They ran north along the footpath through the park. Hundreds of city residents were walking, playing with their kids, fishing from the bridges or just enjoying the weather. Kayakers were navigating the rapids around fishermen in hip waders while a blue heron hunted among the cattails.

"Did you know that Mrs. VanWingen and her high school students fought for this park? Without her, there'd be flood walls and fencing all along here."

"So, how's your diplomatic mission going anyway?"

"It's not. She practically ran me off her land yesterday."

"Oh, come on! With your ass-kissing talents?"

"My boss calls it 'charm.'"

"That's 'cause he's a man. But from what I've seen, Mrs. VanWhat's-her-name'll respect you more if you just lay out the facts."

"I tried that, but she's a science teacher with this *way* of looking at you. Never mind." She slowed down. "Let's get coffee." They re-crossed the river at the next bridge and stopped to stretch against the railing.

"So when she tells you to go to hell, are you going to take it personally?" Bella said. "I *know* you."

"No, I won't," Caroline protested, knowing she might. "Convincing her to support the zoo is my *job*, Bell."

They had reached The Third Base. Bella held the door. "After you, Miss Congeniality. All I can say is your job suits you."

"Miss Congeniality?" Caroline muttered under her breath.

A young barista with a dolphin tattoo on his forearm smiled from behind the counter. "What'll it be, ladies?"

Caroline said, "I'll have a half-decaf Americano with room for cream. And she wants a toffee, caramel, mocha, tutti-frutti—" She turned to Bella. "What's it called?"

"A toffee, caramel, mocha crème frappachino with whipped cream and a blueberry bagel, toasted, with cream cheese." It was her regular order.

"Ah, the Home Run Special," said the barista, looking amused.

Caroline turned to Bella. "Do you have any idea how many calories—?"

"I haven't had breakfast yet!"

Bella waited for their orders as Caroline wove through the crowded café and took a table by the window.

The Third Base had become a regular stop after their Saturday runs, and many of the patrons were familiar. Some came for the gourmet cheeses, wine, overpriced eggs and newspapers that appealed to urbanites too busy to drive to the big box stores at the outskirts of town. Others came for the fair-trade, organic coffees and hot drinks.

Bella set a white mug in front of Caroline, then took her place in front of a mountain of froth in a cereal bowl sized cup and saucer—the Lady Gaga of barista artistry.

"What, no sprinkles or paper umbrellas? Is there any coffee under there?" Caroline dipped a finger-full of whipped cream. The "Miss Congeniality" barb was still stinging and it made her want to identify some flaw in her friend and pick at it.

Bella didn't seem to notice. The fact that she weighed less than most twelve-year-olds further irritated Caroline. Sins and excesses should always have consequences.

Finally, Caroline said, "Say what you will, Bell, but I have a good feeling about Mrs. VanWingen. I really think I can win her over."

Bella looked up—milk froth coating her upper lip. "Or die trying."

On the walk back to their building, Caroline listened to a voice message.

"Hi, sweetheart. It's Mom. What are your plans for the Fourth? Dad's doing ribs. We hope you can come home. Call me!"

12

WILD THINGS

Sunday, June 12

Natural Curiosity: Notes from Willow Creek Farm
Iris Van, *Saskawan Evening Star*

I watched a pair of weasels cavort in my creek this week. They chased each other in circles, up and down the hill and in and out of the water before seeing me and ducking into their burrow under the bank.

What they were doing could only be described as play. These engaging little members of the mustelid family—otters, badgers, weasel, martens, ferrets, mink and wolverines—used to be common in West Michigan. As I watched them enjoying Willow Creek, I thought how fortunate they are to still be wild and free.

Some of you may have witnessed my fifteen minutes of fame last week after a wily little South American monkey ran away from Ridge Park Zoo and took refuge in my barn. How he managed to break out is still a mystery, but the fact remains that by doing so, he was in grave danger. Capuchin monkeys are highly social and intelligent animals and this one apparently wanted to meet the neighbors. I was glad to make his acquaintance, but it's a miracle he came to no harm.

As you know, I'm a fan of anything with fur, scales or feathers. That's why I'll never be a fan of zoos. At best, zoos house animals that have no place else to go. At their worst, zoos are confining and unspeakably cruel. No doubt Ridge Park Zoo is better than some, but in my opinion, that's not saying much.

The whole incident got me wondering why we need zoos at all. Nowadays, they claim to have "natural enclosures," but life in captivity still isn't much fun for wild animals and it certainly isn't natural. The ability to see rare animals on demand may even distract us from the great challenge ahead—halting our own species' headlong rush to destroy the planet. If we don't get control of over-population, pollution and habitat destruction, we endanger *every* species, including our own.

Zoos are big business. A new zoo in nearby Nord Haven would, I'm sure, give a boost to the local economy. But I'd rather get behind organizations that protect rhinos *in Kenya* or tigers *in Thailand*. If I want to see a gray fox, a box turtle, or a pair of bald eagles, I'll visit a state park or a nature center. Who knows? I might even see a pair of playful weasels in my own backyard.

You'll get a rare chance to voice your own opinion this November when the zoo holds its referendum. If you support zoos, you should vote to give animals larger, more natural living quarters, but if you question the premise that wild creatures should be incarcerated for our amusement, you might want to think twice about perpetuating this sad and outdated industry.

Caroline folded the newspaper on the kitchen table and frowned just as her phone rang. Whoever it was, she didn't want to talk. She looked at the caller ID and sighed.

"Hi, Mom. I got your message. I should have called. Sorry."

"That's okay. I know you've been dealing with all that monkey business."

"It's been a rough week. I'm looking forward to a few days off, especially if Dad is grilling ribs. Are you heating the pool this year?"

"I'll tell Dad to crank it up just for you. By the way, we're having a little party on Sunday afternoon for a few friends."

"Oh?" she said, rubbing her eyes. She *really* wasn't up to party.

"Some of them have their kids home for the weekend, too. We thought that would be more fun for you. The Steinberg's oldest son is recently single, too."

Caroline closed her eyes and prayed for patience. "You mean divorced, Mom." Her mother always choked on the D-word.

"Well, anyway, you won't be bored by us old folks." Her mother laughed. "Well, good, honey. Dad will be so pleased."

13

LAKE EFFECT

Monday, June 13

At noon on Monday, a cold front slipped down from Canada over the Dakotas and crossed the prairies of western Minnesota. It glided over Wisconsin and reached Lake Michigan by six that evening.

Warm vapor rose to meet the frigid upper air, creating little popcorn clouds. As they were carried east, they bumped into each other. By the time they reached Michigan, they were a solid gray blanket.

On beaches from Ludington to South Haven, vacationers called their kids out of the water, brushed off the sand and headed home. Boaters sought the shelter of inland marinas from Manistee to St. Joe.

The meteorologist at WSAS, who had seen this pattern a hundred times, predicted lake effect rain overnight throughout West Michigan. Milwaukee and Chicago, he said, would stay dry.

On the Ridge near Saskawan, Iris VanWingen cupped her hand toward the western sky and decided to leave the sprinkler off. At Ridge Park Zoo, volunteers rushed to set up risers in front of Caratasca Island. Caroline checked the weather forecast obsessively and tidied up the Bat Cave in case she had to move her media event inside. When she reached her apartment at six-thirty, the front was announcing itself with distant rumbles.

At ten that evening, wind whipped the treetops and a thunderclap sent Zelda diving under Iris' bed. Little Houdini buried his face in his mother's fur. Mrs. Rojas covered Rafael with a blanket and closed his bedroom window. The thunder did not disturb the boy's dreams of playing hide and seek with Little Houdini.

Caroline tossed and turned. *Warehouses for animals . . . incarcerated for our amusement. . . outdated industry . . .* kept her awake for an hour before she fell into a fitful sleep.

14

ANIMAL ESCAPADES

Tuesday, June 14

Caroline sidestepped puddles on Mrs. VanWingen's driveway and was beginning to question her wardrobe choices: ivory pumps, matching linen slacks and a silk blouse. At least the blue skies promised a dry media event.

Zelda ambled over to greet her.

"Hey, there, Miss Zelda. Look what I brought you." Bending at the waist to protect her ivory pant legs, Caroline held out an omnivore biscuit pilfered from the zoo kitchen. Zelda took the fat kibble daintily between her teeth and dropped to her haunches in the gravel.

"Are we friends now?" she asked, wondering what kind of treat would tame the dog's owner. "So, where is everybody?" There was no sign of Mrs. VanWingen or the boy. If she showed up without the guest of honor, she would look pretty silly. She put her hands on her hips and frowned.

She started for the house but stopped when Zelda trotted off toward the garden. Half-hidden by the low branches of the apple tree near the gate were Rafael and Mrs. VanWingen. They were facing each other, arms bent, palms up, as if receiving some heavenly inspiration.

"Hello?" Caroline called out. Neither of them moved, which peeved her. "*Hello?*" she called out, louder and with an edge. This woman wouldn't win any awards for hospitality and it was rubbing off on the boy.

"Shhh! Stay there." Mrs. VanWingen ordered. "Zelda, sit."

The dog yawned and dropped hind-first onto the grass.

Caroline whispered, "What are you—?"

"Shush!" Mrs. VanWingen hissed.

A tiny black and gray bird swooped down from the tree and landed on Mrs. VanWingen's silver twist of hair and flew off. A second landed in her out-stretched palm and flew to a branch, where it clasped a seed between its feet and began hacking it open.

Rafael's black eyes widened. "I want one!"

"Be still. They'll come," Mrs. VanWingen said.

On cue, a bird landed on Rafael's head. He squeezed his eyes shut and giggled. Now Caroline could see the sunflower seeds in their hair and cupped hands.

"Amazing, " she whispered.

"We're human bird feeders," Rafael said in a stage whisper. "Chickadees aren't afraid of anything!" One landed in his hand. "His feet tickle."

Mrs. VanWingen bent over, brushing seeds from her hair. "Okay, young sir. I believe you have an appointment with, um, Ms.—?"

"Caroline. Caroline Finch." If refusing to learn her name was meant to rattle her, it wasn't going to work.

Rafael shook himself like a wet dog. Mrs. VanWingen tousled his hair. "Careful, or you'll have sunflowers growing out your ears by dinnertime."

"How did you tame the birds?" Caroline asked.

"They're not tame," Mrs. VanWingen corrected. "Just brave and a bit foolhardy perhaps. Any chickadee will do that if you're patient and they're hungry. And chickadees are always hungry."

Caroline looked at her watch. "Are you ready see the zoo, Rafael?"

"Right *now*?" Rafael asked.

"Yup. Right now," Caroline said. "People are coming there to meet you."

He looked at her suspiciously from beneath shiny black bangs. "Me? How come?"

"Because you rescued our monkey. They want to thank you."

"Go along now," Mrs. VanWingen said. "It might be fun."

"It will be. I promise," Caroline said.

"Bye, Zelda." He dropped to his knees to pet her head. "If I come back later, can I play with her? We could have lemonade again."

In the week since the monkey breakout Mrs. VanWingen and Rafael had apparently become quite neighborly.

"Miss Iris helped," the boy said. "Can she come, too?"

"It's just us," Caroline said. She would not give this woman the satisfaction of rejecting her invitation yet again—especially after the diatribe she'd written in the *Star*. Miss Congeniality had her limits.

Thankfully, Mrs. VanWingen was walking toward the side porch, swatting the air over her shoulder. "You two have fun."

"Where's your green car?" Rafael wanted to know. "Do you ever get to drive the zebra van?"

"Both of them are at the zoo," Caroline said, "and no, I don't drive the zebra van."

They reached the sidewalk and walked to the zoo entrance, just a football field away.

"I hope two dollars is enough, 'cause that's what my mom gave me."

"You don't have to pay. You're our guest."

Cars were backed up with their blinkers on. "Are all those cars going there?"

"People saw Little Houdini on TV and want to see him in person."

The WSAS-TV truck had just pulled in.

"All these people are coming to see Little Houdini?" His bottom lip curled into a jealous pout.

"A lot of them. Yes. He's sort of famous now."

"Will *they* get to feed him watermelon?"

"Definitely not. Only Mr. Chappy gets to do that. Maybe you can help."

"Good," he said. He was walking sideways now, sizing her up. "You got any kids?"

"Nope. No kids."

"Why not?"

"Um. I have to find a dad for them first."

"Oh." He considered this. "Too bad."

"I'm sorry your mom couldn't come today, Rafael. But I'm glad about her new job."

Rafael wore a clean, white button-up shirt, a pair of navy shorts and black and silver sneakers that looked new. His black hair had been gelled into a part, but the front was already falling into his eyes. He was a beautiful child.

"How about you, Rafael? Do you have a dad?"

"Nah. He died before I was born."

"I'm so sorry."

"Mmm," he said, ambiguously.

She wondered if ten-year-old boys held hands with women the age of their mothers.

At the gate, visitors were queued up at the turnstile next to the ticket booth.

"This way." She led him toward the admin building. "We don't have to wait in line." Rafael lengthened his stride and pulled himself up a little taller as they passed a long line of visitors.

Peter was coming toward them from the clinic.

"Hi, Doctor Peter. Remember Rafael Rojas?"

Peter offered his hand. "How could I forget the boy who found our monkey?"

Rafael grinned.

"Looks like a full house again," Peter said to Caroline, eyeing the crowd. "Who knew escapes could be so good for business?" Then he laughed. "What am I saying? *You* did."

Caroline flashed a wicked grin. "We're in the monkey business now."

A traffic jam of strollers was lined up at the gift shop where her rush order of Little Houdini tee shirts and monkey plush toys in every size and color had just arrived.

She led Rafael into her office where she gathered up her notes.

Rafael sat down in her chair and picked up her paperweight. "Can I touch this? Wow, this is heavy. Is it glass? Hey, there's fish inside. How did they get in there?" He held it up to his eye. She started to answer when he set it down and stood up again. He leaned on his elbows and watched her laptop shuffling though photos of the ribbon cutting. "Why do those people have such big scissors?"

"We were opening the island where Little Houdini lives with his mom and dad and aunts and uncles and cousins."

"You put a *ribbon* around it?" He shook his head incredulously. "No wonder he got out."

"No, that's . . . " She tried not to laugh. "You'll see."

Next, he patted her desk phone as if it were a small animal. "What are these buttons for?" Before she could answer, he went to the window. "If we climbed that fence, I bet we could see Miss Iris' house. Why does Doctor Peter look like Santa Claus?" He picked up her cell phone. "Are there any games on here? Is there anybody you want me to call?"

"No, but you could put your name in my phone."

She sat down next to him in her chair. He worked for several minutes selecting each letter and number.

"Most people call me Rafa, so that's what I put." He looked up at her. "Does this zoo ever lose goats?"

"Not that I know of. Why?" His hair smelled of peanut butter and shampoo.

"My uncle has goats in El Salvador. So if you ever need someone to catch one, or another monkey, just call me. I'm in the Rs." He set the phone on the desk and stood up. "I could probably catch a donkey, too."

"I'll keep that in mind."

A few minutes later, they left the building together. When Rafael saw the flamingos, he reached for her hand to pull her along.

Derrick Wolcott, the WSAS television reporter, was interviewing a family with several photogenic children near the island. Victor and Gwen were at the back of the crowd trying to be inconspicuous. Caroline was surprised to see Tom Engelsma, the board president, talking to Vic. *Bless him*, Caroline thought. Board members rarely attended daytime events, but Tom was exceptional.

Chappy stood at the railing, no doubt pointing out Little Houdini to several photographers and dozens of visitors. When he saw Rafael, he excused himself and pulled the boy into a back-slapping guy hug. "I'm glad to see you, Rafael."

Rafael beamed. "Can I see the monkey now?"

Caroline nodded. "You two stick like glue while I talk to these people, but be ready to come up by me when I call you, Rafa, okay?" She pointed to the risers. "After that, Mr. Chappy will show you around the zoo."

She waded into the crowd to greet Tom and several journalists she knew. There were three or four media outlets represented and dozens of curious visitors. Derrick waved at her. He looked to be in good humor, but some of the other journalists showed signs they'd rather be covering a car accident. She knew they were hoping for a late-breaking story about the escape—which she'd warned them not to expect. She had merely offered them the opportunity to meet the boy who found Little Houdini.

Caroline caught Victor's eye and nodded as she stepped onto the risers. He and Gwen took their places next to her looking like the Blues Brothers in their dark glasses, wide stance and poker faces—not exactly the way she'd coached them. Neither Gwen nor Tom would speak, but it looked good to have a full podium.

Caroline stepped to the microphone. "Hello, everyone. Welcome to Ridge Park Zoo on this beautiful morning. I'm Caroline Finch, Director of Communications and Development. With me are Dr. Victor Torres, our Executive Director, Gwen DeJonge, our curator and Mr. Tom Engelsma, the president of the zoo's board of directors and the owner of Engelsma Construction.

"Unless you've been living on an island from which there was no escape, you know we had a very unusual incident last Wednesday. One of our youngest capuchin monkeys decided to explore the neighborhood. He did not have his mother's permission—or ours." The audience chuckled and murmured attentively.

"Here at Ridge Park, we nurture the intelligence and curiosity of our animal residents. We provide enrichments and encourage our primates' natural tool-using behaviors. You might see a monkey using a stick like this one. . ." Caroline reached into a box and pulled out a thin bamboo cane, ". . . to dip into honey or peanut butter their keeper puts in a special reservoir inside a tree. In this way, they have to use powers of reasoning and tool-using to reach their food. But occasionally, these powers just cannot be contained."

Several reporters had started to take notes. Two mothers standing at the back of the crowd edged closer, oblivious to the tugging of their preschoolers.

"Zoo escapes are very, very rare. But when one happens , our main concern is the safety of the community and of the animals. Most zoos have excellent safety records. But, as you all know, escapes do happen and primates can be particularly clever escape artists.

"An orangutan at a Missouri zoo was given a truck tire to play with. When no one was looking, he leaned it against the electrified wire around his enclosure and just *climbed* on out."

Caroline smiled brightly as laughter rippled through the crowd.

"This same orang was given a beautiful new enclosure with a lovely tree right in the center. On the day the exhibit opened, the zoo director was addressing a group of visitors when the orangutan in question yanked the tree out of the ground, dragged it to the edge of the enclosure and climbed over the fence."

More laughter.

"A female orang with a habit of wondering, could always be found sitting in front of her enclosure being fussed over by delighted visitors. When a female gorilla escaped, they found her watching the polar bear.

"Not all zoo runaways are mammals though. Parrots—who have big, complex brains—have been known to unscrew the bolts of their cages and then go around opening the doors of other cages. Not all escape artists are vertebrates, either. Who remembers what an invertebrate is? Anybody?"

A young reporter, probably from the university said, "It lacks a backbone."

"Looks like someone was paying attention in biology class. That's right. Workers at one zoo were mystified to find empty mollusk shells in one of their tanks every morning. When the staff rigged up a camera with a motion detector, they discovered that the aquarium's octopus had been pulling itself out of its tank and along a metal platform above the tanks used by the keepers. It moved arm-over-arm-over-arm-over-arm-over-arm and then dropped into the mollusk tank for a midnight snack. Then, it had the foresight to slip back into its own tank before morning."

Visitors pushed closer to hear Caroline.

"Now to our own escape artist, Little Houdini. I can tell you that those of us on this platform haven't slept well since that day. We appreciate your patience as we continue our investigation. Now, Dr. Torres will tell us more."

She backed up and started a round of applause.

She had asked Victor to talk about the AZA panel who would assist with a formal investigation. It would sound responsible and thorough, but few journalists would ask for details, which frankly she didn't have.

Victor stepped to the microphone, palming the index card of talking points she had given him. He cleared his throat and waited too long to speak, making everyone squirm. Then, he glared into the crowd through his sunglasses. She looked down at her hands. She had worked hard to warm up the audience and now he was losing them.

"You can laugh at Caroline's—Ms. Finch's—stories," he said quietly as the crowd fell silent, "but animal escapes are no laughing matter to a zoo director." He leaned too close to the microphone, setting off an excruciating wang and causing on-lookers to cover their ears.

Caroline kept her smile firmly planted. Victor eyed the crowd as if they were a pack of unruly children. Several visitors looked ready to run for cover. He put his notes—*her* notes—in his pocket. What was he doing?

"Do you have anything *new* to report?" one of the reporters asked, with a hint of pique. Caroline dropped her gaze. Her carefully orchestrated love-fest was turning hostile.

"We've ruled out several scenarios," Victor said in a monotone. "The whole troop was in its sleeping area inside when the keeper arrived on the morning of the escape. The monkey did not escape the evening before, nor was he out all night—as some of you have reported." He glared at the journalists over his sunglasses.

A young reporter wearing a Saskawan Community College tee shirt raised her hand. "Dr. Tor—"

"Nor have we found flaws in the design of the exhibit," Victor continued, ignoring her.

The student reporter raised her hand again. "Couldn't a door have just been left open or something?"

Caroline saw Chappy cross his arms at the back of the crowd.

"Our primate keeper is our most experienced employee. Nothing suggests he was at fault."

"Could Little Houdini have unusual jumping or climbing abilities?" Derrick asked.

Victor put a hand in his pocket. "Capuchin monkeys can jump three or four meters, but that's laterally, say, from branch to branch, not vertically. The jump required to get out of this exhibit would be physically impossible, even for an adult monkey. It's not likely this fourteen-month-old is the Michael Jordan of monkeys."

Someone laughed at the back of the crowd. Caroline let the breath go that she had been holding.

"Will the zoo put a fence around the island now?" someone asked.

"Absolutely *not!*" Victor thundered. "Of course, that is what zoos did years ago." He gestured toward the island behind him. "You can see how different this exhibit is from our older ones. Wild capuchins spend most of their time in trees, so we've taken great care to create places for them to climb and perch and even hide. They can also forage for food, as Ms. Finch said."

Victor paused as the reporters fired more questions.

"Will all future exhibits be like this one?"

"How do you think the escape will affect the referendum?"

"What about Iris Van's remarks in the *Star*?"

"Could you make a statement about that?"

Victor took the microphone out of its clip and walked to the front of the platform. "I'll try to address several of your questions at once. Thousands of years ago, zoos began as museums of live specimens. They were entertainment, of course, but they also demonstrated man's dominance over wild beasts. Alexander the Great sent wild animals home to Greece. The Romans pitted human slaves against lions and bears for sport. Louis XIV organized a duel between a tiger and an elephant. There was no victor in that battle. In the 1800s, you could get free admission into the London Zoo if you brought a dog or cat to feed to the lion." He let these images sink in. "Does this horrify you? If it does, we're making progress."

The crowd pressed in on every side.

"We still have a long, long way to go. Modern zoos play an important role in animal conservation and public education. But when I speak of a modern zoo, I'm not talking about this one."

Several journalists stopped writing to look up.

"We do our best, and Caratasca Island is a good start, but Ridge Park is in grave need of modernization. Our animals deserve better. *You*, the public, deserve better."

"Can you give an example?" Derrick asked.

"Sure. Our flamingos and our native turtles have let us know we're not meeting their needs by refusing to breed in their cement ponds. Our wolverine paces around her cage all day—a behavior we call cage stereotypy. She's bored and frustrated. Her enclosure is much too small. I don't know about you, but I think we should change that."

The crowd was quiet now and Victor was so lost in his own thoughts that he seemed to have forgotten them.

"Zoos breed animals because their wild cousins are in trouble," he said. "The main responsibility of zoos today—and the media should be our partner in this—is to raise a public outcry over deforestation, over-fishing, the disappearance of our prairies and savannahs. In Michigan, we are polluting our Great Lakes, mining our dunes and filling in our wetlands. It has to stop.

"We are literally crowding our fellow earthlings off the planet. Do any of you think one species has a right to do that to another?" He looked down at the crowd and walked to the other side of the platform. "I consider it my job to mobilize you."

A reporter's hand shot up. "What about Iris Van's editorial? Would you comment on that?"

"I agree with much of what she says. I always have. We should all support animal conservation efforts around the world. But here's a news flash for you reporters and I expect to see this in every newscast or article or blog post this week: Twenty-five cents of every admission and two dollars and fifty cents of every annual membership to this zoo supports animal conservation programs locally and internationally. How many of you knew that?"

Only one or two hands went up.

"Believe me, we could use every penny right here at Ridge Park, but we think international stewardship efforts are important. People say zoos are only interested in large, furry mammals, like pandas and tigers. But let's remember, when we protect the home range of the giant panda in the mountains of China or the tiger in India, we're also saving thousands of smaller animals, plants and insects in that region. That's a good thing."

He looked over the heads of the reporters to a row of parents standing at the back. "Every time your child sees an owl up close, touches the feathers of a whistling duck at our petting zoo or sees a capuchin mother nurse her baby, a stronger connection to wild animals is created. We hope your kids are conservationists-in-the-making. At the same time, our resident animals are ambassadors for their cousins in the wild.

"Let me leave you with this thought: Ridge Park Zoo exists to encourage kindness and good feeling toward our fellow earthlings, and to remind all of us to tread lightly on the land. There's just no higher calling I can think of. Thank you."

Victor turned to look at Caroline as someone at the back of the crowd let out a whoop followed by enthusiastic applause. Caroline reached for the microphone, but Tom Engelsma lifted it from her hand.

"Thank you, Director Torres," Tom said to the crowd. "I'd like to say just a few words."

Caroline shot a puzzled look at Victor, whose face showed equal surprise.

"This November *you* will decide the fate of this zoo. How many of you will vote yes for a new zoo for these magnificent creatures? *Show of hands!*"

The visitors eyed each other uncomfortably. A few raised their hands. The rest began to disperse.

The spell was broken.

Gwen whispered. "What the hell?"

Tom had his hand raised like an evangelist. "Thank you, everybody. I hope the zoo can count on you in November. Ridge Park is a Zoo on the Moov! Yeah!" He punched the air with his fist then began a round of applause answered by only a few tepid claps.

Reporters began firing questions at him.

"How will the escape affect the referendum?"

"Will the new zoo be more secure than this one?"

"How will the new zoo be paid for?"

Tom's smile took on a panicked look. "That's, that's all of my comments." When he handed the microphone to Caroline, his face was bright pink. *Serves you right*, Caroline thought. The reporters were still firing questions as Caroline walked to the front of the risers.

A firetruck screamed by on Russet Ridge Drive. She nodded at Chappy, who began pushing Rafael ahead of him toward the platform. Under the cover of sirens, she ignored the questions.

"How much will a new zoo cost?"

"Will taxes have to be raised?"

As the sirens faded, Caroline spoke. "I asked you here today to meet a new friend of mine." She put one arm around Rafael's shoulder as the crowd settled down.

"Last week, our Little Houdini was very lucky to be found by this young man. On a trip to his uncle's home in El Salvador, he watched monkeys eating fruit in the trees. So, when he saw our Little Houdini, he knew what to do. You all know the rest of the story. It was his quick action that helped bring our monkey home to his mother. I'd like to introduce him now. His name is Rafael Rojas, or Rafa to his friends. He is ten years old."

Caroline's applause was quickly answered by the crowd. Cameras clicked and a reporter shouted, "What do you think of Little Houdini's island, Rafa?"

Rafael looked up at Caroline, who nodded.

"I think he likes it. It's sort of like the playground at my school."

"Were you scared when you saw the monkey in the barn?" another reporter asked.

"No," Rafael said, taking affront. "He's as small as a kitten."

The crowd laughed as Caroline raised her hand for silence. "No more questions now, please. In a few minutes, Rafael will get a private tour of the zoo. But first, we want to thank him officially." She held up a certificate with gold lettering. "It reads, 'In recognition of your outstanding contributions to the welfare of animals at Ridge Park Zoo, we honor Rafael Rojas with the honorary title of Junior Zookeeper.' It is signed by Director Victor Torres and our board president, Tom Engelsma."

She shook the boy's hand as cameras clicked. On cue, Gwen handed Rafael a zoo cap, a tee shirt and a family membership to the zoo. Rafael smiled shyly as Gwen and Victor shook his hand in turn. Tom had slipped away.

"And now," Caroline said, "since this escape is still a mystery, I need the help of the children who are visiting today." She reached into the box and pulled out a roll of vinyl. She handed one end to Rafael and unrolled a banner with large green lettering, "THE CASE OF THE RUNAWAY MONKEY." Smaller lettering read, "How Little Houdini Escaped from the Zoo."

Caroline spoke over the heads of the journalists to the families, playgroups and campers behind them. "Children are welcome to visit our art tent to draw a picture of how they think Little Houdini escaped. We'll display the drawings this week and post some on Facebook. So think hard, get creative and help us solve this monkey mystery. Thanks for visiting the zoo today. And come back soon!"

Dozens of children bolted ahead of their parents to get a better look at the island. Others headed for the art tent.

Chappy beckoned to Rafael as Caroline stepped off the risers. She talked to several children and successfully avoided reporters' questions. She was rolling up the banner when Victor leaned over her shoulder.

"Nicely done, Director Finch."

"You, too, Director Torres. You had me worried for a minute, though."

Victor was actually smiling. "Yes. Well, I thought it went well." After a beat, he asked, "Did you know Tom was going to speak?"

She frowned. "I didn't even know he was coming."

Victor shook his head. "I don't know what he was thinking, bringing up the referendum."

"He made it sound like the escape was a publicity stunt."

Victor squinted into the distance. "Tom really wants this vote, but we may need to rein him in a bit." Caroline noted the "we." She had her hands full with Mrs. VanWingen."

"And speaking of reining people in,'" Victor said, "how's it going over at Willow Creek Farm?"

She shook her head. "She's a tough old bird—a member of the raptor family, if I had to guess."

"She made some good points in her Sunday column. Damn it. We don't want her as an adversary."

Derrick was standing to the side, waiting, and sporting his TV grin.

Victor lowered his voice. "Okay. Well, I'll leave you to the reporters." He walked briskly toward his office.

"This was fun," Derrick said, looking around at the crowd that was now six deep at the railing of Caratasca Island.

"Did you get some good footage?"

"Sure, but not the How-in-the-Hell-Little-Houdini-Flew-the-Coop story."

"Oh, *that* old thing?" she said, coyly.

"Don't you have *any*thing for me?"

"Well." She looked behind her to make sure no one was listening. "I can tell you exclusively and off the record, that Little Houdini did *not* fly off the island."

Derrick laughed. "Those stories were fun. Looks like escapes sell tickets."

"They don't hurt TV ratings, either, I suspect."

"Touché." He started to say something, but changed his mind. "Yeah, I don't mind peddling your escape stories for a while. But if you think you're going to distract any of us much longer—"

"Don't forget kids' wacky escape theories. Stop by our art tent on your way out. That should be good for a few more segments."

Derrick nodded toward a knot of spectators reacting with laughter to whatever the monkeys were up to. "If I didn't know better, I'd say you pried opened the cage door yourself. How about this headline: 'Crazed P.R. Director Springs Monkey to Boost Zoo Attendance. Details at eleven.'"

She countered, "'TV Journalist Frees Monkey to Boost Ratings.'"

"Touché again. Seriously, this was interesting," he said, looking at the crowds of visitors. "Most people don't know half of what happens on the other side of those railings. And I don't know who's cuter: the monkey or that kid."

Caroline smiled, but didn't respond. She was ready to bring this conversation to an end. Her regular work had piled up since the escape and nervous exhaustion was setting in. "Thanks for coming out, Derrick," she said, turning to leave.

"Um, Caroline. Would you, uh, like to get a drink with me sometime? After work, off the record, strictly non-business."

She had not seen this coming. Derrick was about her age, definitely attractive in a preppy, frat-boy kind of way. She pictured drinks, then her mind raced ahead to dinner, then *way* ahead to sex. *Not going to happen. Ever, ever, ever.* The man was ambitious and worked odd hours. She wasn't falling into *that* quagmire again.

"Wow . . . Derrick. This is a total surprise. I'm—I'm flattered." She looked past him for the right words. "I like you, but I'm only recently single. I'm just not ready."

Derrick took a step back. "Say no more. Call me if you change your mind." Then he winked, which erased all remaining doubts.

Caroline walked toward the art tent with Derrick's surprise flirtation on her mind. He wasn't her type, but that didn't mean his interest wasn't appreciated.

Back in college the unwanted attentions of men annoyed her. But the moment she put on a wedding ring, she became an androgynous, invisible creature—*persona non grata* to the opposite sex. Then, when her own husband had lost interest in her, she had stopped feeling attractive altogether. Though she couldn't reciprocate, Derrick's interest felt good.

She passed the bear enclosure and caught her reflection in the thick glass. She stopped. Anyone seeing her would think she was watching the bears. The straight lines of her ivory outfit were stylish and sophisticated, not to mention slimming against her olive skin and dark hair. She smiled, and her reflection smiled back.

In the art tent, four long tables were already filled with children working on their pictures. A clothesline strung between two trees had several finished drawings attached with clothespins.

A girl of about six waved her picture. "*I* know how the monkey escaped!" She held up her drawing of an upside-down stick figure monkey drawn with brown crayon. A tree looked like it was falling over and there was a large black squiggle behind it.

"Okay. Tell me," Caroline said.

The little girl traced it with her finger. "This is a tornado. It came down out of the sky and took that monkey right outta there." She circled one arm over her head to demonstrate.

Caroline nodded solemnly. "Wow! That's a really interesting theory. Let's put your drawing up on the clothesline. Thank you."

Back in her office, Caroline was surprised to find a voice message from Iris VanWingen asking her to drop Rafael off at the farm instead of his house. She explained that Mrs. Rojas had asked her to watch Rafael until she got home from work at six.

Perfect, Caroline thought. *And she really does know my name.*

15

SHUTTLE DIPLOMACY

Before Caroline's lime Fiesta had rolled to a stop in the driveway of Willow Creek Farm, Rafael was already yelling out the window.

"Miss Iris! Miss Iris, guess what?"

Zelda bounded down the porch steps with Mrs. VanWingen close behind.

He bolted from the car holding his certificate out of Zelda's reach. "I saw Little Houdini! And I got this shirt and a whole *bunch* of stuff. Look! I'm a junior zookeeper with a badge and everything."

Caroline watched from the car as Mrs. VanWingen examined the gold-rimmed certificate. "My my, isn't this *fancy*? Make sure you translate every single word for your mom tonight, okay? I told her you could stay with me until six." She glanced at Caroline. "At least I think I did. My Spanish is a bit . . . non-existent."

"Good, because he wants to tell you all about his day," Caroline said.

Mrs. VanWingen poked a spot on the front of his shirt. "I see you hit the concession stand or it hit you."

Rafael pointed to each stain in turn. "Mustard. Snow cone. Ice cream."

"So? How's our monkey?"

"I couldn't go on his island because the other monkeys might be scared of me," he said, looking disappointed.

"I bet when he saw you he said, 'Look! That's the boy who gave me watermelon.'"

He nodded. "I got to help make their dinner in the kitchen. They get nuts, oranges and carrots. A lady brought branches with berries, too."

"Mulberry branches," Caroline said. "One of our volunteers brings them in every year from her yard. Some people mistake them for jelly beans," Caroline added, pointedly.

"Then we cleaned their bedrooms," Rafael said. "They sleep in straw. We also took care of the owl monkeys."

"Which? Owls or monkeys?"

Rafael looked puzzled, then rolled his eyes. "Owl *monkeys*! They have big eyes, like owls."

Zelda nuzzled the edge of his tee shirt, enjoying the aroma of ice cream with monkey overtones.

Caroline got out of the car. "I'm sorry you couldn't come, too, Mrs. VanWingen. But, we brought you something."

"A senior zookeeper badge?" Mrs. VanWingen asked dryly.

Caroline took a long, rectangular box wrapped in spotted leopard paper from the back seat.

"We bought it at the zoo," Rafael said, starting to bounce. "You should open it."

"Why, I—." She pursed her lips, caught off guard by the fuss. "My, it's heavy. Let's go sit."

On the deep wrap-around porch, two vintage lawn chairs faced the yard. At the far end, a metal glider with cracked red vinyl cushions sat with its back to the barn. Exuberant peach and white impatiens spilled over their baskets hung from the porch soffit.

Mrs. VanWingen directed Caroline toward the glider and lowered herself into the chair nearest the screen door. Zelda took a drink from a crockery bowl by the door before sitting down on a thick rug next to Caroline.

Iris' eyes twinkled mischievously as Rafael helped unwrap the box. "From the zoo, huh? I bet it's a barrel o' monkeys." She put her ear to the box and shook it, making a show of things.

Rafael giggled. "Nope. It's not."

She set the box on the floor and pulled out a long copper bird feeder.

"Why, how about that! Isn't this lovely. Now we won't have to stand out there all winter with seeds on our heads." She gave Caroline a polite nod. "Thank you." Then, she slapped her knee. "Okay. Who wants lemonade?"

"Me!" Rafael's hand shot up. "Do you want some, Miss Caroline?"

"Oh, I should go," she said. Her response was instinctive—and incredibly stupid.

Mrs. VanWingen gave a shrug that implied, *Suit yourself.*

"Pleeease, Miss Caroline. Stay!" Bless the child for giving her a second chance to seize the moment.

"Well, maybe just for a *few* minutes."

Rafael announced, "I'm a little hungry, too."

Mrs. VanWingen poked at the stains on his shirtfront again and tugged on his cap. "Is that right?"

"They gave me this hat, too," he said. "And a ticket to the zoo. Yup."

"A family *membership*," Caroline corrected. "Be sure to give it to your mom and don't lose it. It means you can come anytime for free. Maybe you can bring Mrs. VanWingen sometime."

Mrs. VanWingen got up and opened the screen door. "Come get the glasses, Rafa. I'll get the pitcher. I'll see if I can find some cookies."

"Can I help?" Caroline called out.

"Nope. Stay there."

She could hear Rafael in the kitchen going on about mulberry branches and how Chappy whistled at the monkeys. *The kid deserves a junior PR Director badge, too,* she thought.

Zelda stretched her wet nose to within inches of Caroline's ivory panted thigh. Caroline shifted away. "Sorry, girl. Nothing personal."

Rafael made several trips from the kitchen to the porch with glasses and a plate of windmill cookies. He set them on a glass coffee table. Mrs. VanWingen followed with a pitcher of lemonade with real slices floating on the top.

"The real thing," Caroline said. "And cookies before dinner. I feel decadent."

Mrs. VanWingen sniffed. "I gave up being a role model when I retired and my girls left home."

"That's not what *I* hear," Caroline ventured. "And you're not exactly retired."

Mrs. VanWingen filled three glasses.

Caroline struck out boldly. "In fact, I hear a lot of folks in this town pay attention to what you have to say."

She handed Caroline a full glass. "Ah, my column. I'm not sure who reads it, but it helps keep my mind sharp. And they pay me. Imagine that."

Caroline sipped the lemonade. "Delicious. Thank you." She settled against the cushions. "I read '*Natural Curiosity*' for the first time on Sunday. We aren't as far apart on zoos as you think, Mrs. VanWingen. Our director talked about the same conservation issues at our press briefing today."

Rafael palmed a handful of cookies.

"Leave some for our guest, please," Mrs. VanWingen said.

"Oh, sorry." He dropped all but one cookie back on the plate.

Mrs. VanWingen sat back in her chair. "So tell me, Rafa, what was our monkey up to today?"

Through a mouthful of cookie, he said, "Well, he played with his friends and sat on his mom's lap a lot. He lives on an island with water all around and a tall, tall, tall wall all around, like this," demonstrating the negative angle. "No monkey could get out of that!"

"And yet," Mrs. VanWingen said, arching her eyebrows over her glasses, "one did."

The boy shrugged. "Yup. It's a mystery." He downed his lemonade in one long gulp and set his glass down with a bang. "Can I play with Zelda now?"

"Her ball is under the lilac there." Iris pointed toward the corner of the porch.

He jumped off the porch, crawled under the bush and stood up, holding a dirty yellow tennis ball over his head as Zelda jumped off the porch and began prancing backwards. Rafael pretended to throw it several times, but hid it behind his back when Zelda tore off, waiting for it to land. Finally, he heaved the ball and it rolled into the barn. Zelda disappeared inside and they could hear shovels and rakes clanking together and falling to the floor.

Caroline and Mrs. VanWingen laughed.

"That dog hasn't had this much exercise since my grandchildren visited last Christmas."

A moment later, Zelda reappeared triumphantly in the doorway with the ball in her mouth.

"Here, Zelda!" Rafael commanded.

She trotted obediently to where he stood. But when he reached for the ball, she tore off again, holding her head and tail high and sassy.

Mrs. VanWingen laughed.

Rafael staggered around the yard, yelling, "Zel-el-da-a! Come back here." The dog stopped and let Rafael touch the ball and a game of tug-of-war ensued. At the end of the round, Rafael was straddling her back, trying to pry the ball out of her mouth as she growled menacingly. Then the whole game began again.

"Some retriever," Caroline laughed. "Where'd you get her?"

"My daughters gave her to me after my husband died. She's probably Labrador, with some springer spaniel or border collie. My grandson says she's pure splab."

"Splab? Or maybe La-border? Or, . . . spring-ador?"

"Something like that. She's a good barker, but she wouldn't fight off attackers if there was a bed to hide under."

"You're pretty isolated back here," she said, wondering if Mrs. VanWingen was ever afraid to be so alone. Except for the distant drone of traffic, there was no sign of other human presence.

"True. But I enjoy it." A flicker of something—concern or worry—crossed her face and she started to say more, but stopped. She set her glass on the table with a soft clink.

Rafael and Zelda were still rolling in the grass.

A breeze kicked up and the lilacs exhaled their perfume onto the porch. Caroline sighed, gliding herself into a stupor and hoping this small truce would hold. She was happy to let Rafael take the lead on zoo diplomacy. But now the conversation had shifted, and she needed to direct it back to the merits of zoos in general and Ridge Park in particular. Then again, she had no desire for another confrontation and the glider was so comfy.

"It's so quiet," she said, finally.

"Mm. That all depends on how well you listen." She tilted her head to one side. "Hear that?"

"What?" Caroline heard only distant traffic.

Mrs. VanWingen pointed toward the pine tree behind Caroline's head.

"A house wren has been singing non-stop all day. He's got a nest in that pine. And there?" There was a *chur-chur* somewhere. "The red-belly."

"A red-bellied what?"

"A good-sized woodpecker. They like my dead ash trees."

There was a *heh-heh-heh* in the distance. "Hear that?"

Caroline nodded. "What is it?"

"Don't ask *me*," Mrs. VanWingen said with shrug and a wry chuckle. "That's coming from your side of the fence."

"Oh. Right." Caroline concentrated. "Oh, I know that! That's a flamingo. They sound like they're laughing. I never realized you could hear them way over here."

"I wonder what they have to laugh about."

"Not much, to be honest," Caroline said, seizing the opportunity. "Their enclosure is too small and their pond—the one that feeds Willow Creek—has an old cement bottom. At the new zoo, they'd have a natural pond with vegetation all around."

Mrs. VanWingen didn't respond.

Caroline tried a different tack. "I bet you hear Goldwyn, too."

Mrs. VanWingen looked mildly interested.

"Our four-hundred-and-fifty-pound lion. When he roars, they can probably hear him in Detroit. He has a habit of roaring at ten o'clock every morning."

"Ah, yes. I do hear him sometimes."

"One of our zoo volunteers mentioned his habit to a Japanese tour group. They were so fascinated that they promised to come back the next morning, just before ten. Our poor volunteer tried to explain that Goldwyn *occasionally* took the off day and he *might* not roar *exactly* at ten, but they insisted. The next day the whole group lined up in front of the exhibit with their cameras ready."

"Was the volunteer there?"

"She was hiding in the bushes!"

"And?"

"So, at *exactly* ten, Goldwyn gets up, stretches and climbs up to the highest rock in his enclosure. He gazes down at his audience lined up at the railing, all with their cameras pointed at him, and then, he lets out a roar that *shook the zoo!*"

Mrs. VanWingen slapped her knee. "What did the volunteer do then?"

"She came out of the bushes to take her bows, of course."

Caroline watched Mrs. VanWingen's smile fade into a scowl. "Goldwyn. Little Houdini, indeed. Such anthropomorphic sentimentalism."

"You're right," Caroline nodded. "Officially, we don't name our animals, but sometimes the public does, and even the zookeepers can't seem to help themselves. Everyone—besides my boss and the monkey keeper—seems to be enjoying this Little Houdini business."

"I bet it hasn't hurt zoo attendance either."

"You're right about that, too."

Caroline sat in the silence that wasn't really silent, she realized, but an eclectic chorus of their wild and captive neighbors.

Rafael crawled up the porch steps and lay on his stomach, panting.

Zelda sank into her rug with a grunt.

"You've got a little slice of heaven here, Mrs. VanWingen," Caroline said. "The city just grew up around you, but *this*—this is so unspoiled."

"I wish that were true." She pointed toward the woods beyond the garden. "We lost a whole grove of elms in the seventies, and now the ashes are going. I pull garlic mustard and English ivy from the woods. English sparrows take over every bluebird house I put up. My mother planted Eurasian yellow iris in the stream back in the fifties that's crowding out the native blue flag. I'll probably never be rid of it." She raised a hand and dropped it back in her lap. "It's more than one old person can handle, sadly."

"I wish I could send over a crew of our volunteers," Caroline said. She set her empty glass on the table. "We have a whole team replanting the zoo with native plants. It's a big job." Caroline sat back, feeling proud to have found some common ground.

"But meanwhile, your plastic cups and pond scum are polluting my turtle pond," Mrs. VanWingen snapped.

So much for common ground, Caroline thought. "I'm sorry about that," Caroline said. "We sell all our beverages in souvenir cups so visitors will reuse them instead of littering. Sometimes we can't keep ahead of it, though. Anyway, with any luck, we won't be your next-door neighbors much longer."

Rafael was balancing on the porch railing, inspecting the hanging baskets and bringing to mind Little Houdini. "I threw raisins to a different kind of monkey today. They have long white mustaches," he said, "What are they called, Miss Caroline?"

"Emperor tamarins."

"I threw raisins on the ground, and Mr. Chappy hid some of them under the leaves. Wanna know why?"

Mrs. VanWingen raised her eyebrows.

"It's like a game," he said. "Sometimes they play with baby toys, too."

"That doesn't sound very natural," Mrs. VanWingen pointed out.

"It's not," Caroline said, "but it provides mental stimulation. Our vet says it only takes about four weeks for brain function to improve when zoo animals are given enrichments."

"Enrichments?" she said. "No surprise there. I used to tell my students, 'Either use your brains or they'll turn to mush.'"

"And you know what else?" Rafael flung himself into the glider practically giving Caroline whiplash. "Mr. Chappy gives the monkeys really hard nuts so they have to crack them open with stones."

Mrs. VanWingen gave a look that passed for approval.

"I think Zelda likes it when I throw her ball into tall grass where it's harder to find," Rafael said. "Mr. Chappy asked me if I had to think hard to figure out how to catch Houdini. He said that was like an enrichment. We did think hard, didn't we, Miss Iris?"

"Indeed, we did. We had to use *all* our smarts that morning."

Rafael climbed up on the railing again to examine a heavy brass bell that hung from the post. "Can I ring this?" He gripped a rope attached to the clapper.

Mrs. VanWingen grimaced and covered her ears, "Just two times. It's *very* loud."

Rafael yanked the rope twice, leaving a deafening hum in the air. Then he jumped down. "What's it for?"

"It's a dinner bell. My grandmother used it to call my mother. Then *she* used it to call me and my sister, then *I* used it to call my daughters. It was sort of an alarm, too."

"What for?"

"Well, we didn't have cell phones back then, so if my dad was off in the orchard and the house caught fire or one of us got hurt, my mom could call him with a special ring. Three quick, then three slow rings meant, 'Help! Come quick!'"

"Did she ever use the special ring?" Rafael asked.

"Just once. My little sister got her head stuck between those two spindles in the railing." She pointed at a spindle on the steps that didn't quite match the rest. "I thought we should leave her there, but my mom called my dad and he sawed her loose."

"You wanted to leave her with her head stuck?" Rafael asked.

"You'd understand if you had a little sister," Mrs. VanWingen said.

Rafael, on his knees now, tried to push his head between the slats. "My head won't fit."

"That because your brain has been enriched," Mrs. VanWingen said.

Rafael jumped off the porch and ran toward the barn with Zelda at his heels again.

Mrs. VanWingen squinted at Caroline. "More lemonade, Ms. Finch?"

"No thank you, but it was delicious. I wish you'd call me Caroline."

"All right then. Call me Iris." She shifted in her chair to face the glider. "So, *Caroline*. You've been doing your best to steer the conversation to zoos. So, go ahead, tell me why we need them."

Caroline sat up straight. "Zoos? Well, uh, there's, I mean, there's a lot—" She collapsed against the cushion and clapped her hand over her forehead and laughed. "You've caught me off guard and completely tongue-tied. Let me think. Why we need zoos… There are a lot of zoos we don't need, but we *do* need well-run, humane ones. I mean, we don't need farms that misuse herbicides and chemical fertilizers or mistreat animals, either. Am I right? But no farm can become sustainable and organic overnight, either."

"True."

"Zoos are having to correct mistakes of the past, just like you have to work at eradicating the yellow iris your mother planted. It takes *time* and a lot of resources."

Iris' eyes bore into Caroline. "So, describe this so-called 'well-run, humane zoo.'"

"One with naturalized exhibits, like our new Caratasca Island monkey exhibit. It offers space where monkeys can forage, run, climb, interact—whatever they do in the wild. To do that for all our animals we need more space than we have here in the city."

"Aye, there's the rub." Iris folded her arms. "Just to be clear, I'm *not* selling."

Caroline replayed what she just heard. "Wait. Wait a minute. Selling your *land*? You think Ridge Park wants Willow Creek Farm?"

Iris shrugged. "I've gotten letters and phone calls from agents who say they represent 'interested parties.' I figured it was you zoo people."

"No. Ridge Park is planning a move to Nord Haven. We're not—"

"Miss Iris! Miss Iris!" Rafael was pushing the blue Schwinn out of the barn. "Can I ride it?"

"Just stay in the driveway," Iris said.

Rafael wobbled across the gravel as Caroline tried to make sense of Iris' accusation.

Iris turned to Caroline again. "Go on. Tell me more about 'well-run, humane zoos'—which, by the way, is a laughable oxymoron."

Caroline stifled a sigh. "Traditional zoos are built like strip malls—rows of enclosures viewed by visitors from paved pathways. But in modern zoos visitors interact with the animals. Humans can even enter the habitats."

Iris chuckled. "So your Goldwyn could choose his dinner from a parade of tasty visitors?"

Caroline rolled her eyes. "No, but he might be able to wander throughout the zoo in a series of enclosed walkways."

Rafael careened into the lilac bush.

"Careful," Iris called out. "Practice using those hand brakes."

"At some aquariums, visitors walk through glass tunnels with the otters, penguins or fish swimming around them."

Rafael righted himself and pushed off again.

Iris nodded. "I've seen pictures. But what's the point of that, other than entertainment? How does that benefit the otters, say?"

"Would people care as much about the extinction of sea otters if they've never seen or interacted with them? Zoos are the classrooms of worldwide animal conservation efforts. We provide a window into a disappearing world. Zoo breeding programs have saved several species from complete extinction."

"Like?"

"Like the Arabian oryx, Przewalski's Mongolian horse, Guam rails, black-footed ferrets—"

"He should probably have a helmet," Iris said, nodding toward Rafael, who had just fallen again. "My girls never wore 'em. Anybody'd think kids have turned to glass. So, what about North American animals?"

Caroline struggled to follow Iris' train of wandering thoughts. "Uh, well, the Detroit Zoo, for example, breeds endangered native Karner blue butterflies and trumpeter swans for release around the state. Our own reptile keeper, Kirby, tags wild rattlers for study, and we're starting a turtle prog—"

"Zelda, come!" Iris commanded of the dog, who had been chasing the bike and causing Rafael to swerve dangerously. "Come lie down. What's your title?"

"Mine? Director of Communications and Development."

Iris nodded—which Caroline took to mean that either she was good at her job, or that all this was candy-coated (probably kiss-ass) nonsense.

Iris leaned back to look through the screen door. "It's almost six, Rafa. Put the bike away. Your mother is expecting you home."

Caroline said, "Why don't I walk him?"

Iris eyes ran the length of Caroline's ivory ensemble. "That your idea of hiking gear?"

"It's my meet-the-press gear, actually, but the path will be dry by now. I'll be fine."

"Can Zelda come, too?" Rafael asked, running out of the barn.

Caroline asked hesitantly, "Does she have a leash?"

"She doesn't need a leash," Iris said.

She doesn't need a leash. Those, Caroline would recall later, were Iris' exact words.

16

MUD THING

Caroline, Rafael and Zelda headed down the now-familiar path along the top of the ravine. Zelda zigzagged along, a few paces ahead, well clear of Caroline's slacks. Rafael couldn't stop talking about his day, the ice cream, the lemonade, Mr. Chappy and Little Houdini.

"Be sure to tell your mom everything." She thought of how he would so effortlessly repeat the entire day in Spanish. "You should be proud, Rafa."

He kicked a pine cone down the path and ran after it to kick it again.

When they reached the corner of Iris' property, the mine fence and Rafael's backyard Caroline pointed to the sign on the mine fence. "You know what that says?"

"Sure. Danger. *Peligro*. Same thing. Why'd they say it twice?"

"Because, it's really important that you never go in there. There are holes you could fall into." She didn't want to get into the gory details.

"Miss Iris says that's just an old wise tale."

"That's old *wives* tales, Rafael, but it's not—I mean—there's a reason for this tall fence and those warning signs." She felt suddenly irritated by Iris' many iron-clad opinions. "You should obey the signs. I know *I* will, just to be safe. Okay?"

"Yeah." He was petting Zelda's tail, half listening. "I think Zelda has an old wise tail, don't you?"

Caroline tapped his shoulder. "Hey! Promise me?"

"Promise."

Caroline squeezed his shoulder. "Okay, Mister Junior Zookeeper Rojas. Thank you for coming to the zoo today. Give your mom that membership card. It means you can come to the zoo anytime for free, so don't lose it."

A second later he was tearing across the backyard yelling, "Mom! *Mira lo que tengo!*"

Caroline called to Zelda who was standing at the top of the slope at full attention. Below them, the golden retriever she'd seen the week before was bounding up the hill toward them on their side of the fence. He was covered in mud. He came to a halt nose-to-nose with Zelda. Caroline scanned the woods, but didn't see the owner.

The dogs' face-off turned into mutual butt-sniffing, then playful bowing. Before Caroline could come to her senses, both dogs tore down the hill.

"Wait, no!" she yelled. "Come back here. *Zelda!*"

The dogs spiraled around each other and were soon belly-deep in Willow Creek.

Caroline sized up the situation. She was alone at the top of a hill dressed from head to toe in ivory. Two strange dogs—one that *she* was responsible for—were at the bottom of the hill wallowing in muck.

"Zelda! Come here. *Right* now!" She clapped her hands and called several times, each time with more urgency. The dogs, in their rapture, ignored her. She raised her hand to her forehead, trying to think.

She could run back and get Iris, but she couldn't leave Zelda here. What if Zelda ran off with the other dog and got lost, or worse? Iris would never forgive her. The ravine was steep—at least thirty feet above the rain-swollen creek. She weighed the possible effects on her outfit against explaining to an elderly widow how she, Caroline, had lost her only companion.

She rolled up her pant legs to the knees and started picking her way down the slope, easing herself from tree to tree and stopping to bark angry orders at the oblivious dogs. The ground got softer as she edged down the hill. She gripped one sapling, then another, letting herself down slowly.

"Zelda!" She called again and again. Mud began caking on the bottom of her shoes, which admittedly, she should have removed.

She was really mad now. "'She doesn't need a leash,'" she mimicked Iris in a tone she wasn't proud of. "Zelda. Bad girl!" She let go of the tree she was clinging to and clapped her hands. Her feet slid out from under her and in an instant, she was skidding down the rain-slicked slope on her backside, pushing wet leaves and sticks ahead of her. She came to an abrupt, bone-shattering halt with her heels plowed deep into black, gelatinous bleck at the edge of the creek.

She heard curious, banshee keening before realizing *she* was the source. She lifted her mud-caked hands to be sure they were still attached. She tested one leg and then the other for functionality. *Everything* hurt, but seemed to be more or less working.

The same could not be said for the ivory, meet-the-press PR gear.

"Crap!" she said loudly. "Crap, crap, crap!" She shook her hands and flung more mud across the front of her silk blouse. She felt water seeping through the seat of her pants. "Shit!"

She tried to get up, but had no traction. She rolled onto her knees and pulled her shoe out of the mud and poured out a half cup of muddy water. Her other foot was unaccountably bare. She twisted around and saw it halfway up the hill sticking out of the mud like a dinosaur tooth.

"Shit and crap!"

Both dogs were watching her curiously.

"Ze-el-da-a," she whined, rolling onto her hands and knees. She tried to get up, but slipped again. Then the two dogs were upon her, all paws and tongues.

"Get away from me!" she shouted. "No. I mean, come here!" She lunged for Zelda and made contact with her collar. "Ah! I've got you. BAD DOG!"

Pulling against sixty pounds of canine, she achieved an unsteady upright position. Up the hill, she examined the skid marks of her descent. Then she assessed her shoe (wet and caked), her blouse (Jackson Pollock-esque) and her linen slacks (unrecognizable). Then, oh God, she felt a cool breeze on her backside and felt the silk of her best, lacy, formerly white panties.

"Shit! Shit. Shit. Double SHIT!"

"Are you okay?" A voice called out from somewhere above. The sandy-haired jogger was standing on the other side of the mine fence at the top of the ravine holding a dog leash.

"Did you fall, miss?"

"Is that your dog?" she demanded, keeping one hand on Zelda and the other on the seat of her pants. It was an awkward posture she wasn't sure she could hold for long. She needed a third hand for her shoe. A prehensile tail to grab a tree would be nice, too.

The jogger seemed to be considering his answer carefully.

"That dog!" She sputtered, pointing. "Is he yours?"

"Not if you'll be calling your lawyers," he said, offering a guilty smile. He put both hands on the fence. "It looks like you took quite a spill. Are you hurt?"

She glared up at him. "My dog chased after yours. I was trying to get her—and I slipped. But I'm fine."

She brushed hair out of her eyes before realizing she had probably muddied the last piece of clean real estate on her entire body. Her elbow was starting to throb and was probably bleeding. When she tried to lift her foot she felt the mud sucking on her foot. She was sinking into oblivion as she chit-chatted with this stranger. Any movement now would only bring more humiliation—although, she couldn't imagine how she could look any more ridiculous.

"Just call your dog. *Please.*"

The man clapped. "Magoo. Here, boy."

The retriever bounded up the hill and greeted its owner through the fence.

"Not here, goof ball," the man said. "You have go back under the fence down there." He sidestepped down the hill on his side of the fence with a grace that mocked her. Magoo followed, enjoying this new game. Where the creek ran under the fence, erosion had created a dog-sized hole that Magoo must have breeched, then quickly forgotten about. It took a while for the man to coax the dog back under the fence.

Zelda whined to join them.

"Oh, no, you don't," Caroline warned.

The man stood on the other side of the fence, looking at her. "I'm sorry about my dog. He usually sticks right by me. I guess he likes your dog."

"She's not my dog actually. I'm, just, never mind."

"Well, Magoo is an excellent judge of character." He showed no sign of leaving. "Do you need some help getting up the hill?"

"No. I'll manage. You go on."

He wasn't moving. He was apparently waiting to see proof of her mountaineering skills. She wasn't falling for that. She pretended to adjust Zelda's collar. She rolled down the cuffs of her slacks and rolled up the sleeves of her blouse, which wasn't easy with only one free hand. When she looked up, he was still there. *Damn!*

"I'm going to walk along the stream," she called out, gesturing ridiculously in the direction of the steep, flooded bank. She waved casually and forced a weak smiled, hoping to be rid of him before her feet went out from under her again.

"But your shoe . . ." he said, pointing to the visible half of her ivory pump. "Should I get it?"

"No!" she said, too loudly. Adjusting the volume, she added, "No. No, thank you."

"Well, I can't just leave you here. This is my fault, or Magoo's. Bad boy."

"Thanks for the offer, but no thanks." She said this with finality.

He just stood there, looking crushed. "My name is Neil."

Great. Now he wanted to chat.

He asked, "What's yours?"—as if they'd just met at the dog park.

Her possibly concussed brain conjured up some human butt-sniffing involving her ventilated backside. Suddenly it all seemed hilarious.

"What's so funny?" he asked.

She shut her eyes. "Caroline. That's my name. It's been just *lovely* having this time to chat, Neil and Ma—Magoo," she sputtered. "But you see, I've skinned my elbow, lost my shoe, ruined my clothes and ripped the seat of pants *wide* open. So, I'm not—I repeat—I am *not* going to *crawl* up this hill with *you* standing there! So, feel *free* to take your dog and *run along* home!"

Neil rocked from foot to foot indecisively. Then he backed away from the fence and was gone.

She sighed. "Okay, dog. Let's get out of here. *Mush.*" She urged Zelda up the steep slope, holding her collar with one hand and her shoe with the other. They were closing in on the mate when she slipped to her knees.

"I'm coming down!" It was Neil. He now stood at the top of the hill on her side of an eight-foot, chain link fence topped with rusty barbed wire. Magoo was tied to a tree.

Neil pulled his tee shirt over his head.

"Whoa there, fella. What are you *doing*?"

"I'm tossing you my shirt. Tuck it around you. You know, in your pants," he shrugged, looking flustered.

"Oh, for *Pete's* sake," she said, as the shirt landed at her feet. She set her shoe down, picked up the shirt and began tucking it awkwardly into her waistband, muttering mild expletives while keeping a stranglehold on Zelda. When she looked up again he was standing a few feet above her, bare-chested, flat-bellied, glistening with sweat and holding her other shoe. (A ridiculous flashback to Prince Charming and the glass slipper made her want to giggle.) He heaved the first shoe to the top of the hill and turned toward her.

"Give me your other shoe," he said. She watched him heave the other one to the top of the bank. He turned back to her, offering his hand. Veins stood out on his forearm.

She hesitated.

He looked up, probably hoping to find patience somewhere in the treetops. "I'm not going to leave you down here," he said. "Take my hand, please Caroline."

She lifted her arm and felt his firm grip on her wrist. "I can do this on my—*oh!*" Her body rocketed upward, past running shoes with green soles, calf and thigh muscles covered with gold hair that disappeared into shorts and reappeared darker above the waistband. She looked away quickly.

She felt strong upward pressure in the small of her back.

"Grab that tree. Got it? Now don't move."

He scrambled upward to the next sapling and turned again to offer his hand. "This way. You got it."

Zelda clambered up the hill next to her.

"If I had on decent shoes," she huffed, "I wouldn't have fallen."

His face was pink with effort and pulled taught over his jaw. (*Late-thirties,* Caroline thought.) There was a hint of gray in the sideburns. (*Early forties, tops.*) No wedding ring. Why was she even looking?

"I, uh, wouldn't have fallen except for the mud," she heard herself explaining. "I usually don't wear heels, except I had a thing at work." She looked vaguely in the direction of the zoo.

He nodded as if she were making perfect sense. Locks of damp, strawberry-tinged curls poked from under his baseball cap.

"I had to walk a neighbor boy home," she continued, gasping for breath as if she'd never seen the inside of a gym.

His skin was flawless. A mosquito landed on his shoulder. Without a free hand, she blew on it. He turned in surprise.

"Sorry, there was a bug."

His eyes were amber, flecked with green.

"The path was pretty dry," she babbled on. "So I didn't expect so much mud down here. I should have realized, after that rain. I had to get the dog though."

He was muscular for a jogger. (*Thirty-seven.*) "Your dog came out of nowhere and I couldn't get Zelda to listen. She's not my dog." Had she already said that? She listened in horror to this nervous gush of words, but was incapable of turning it off. She looked hideous and sounded insane. She was being hauled uphill like a wrecked vehicle by a benevolent, thirty-sevenish, not-bad-looking, possibly single stranger.

When they reached the path, she stepped back and raised her free hand to smooth her hair. A clod of drying mud was stuck to her bangs.

He was breathing hard now. His eyes swept her from head to toe. "You're pretty scraped up. Are you sure you're okay?"

Caroline rubbed her elbow, which hurt like hell. "I'm *fine*," she insisted too loudly.

He exhaled a long breath and handed over her shoes. "Magoo usually stays close by, but I guess he saw your dog and went under the fence down by the creek. I'm really sorry."

She nodded. "S'okay. Thanks for the, um, hoist," she said, punching the air for emphasis.

He untied Magoo. "My pleasure."

"Uh, your shirt," she said, hoping he'd tell her to keep it.

"Keep it," he said.

Caroline nodded. "Thanks. It'll come in handy on the way home."

"Is that far from here? I could walk you."

"No. But, thanks."

He nodded, "Okay, then." At the corner of the fence he disappeared into the undergrowth behind a red-lettered No Trespassing sign.

She called out. "You shouldn't be in there, you know. It's dangerous."

In a few seconds, man and dog reappeared inside the fence. "Really?" he said, smiling now.

"There's a mine under there," she said, pointing to the signs. "The ground is unstable. Didn't you notice the signs?"

"Thanks. I'll be careful." He was showing no concern whatsoever. She watched him turn and climb to the top of the rise and vanish again.

She sighed, looked down at Zelda and shrugged, "Why would anyone believe a pathetic mud thing?"

Iris was still on the porch when they reached the driveway. Zelda bounded up the steps as Caroline opened the car door, tossed Neil's tee shirt on the seat and hurled a look at Iris that said, *Don't ask*.

As she threw the car into reverse, she heard Iris say, "Zelda! You're covered in mud. What on earth . . . ?"

༺

That evening after supper, Iris came out to the porch again. It was after eight, but the long dusk would linger until nearly ten. The eastern clouds were turning from magenta to deep lapis.

The *Saskawan Evening Star* lay in her lap unopened. The mating calls of the katydids caught her attention. If she listened, she might hear the raspy bark of red foxes over on the mine property or the music of the wood thrush singing his haunting love song from his hiding place in the treetops.

Iris, so fluent in animal languages, was troubled by the exotic chuffs and chortles coming from the zoo. What was their meaning? At least, she no longer had to listen to the solitary young elephant whose nighttime lament needed no translation.

Judy. That's what the zoo had called her.

17

PRINCESS OF PACHYDERMS

Summer, 1941

Iris and Lillian lay awake in their thin summer nightgowns listening to the hum of circus wagons in the field beyond the orchard. Animal handlers and performers shouted orders as they set up camp around the spring-fed pond. By morning, a whole little village would have sprung up, more colorful and alien than any Iris had ever seen in her *National Geographic* magazines. Sleep was impossible.

For the third summer, their father had rented out their west meadow to the circus people who came to Saskawan each August. Her parents no longer kept horses, and the pasture was too wet for fruit trees, so it stood empty. The circus people could set up camp, feed and exercise their animals just a couple of miles from the fairgrounds where they performed for a week.

Mother took a dim view of these "gypsy show people." Her greatest fear, in fact, was that somewhere someone was having fun. She saw nothing to admire in their pierced ears, tattoos, strange accents and "unchristian ways." But in the end, her Dutch frugality trumped her Calvinist moral certitude, and so, the circus came to Willow Creek Farm.

It was too exciting for words. By eight o'clock, Iris was out of bed, putting on her blouse and dungarees as if the house were on fire.

"Mother said we can't go near the circus camp," Lillian whispered nervously, pulling the sheet up to her chin.

"I'm just going to check on the apples for Daddy." She braided her gold hair without brushing it first.

Lillian brightened. "I'll come with you." She swung her feet out of the bed and let her nightgown fall to the floor.

"If I watch the circus people at all," Iris said, feeling a pang of guilt, "it will be from afar." "Afar" was a wonderful new word she'd learned in the sixth grade, and she was proud to find reason to use it.

Lillian stopped buttoning her checkered blouse, not liking the sound of this. But as Iris pounded down the stairs, she yelled, "Wait for me!"

On most August mornings, the girls would have to wait until they'd fed the chickens, weeded a row of the garden, brushed Calamity Jane, their one-eyed cat, and helped their mother hang a load of laundry before they could play. But Mother had gone to the market early and wouldn't be back until noon. If they didn't stay in the orchard too long, they would have their chores done before she returned.

Later, after the supper dishes were done, they would come back to their apple tree perch and stay until the dreaded "clang-clang-clang!" of the bell on the side porch signaled that their day was over, and baths, bed and prayers awaited.

On this first morning of the circus' third summer at Willow Creek Farm, the red and gold trailers were parked in rows. Some were piled high with canvas tenting and posts the size of telephone poles. People slammed doors and barked out orders. A woman with long black hair was hanging laundry on a clothesline strung between two wagons. Hidden in the apple tree, the girls saw an odd little man almost as small as the monkey he was feeding.

"Look, a midget!" Lillian whispered. "I learned about them in the encyclopedia. He was born that way."

"How else, silly? Did you think he shrunk in the wash?"

A man and a woman had set up a huge metal cage on the grass and shouted commands as lions and tigers jumped through golden hoops. Terriers with springs for legs did back flips or ran up their trainers' legs to sit on their heads. Several boys, not much older than Iris, led dappled gray horses to the pond to drink.

"I think Heaven will be like a circus every day," Lillian said dreamily, swinging her legs on the branch next to Iris. Their teacher at Vacation Bible School, Mrs. Ten-Boer, had described Heaven in colorful detail. "Only *I* think we'll *all* have wings—even the horses—and the grass will be made of gold."

"How could horses eat metal grass? And they're much too heavy to fly. Would their manure be gold, too?"

Lillian puckered her lips to work out this problem. "Well, angel horses can do anything they want. Besides, I don't think you have to go to the bathroom in Heaven—even horses."

Iris rolled her eyes. She wanted to remind Lillian that, according to Mrs. Ten-Boer, animals don't have souls, and therefore wouldn't be joining Lillian in Heaven. She *almost* said, *If animals aren't going, I don't care if I do, either,* but she held her tongue (something her teachers and parents suggested she do much more often.) Besides, a horseless, dog-less, cat-less Heaven would just give Lillian nightmares.

So, she said to her sister, "Well, *I* like horses just fine without wings," which showed excellent tongue-holding skills.

Iris suspected her father didn't care much about going to Heaven either. He only came to church when she and Lillian were singing in the Junior Choir. She knew her mother prayed for his soul. Recently she, Iris, had decided that she'd rather go wherever her father was headed than spend eternity with Mrs. Ten-Boer. Lillian didn't seem to have any of Iris' misgivings. At least she and her sister agreed about the circus camp.

If it wasn't Heaven, it was surely the next best thing.

Lillian's favorites were the acrobats who practiced leapfrogging and tumbling in the grass. She practiced standing on Iris' shoulders in the hayloft until they fell into the soft hay, weak with laughter.

But for Iris, the lure of the circus was a pair of trained elephants. In that third summer, they arrived with their newly arrived baby. The proud parents picked daintily at a pile of hay with their trunks as the baby butted against her mother's round belly and reached up now and then for a reassuring touch or a drink of her milk.

"They sure have a lot of skin," Lillian said. "Maybe they just keep growing into it, like new school shoes." Mother always bought their shoes so big they had to stuff the toes with newspaper until Christmas.

"Don't be a ninny," said Iris, rolling her eyes again. But she did wonder if it was true, and if there was a book in the library that might tell her more about elephants.

"Their wrinkly bottoms look like Grandma's."

"You don't know what Grandma's bottom looks like."

"Do so! I saw her in the bathroom once." Lillian covered her mouth and they got to laughing so hard Iris fell out of the tree, and Lillian wet her pants.

One evening after dinner, as the girls kept their vigil in the apple tree, the mother elephant stretched her trunk toward a fringe of fresh green grass their father's tractor had missed. Held fast by a short tether around her back leg, she couldn't reach.

"Look," Lillian said. "Mrs. Elephant wants our grass."
Iris dropped to the ground.
"What are you doing?" Lillian asked, her voice rising.
"Stay here."
"Oh, no! You better not. Mother said!"
"'Mother said. Mother said.'" Iris mimicked.

Under the apple trees she began pulling the long orchard grass until she had a heavy armload. She crouched at the end of the row until the coast was clear. Then she ran full-tilt toward the elephants.

The sight of a skinny creature charging pell-mell out of the woods startled the elephants. They backed up, shielding their baby with their huge ears and trumpeting in alarm. Iris threw down her armload at the elephants' feet and sprinted back to the tree.

"Let's get out of here!" She yanked on Lillian's foot until she tumbled out of the tree. They bounded between the rows and didn't stop until they dove into the glider on the side porch, giggling uncontrollably.

"What are you girls up to?" their mother called from the kitchen.

"Nothing," they said in unison.

"Well, it's time for bed. Baths first."

That night, and many others before, Iris and Lillian begged their parents and prayed to the Heavenly Father and Jesus—within earshot of their mother—to go to the "real" circus. Their mother was unmoved.

"But why not?"

"Because we said so," was their mother's final and completely inadequate response.

"We have a circus in our own pasture," their father offered.

The difference between overalls and sequins, sleeping lions and leaping lions, practice and performance was lost on their practical, frugal parents. It was exasperating, infuriating and completely unfair.

But that summer—the summer the baby elephant came to Willow Creek Farm—a man from the circus knocked at the kitchen door.

"I have tickets for your girls," he said, chewing a plug of tobacco and pulling a strip of pink tickets out of the pocket of his coveralls.

Lillian grabbed Iris' hands under the table. Iris would have crossed her fingers if Lillian weren't squeezing the life out of them. Life would not be worth living if her father said no. Iris prayed silently, "Please, God. Please, God. Please, God." She was about to promise never to complain about evening church again, when her mother pushed back her chair and began clearing the table. Their father winked in their direction.

The center pole of the "Big Top" was, by Iris' reckoning, taller than the Great Pyramid or the Eiffel Tower. She and Lillian held their father's hands as they climbed to the top of the wooden bleachers for the best view. Clowns in oversized shoes, floppy orange wigs and three-fingered gloves worked the crowd, hawking cotton candy and teddy bears hanging from sticks. The girls knew better than to ask.

Finally, a band in red uniforms with gold buttons as shiny as their instruments marched in leading a parade. A white poodle in a turquoise dress and matching hat walked on its hind legs and flipped over and over without taking its eyes off a pretty girl wearing an identical outfit.

Lillian pointed to the little man with a monkey on his shoulder. She cupped her hands around her sister's ear and whispered, "That's our midget."

Iris shrugged. "Don't you think I *know* that?"

The same dappled gray horses high-stepped in their feathered plumes. Girls wearing almost no clothes at all stood on their backs. There was so much to see Iris didn't know where to look first. Then the music stopped and the ringmaster walked to the center of ring.

"LAY-dies and GEN-tlemen!"

Iris cupped her hands around Lillian's ear, "I saw him shaving yesterday."

No one else in the audience knew that the boy doing handstands on a bicycle was a crackerjack horseshoe player, or that the kid doing flips wore a knee-brace under his white pants. Iris had to remind Lillian that the diapered "baby" about to take a "death-defying leap" from a burning cardboard building on a tall platform was the same bald midget who fed the monkeys.

For the grand finale, the ringmaster announced, "Now! Direct your attention, please, to the center ring for the sen-SA-tional, the SPELL-binding, the stu-PEN-dous pa-RADE of PACH-yderms!" The crowd roared. "Here comes Papa Phineas, Mama Penelope and the brand new baby, PRIN-cess!"

The elephants lumbered into the ring with the baby running along behind. Princess wore a pink baby bonnet and a diaper as big as a bed sheet. Penelope wore a white ruffled apron and carried a baby bottle the size of a milk jug in her trunk. Phineas wore enormous red pants held on with suspenders.

The elephants pirouetted in unison while the trainer waved his stick like a magic wand. Finally, they stopped in front of three stools. A trainer waved the stick and yelled, "HUP! HUP!" The adults swayed back and forth backing up to the stools. When the trainer tapped his stick on Penelope's knee, both elephants sat down. The crowd roared. Right then, Iris decided to be an elephant trainer when she grew up.

On the short drive home, she leaned against her father's shoulder in the front seat of their green Ford pickup. Her father patted her knee. He must surely have known about their clandestine surveillance of the meadow. Iris reached around his arm and gave it a hug. This was their very own circus from their very own farm. And she had the best father in Saskawan, Michigan—and probably the whole, wide world.

The next night, after the summer sun had slipped behind the orchard, Iris and Lillian set out with their father for the pasture. The circus was packing up and moving on to Lansing. Across the pasture, the elephant trainer, looking bald and ordinary without his plumed hat, and some other men had just put Phineas into the back of the biggest truck. Now they were struggling to get Penelope up the wooden ramp too, but she wouldn't budge. She flapped her ears. She stomped her feet and bellowed.

"She doesn't want to leave our meadow," Iris said, remembering the tasty grass she'd picked for her.

"The animals like it here," her father agreed.

"But where's Princess?" Lillian asked.

The circus people were gathered in a tight circle around Penelope. They were yelling, "Hup! Get in there! Hup." They were swatting at her flanks.

Their father stopped in the middle of the pasture and reached for the girls' hands.

"Daddy?" Iris couldn't read his shadowed face under the brim of his hat.

More circus people gathered around the mother elephant.

Her father tugged on her hand. "They're busy. We'll come back later."

"No! I want to stay!" Iris pulled her hand away. Lillian stared, transfixed.

Some of the men had long wooden poles and were whacking the back of Penelope's wrinkled hind legs. Each time the stick made contact, Penelope's ears flared and her head and trunk swung to the right or the left, but she refused to budge.

One of the men pushed back his cap and laughed. "Who's the boss here, George?"

"Got a mind of 'er own, this one does," another observed.

Her father took Iris' hand again, "Let's go, girls." But Iris' eyes were locked on a rivulet of blood running down Penelope's ankle. For the first time, Iris saw the sharp metal barb at the end of the men's poles.

"Daddy, they're hurting Penelope!" Iris' voice was shrill now. "Make them stop!" She tried to pull away, but her father gripped her hand until it hurt. He picked Lillian up with his free arm and she buried her face in his shoulder.

Iris looked up at her father's angry face. He would do something.

But her father only turned and pulled her toward the darkness of the orchard. "Iris, I said *now!*"

Iris glared fiercely up at him.

A woman's voice called out. "Hold up, Mr. Walker. I have your money."

Her father stopped, but looked past the woman who was coming toward them. Iris recognized her as a grotesque and much older version of the beautiful lady on the flying trapeze. That woman wore a beautiful, sparkly green leotard, shiny black boots and feathers in her jet-black hair. This woman's brittle gray hair poked out from under a faded red bandanna. One bra strap dangled off her shoulder under a pair of faded overalls.

"So, how'd you like the circus, girls? Did you see me up there on the trapeze?" She leaned toward Iris, baring her broken yellow teeth.

Iris glared up at her. Lillian whimpered into her father's shoulder.

"What's the problem with the elephant?" her father asked.

The woman looked at the knot of men and shrugged. "Penelope? Aw, she's just mad 'cause we sold her baby this morning. No room for three elephants in this little circus."

"I hate seeing an animal treated like that," her father said, pulling Iris closer.

"Aw, she'll get over it in a few days and Princess is getting a nice, new home at the Detroit Zoo." She looked over her shoulder at the men who were still jabbing Penelope's ankles. "George! Take it easy, for Christ's sake."

The men leaned on their sticks. The circus people dispersed and went back to their packing, leaving Penelope on the ramp with her trainer. Their father took an envelope from the woman without saying another word. He carried Lillian in one arm and never let go of Iris' hand on the long walk back to the house.

That night, Iris lay awake by her open window reliving the dazzling, horrifying events of the last two days and listening to the frantic, unanswered cries of a mother calling for her baby. Iris sobbed until her insides ached.

She had thought the circus people loved their animals as much as she did. A trickle of blood changed everything.

She didn't speak to her father, or even look at him for days afterward. He had witnessed an injustice and done nothing to stop it. His sin, she thought, was unforgivable.

More than sixty-five years later, Iris regretted that harsh judgment. For although the farm badly needed the money and the circus returned to Saskawan for many more summers, it never again camped at Willow Creek Farm.

18

UNREST

Wednesday, June 15

It was eight-fifteen and Caroline's early start was already in jeopardy as she sat in a snarl of traffic on Russet Ridge Drive. Before leaving work the night before she had pushed a dozen new green and white yard signs into the grass along the curb that shouted, Zoo on the Moov. Vote Yes! Nov. 2. This morning she wanted to assess their visual impact from the street along with thousands of commuters. She imagined drivers saying, "Hey, did you see all those signs in front of the zoo? I'm voting yes on the referendum, how about you?" At least, that's what she hoped.

She suspected there was an accident ahead, but a delivery truck was blocking her view. She crept by the Rojas' driveway and made a mental note to bring them a couple of signs. Iris was another story.

She drummed the steering wheel. *What is going on?* she fumed. She heard honking—something polite West Michiganders rarely did. When the truck ahead changed lanes, she could see about a dozen people standing on the curb outside the zoo, waving homemade signs. She couldn't read the hastily written lettering, but several women were shouting at passing cars. She rolled down her window.

When Caroline reached the zoo entrance and turned in, two women ran alongside her car, chanting, "Don't move the zoo! Don't move the zoo!"

She sped up and parked behind the admin building. Then she walked back to the front and hid behind a bush to watch the commotion. The largest sign read, Honk, if you love our CITY zoo! Another said, Don't Close Our Neighborhood Zoo! Two other protesters, standing off by themselves, held signs that read, End Jails for Animals! and Free Little Houdini! Close the Zoo!

"You've *got* to be kidding!" Caroline said to no one.

The WSAS-TV truck must have been right behind her. She could see Derrick and his cameraman getting their equipment set up in the parking lot. Several drivers slowed down to wave and honk, while a man driving a delivery van shouted for everyone to move along.

As she walked back toward her office, she saw a cardboard sign hung on the fence by the flamingo pond. It read, "Don't make us move!" Caroline yanked it down and dropped it in the trash. It was going to be a long, hot summer.

Victor was standing at his office window with his hands shoved into his pockets. "They were there when I got here a half hour ago," he said without turning around. "I didn't expect they'd get sentimental about this old place."

"Me neither. We've been so focused on the needs of the animals."

"Well, shame on us," he said sarcastically. "So, what do you make of this?"

Caroline shrugged sheepishly. "They love the zoo?"

"Damn it. I won't let this zoo go to hell so that a few neighbors can have a handy place for a picnic." He sat down so hard that she thought the chair would break.

A set of blueprints, unrolled and weighed down with a stapler and a tape dispenser, were spread across his desk.

"What are these?" she asked.

"I borrowed them from Cincinnati. It's their new Africa exhibit. Over eight acres. They've got giraffe, cheetah, lions and a water collection system with buried tanks. They reuse every drop to irrigate and fill the polar bear and sea lion pools. Image how little sewage is coming out of that zoo." He jabbed the desk with his index finger. "Even the construction waste was recycled. Doesn't anyone care about that? In Nord Haven we can do this—I'm thinking maybe a South American equivalent, with llamas, maned wolves, capybaras. Maybe integrate a couple of monkey islands connected by swing bridges." He stood up and began pacing. "What's wrong with people, Finch?"

Caroline held his gaze with difficulty, shocked at his sweeping generalization and wondering why she was suddenly "Finch."

She swallowed. "We have our work cut out for us."

He motioned toward the street. "Go talk to them. Find out what kind of bug crawled up their asses."

"I will, but I'd like to wait a half hour. Besides WSAS just pulled in. If I showed up now, it would just fan the fire."

She was pretty sure she heard him growl, but he was already leaning over the drawings, lost somewhere between South America and Nord Haven.

An hour later, Caroline invited the protesters' self-proclaimed leader into her office. She introduced herself as Missy Grove, founder of CAUZ, Citizens Allied for an Urban Zoo. Caroline listened politely, then offered to host a neighborhood forum the following Monday evening. Missy promised a large crowd.

After lunch, Caroline phoned in a statement to Derrick that was so dry, politically correct and filled with PR platitudes ("Ridge Park Zoo welcomes the public's input... We encourage spirited public discourse...") that it wouldn't bring unwanted attention to the story.

At two o'clock, Chappy called. "Hey, Caroline. Guess who's here?"

Caroline rubbed her temples where a raging headache was getting organized. "No clue."

"Rafael."

"With you? Now? Where?"

"Yes. Yes, and here." He was laughing.

"Uh... *why?*"

"He's keeping."

"Keeping what?"

"*Zoo*keeping. You made him a junior zookeeper, remember? It is a job this young man takes *very* seriously. He showed up a while ago wearing his badge with his lunch in a paper bag. He's helping Julie at the clinic now."

Caroline covered her eyes and laugh-groaned. "I should have seen this coming. I told him to come by anytime. Sorry. I'll come get him."

"No, no. We have plenty for him to do—as long as his mom knows he's here. I'll bring him by your office when we're done at five, if that's okay."

Caroline dialed Mrs. Rojas. There was no answer. Then she dialed Iris.

"He's not supposed to be there?" Iris laughed out loud. "I wondered when his mother walked him over this morning before work. Apparently something got lost in translation. I told her he could stay with me for a few minutes after he's done at the zoo until six when she gets home. Anyway, I'm pretty sure that's what I agreed to."

"Thank you, Iris. I'll drop him off a little after five."

Rafael burst through her office door, with Chappy panting heavily a few seconds behind.

"This guy was a really big help today," Chappy said. "I even got to sit down a couple of times. Now would be a good time, too." He fell into a chair and propped his elbows on his knees to catch his breath. "Peter and I were talking. We'd like to offer Rafael some regular volunteer hours—sort of a junior zookeeping internship. He could come by, say, two afternoons a week." He turned to the boy. "How would you like that?"

Rafael shrugged. "Sure. I can come *every* day."

"Let's make it just two days," Chappy said. "You can spend part of the time with me and the rest in the clinic with Dr. Peter and Miss Julie—if your mom agrees."

Rafael brightened. "If we leave now, we can stop at Miss Iris' and I can play with Zelda, then ask my mom. I know she'll say yes."

And so, a junior zookeeping career was officially launched.

19

PEACE TALKS

Thursday, June 16

Iris was on the porch reading the *Evening Star* when Caroline and Rafael walked up the driveway the next afternoon.

The previous evening Victor had telephoned Mrs. Rojas and explained in Spanish the terms of Rafael's Tuesday/Thursday volunteer program. Caroline would escort Rafael to Iris' about five where he would stay until Mrs. Rojas arrived home at six.

But as Caroline stood at the bottom of the porch steps, Rafael tugged on her hand. "But, can't you walk me to my house when my mom gets home in a little while?"

Caroline looked from Rafael to Iris, "Well, I don't know—"

"*Pleeease?*" he said, actually fluttering his eyelashes. *How naturally children take to being the center of attention*, Caroline thought.

"I'm sure Miss Caroline is too busy for that," Iris said dismissively.

"No. I'd be glad to walk him—today, at least," Caroline said, recognizing the opportunity for extra face-time with Iris that had just presented itself. "I can't promise *every* time though."

Iris nodded toward the glider and let out an almost imperceptible sigh. "Sit" she said and disappeared into the house.

Caroline took a seat feeling satisfied with this latest development in what Victor was calling "monkey peace talks." Rafael took a seat next to her. She patted his knee.

When Iris returned with three tumblers of lemonade Caroline prompted Rafael, "What did you and Chappy do today?"

"We made monkey food. Lettuce, spinach and grapes," Rafael said. "We chopped apples and Mr. Chappy put some in places only the littlest monkeys can fit. Wanna know why?"

Iris lifted one eyebrow.

"So the big monkeys can't get all the food. That's why."

Rafael downed his lemonade in long gulps, and then climbed up to the porch railing and reached for the bell. "Four times?"

Iris held up three fingers and said, "Go," as metal clanged against metal.

When her ears stopped ringing, Caroline said, "I heard you helped out at the art tent too, Rafa."

"Yup. I gave out crayons and paper and hung up the pictures on a string, but, oh man," he said, slapping his forehead, "some kids have crazy ideas!"

"Like what?" Caroline asked.

"Like, Houdini flew out on the back of a bird or he dug a tunnel right under the water. Mr. Chappy says there's cement under there, so he couldn't do that, and besides, monkeys aren't really diggers, like meerkats or prairie dogs. Now, *they* can really dig and you have to watch out for them. That's what Mr. Chappy told me."

"What else?" Caroline asked, keeping an eye on Iris, who seemed to be listening.

"We put fish in the otter pool. They like to chase after them."

"*Live* fish?" Iris asked, expressing surprise.

"Usually they get flash-frozen fish," Caroline explained. "But every week or so they get live fish to hunt."

"The zoo has a freezer bigger than this whole porch!" Rafael said with a sweeping gesture.

Zelda had gone into the yard and returned with the slimy, yellow tennis ball, which she dropped at Rafael's feet. The two of them ran off into the yard.

Iris gave Caroline an appraising look. "So, I saw the picketers. I couldn't read their signs. What's their position? Free Houdini?"

"A few. Most want to keep the zoo in the neighborhood."

"Really? That's a bit self-serving."

"I met with the leader and promised to meet with a group of neighbors next week. Want to help shake them up? Might be fun."

Iris looked surprised. "Thanks, I'll pass."

"This referendum question has so many sides, I've lost track."

"So, what happened to you and Zelda yesterday?" Iris said, changing the subject. "Were you mud wrestling, or what?"

Caroline laughed weakly. "She ran after another dog and forgot her manners. We—I—fell trying to get her back." Caroline rubbed her elbow. "I got pretty banged up."

"Miss Iris!" Rafael was running toward them holding out his hand. "Look, I found a *diamond* in your driveway!" He ran up the steps and handed her a gum ball-sized stone.

She inspected it closely. "Hmm. Looks like granite, with flecks of mica. As pretty as diamonds."

"Can I keep it?"

"It's all yours," she said.

He leaped off the top step. Zelda trotted behind with the tennis ball.

Caroline rolled up her sleeve to show a large bandage. She wasn't ready to change the subject. "See? I scraped my elbows chasing after your dog."

Iris tipped her head back to take a look.

Caroline waited for an apology, or some show of sympathy, but Iris only eyed her khaki slacks and running shoes and said, "I see you dressed sensibly today." She got up, took a pair of clippers from her skirt pocket and went down the steps to snip off several spent peony blossoms.

"You said Zelda didn't need a leash," Caroline reminded her.

Rafael ran over with another pebble. "Look! Here's a red one, Miss Iris."

"Ah, yes. This one's a keeper." Iris held it up to the light. Rafael came around to stand beside her. "This, my dear, is jasper. A glacier pushed it here from Canada."

"Canada!" he repeated as he put the pebble in his pocket and ran back to a sunny patch in the driveway. Zelda trotted along behind, looking puzzled.

"Here's another one," he announced, coming close for an appraisal.

"Why, forever more! You've got yourself a little piece of the moon."

"The moon? Did it fall off?" His mouth opened, and he looked up at the sky.

Zelda dropped the ball at his feet and watched it roll unnoticed into the gravel. She looked positively woebegone. Caroline came off the porch and tossed the tennis ball across the yard, making her elbow smart.

"It didn't fall off the moon," Iris was explaining, "but it's what the moon and most of the earth is made of. It's called feldspar."

"So, not blue cheese, eh?" Caroline said, feeling a little woebegone herself.

Iris and Rafael huddled together. "If you know what to look for," Iris was saying, "there's a story in every pebble."

Zelda dropped the ball at Caroline's feet. She cupped the dog's muzzle in her palms. "Good girl. Is this your idea of an apology, Miss Zelda? Huh?"

Iris straightened up and looked at her watch, "It's time you two ran along."

"Can Zelda come?" Rafael asked.

Caroline saw Iris nod.

"Iris," Caroline said, "about that leash . . ."

Zelda moped at the humiliation of the leash, but stood stoically at the fence corner as Rafael disappeared into his back door. Before turning back toward Iris', Caroline paused to inspect the mud slick she had left the day before.

"See what you made me do, Zelda?" The dog stomped hopefully, ready for another off-leash adventure. "Oh no, we're not playing that game again!"

The woods was quiet. The jogger and his dog—Neil and Magoo—were nowhere in sight. She was sort of hoping to show him she didn't always look like an overdressed, sci-fi swamp thing.

She listened to the breeze stir the leaves of the walnut trees on the other side of the fence. The trees looked ancient and permanent, although they were surely clinging for dear life above a subterranean chasm. She thought of the man in Florida whose whole house had been swallowed up with him in it. She shuddered.

Why would anyone jog through a Swiss cheese landscape? And how did he even get in there? And how did he get out to rescue her?

"Come on, Zel." She walked along the fence where it continued into the next backyard. In a horror movie, this is where a creepy soundtrack would begin to play and the audience would squirm in their seats. Don't go in there! She was doing this for Rafael. What if there were holes in the fence for a curious boy to crawl through?

She ducked under a broken limb before coming upon a wide gate secured with a padlock. This looked to be an old entrance that was now blocked by houses. She rattled the gate and inspected the padlock. It was rusty, but intact. As far as she could see in either direction, the fence had no gaps or holes. Unless the jogger had a key, or could pole-vault—she pictured his muscular thighs—nothing explained his sudden appearance on her side of this fence.

She turned Zelda around and started back down the path.

"What do you think, Zel? Did you and I meet a guy and a dog yesterday, or were they figments of our imaginations?"

Zelda yawned, but didn't answer.

"Yeah, I'm not sure, either."

20

DOG MINUTES

Friday, June 17

Zelda sat at full attention looking down the gravel driveway toward the street. Iris had disappeared below the hill—a place strictly off-limits to a dog. Almost every day, Iris disappeared there and Zelda had to wait. Momentarily, there would be a joyful reunion—since the length of the separation bore no relation to her supreme discomfort at being left alone, or to her elation at seeing her human again. There'd be ear scratching and soothing words before they'd walk together to the house.

But until then, she'd have to wait. She turned in a circle, whined, yawned twice and lay down on the warm gravel with her chin on her front paws.

Iris' mailbox was on a post at the curb—a leftover from the days when Russet Ridge Drive was a rural road. Her daughters thought she should get a post office box, but it seemed just one more capitulation to old age. Besides, the daily walk down the driveway was good for her.

Iris waited for a bus to pass before pulling down the metal door and extracting a stack of mail. Then she walked slowly up the drive, examining each piece until she found what she had been waiting for—a letter from the Michigan State University Cooperative Extension Service.

Three weeks ago, she had exhumed the shriveled roots of several dying asparagus plants and a tomato vine. She'd mailed them with a soil sample and twenty-five dollars to the lab in East Lansing.

She opened the letter and read the contents.

"Findings of Soil Test for I. VanWingen, Saskawan, Michigan: Sample shows significant sodium chloride (salt) content. Remediation:

Remove soil or saturate area repeatedly with water. Allow to remain fallow for several years prior to replanting . . . "

She stopped mid-stride. *Salt?* Iris read again. Then, "Add calcium amendment in the form of gypsum. This is readily available. . . "

She continued walking, piecing together recollections.

The death of those plants was just the latest in a string of mishaps, she reminded herself. First, her peripatetic watering went missing then materialized again exactly where she'd left it three days earlier. The up-ended compost bucket she'd blamed on raccoons or neighbor kids, but she'd also ran out of gas when she'd just filled the tank. Was her memory playing tricks on her or was something more sinister going on? Some nights, Zelda growled at the empty yard or barked at the open barn door.

Maybe they were both losing their marbles.

She looked at the letter again. *Salt in the garden?* Could she have confused a bag of water softener salt for a bag of fertilizer? That didn't seem likely.

She headed back up the driveway.

When the top of Iris' silver head bobbed above the crest of the driveway, Zelda sat up and barked a greeting.

Iris patted the front of her denim skirt as the dog shot forward like a thoroughbred out of the gate to dance circles around Iris' legs.

"Good gracious, I missed you, too." *Dog years may be short,* she thought, *but dog minutes must be very, very long indeed.*

On the way to the house she fingered the letter in her pocket and tried to pictured herself spreading salt on the garden.

"We're a pair, you and I."

Zelda bounded up the steps and waited there with a worshipful expression.

21
WHAT THE LAND TEACHES

Sunday, June 19

Natural Curiosity: Notes from Willow Creek Farm
Iris Van, *Saskawan Evening Star*

More than two hundred million years ago, my little farm sat on the shore of a small, salty sea which covered most of our Michigan mitten. It was the last puddle of an ocean that inundated Michigan at least six times. As the water dried up, the sea became a very salty, mineral-rich soup. These minerals sank to the bottom and gradually dried into layers of sediment which hardened into rock. Michigan was left with limestone, shale and some of the world's richest deposits of gypsum. The east Michigan town of Alabaster is named for its purest form.

Eventually, tropical plants, like those we see in Florida today, took root. Our hottest, most humid summers are nothing compared to the heat waves of that time. These vast jungles added a layer of rich soil on top of the gypsum.

Just one million years ago—the blink of an eye in geological time—the weather turned colder. Snow fell and fell—and fell some more. In fact, the snow got so deep that it was a mile deep! Snow covered everything from the North Pole to Kentucky. Over time, the snow packed into ice. It slipped and slid and broke apart and the pieces collided like bumper cars. The glacial ice ground some rocks into sand and dragged others along, leaving giant skid marks and deep furrows in the landscape. Some became our river valleys, while the biggest become our Great Lakes.

Sometimes, the glaciers grabbed a Canadian rock and hauled it all the way down to the state. How do I know this, you might ask? Because rocks carry their life stories around with them, just as trees tell stories with their rings.

One stone with a tale to tell is the wandering pudding stone. These pretty speckled boulders are quite common in Michigan but are rare in the rest of the world. They are smooth and gray with brilliant red and black pebbles scattered all through them. Some hungry geologist must have thought they looked like nuts and raisins in a pudding.

The "raisins" are actually red jasper, which comes from just one place in the Midwest—the North Channel of Lake Huron. So, when you find a pudding stone near Saskawan, or even down in Indiana, you know the glaciers hauled it all that way! (One exception is the football-sized pudding stone in my garden which rode down from the U.P. in the back of my dad's Packard in about 1948.)

We have geology to thank for much of what we love about Michigan. We wouldn't have the Great Lakes or our lovely sand dunes without our glaciers. Many of our inland lakes—we have over 11,000—were formed when huge ice chunks broke off and were left behind to melt. Did you know that poor Maryland has not one natural, inland lake? Virginia used to have two, but one recently sprung a leak and dried up. Sometimes that happens here, too. At Yankee Springs State Park, not far from here, are deep, dry craters that were once thought to be made by meteorites. We now know that these "Devil's Soup Bowls" are glacial lakes that dried up.

And, don't forget those ancient seas, which left gypsum under our feet. If you dig it up, grind it up, heat it up, and add water, it becomes very useful indeed. You may know it as "plaster of Paris." Everything from industrial molds to fertilizer to sidewalks to matchstick heads utilize gypsum. Here in Saskawan, a whole industry grew up around mining it. If your house was built before 1950, chances are your walls are made with local gypsum, a gift of Michigan's ancient, inland seas.

22

DELUGE.

Tuesday, June 21

The window fan had been going since bedtime, but it was now 3:00 a.m. The house had finally cooled down, so Iris got up to turn it off. Zelda was already up, standing in the hallway and looking down the dark stairway into the kitchen.

"Out?" Iris asked, hoping that wasn't the case. One daily round trip on the stairs was enough these days. The dog sat down as if to say, *No, that's not it*, and growled at the dark.

Iris listened. She heard a clunk on the back porch. She reviewed her nightly rounds: closing the downstairs windows, turning out the yard light, locking the back door. *Or was that yesterday?*

Zelda descended three steps and stopped to see if Iris was following.

Iris sighed again. "Who's the watchdog around here anyway?" She grabbed her robe from the back of the rocking chair and took her cell phone from its charger on the dresser.

"Lead on." She gripped the handrail and tested her hip before starting her descent. In the kitchen, she peered through the kitchen door into the darkness. She flipped on the porch light and looked again. She opened the door. The yard was still except for a couple of tree frogs signaling each other, a single car whooshing by on the street and a freight train signaling somewhere in the distance.

Zelda sniffed the air through the screen.

"We've got a pair of healthy imaginations," Iris said, shutting the door and locking it again. Then she went to the living room sofa and pulled the afghan over her, while Zelda made the rounds of the downstairs windows, keeping watch over the quiet yard.

Iris woke to the sound of the well pump humming in the basement. She sat up and listened. *The toilet must be running.* But in the bathroom, the tank was quiet and the faucet was off. She looked through the kitchen window toward the barn and saw the garden hose snaking across the driveway into the doorway. A rivulet of water ran out of the barn and into the grass.

"What in heaven's name?" She hurried down the porch steps in her moccasins to turn off the faucet at the corner of the house. She could see a dark stain on the barn's dirt floor.

She rushed to barn and stood there with her hands on her cheeks. Bags of manure, topsoil, peat moss and organic fertilizer were soaked with water. Bales of straw in one corner were dark and sodden. Her grandmother's walnut dresser was resting on its makeshift platform of bricks—just a few inches above the mud. She drew back the tarp and ran her hands lovingly over its marble top and burled drawer fronts.

The old Schwinn, the Radio Flyer, her garden tools, tarps and paint cans weren't so lucky. She yanked angrily at the offending hose and pulled it back toward the house. She was sure she had left it coiled by the house after she watered the tomatoes. When had she let Rafael wash the bike? *That was days ago*, she thought, but she wasn't sure.

Zelda found the muddy barn less interesting than the prospect of breakfast, which seemed to have been forgotten. She whined until Iris came to her senses and walked slowly back to the house.

Iris spent the rest of the morning dragging what she could out of the barn to dry in the June sun, all the while, wondering what was happening to her quiet life.

Caroline spent the same morning selecting photos for the *Ridge Park Zoo Nooz*. One thought led to another and pretty soon she was thinking about Little Houdini's escape and Rafael which led to the charming jogger/rescuer and what to do with his tee-shirt—anything but the task at hand. At two, she headed to the Bat Cave where she found Julie eating a late lunch.

"Want some company?"

"Sure. Haven't you eaten?" Julie took her boots off the chair across from her.

"Hours ago, but the fundraising gods are not smiling upon me today. I need a break." She searched the counter for something fresh baked, gooey and high carb. *Nothing.*

She opened the refrigerator and closed it again. She wasn't hungry but she wanted something to eat, anything. She sniffed the coffee pot and nearly gagged. "Oy! I can't face that computer anymore today. And I have a serious compulsion to pace and gnaw."

Julie nodded knowingly. "Classic cage stereotypy. What's up?"

Caroline searched the cupboard. "I need an enrichment."

"I can imagine," Julie said through a bite of sandwich. "Why do you think I wrestle Chinese water dragons for a living?" She held up a heavily bandaged pinky. "Anything to avoid a desk job."

"Ouch! What happened?"

"That guy did *not* want me poking around his injured claw this morning."

"Are you okay?"

"Fftt," Julie said with a shrug. "Part of the job."

"Chinese water dragon, eh?" Caroline rooted around a cupboard for a tea bag. "Big lizard, right? How big?" She put a mug of water and a tea bag in the microwave and leaned against the counter.

"Like this," Julie said, indicating a foot and a half. "With scalpels for claws, by the way. Usually he's as lime-green as your Fiesta. But today he was so freaked he went all pale greenish-gray. I was feeling sorry for him when he nailed me, the ingrate."

Caroline added sugar to the hot tea.

"Sit. Sit," Julie commanded, pushing the chair opposite her with her foot. "I have goldfish and carrot sticks to gnaw on."

Caroline discreetly brushed something dry and brown off the seat where Julie's boots had been and sat down. "I am supposed to be choosing photos of the ribbon-cutting for the newsletter, but I keep trying to see what the monkeys are doing in the background of every shot. I'm getting nowhere in either case."

"It's been, what, a week and a half?"

"And Houdini *still* refuses to talk. Don't you guys have some truth serum over at the clinic?"

Julie shook her head. "Maybe we'll never know how he got out. That would be frustrating." She opened the second half of her sandwich and arranged goldfish on top of the butter and pressed it back together. "Old family recipe," she said, by way of explanation. "Oh. I've been meaning to tell you. Rafael is such a hard little worker! I saw him washing windows today with Chappy—a lot of volunteers would quit if they had to do that."

"When I walk him to the farm he tells me everything about his day. He tells Iris VanWingen too, which may help convince her we aren't running Animal Alcatraz over here."

"At least she left us out of her column this week," Julie said. "Who knew all that stuff about gypsum, though?"

She sipped her tea and thought about the mine again. "You grew up near here didn't you?"

"The Ridge? Yup. Born and bred."

"What do you know about the Stoddard Gypsum Mine?"

Julie cringed. "Enough to steer clear. Why?"

"Rafael lives right at the fence corner. There are all kinds of warning signs. I was just wondering how dangerous it really is in there."

Julie pushed the bag of carrot sticks toward Caroline. "Most kids grow up afraid of the dark or the boogie man, but for Ridge kids, it's that mine. We had the fear-a-God pounded into us about those sinkholes. My brothers used to threaten to toss me in there all the time. My parents would have grounded me for life if I ever even touched that fence. I was no saint as a kid, but I never went *near* that mine, not once. Gives me the willies even now."

"Did anyone ever fall in?"

"Oh, sure. Well, I mean, if someone's dog or cat disappeared, we figured they got buried alive in there. Once a kid got lost and I remember seeing the cops shining flashlights through the fence. Even *they* didn't want to go in there."

This wasn't exactly hard evidence. "So you believe the warning signs?"

"You betcha. I wouldn't step foot on that mine property." She got up and tossed her crusts in the garbage.

"Too bad. It's a beautiful woods in there."

Julie shuddered. "Don't be fooled. That place is one big booby trap."

When Rafael arrived at her office a little after five, Caroline was proofreading the *Zoo Nooz*. She kept him occupied looking at the children's drawings of Houdini's escape. Then she emailed the newsletter to more than six thousand subscribers, plus one. She had found Iris' email address at the bottom of her Sunday column and added her to the list.

She looked at the time. "It's late, Rafa. Your mom will be home in ten minutes."

"Does that mean there won't be time for lemonade?"

"Sorry, kiddo, I had to finish my work. We'll stop at Miss Iris' to explain, and then I'll walk you home."

The entire contents of Iris' barn seemed to have spilled out onto the gravel driveway. Iris was standing inside the kitchen door, watching them through the screen.

"Having a yard sale?" Caroline called out.

Iris didn't answer.

"I'm sorry we're late." Caroline said, sensing something. "I had to finish a project, but I should have called. Anyway, I wanted to stop by and explain before I walk Rafael home."

Iris stepped out onto the porch and crossed her arms over her checkered shirt. She glanced toward the barn. "Rafael, did you use the hose yesterday?"

He froze. "No," he said.

"Well, *somebody* left it running all night. It's made a terrible mess in the barn."

He shook his head. "I didn't. It wasn't me."

Iris eyed both of them suspiciously.

Caroline put her arm around Rafael's shoulder, feeling protective. He was standing his ground, though, folding his arms to mirror Iris' body language. His eyes met hers, giving her a chance to rescind the accusation.

Now Iris was glaring at Caroline. "Remember that odor I told you about? You can smell it now."

Caroline inhaled and smelled something delicious wafting through the screen door. "I don't smell anything." She patted the boy's shoulder and said quietly, "Come on. Let's get you home." They turned and began crossing the gravel with Zelda at their heels.

"Don't you people ever *clean* those cages?" Iris called after them.

You people? It would do no good to argue right now. *Two steps forward, one step back, or was it to be the other way?* She turned to look at Iris again, but couldn't manage a smile. "Iris, I will check into it and get back to you."

"I know cat urine when I smell it." Iris shook her head, incredulous at the world's general stupidity, and Caroline's in particular. "Zelda, stay."

The dog stopped, confused by the change of routine. Then she dropped her head and turned back toward the house, stopping several times to look longingly at Rafael and Caroline.

Rafael shuffled along beside Caroline, whacking at pine cones with a stick.

Caroline said, "You know, I think her hip hurts her sometimes."

"I didn't leave the hose on," he said, decapitating an innocent May apple.

"I believe you."

"*She* doesn't." A few steps further on, he added, "My mom's feet hurt her sometimes."

"I bet it makes her a little grumpy sometimes."

They walked along silently until they reached the fence corner. She traced the halo of shine in his jet-black hair with her fingers. "I'll see you on Thursday in my office, Okay? We'll leave at 5:15 sharp, so you can have time to play with Zelda."

"What if Miss Iris is still mad at us?"

Caroline shrugged. "We won't let that happen. We'll use our charisma."

"What's charisma?"

"We will be so nice to her that she won't be able to stay mad. You and I, we're good at that." There was nothing wrong with wanting to please others, no matter what Bella said.

"Okay, but will you walk me home after that?"

"We'll see."

He exhaled until she thought he might deflate like a flat tire. "Why do grown-ups always say, 'We'll see. We'll see,' instead of giving a real answer?"

"Because it's not good to make promises you might not be able to keep. But there would have to be a very good reason not to walk you home next time. How's that?"

"That's almost a promise."

"Yes, and that's the best I can do."

"Okay, bye," he said, suddenly tearing off across the yard. The patio door slid opened. A woman's hand waved and the door closed.

Leaves rustled overhead. A red-shouldered hawk glided over the house and landed in a cottonwood tree at the bottom of the ravine with a descending *keeee-aah*.

Caroline drew a breath, stopped and wrinkled her nose. There *was* an odor. She sniffed several more times. Faintly feline. Then the breeze died and it was gone.

She heard distant barking coming from inside the fence. Her heart shifted into overdrive. If she left now, she'd miss him, but she couldn't just stand here. She faced the house, pretending to be watching Rafael safely home. She glanced over her shoulder, hoping to see Neil's red cap coming over the rise. She took out her ponytail holder, shook her hair free and ran her hands through it, keeping her eye on the fence. She bent down to untie and retie her shoe. Then she untied and retied her other shoe, then the first one again.

"My mom wants to know if you're okay." It was Rafael.

She jumped. "You scared me!"

"Do your feet hurt, too?"

"No. No. I'm fine. There was a stone in my shoe." *Lying to a child. Shameless!* "I'm good, thanks." She waved to Mrs. Rojas, who was watching from the kitchen window.

Neil and Magoo were approaching from the inside of the fence. Magoo barked twice and rattled the fence with eighty pounds of dog power.

"*You* again?" Neil said, grinning widely.

"No, *you* again," she said, hoping she looked surprised, yet coolly casual.

Neil threaded his fingers through the fence and twisted to stretch his back. "So, are you stalking me?"

"Stalking you?" Caroline let out a laugh, which probably sounded forced. She wondered if he was serious and wondered what qualified, exactly, as stalking. Adjusting one's schedule a minute or two in hopes of seeing someone didn't count as stalking, did it? She was new at this.

"I could ask you the same question," she said too late to be witty.

"I told you, I jog here."

"Well, *I* told *you* I walk my friend home every Tuesday and Thursday—at six."

He removed his cap, revealing the nicest hat-hair she'd ever seen. He ran a forearm over his brow. "You never told me that. I would remember, because that's my exact jogging schedule—Tuesday and Thursday, sometimes Saturday." He glanced at his watch. "Just before six."

Rafael reached through the fence to scratch Magoo's chest. "Can I pet your dog?"

"Uh, this is Rafael," Caroline said. "Rafa, that's Magoo and his friend, Mr—" Only a real stalker would readily recall a detail like the stalkee's name, plus she was hoping for a last name.

"Neil," he waved. "Howdy, Rafael."

"I like your dog. He's bigger than Zelda."

"So, where is Zelda today? I hope she's not grounded."

"She couldn't come on our walk today," Rafael explained, scratching Magoo's neck.

Magoo pressed himself into the chain links and dripped saliva on Rafael's forearm, drunk with joy. Mrs. Rojas opened the slider and called to Rafael in Spanish.

"Bye, Mr. Neil. Bye, Magoo. Bye, Miss Caroline." He bolted across the yard.

When Caroline looked up, Neil was watching her with that intent look of his. The corner of his mouth twitched. "So, your hiking clothes are in the wash today?"

She laughed. "The white ones?" A clever retort was called for here, but nothing came to mind. Of course, she'd think of one in an hour or so. She grinned stupidly, twisted a lock of her hair around two fingers, then shoved her hands in her pockets. Neil, she noted, was having a hard time maintaining eye contact. So, he was nervous, too. This was a good sign. There was no hint of the brashness of the men who frequented Bella's favorite bars. Neil was early forties, for sure. Perhaps his sharp edges had worn down.

"Any permanent injuries?"

"Um," she said. Now, there was a snappy rejoinder. "The blouse made a full recovery. The pants and shoes, sadly, didn't make it." *Better.*

Neil's face lit up, which meant, specifically, that there was crinkling around the eyes and his cheeks creased from the corner of his eyes to his jaw line. His teeth were white, but not fake, glow-in-the-dark white. His bottom teeth overlapped, but the top ones were straight. His skin was flushed from exertion, or maybe, she hoped, from nerves. She had to look away to stop grinning like an idiot. She felt as transparent and happy as a lime-green Chinese water dragon.

Magoo whined for attention. Caroline moved where she could reach his chest, hoping to prolong the conversation.

"My pride," she said, "needs some serious rehab, though." She pulled on Magoo's ear. "And it's all your fault, Mr. Magoo. Yes, it is."

Magoo snorted softly.

"He's sorry," Neil translated. "But, he'll tell you anything you want to hear. He's a golden."

Magoo backed up and began lumbering sideways up the rise.

"Okay, bud, we're going." Neil seemed ready to say something, but stopped. He took a couple of steps backward and raised his hand. "Well, I'm glad you're okay."

"Thanks." She nodded. "I am."

"So, maybe I'll see you on Thursday?"

"It's a date," Caroline said cheerily.

As soon as he disappeared over the rise, Caroline smacked her forehead. *It's a date?* Did she *actually* say that? She couldn't have, yet she'd heard the words tumble out of her big, stupid mouth. She might as well have asked, *Wanna be my boyfriend?*

She hurried down the path, away from him. Now she would have to skip Thursday entirely to compensate for her puppy-dog eagerness. Her inner adult weighed in. *Caroline, you like this man.* She counted to ten and slowed her pace. *Let him know. Take the risk.*

But then adolescent Caroline butted in. *But what if he doesn't like me?* She smacked her forehead, harder this time. Maybe she should pass him a note before gym class.

She definitely needed to upgrade her game.

23

EAU DE NEIL

"Can't this wait for the weekend?" Caroline was giving the evil eye to a mountain of unfolded laundry on Bella's sofa. Her friend had offered iced tea and a view of the sunset from her riverside balcony in exchange for Caroline's folding services.

"No way!" Bella said, emphatically. "I'm down to my Christmas socks."

The dryer buzzed and Bella went to get yet another load. Caroline filled a basket and took it to the balcony. Across the wide boulevard, Riverbend Park was busy with skateboarders, cyclists, walkers, joggers and picnickers. A man and a woman on a red blanket were tossing crumbs to a family of mallards.

Caroline shook out a pair of Bella's yoga pants. She didn't mind really. The weather was perfection and the sun would take its sweet time setting on this, the summer solstice. Across the river, urban rooftops and the strings of power lines ran up the gentle rise of the flood plain and abruptly stopped at an unbroken shag carpet of green that she now understood was the mine property, Willow Creek Farm and the Ridge Park Zoo beyond. She wondered idly which of the huge white pines she could see was the one next to Iris' porch.

Bella came onto the balcony and sat down.

Caroline asked, "So, what are you doing on the Fourth?"

"My sister wants me to drive up to Ispeming see her baby bump. But it's, like, a six-hour drive and there could be a backup on the bridge. I think I'll wait for the real thing in September. Besides, a guy I met asked me to his cottage for the weekend."

"A guy? What guy?"

"Mark Sss—omething. I met him last Tuesday, when you stood me up and I had to run alone. I turned my ankle just as he ran by."

Caroline laughed. "How convenient."

"Anyway, we went to the Third Base."

"On your first date? Bad Bella!" Caroline teased.

"Funny. We just had coffee, actually. He lives in the next building. His parents have a place up north. Crystal Lake. His friends will be there, too. You should come."

The idea of a weekend, probably a drunken weekend, with strangers had no appeal. "I'm going to see my parents in Evanston," she said, letting go of a long, pent up sigh.

"Bummer." Bella never saw the need to hide her feelings.

"Actually, I'm looking forward to it, sort of." Caroline folded a third and fourth pair of yoga pants. "It's just that they're having a party and there will be people there who haven't heard about my divorce, or who have, and will give me pity looks. My mom also invited a guy she euphemistically calls 'recently single.'"

"So, don't go."

"It's not that simple." In fact, things were never as simple for her as they were for Bella. "My parents have been really supportive this year. I should go."

"So many shoulds, gottas and have-tos. Don't you get tired of that?"

Caroline dropped her hands into her lap. "You know what I am *really* tired of?"

"What?"

"Folding yoga pants. Don't you own any jeans?" She tossed another pair on the pile and frowned. "You may be right, Bell. But I hate to disappoint my family—unlike someone *else* I know, eh? Poor li'l baby bump."

Bella lifted her chin and shook out a towel. "I am not moved by guilt—unlike someone else I know."

The darkening silhouette of the Ridge rose to meet clouds in a hundred shades of orchid and amethyst. Caroline wondered if Neil lived somewhere over there.

After a long silence, she said casually, "I met a guy, too."

Bella tossed a towel onto a towel mountain. "Say more."

"Only if you promise not to go all Bella on me."

"'All Bella?'"

"Just don't overreact. You'll have me sending him roses or leaving my panties on the fence."

"Panties?" Bella's radar was up. "How are panties involved?"

While they folded fifty more pounds of laundry, Caroline related every humiliating detail of her Slide of Infamy and Mystery Man's

Daring Rescue. She showed Bella her scraped elbows. She may have given some poetic license to the angle of the hill, the size of Neil's biceps and the definition of his abs for its entertainment value. Bella was such an appreciative audience.

Bella was still laughing. "Does this guy have a name?"

"Neil."

"Neil what?"

Caroline shrugged.

Bella rolled her eyes. "I guess that's top-secret intel, eh?" She picked up another towel and shook it. "But he *is* single, eh?"

"Sure," she shrugged again. "Maybe. I don't know."

"Did you get his cell number? Email?"

She shook her head.

"Give him yours? Arrange to meet again?"

"Okay. Stop. I get it. I suck at this."

Bella sighed. "Is he *straight*, at least?"

"Look, I said I *met* a guy. I didn't say I got his life story." She fished a neon pink thong out of the basket and twirled it on her index finger, feeling peeved. "Don't these get stuck?"

Bella snatched them away and pushed them under the folded towels. "So, anyway, you got a good vibe from this guy, eh?" Her tone turned conciliatory.

"Maybe. He refused to leave me there—even though I told him to. He seemed concerned that I was okay."

Bella nodded. "Well, that's . . . something."

Caroline stood up and leaned into the balcony railing. "Never mind. It was nothing." The couple on the red blanket were kissing now. "It's just that, he seemed . . . *interested*. He was apologetic about his dog, too." She turned to face Bella. "He has these deep laugh lines— like parentheses." She traced brackets on her cheeks with her fingers. "And curly hair that's sorta shaggy. He seemed not macho, but not the opposite of macho, either—just mature."

Bella grimaced. "*How* mature?"

"Forty, maybe. Maybe a bit beyond." She sat down again. "That's all I know. Enough with the questions. Let's talk about something else." She held up three anklets, one pink, one white and one green striped. "These don't have mates."

Bella held out her hand. "Into the singles drawer."

"You have a singles drawer?"

"Single socks go there to wait for their mates. I've got a strict policy."

Caroline patted the three socks gently before handing them over. "Poor socks." This orderliness seemed uncharacteristic for someone whose housekeeping standards required a new word—something beyond chaos, anarchy and pandemoniacal uproar—to accurately describe it. "I'm afraid to ask, but what happens if the mate never shows up?"

"Rag bag." Bella tossed an imaginary sock over her shoulder.

"Heartless bitch," Caroline muttered under her breath.

"Hey, single-sockness is *highly* contagious. You can't let it get a foothold. Ha!" Bella laughed heartily. "If you let the odd one slip in, it upsets the balance and pretty soon, you have nothing but singles."

Caroline nodded pensively. "You may have solved one of the universe's greatest mysteries—except for where lost socks actually *go*."

Bella wiggled her eyebrows knowingly. "What do you think black holes are for, eh?"

Caroline tackled a pile of towels next. "But as a metaphor, a single sock drawer... well, no, it's just *not* a metaphor... for *anything*."

Bella shook her head emphatically. "Absolutely not a metaphor."

The setting sun was turning a Chicago-bound jet trail into a bright orange pipe cleaner. The woman on the red blanket slapped at a mosquito and began tugging on the blanket until her companion rolled to a stand.

Bella pushed her feet into the railing and tilted her chair at a precarious angle. "So. Let's review: A semi-anonymous, nicely dimpled, obviously athletic, slightly older gentleman appears out of nowhere to rescue you from death-by-mud."

Caroline groaned. "I thought we changed the subject."

Bella drummed her fingers on her tumbler. "Not a lot to go on."

"Bell."

"Was there lingering eye contact?"

Caroline ignored her.

"You were wearing good underwear, eh?"

"He didn't see my underwear."

"He was checking you out, though, eh?"

Caroline stood up and wrapped a towel around Bella's head. "I'm going home," she said.

Nothing intelligible came from underneath.

Caroline turned in the doorway. "I almost forgot. He gave me his tee shirt when my pants ripped. Kind of chivalrous, don't you think?"

Bella's chair came down with a bang. "You still have it?"

"In my laundry."

"Did you smell it?"

"Ew! Of course not."

"Pheromones, my little friend. What's the strategy for returning said tee shirt?"

She shrugged. "He said I should keep it."

Bella huffed loudly. "This calls for the classic drop-the-hanky move. The oldest courtship move in the history of... courtship—although it might have started as drop-the-mastodon bone or something."

Caroline stood with one hand on her hip and the other on the sliding door. "You're making no sense."

"Let me spell it out for you, oh Clueless One: Boy lends shirt, girl returns shirt, *et voila!*—into bed they go, eh?"

Caroline looked heavenward.

"Okay," Bella said, "in *your* case, you date for six months, get engaged for a year, have a big white wedding and buy a house with a picket fence. Are you following now?"

"Pretending for a moment that I want to see this 'gentleman' again, he did say he jogs on Tuesdays and Thursdays."

"That's a start."

"So, I might see him later this week."

Bella was thoughtful for a moment, before she twisted to face Caroline.

"What?" Caroline asked.

"Just—" Bella hesitated, then frowned.

"Just what?"

"Like Grandmama Canelli always says, 'A rich coat may hide a poor heart.'"

"Huh?"

"I'm just saying, this guy could be married, like, to a supermodel. Even a pregnant supermodel, eh? Or, the supermodel could be a guy. You never know. Probably not pregnant then, but maybe they're planning to adopt, or—"

"Ok, I *get* it."

"Forget what I said before. Just take it slow. Okay?"

Across the street a woman with a blonde ponytail was walking a golden retriever that looked exactly like Magoo. Hell, it probably *was* Magoo, Caroline thought, and Neil's supermodel girlfriend, who looked about sixteen. Or, maybe she was Neil's daughter. *Even worse.*

Caroline sighed again. "First, you tell me to set a trap, now you're saying take it slow. And why am I taking advice from someone planning a two-night stand with a guy she just met?"

"I know." Bella tucked the last pair of yoga pants into the basket. "You're not me. Sometimes I forget that."

Caroline reached out and patted the top of Bella's crunchy orange spikes. "Thanks for keeping that in mind."

"I just don't want you spending another summer under a blanket on my couch."

"I know. I won't."

The washer in Caroline's utility closet was filling with water as she lifted the green and white tee shirt out of the dirty clothes basket with two fingers. She held it a few inches from her face and sniffed. Then she buried her face in the soft cotton and inhaled. Eau de Neil.

24

RUFFLED FEATHERS

Thursday, June 23

The contents of the barn were back in place when Caroline and Rafael drove into Iris' driveway well before six. Zelda escorted them from the top of the rise as Iris came out onto the porch. Caroline let the car idle, unsure whether they would be welcome.

As usual, it was Rafael who broke the ice, announcing that Miss Caroline "needed" to walk him home because a big dog had lunged at him from one of the yards.

"Since when are you afraid of a fenced dog?" Iris wanted to know. She shot a glance at Caroline, which, if it wasn't exactly friendly, was at least expectant. "I made drinks," she said.

A breeze stirred up the leaves on the cottonwoods above the barn, sending a blizzard of white fluff into every corner of the yard. Caroline took her place on the glider.

"I'm having a tonic," Iris called from the kitchen. "Care to join me?"

"Sure," Caroline said, not knowing exactly what "a tonic" might be.

A minute later, Iris stood over her with a tall glass topped with a lime wedge.

"Lovely. Thanks." She took a sip. *Gin* and tonic. And a double, if she was any judge.

"My husband's favorite, with Beefeaters."

Caroline lifted her glass. "Here's to your husband."

"Yes," Iris said with a smile.

Rafael dispatched his lemonade quickly and was soon balancing on the railing and reaching for the bell.

"Let's not ring the bell for a while, Rafa. The phoebes have returned to their nest again this year." Iris pointed to a tidy half-bowl made of grass and moss that seemed glued to the corner porch column. "This is their third year using the same nest. Built to last and just imagine, they've been to Florida and back twice!"

Rafael pulled himself up to see inside. A little gray bird watched from the apple tree, bobbing its tail.

"And look, Rafa," Caroline said. "There's a monarch, there on the lilac." The butterfly opened and closed its orange wings as it crawled over a fragrant purple cluster.

"The first of the season." Iris said. "This one's on its way north."

"Did it come from Mexico?" Caroline asked.

"Not this one, but perhaps its grandparents did. Not every monarch goes to Mexico. It's complicated."

"We plant a lot of wildflowers for the butterflies and bees at Ridge Park."

"You have caged butterflies over there?"

"No, no. They're just passing through, same as here."

Iris' look revealed surprise and skepticism all at once.

Rafael jumped from the railing and landed with a thud. "Hey, guess what I did today? I helped give the meerkats their check-ups. Yup. Doctor Peter and Miss Julie made them sleepy so they wouldn't be scared. They got their toenails clipped and their teeth cleaned. One of them got a tooth pulled. She has to take medicine for a while. They hide it in a treat. You wanna know how they know which one gets the medicine?"

"How?" Iris asked.

"They shaved a spot on her leg. "

Caroline watched this exchange. If Iris wasn't interested, she was pretending to be for Rafael's sake.

Iris went into the kitchen and came out with a basket. "Rafa, see if you can find some strawberries in the garden."

Rafael went off with Zelda tagging along.

"I enjoyed your column last Sunday," Caroline said. "Who knew we're sitting on the shore of an old sea?"

"Mmm," Iris nodded. "That's why the gypsum is so close to the surface around here and easy to mine."

"How close to the surface is it? I saw those warning signs on the mine fence. How dangerous is it inside the fence?"

Iris shrugged. "Oh, I'm not sure."

"I saw a guy and his dog in there. I warned him about the sinkholes, but he seemed unconcerned."

"A few people go tramping around those woods, if they can find a way in. But most stay away, which is just as well. It's a lovely, unspoiled woods."

"But is it dangerous, or not?"

"The mine's been there almost as long as this farm. There were cave-ins years ago. They stopped mining a few years back, so if the land was going to give way, it probably would have by now."

"Why all the warning signs?"

"Probably to keep trespassers out," Iris said, smiling. "Wish I'd thought of that."

"Is that why the land was never developed?"

"Well, walking on it is *one* thing, excavating a building foundation is something else entirely."

"So, mining below, untouched wilderness above, city all around. What a strange combination."

"A lot of my birds nest over there, I suspect." She nodded toward a woodpecker making its way up the dying ash tree behind the garden.

Rafael and Zelda came back and handed Iris a basket with a handful of berries. "Is that all you found?" she asked.

"Well, there were more, but Zelda had some." Rafael eyes darted guiltily before he added, "I ate a couple, too."

Iris sat back. "We call that a picker's fee. You can take the rest to your mom. Let's go inside and wash them." She leaned forward to get up, but winced and sat back.

"Rafa," Caroline said, "why don't you wash them when you get home?"

"Okay, but can I ride the bike now, Miss Iris?"

"There's a pump for the tires between the tractor and the paint cans," Iris said. "I know where every blessed thing is in that barn for the first time in forty years."

"Sounds like the barn was quite a mess. I'm so sorry."

"Yes," she said quietly. "I don't know how it happened."

A nuthatch landed on the copper feeder, scattering a half dozen seeds to a waiting chipmunk before finding one to its liking.

"By the way, my birds love the new feeder, but the squirrels are outraged. They keep looking at me as if I've made a terrible error in judgment, putting the seed out of their reach."

Caroline smiled at the thought. "A lot of animals depend on you. It must be a lot of work."

Iris blew out her breath. "That it is."

"What will happen to this place when—" Once she began, she didn't know how to finish her sentence.

"My daughters will inherit the property. They both live out-of-state with their families. They'll sell it and it'll get developed." She shrugged.

Caroline suspected Iris' feelings were far stronger than she was letting on. "I'm sorry to hear that."

Two fox squirrels spiraled up an elm snag and back down again.

Iris sighed irritably. "Remember I told you about the people who tried to pressure me into selling—the ones you said *weren't* zoo people?"

"Yes."

Iris looked away. "Well, I still don't think you know everything that's going on at that zoo of yours. There are people who want my farm—and I think they want it for the zoo."

"I doubt that. Ridge Park is planning to move, remember?"

"Maybe, but I'm pretty sure at least one of my so-called 'buyers' is connected to the zoo in some way."

"Who?"

"I can't remember his name, but I saw his picture in that newsletter you sent me yesterday. There's a picture of him at your ribbon-cutting. He sent me letters last fall and came by twice this spring. He made me so mad, I told him he could have this property over my dead body." She laughed dryly. "I think he took that as a challenge."

Caroline sat up straighter. There must have been sixty or seventy people in all the shots she included in the *Zoo Nooz*. "Can you show me?"

Iris started to get up, but winced and sat down again. "Damn my hip. Go get my laptop from the dining room."

"Your laptop?" Iris seemed more the typewriter sort.

Caroline stepped into the kitchen, feeling like a cat burglar. The floor creaked, and there was a vague whiff of chicken broth, lavender and mothballs. A pair of sheepskin moccasins lay by the door. The one window faced the barn and had a valance of white Dutch lace. *Classic Saskawan*, Caroline thought. Below the window was a well-used porcelain sink with a built-in drain board. White cupboards and scalloped white trim above the sink—circa 1940, she guessed—brightened the room. A set of narrow stairs ascended at the opposite end.

Against the wall a drop leaf table was set with a single, quilted placemat in a daffodil print. At the sight of it, something sank inside her. What was it? Sympathy for a solitary widow or a sense of personal dread? She turned her attention to several photographs held by magnets to the refrigerator. A photo of a family in matching Christmas sweaters read, "Hi Mrs. Van! Just wanted you to see my family. Your favorite student, (Ha-ha!) Joey M. Class of '82." Below it was a set of small blue hand prints on yellowing newsprint that read, "I love you, Grammy Van! From Sophia."

"The dining room's to the left," Iris called from the porch.

She focused. "Okay." She passed through the door into the dining room. An antique pendulum clock with a hexagonal face counted out seconds from the corner. It was about twenty minutes fast. She flicked the wall switch, and a blue and gold Tiffany lamp lit up a trestle table piled with folders and books. In the adjoining living room was a green couch of uncertain vintage with a crocheted, multi-colored afghan tossed over the back. Next to it was an ornate loveseat with carved wood trim.

"See it?" Iris called. "It's in the corner." It sat in the middle of a leather-topped wooden desk.

"I see it," Caroline called out.

Next to it a cell phone blinked in its charger. This felt like entering Superman's phone booth—where an ordinary (not so mild-mannered) farm widow morphs into "muckraking, anti-zoo Nature Woman!"

A row of books—*Life in the Michigan Woods, Birds of the Great Lakes, A Practical Guide to Mushrooms*—was squeezed between bronze bookends. She stood over the desk, unable to touch anything.

"This room's a disgrace," Iris said from the doorway, making Caroline jump. Iris smoothed an errant wisp of white hair and hobbled over, gripping the chairs for support. "Let's see now." She bent over the desk and moved her thumb and forefinger over the track pad. "I can never find anything on this thing."

"You seem to know what you're doing."

Iris opened her email and waited. "Mostly, it's a bunch of gobbledygook to me. If you're over forty, you'll never speak Computer without an accent. I harbor a deep resentment of technology. It's so damned addicting but completely unreliable. One day I'll write an essay on that." She pointed an accusing finger at the cell phone. "And *that*! It's like a spoiled child—forever getting lost, falling asleep at the wrong time or needing more juice. Don't get me started." She leaned closer to the laptop and tapped a few keys.

Caroline, who was smiling now, pointed out an email. "There. That's it."

Iris opened it and scrolled to photos of the ribbon cutting: "Ridge Park Welcomes Capuchin Monkey Troop," said the caption.

Iris stopped on a photo of Victor, Tom, Paddy and the woman known only as "the bimbo." They were grinning and holding brats and red plastic cups of beer. Iris' finger made contact with Paddy's face. "Him." In a few deft strokes, Paddy's round face filled the screen.

"That's Paddy Malone," Caroline said. "He owns the Pizza King chain. He's not a developer or a realtor."

"Well, he wants my farm, I can tell you that," Iris said. "And he obviously likes the zoo."

Caroline frowned. "How many times have you spoken to him?"

"Well, first he sent me a letter, which I ripped up. Then he started calling me and leaving messages, then one day he and another guy just showed up in the driveway."

"What did he say?"

"It wasn't what he *said*, exactly. It's just . . ." Her voice trailed off.

"What? Iris, you have to *tell* me."

"At first he was friendly, but a little oily, you know—*too* polite." She shook her head and laughed unconvincingly. "Things like this don't happen in Saskawan."

"Things like what?"

"Broken knee caps, guns with silencers, shallow graves in backyard gardens." She waved her hand to erase everything she had just said. "I'm making no sense."

"Are you saying he *threatened* you? Tell me *exactly* what he said."

Iris took a deep breath and thought. "'Why would a woman your age want to live back here all alone?' And 'A lot of things could happen to an elderly woman back here with no one around.' Stuff like that."

"I'm sure he didn't mean anything."

"No, no, probably not." Iris bit her lip. "Anyway, what's his connection to the zoo?"

"He's a friend of our board president, Tom Engelsma." She pointed to Tom. "Tom is the donor of the land in Nord Haven. Paddy has pledged a lot of money to move the zoo and help get the referendum passed. So, if he wants your land, it isn't to expand the zoo."

Iris crossed her arms and thought. "Maybe he thinks if the vote doesn't pass, he could buy my farm and give it to the zoo."

Caroline considered this. "That would be news to us. How many acres do you have?"

"Twenty, give or take."

"The zoo has twenty, too. That would make forty. The land in Nord Haven is a hundred acres."

"Could it be just his idea of a back-up plan?"

"I suppose. But our problem isn't just being small, it's being *old*. Many of our enclosures, our clinic, where our animals sleep at night and stay during cold weather are inadequate. Many of our buildings would have to be replaced or renovated and we'd still be too small to do the kind of conservation work we should be doing."

"Maybe he wants to build himself a mansion back here, or open a new pizzeria or something. Who knows?"

"Well, *I* sure don't," Caroline said, but she planned to find out.

On the walk home, Rafael described his morning at the clinic for the third time. It seemed meerkats were displacing monkeys on his list of favorite animals. Caroline's mind jumped back and forth from one mystery man who threatened elderly widows to another who leapt sinkholes and fences in a single bound.

That morning, Caroline had folded Neil's shirt—which now, sadly, smelled of fabric softener—and brought it to work. She had considered Bella's shirt-returning-hook-up-scheme, but chickened out and left the shirt in the car. After calling today's rendezvous a "date," she couldn't appear too eager.

In the distance, she heard Magoo's low bark. Zelda cocked her head and answered with a sharp retort as she pulled Caroline forward. *How uncomplicated to be a dog*, she thought, as she reined her own impulse to break into a jubilant run. At the end of the leash, the white tip of Zelda's tail began whirling in wild anticipation. On second thought, Caroline was grateful not to have such an undignified, tell-all appendage.

Neil and Magoo were waiting just inside the fence—paws and fingers clinging to twisted wire. The sight of him shifted her heartbeat into overdrive and her knees threatened to buckle. These sensations shocked her. A case of the wobblies at her age? Her body seemed to be in charge now.

She watched Neil stretch against the fence—Pyramis awaiting Thisbe at the chink in the wall. He wore the same Tigers cap and running shorts, but this time with a Chicago Cubs tee shirt. (He was an undiscriminating sports fan, or perhaps confused.) His running shoes were covered with white dust. *Gypsum?* she wondered.

"Hey!" Neil called out, dropping one hand to his hip.

"Hey, yourself." She stopped a few feet from the fence and self-consciously pushed a lock of hair behind her ear.

He touched his cap and grinned a little nervously, she thought.

"Hey, Mr. Neil, does Magoo like strawberries?" Rafael pushed one through the fence into Magoo's mouth.

"I guess so," Neil said, laughing.

Across the yard, Mrs. Rojas opened the slider at the back of the house and called for Rafael.

"Bye," he yelled as he ran across the yard.

Caroline let Zelda follow Magoo along the fence to the end of her leash. He stopped occasionally to lift his leg on one of the posts, reminding Zelda whose territory was whose.

Caroline fixed her face in a Mona Lisa smile. "So, it's your day to run, huh?" she said, stating the obvious.

"Yup. And yours to walk Rafael home?"

They nodded at each other.

"Maybe it's providential," he said.

"What is?"

"That we keep running into each other. Maybe it's a sign."

"A sign of what?" She wanted to hear him say it.

He looked away, licking his lips. *He's as nervous as I am*, she thought.

He said, "I was just thinking that you're someone who, like me, likes to hike in the woods—despite some odd wardrobe choices. By the way, I see you've learned your lesson."

She felt his eyes sweep downward over her navy and white striped cotton V-neck, khaki slacks and sensible leather moccasins. She felt her cheeks light up.

"Anyway," he added quickly, "I was thinking you might like to hike on *my* side of the fence," he said, gesturing over his shoulder.

"In Jell-O-Land?" she said, taking a step back. "I-I don't think so."

"Oh, but you'd like it." He swept his arm expansively as if he were selling a kitchen appliance. "There is a valley of ferns that would take your breath away."

"It's probably a sinkhole. Of *course* it would take my breath away."

He leaned closer, "I'll let you in on a little secret." (Now he sounded like a used-car salesman.) "Those sinkholes are urban legend. I've been playing in these woods since I was a kid. And besides, I know the owner."

She gripped the chain links and pulled herself up to look into the solid wall of greenery. What dangers lurked inside?

"Have you got a lair in there?" she asked, only half kidding, although no *actual* pervert would admit it if he did.

"Well, I used to have a fort, but it's been gone for years. It was off limits to girls, anyway, but recently I've softened my rules." His parenthetical dimples were showing most appealingly.

Her restrained smile had at some point become a full, toothy grin. She bit her lip and pointed to the rusting signs on the fence. "Those are, what, just decoration?"

"To discourage riffraff, ATVs, teen partiers, litterers—you know. No sinkholes or lairs. Promise. And don't forget, I'm an experienced rescuer." He tugged at the hem of his tee shirt. "I brought this special piece of rescue equipment, see?"

"Oh, I forgot to bring your shirt!" Caroline fibbed. "I'll bring it with me next time, um, that is, if I should ever, if I should decide to, um, run into you again." She wanted to roll up that tangle of words and send it back where it came from.

"Ah, my lucky shirt. Yes, I really need it back," he said.

"Wait. You said I could keep it," she said, lifting her chin.

"That was before I knew it was lucky." He was grinning again. (It was true: people really did look like their dogs.) "So, how about just a quick hike? I can open the gate for you." He pulled a set of keys out of his pocket.

"*Now?* Oh, I can't *now*." What if this guy was a serial killer? No one would even know where to look for her decaying body.

"Okay. What about next Tuesday then? You can bring my lucky shirt, because I *really* need it back."

Dear Bella. She was right about so many things.

"I'll bring it when I drop off Rafael, but I can't promise I'll hike in there." She glanced up at the red letters. They still said, DANGER! Unstable Ground. KEEP OUT!

Neil shrugged amiably. "Okay. I'll run by at six, get my shirt and we can hike if you're feeling brave."

"Brave?" She put her hands on her hips. "Is that a dare?"

"A *double* dare."

"A double-*do*g dare?"

"If you bring Zelda."

She laughed. "I'll think about it." She tried to dial back her smile into something more enigmatic, but it was a losing battle.

He began walking backwards up the rise. "No pressure." He adjusted his baseball cap to shield his eyes from the sun. "I'll take that as a definite probably. Come on, 'Goo!"

Caroline and Zelda walked side by side away from the fence. Before the path took its turn into the underbrush, Zelda stopped for a last look at Magoo.

Caroline whispered, "Are they watching us, Zel?"

She would have given anything to know.

25

TROPHIES

Friday, June 24

Ridge Park Zoo had yet to see a penny promised by one Patrick "Paddy" Malone, the flamboyant (and possibly shady) Pizza King of Saskawan, Michigan. Caroline had left several polite messages on his office voice mail. Finally, she called Tom Engelsma, who gave her Paddy's home phone. Someone sounding like his daughter answered, but she suspected it was the young woman known to the Bat Cave crowd as "the bimbo." Caroline had scolded them for being judgmental and ungrateful, but she had to admit, the nickname fit.

The bimbo, she soon learned, did not have a stripper name, like Angel or Bambi, or an edible name, like Brandy, Taffy, Cherry or Candy. Her name was Sarah—sweet, respectable and Biblical.

Paddy, Sarah said in an over-the-top Southern accent, was on safari in Africa, "for, like, the *whole month!*" And oh yes, maybe he *did* leave a check for the zoo before he left. Actually, she giggled, he might even have, like, asked her to send it, and she was, like, *super* sorry! She would look for it, and call back if she found it, or anything. Caroline repeated her own phone number several times before Sarah put down the phone and rummaged around for a pencil and paper.

Caroline frowned and hung up, super sure she, like, had heard the last of Sarah. She was considering her options when Sarah called back. She had found the check and would put it in the mail as soon as she found a stamp.

"No! No. Don't mail it. I'll be right over to pick it up."

Caroline parked her Fiesta in the brick driveway of Paddy's mansion not far from her old apartment in the historic district. The place looked fit for bonafide royalty. It sat at the end of a narrow brick street in a six-block area of homes built by nineteenth-century lumber barons. After they deforested the state, they began making paint, paper, furniture, automobile parts and plasterboard and flushing the waste into the Saskawan River. West Michigan's glory days and its lumber barons, were long gone, and its forests and rivers were the better for it.

Paddy's house was a two-story Italianate villa flanked by matching leaded-glass sun porches. A row of well-behaved boxwoods guarded a classic stone railing around the front porch. A brass plaque beside the massive front door read, "Historic Home, 1901."

Caroline rang the doorbell, triggering a carillon somewhere deep in the house. She half-expected Jeeves to answer the door, but soon heard the slap of flip-flops. Sarah opened the door wearing something stretched across her richly endowed front, which, if it was supposed to be a shirt, wasn't quite up to the job. She wore cut-offs so short they must have required a bikini wax. She looked at Caroline through heavy blonde bangs.

"Ha!" she said brightly. It took Caroline several seconds to translate this to, "Hi!"

"Hi, Sarah. I'm here to pick up Mr. Malone's check."

"Come on in." She stepped back and opened the door wider. "Can ya believe I found it? Paddy's study is such an old pigsty. Stay rot here. I'll go fetch it."

As Sarah disappeared into the house, Caroline wondered if Paddy had borrowed her from the set of *The Beverly Hillbillies*.

As her eyes adjusted to the darkly paneled foyer, she saw a pair of staircases winding upward on either side to meet at a second floor balcony. Caroline gasped. A dozen animal heads looked down at her with fixed stares. A cougar with fangs as long as her thumbs appeared to be jumping through the wall at a moose, an elk and some kind of small antelope. She recoiled, nearly knocking over an umbrella stand—which on closer inspection turned out to be the lower leg of an elephant. Her jaw went slack.

On the opposite wall, a kudu with its distinctive spiral horns kept company with several smaller ruminants. Hides and pelts of every description hung over the railings.

Sarah approached, waving an envelope. "Got it! I made some iced ('ahst') tea. Ya'll want some?"

Caroline could only point. "What is all this?"

Sarah followed Caroline's gaze. "Oh, that. Creepy, huh? I dunno," she shrugged. "Some of them were his daddy's. But not that one." She pointed over Caroline's shoulder.

Caroline turned and jumped simultaneously at a seven-foot grizzly in full attack pose.

"Paddy bagged 'im in Alaska last year. He *loves* that thing! He's bringing home an onyx this time."

"I think you mean an oryx," Caroline said, thinking of the three handsome antelopes at Ridge Park, with their magnificent spear-like horns.

Sarah giggled. "Yah."

Caroline pushed her fingers into the grizzly's course fur.

"Paddy emailed me last night. He bagged a lion this time. He's having it made into a rug for the study." She pointed into the interior of the house.

"When you said he was on safari, I thought you meant he was taking pictures."

Sarah's underdeveloped brain chugged along, finally putting together the two-piece puzzle of a zoo representative's horrified expression and a room full of animal remains.

"Oh," she whispered, tucking a lock of hair behind one spangled ear. "You probably think, um, well I know what it *looks* like." She sighed, looking around the room. "Paddy *loves* animals. *Really*, he does!"

Sarah looked at Caroline with the gentle, vulnerable eyes of a ruminant.

"Thanks for the check, Sarah. I'll send an acknowledgment letter next week." She turned to go, then stopped. "Have you ever heard Mr. Malone talk about wanting to buy land near the zoo?"

Sarah tilted her head to think. "I don't know. I mean, he's always wantin' to build new pizza places, but I don't know where. He doesn't talk about that with me." She reached out to touch the grizzly's giant paw and said, "I don't know why Paddy has to kill 'em."

Caroline shook her head. "I don't either, Sarah." Then she let herself out.

"Did you know you can *still* hunt big game in Africa? *Endangered* big game!" Caroline told Bella as they ran along the river that evening. "I mean, I know Africans sometimes kill bush meat for food, but I had no idea some *white* guy from *Saskawan, Michigan*, could *legally* kill a rare animal the size of a refrigerator and have it stuffed with sawdust or flattened into a rug."

"Neanderthals are still among us," Bella observed.

"I thought über men like Teddy Roosevelt and Ernest Hemingway were as extinct as the animals they hunted."

"What about Dick Cheney, Ted Nugent and half the NRA?" Bella was never shocked by malfeasance of any kind.

"Hunting must feed some primal instinct to dominate or assuage some fear of being eaten," Caroline mused.

"Don't overthink it. Some people *like* to kill and others like living by their wits. It's no different than growing your own food."

"A carrot doesn't scream when you pull it. Anyway, I don't object to hunting over-populated animals, like deer or geese, if you plan to eat them. And I'm not a vegetarian, but just to hang a severed head on your wall? It's barbaric."

"They're *trophies*."

"Yeah, whatever you call them, it's anachronistic and pointless, not to mention immoral and shocking."

Bella sniffed. "The only thing that shocks me is that this Great White Pizza King would donate money to a zoo."

"I know . . . Maybe he feels guilty."

"Trust me, guys like Paddy don't do guilt. He's more like a pedophile hanging around a playground."

"It sickens me to think he even *looked* at Goldwyn."

"His pizza is pretty tasty, though," Bella noted. "Let's order one this weekend."

"Are you *serious*? We're boycotting Pizza King from now on."

"You've never even been there," Bella pointed out.

"Still."

As they ran in silence, Caroline tried to purge the image of Goldwyn as a rug. It seemed that everyone had misread Paddy's enthusiasm for a new zoo. And why did he want Iris' property? People were hard to read, Caroline was thinking. Bella was right, she needed to stop being so trusting—which brought her around to Neil.

Should she trust the guy? His invitation hung in the air like a brightly colored piñata—so tempting and full of promise.

"Hey!" Bella called from behind. Caroline had missed their turn. "Are you lost?"

"Sorry." Caroline turned around. "You know, I actually believe Sarah when she says Paddy loves animals. But he loves them like he loves his over-sized house or his pizza empire—or her. They're all part of a vast collection. But I honestly don't understand how that man sleeps at night."

"I'm sure he sleeps just fine on his nice trophy rug with his nice trophy girlfriend."

It was Caroline, not Paddy, who couldn't sleep that night. At 2:45 a.m., she Googled "hunting big game in Africa."

By 3:10 she had learned that she, Caroline Finch, could for as little as $350 a night, have an "Unforgettable Big Game Experience" in Tanzania, South Africa, Namibia or Zimbabwe. Accommodations, catering, transportation and the services of a professional hunter, tracker and skinner included. Liquor provided in moderation. Taxes, license and permit fees included. For an additional fee, they would prepare her trophy, do her taxidermy work and dip, pack and ship her trophy back home to Saskawan, Michigan.

26

THE SECRET LIVES OF MONARCHS

Sunday, June 26

Natural Curiosity: Notes from Willow Creek Farm
Iris Van, *Saskawan Evening Star*

Along with the hordes of human tourists this summer, monarch butterflies will soon be arriving in West Michigan. These orange and black beauties delight us with their seemingly aimless fluttering in our gardens. But don't be fooled, these insects of the order *Lepidoptera* lead a purpose-driven life.

You probably know that monarchs winter in Mexico. But how exactly such a fragile creature accomplishes this epic journey was a mystery until quite recently. We now know that this annual migration is sort of a multi-generational relay.

To explain, I'm going to tell the story of one monarch family. Their saga began fourteen months ago, in April of last year, when one female emerged from her jade-green chrysalis near San Antonio, Texas. I will call her Antonia. She flutters off in search of three things: nectar, a healthy mate and milkweed plants on which to lay her eggs. Her quest brings her northward with the spring. Along the way, she lays hundreds of eggs on young milkweed plants in Texas, Oklahoma and Missouri. After a natural life span of about six weeks, she dies.

One of the eggs she laid in Missouri hatches. She's Dixie, our next butterfly. Dixie continues north through Illinois and Indiana into

Michigan. One day in mid-June, she stops on a lovely red milkweed growing behind my barn. She lays an egg on the underside of a leaf, then she feeds on the nectar of a yellow coreopsis before she flutters off. She continues north and into Canada, where she, too, will end her days.

Three days later, I notice tiny holes in the leaves of my milkweed plant. A tiny, caterpillar with pretty black and yellow zebra stripes is busy eating. For two weeks I watch it munch through one leaf after another until its body is plump and nearly two inches long. Then one day, I find it hanging on the dried stem of a bush nearby. By morning it has encased itself in a sea-foam green sleeping bag decorated with a ring of gold—truly one of nature's most elegant creations. For the next two weeks, nothing happens that I can see. But one morning, the casing has become transparent. Inside, I can see tightly folded orange wings. In a few more hours, Dixie's daughter, Willow, emerges. She rests in the sun until her wings are dry and strong, then, lifts off in search of a nectar meal and a mate.

Her quest takes her to the Lake Michigan shore, where she joins other monarchs feeding among the dunes on fragrant raspberry-colored milkweed blooms. With fresh water as far as the eye can see, this is a monarch paradise, to be sure. Willow lays several eggs near the Little Point Sable lighthouse. These butterflies will be the fourth generation of this monarch family. One of them I will call Rosaria.

Rosaria is a late-season monarch. This means her life will be nothing like Willow's, Dixie's or Antonia's. She has no interest in finding a mate or a milkweed nursery. Some say she's bigger than her mother, but she's immature, like a robust teenager. Unlike her mother and grandmother, she's equipped with a strong homing instinct. In the fall, she will join millions of her generation who will ride southbound winds, covering as much as twenty miles a day and stopping only for nectar and brief rests. For if this monarch family is to survive, Rosaria must fly over two thousand miles!

By November, Rosaria has miraculously reached her destination high in the mountains of Central Mexico. Today, the area is a Unesco World Heritage site known as El Rosario Monarch Butterfly Reserve.

Just how Rosaria finds her way to these mountains is still a tantalizing scientific mystery. Perhaps she follows markers left by northbound monarchs. No one knows for sure. But we do know she will spend the entire winter clinging sleepily to a pine tree high in the Reserve, living only on her own stored fat.

Then, in February, Rosaria will begin to stir. One day, she and millions of other butterflies will leave the Reserve and head north. Now a mature adult, Rosaria needs a mate. When she reaches Texas, she will be ready to lay her own eggs not far from her great-grandmother Antonia's birthplace. In the eight months of her life, she has covered more than 3,000 miles. There in Texas, her remarkable life will come to an end.

My story ends here, too, but remember, it is just one chapter of a family saga that has been repeating itself for thousands of years. Perhaps this summer one of Rosaria's offspring will find that little patch of milkweed behind my barn. I'll be watching.

So, my good readers, are you ready for monarch visitors this summer? You can welcome them to your yard by planting native flowers that adult monarchs love, like purple blazing star, red or lavender bee balm or yellow black-eyes Susans. But remember, monarch caterpillars, like persnickety toddlers, eat *only* milkweed leaves. So no butterfly garden is complete without this vital "host plant." A shallow saucer of water with a few pebbles for landing pads will complete your butterfly rest stop.

Attracting monarchs is more than mere summer entertainment. Monarch numbers have plummeted more than ninety percent in the last twenty-five years. The reasons are many: Our great Midwestern prairies are being paved, plowed and mowed at a rate of six thousand acres per day. Indiscriminate use of agricultural herbicides kills milkweed along field edges where these hearty plants used to flourish. And mind you, that bug spray in your garage doesn't know a butterfly, ladybug, dragonfly or honeybee from an aphid; so please, don't use these products.

My fellow Saskawanians, we are fortunate to be on the monarch's migratory path. So, let's get planting and help our monarchs on their incredible journey.

27

ANIMAL CRACKERS

Monday, June 27

A lightning bolt of pain shot from Caroline's jaw into her left ear, telling her she was clenching her teeth. She tried to relax and concentrate on the argument that raged around her—one that clearly called for calm leadership.

Forty-five minutes earlier, a couple dozen Ridge residents had filed into the Bat Cave for what she'd billed as a "Neighborhood Forum." Some had been recruited by Missy and her CAUZ group of anti-move picketers, others had seen flyers Caroline posted around the neighborhood.

She had scrubbed every inch of the Bat Cave, (Was that guano on the floor?) brewed a large pot of coffee and filled bowls with animal crackers—the zoo's signature dish. She set out flyers and hung architectural renderings of the new zoo showing trees arching over vast veldts and lush jungles filled with happy animals.

The group had seemed cordial enough as she welcomed them, but their mood deteriorated after she introduced Commissioner Edward Szczesny, the Ridge's city councilman. His endorsement of the new zoo was enthusiastic, but he came across as arrogant and patronizing.

When she opened the floor to questions, all hell had broken loose.

"Why do we need a big, fancy zoo anyway?"

"Why do we need a zoo *at all*? I say, shut this place down!"

"I liked this place just fine when it was just a couple of bears and an elephant."

"Why do you want to gawk at imprisoned animals, anyway?"

"How are people without cars supposed to get to Nord Frickin' Haven?" That question prompted the commissioner to pontificate further on the county's transportation funding.

Caroline had to cut him off to give Victor a chance to show the plans for the new zoo.

"Will there be baby bears at the new zoo?" a little girl wanted to know. This gave Victor an opening to explain that bear families need more room than the current zoo could offer, but that Nord Haven would provide that. He did an able job, but it was clear the merits of a new zoo were beside the point.

Next, a Parks Department employee went over the city's plans for the park that would replace the zoo if it moved. She had described wading pools, Frisbee golf, basketball courts, a state-of-the-art playground and picnic areas.

The room erupted again.

"This referendum is a sham."

"Why don't you just admit it's a done deal?"

This got general applause.

"The city just wants to move the zoo closer to the money."

At that, Caroline had reminded everyone of the money saved by Tom Engelsma's gift of land. Victor had said his only goal was a better, more humane zoo.

"This whole thing reminds me of the Blues Festival, the Hilltop Grill and the Ridge Top Bakery. We helped 'em all get their start on the Ridge, then they moved to fancier parts of town."

"That's right! It happens every time!"

"Nobody gives a rip about working class neighborhoods."

"But what about these poor animals?"

"Has anyone thought about what this move'll do to property values around here? It won't be good."

"Can you tell us when we'll have this so-called park?"

The commissioner talked about "laying the groundwork," "a citizens' advisory committee," and doing a "needs assessment." When he started in on the city's "2020 Plan," one woman at the back interrupted.

"So I'm hearing that this here'll be a weedy eye-sore until my kids have gray hair," to which the commissioner replied, "Well, I, for one, fully support the concept of a neighborhood park."

"The *concept*?" her husband roared. "How gullible do you think we are? Our kids can't swing on a concept."

And that was when Caroline realized she'd been clenching her jaw.

She took a step closer to Commissioner Szczesny to take the floor. "It's almost eight o'clock and I promised we'd take no more than an hour of your time tonight."

Another woman raised her hand. "I want to hear about the monkey escape."

Several people groaned.

"It's a fair question," she protested. "What about security around here? Maybe we'd all be better off without wild animals in our backyards." She crossed her arms and glared at Caroline.

Everyone, in fact, was looking in her direction, which she found odd—until she realized Victor had slipped out. She felt a prick of irritation, but given half a chance, she'd have been right behind him.

She repeated what she'd already said dozens of times since the escape: No obvious design flaws, a functioning security system, a full investigation underway. Finally, "That's all I can tell you now, but I promise to keep you informed." Even to her own ears, it was beginning to sound like stonewalling.

At this, several side conversations broke out and a toddler who had been stuffing herself with animal crackers began whining loudly. People got up to leave.

Caroline said, "I want to thank you again for coming. Please pick up some literature on your way out. I have left my business cards on the table—" Her eyes swept the room and locked in on a man leaning casually against the back wall.

It was Neil.

"—um, so you can," she said, "uh, contact me. We also have, uh, more drawings on display along the back, along the back wall." Her mouth dried up and disengaged from her brain. "Uh, um, if you haven't signed in make sure you—" He was grinning at her. "—uh, give us your, uh, contact information. Thank you. Thank you again."

With her linguistic abilities incapacitated, she gave up.

The crowd began shuffling out the door.

A young woman holding a sleeping infant approached Caroline. "I hope we weren't too disrespectful."

"No, not at all," Caroline said, smiling.

"I hope we didn't offend you. We're all good people who've worked hard to get where we are." She took a step toward the door, but turned back. "I grew up on the Ridge. I used to walk to the zoo with my brothers every Saturday. I always thought my kids would be able to do that."

She stroked her daughter's hair.

Caroline touched the baby's warm head. "I hope she'll still be regulars at the new zoo. Maybe we'll have bear cubs for her to see."

The woman nodded, and left.

Neil had taken a seat on a tabletop at the back and was swinging his feet, still grinning.

"I'm surprised to see you here," she said, gathering up the literature on the display table.

He hopped off the table and began picking up empty cups from the rows of tables, working his way toward her. "Likewise," he said.

They were alone in the room.

He pulled a card out of his shirt pocket and read, "Caroline Finch, Director of Communications and Development."

Caroline felt the ache in her jaw. "Were you one of the picketers?"

"Picketers? Hardly. I saw a flyer at the gas station and was curious. Imagine my surprise to find you here."

"So, you're a neighbor?"

"I work nearby."

"And jog nearby."

"Yup. After work."

"On private property riddled with sinkholes."

"I work there, at the mine."

"You're a miner?"

He laughed. "Sort of. The mine is—*was*—a family business."

She wasn't expecting this. "What's it called?"

"It used to be the Stoddard Brothers Gypsum Mine. That was my great-great-grandfather and his brother. Now it's just my cousin and me. We're developing a storage business—Stoddard Cold Storage."

"So, your last name—?"

"Stoddard. Neil Stoddard."

"A miner, huh? Do you, like, have a headlamp and a pick ax? A pack mule, maybe?" She laughed, picturing this.

Neil laughed, too. "I'm a geologist by trade. Seemed like a good idea back in college when business was good, but when the mine went belly up, well—" He shrugged. "Mostly, I teach at Sas-U. Anyway, my invitation still stands. I know that mine like the back of my hand, and we'll steer clear of sinkholes. Promise."

She stacked the brochures into a pile. "So, how many Stoddards are there?" She was thinking of little Stoddard children and perhaps a pregnant, supermodel Stoddard wife.

"Just my cousin Davy and me."

"So, not, like, say, your wife and kids?" She could be direct when she needed to be.

"Oh," he said, catching her meaning. "No. No kids. But if there were, I'd have them swingin' their little pick axes day and night to keep 'em out of trouble. My wife, too—if I had a wife—which I don't."

Caroline turned away to put the unused coffee cups back into their plastic bags at the counter—and to hide a look of satisfaction.

"And for the record," he leaned around her, trying to make eye contact, "if I did *happen* to have kids—and the wife to go with them—I wouldn't be asking you to hike with me tomorrow."

She met his gaze. "Thank you." Then she turned away again, feeling self-conscious. "It's just that, uh, I'm sort of new at this, whatever *this* is."

"Me too, if that's any help." He leaned against the counter. "Full disclosure? I was divorced four years ago."

She frowned. "I'm sorry, Neil. I've been there—just last summer. It's like a death."

His eyes dropped from her for the first time. "That's a good way of putting it."

She picked up packets of creamer and sugar and tossed them into a box.

"I never would have guessed you worked at the zoo," he said. "I figured you were Rafael's teacher, or maybe a social worker."

"So, supermodel or pop diva never entered your mind?"

He laughed. "No, but I toyed with dryad."

"Dryad? Let's see," she looked at the ceiling, "a wood nymph?"

"Ah, you know your mythology."

"I was an English major, but never a wood nymph. A wood nymph would never be so clumsy . . . and mud-covered."

"Maybe, but you *were* in white. A guy doesn't see something like that every day. I half expected a unicorn." He crossed his arms, making a study of her. "You know," he said. "I keep thinking I know you. Were you a TV reporter or something?"

"I worked for MidWest Energy."

"*Stormy!* You're that *girl.*"

She groaned and felt herself flush. "*Sunny,* if you please."

"No, everybody used to call you Stormy."

"No, they didn't!"

"Well, *I* did," he said, laughing.

She picked up the box of coffee supplies, straining to reach the top shelf. Then, she felt the pressure of his shoulder as he pushed it into place.

"Thanks," she said, withdrawing from the unexpected current of him.

He spread his arms wide. "Just trying to show you what a stand-up guy I am. How am I doing?"

She nodded. "Pretty convincing."

"Does that mean you'll go hiking with us tomorrow?"

"Us?"

"Magoo and me. He's excited about seeing Zelda again."

"Oh, he's invited Zelda, has he?"

"Yes, but they need chaperones."

"I can't promise Zelda," she said. "She belongs to an interesting, but kind of cranky, woman who lives in the farmhouse." She wondered if she and Neil would need chaperones.

"Mrs. VanWingen? She caught my cousin and me pilfering strawberries from her garden when we were kids. Not happy. I read her tirade about the zoo. I see she hasn't changed." He cocked his head and studied her. "So, tell me, what brings a zoo director, a farm dog and a young boy to my corner of the woods every Tuesday and Thursday evening about six o'clock?"

"Long story," she said, opening the coffee carafe to dump it in the sink. "Hey, would you like a cup? It's ground monkey chow and penguin feathers—but it's hot."

"If it's the only way you'll have a drink with me tonight, then I'm in."

He sat across from her in the empty Bat Cave, palming a ceramic mug and eating animal crackers as she recounted the events of the previous two weeks. She described the ribbon cutting and the Zoo on the Moov referendum campaign. When she mentioned the zoo's security system, he began to frown. She was boring him. Rob would have been comatose by now, she thought. But Neil only wanted to know more about capuchin monkeys.

Between cracker donkeys and cracker hippos—for she had never been able to eat an animal cracker without identifying it first—she outlined her efforts to turn the escape into something positive for the zoo. ("Brilliant!" he said.) He stopped her occasionally to ask about zoo attendance, the vote or plans for the new zoo.

Then she told him about her faltering attempts to win over the temperamental Mrs. VanWingen, Rafael's volunteer work and their walks along the ravine.

"And *that's* how I ended up soaking my ass in Willow Creek."

Neil shook his head. "You have a really challenging job, Director Finch. And don't forget the neighbors who think this zoo is their personal playground." He glanced around the room. "This forum was a good idea."

She bit the trunk off an elephant and let it dissolve on her tongue. "I still know a lot more about utilities than zoos. Sometimes, I'm afraid I'm in over my head."

That was more than she should have said. Neil was a perfect stranger (though, becoming more perfect and less strange by the minute).

"But, I love my job and I'm a fast learner," she added quickly. "I hope you're not friends with any of our board members, or something. Oh no!" she gasped, "You aren't, like, a major anonymous donor, are you?"

He laughed. "Nothing so interesting or mysterious—or rich." He took both mugs to the sink and began to wash them. *Is there anything more attractive than a man with a dishrag?* Caroline sighed to herself.

He dried the mugs, facing her now. "I see why walking Rafael home would be a pleasant end to your day. You have a stressful job, especially with the referendum and the monkey escape." He folded the dishtowel and hung it to dry. "I should let you go home now, but I'm looking forward to our hike tomorrow evening."

"Me, too," she said.

That night before bed she Googled "Neil Stoddard, Saskawan, Michigan." Nothing on Facebook or—thank God—the Sex Offenders Registry. But on the Sas-U website, she found an image of a tanned Dr. Cornelius J. Stoddard, with sunglasses pushed up into his curly hair.

"Associate Professor of Geology. Doctorate received, Michigan State University. Member, American Association for the Advancement of Science. Author, *Glaciations and Landforms of the Midwest.* Courses: Environmental Geology, Exploring Earth, Glacial Geology and Wetland Geology."

Impressive. Then, she imagined her ex's hospital profile: *Robert G.*

Finch, M.D., Board certified misogynist. Residencies in narcissism, parsimony and ignominy. Member, Alpha Male Medical Society, American Congress of Medical Misanthropes (ACMM). Blah blah blah."

Caroline stared at the screen. Like Bella's Grandmama Canelli said, a rich coat (or in Neil's case, a disarming demeanor and sexy hair and a great smelling tee shirt) could indeed, hide a poor heart.

She would not rush into anything.

She checked the forecast—highs in the nineties with ninety percent humidity. She packed a tote bag with a change of clothes, bug repellent, a zoo baseball cap, her running shoes and one lucky tee shirt.

28

DOG DAYS

Tuesday, June 28

Caroline's ten-o'clock coffee sat untouched on her desk. The air conditioning in the admin building wheezed and clanked, but was barely staying ahead of the outside temperature of eighty-five.

Victor walked by her door, grunted, then backed up. "What's your take on last night?" he asked.

She propped her chin on her hand and frowned. "I'm not sure."

He set his coffee mug on the edge of her desk and took a seat. "Is the referendum in trouble?"

"I'm not sure of that, either."

He didn't respond. She knew this trick—letting a long silence force her to spill her guts. He breathed. She breathed. It was way too hot to play this game.

Finally, she dropped her pen on the desk and sat back. "There's a lot of opposition out there, but it's coming from so many different directions, it's harder to manage."

He crossed an ankle over his knee, making it clear he wasn't going anywhere. "Say more."

"There are neighbors who want us to stay because they love this zoo. Others want us to move, for the sake of the animals—or shut down entirely, again, for the sake of the animals. Some don't like zoos at all, but prefer a smaller zoo over a larger one. Others just think we torture animals for the hell of it. *Still* others just think zoos are passé. I talked to a couple of former donors who said they'd rather fund a new arena or a science museum."

"Where does that leave us?"

"Like I said, I'm not sure. You always say people need to *see* rare animals to get behind conservation efforts, right? 'In the end, we will conserve only what we love?' Most of the neighbors at the forum last night *want* a better zoo. The whole debate was about the access you say is so important. They don't want us to move the zoo out of their reach."

Victor paused to process this. She liked this about him. He took a slow drink of his coffee, eying her critically. She sensed his disappointment in her. A few months ago she had assured him that building a new zoo would be a slam-dunk. Now, she was doubling back and second-guessing, which she had to admit was par for the course for post-divorce Caroline.

Victor folded his arms across his chest. "Okay. So, do we need to rethink this? Regroup? What?"

"We need to take the cubist's view."

His upward glance was just short of an eye roll. "Meaning?"

She raised her palms. "Look at the issue from all sides."

Victor lowered his chin. "But you can still sell this referendum, right?"

"Yes, of course." She drew a series of tight scribbles on a scratch pad, delaying the eye contact. "I have no problem representing the interests of this zoo. But, after last night, I realize this isn't a simple right-wrong, yes-no issue."

"Hmm," he said—something short of full agreement. "As long as you don't forget who signs your paycheck."

She smiled. "I won't. Actually, I can do my job better after hearing all sides. I'll develop some ideas and get them to you next week."

Victor slapped the arms of his chair and got to his feet. "Thank the Lord. You had me worried, Finch." He stepped into the doorway, but turned back. "So, who was that guy you were talking to after the meeting?"

"Uh, that was Neil Stoddard. He owns the gypsum mine on the other side of Iris' farm."

"Iris? Are you two on a first-name basis now?" he asked, raising his eyebrows approvingly.

"As a matter of fact, we are," she said, grinning like the Cheshire Cat.

"And?"

"Turns out young Rafael has enough charm for the both of us, bless him. He goes on and on about taking care of the animals when I drop him off at the farm. But I don't expect we'll see a change of heart about zoos anytime soon. She has some *pretty* strong opinions."

"Can you get her over here?" he asked.

"No luck so far, but I'm not done with her."

"That's the spirit." He started to leave again, but stopped. "So, I saw that guy, Neil Stoddard, getting into a red pickup last night after the meeting. I also saw him leaving Tom's office a few weeks ago. I remember that white logo on the door. Do you think Tom's hitting him up for a donation?"

Caroline shrugged. "I have no idea." What had Neil said when she asked if he knew anyone on their board? He hadn't exactly denied it.

"—where he stands on the move?" Victor was asking.

"What?" she blinked vacantly at Victor before coming back to the present.

"This Mr. Stoddard," he repeated. "Where does he stand on the move?"

It hadn't occurred to her to ask him—which was a strange oversight when she thought about it. Neil could be so distracting.

Victor was looking at her as if a wart had sprouted on the end of her nose.

"Uh, I, uh, I'll ask him tonight," she said.

"Tonight?" Victor's expression morphed from surprise to confusion to amusement in an instant.

"I'm seeing him, um, later. After work."

Victor waited for more, but she returned a deadpan stare. That was all he was going to get.

"Okay, then," he said finally, lifting his mug. "Here's to 'later after work.'"

By noon, the temperature hovered at ninety-three. Caroline regretted not refilling the literature racks before this heatwave, but with large holiday crowds expected, that task couldn't wait. She filled a carton with flyers about zoo membership, the adopt-an-animal program and volunteer opportunities and headed up the scorching asphalt path into the zoo.

At the bear exhibits, Donna was standing on the rocky ledge between two enclosures. Below her, a pair of Asian sun bears with necklaces of yellowish fur were opening coconuts with their long, ivory claws. They seemed oblivious to the heat.

She greeted Donna and headed to a spot of shade when a loud splash startled her. She was relieved to see Donna still on the ledge.

"Thank goodness, Donna! I thought you fell in."

A block of ice the size of a basketball was bobbing in the pool below the rocks as two Michigan black bears plunged into the water after it.

"Tempting, but I prefer pools without bear poo—or bears."

"They're having some fun."

Donna pulled the front of her shirt away from her damp skin and frowned. "Some zoos have temperature-controlled rocks for their mammals, but here at Ridge Park, we do things the old-fashioned way." She forced a smile.

"Well, they look very appreciative."

"Maybe. But they don't like the heat. They're Yoopers, you know."

The first bear stood on its haunches and pawed at the ice, but only pushed it deeper into the pool. Then, he plunged headlong at it, creating a tsunami that sent the block into the arms of the second bear. The first threw back his head and bellowed in frustration.

Caroline smiled at the idea of Bella tussling over a block of ice with her fellow Yoopers. "It looks like they're playing water polo," she said.

"Yes, but they're *very* sore losers."

The second one was bellowing now. "He sounds like Chewbacca."

"Actually, Chewbacca sounds like *him*," Donna corrected. "*Star Wars* recorded bears for Chewie's voice—with a little walrus, lion and a few others thrown in." She dipped her red bandanna into a cooler of ice water at her feet and wrapped it around her neck. "Man, I've got to get out of this sun."

Caroline trudged from kiosk to kiosk, trying to ignore the heat. She was looking forward to her walk with Neil, but wished it were cooler. Her makeup had long since slid off her face, and she hadn't thought to bring back-up. At MidWest, she had always kept a makeup kit, hairspray and a clean, silk blouse in her office—but that seemed like eons ago. Neil would just have to settle for a clean, honest—albeit wilted—look. Besides, he'd already seen her looking much worse.

Not everyone was suffering from the heat. Besides the sun bears, the kangaroos and wallabies didn't even seek out the shade. The capybaras were up to their ears in their pool, and the river otters floated on their backs again, using their stomachs as snack trays. Ralph the camel stood on his wide, webbed feet in his sandy, sun-baked yard, ruminating happily and flicking flies with his tail.

At Caratasca Island, Chappy came up the walk with Rafael trailing behind like a trusty caboose. They both carried heavy buckets.

"Look, Miss Caroline!" Rafael said, hurrying toward her. "We made popsicles!"

"Thanks, I'd love one," Caroline said.

Chappy set his bucket next to her and laughed. "Help yourself." Inside were ice cubes encasing omnivore biscuits, peanuts and grapes in their centers.

"What? No Creamsicles?" Caroline sighed.

"These are for the monkeys!" Rafael said, laughing.

"Why do *they* get all the treats?" she whined, brushing Rafael's damp bangs off his forehead.

"Mr. Chappy says if we throw 'em in the water, some of the monkeys might even go wading. And guess what? Mr. Chappy's going in the water tomorrow, too."

"The drain in the moat is slow," Chappy explained. "I need to get it cleaned out before the weekend." He cocked his head toward Rafael. "But it's kind of a one-man job."

Rafael took his bucket to the railing and began making passable monkey calls as he heaved the ice cubes at them one at a time. "Hey look! They like 'em!"

"He loves those monkeys, Chappy, but I think he loves you more."

"Well, he doesn't have a dad. That's hard for a boy."

"Speaking of drains," Caroline said, "Mrs. VanWingen thinks we flush our waste into her creek. I have to admit there's a cat smell over at the farm, and even way down by Rafael's house."

"Hmm," Chappy said, pushing out his bottom lip. "All our waste water goes into the city sewer system—same as the restrooms. I don't know what to tell you about a smell. I haven't noticed it myself. Our larger animals can get a bit, um, foul in hot weather, but nothing you could smell way over there."

"So, we're not polluting Willow Creek?"

"Well, the creek starts under the flamingo pond, so the water's not exactly clean when it leaves here. I've always wanted to remove that cement bottom and get some aquatic plants going. Willow Creek and the birds would be a lot better off. But it makes no sense now, if we're going to move."

Caroline nodded. "I have another question. At the staff meeting right before Julie came in to tell us about the monkey escape, Gwen asked why people would oppose the move. Remember?"

He nodded.

"You said some people like Ridge Park 'for what it is'—before she cut you off and Julie burst in. What did you mean?"

He rubbed the back of his neck, looking uncomfortable. "I hate being a naysayer with everybody so excited about a new zoo."

"You're not?"

He sighed. "My wife's family has rented the pavilion every summer since the world began. They take a family picture in front of the lion enclosure every single year. I can tell you, they're all just sick about this move."

"Even if the new zoo is bigger and has *several* picnic areas?"

He pointed toward the center of the zoo. "See that beech? It was just a sapling when Abe Lincoln came through on a whistle stop tour in 1856. It shades Goldwyn every afternoon. You can't buy a tree like that, or the giant black oak by the barn, or the red maples around the pavilion." He pushed back his cap and pointed up the sloping sidewalk. "And that wall? That's cut fieldstone taken right off the property."

They watched as a grandfatherly man held the hand of a small girl as she leaped along the top of the wall. Flecks of mica in the granite boulders caught the afternoon sun.

"Nobody builds walls like that anymore. You've seen the site in Nord Haven, Caroline. It's just a flat agricultural field that's too wet for condos, and not zoned for retail. Everybody's focused on the acreage, but it's not a great piece of real estate, if you ask me. Sure, we can build bigger exhibits—God knows, these animals need them, but there's a lot that's right about this old place."

The little girl reached the end of the wall and leaped into her grandfather's arms.

"But when it's a park, the pavilion and the trees will still be here," she pointed out.

Chappy shook his head in a gesture of resignation she saw too often in him lately. "Condos or a strip mall, more like. Once the city realizes the true cost of tearing this place apart, they'll sell to the highest bidder. Mark my words." He paused. "I've said too much. With all the suspicion I'm under right now, I'd appreciate it if you didn't repeat what I just said." He bent to pick up the bucket. "I don't know what will become of this place, but I'll miss it. Not everybody agrees, but I think something will be lost."

Rafael ran toward them, shouting, "I'm all out of popsicles and they want more!"

Chappy picked up his bucket. "Come on. We'll toss the rest on the other side."

All the way back to her office, Caroline thought about the bleak, snow-covered cornfields she'd hiked over last winter while the architect described shady, tree-lined walkways and lush "natural habitats." She had to admit, that would take decades to achieve. Something would, indeed, be lost.

She sat down at her desk, feeling like a lawyer who had just found another hole in her case.

For the rest of the afternoon, she attempted to work on the media kit for the black-footed ferret acquisition that would go public in a few weeks, but the neighborhood meeting, Chappy's surprising views on the new zoo and her own nervousness about seeing Neil overrode her work ethic. She checked the Sas-U website again. Sure enough, Cornelius J. Stoddard was still a geology professor there. Still athletic. Still with great hair.

She checked on her orders for a banner for the ticket booth (Black-Footed Ferrets: Coming to a New Zoo Near You!) and a gross of ferret plush toys for the gift shop. She texted Bella, "Can't run 2nite. Returning hanky. Wish me luck!"

She wrote a first draft of her blog: "How Animals Cope with the Heat."

On her calendar, she wrote "Neil, mine hike"—creating a record in case a sinkhole swallowed them or Neil turned out to be a serial killer after all. Then, she finished a half-dozen donor letters and arranged to drop off several yard signs to zoo members.

It was still only 2:52.

She zoomed in on Neil's picture and her cheeks flushed.

She tapped impatiently on her phone clock, which didn't seem to be working. She rearranged the piles on her desk, dusted her shelves, went for coffee, washed all the mugs in the sink, polished her fish paperweight and sharpened every pencil in her drawer. Then, she walked to the gift shop, her heart set on a Creamsicle, but settled for an Eskimo Pie.

It was still only 3:24.

The trip to the gift shop made her sweaty again, so she went into the staff bathroom, wiped her face and rubbed pink lipstick on her cheeks. She let her limp hair out of its ponytail, thought better of it, and put it back. She took off her damp zoo polo shirt, and gave herself a paper towel bath. This morning, she had rashly opted for a lacy white bra with violet trim and matching panties, which now seemed forward and brazen—not that he'd be *seeing* them, but still, what was she thinking? She changed into the bright purple V-neck tee and pair of khaki shorts she'd packed.

She was ready. It was 4:30.

She made a few more phone calls, but when she heard Kirby and Donna going into the Bat Cave, she gave up and joined them.

Their faces glistened as they headed for the refrigerator. Kirby stood with his head in the freezer compartment, peeling his shirt away from his skeletal frame. He took out two cans of Vernors and slid one down the counter to Donna, who was splashing water on her face at the sink. She ran water over her bandanna and wiped her face before collapsing into the nearest chair.

"You look cool," she said, eyeballing Caroline from head to toe with a hint of judgment.

"I just washed up. It's a steam bath out there," she said, to remind her colleagues that she hadn't been in her air-conditioned office all day.

Kirby took a seat at the far end of the table. "I'll sit downwind."

"Not far enough," Donna said, holding her nose.

Caroline smiled. He and Donna bickered like siblings. "I'm sure Kirby's reptiles love the way he smells."

"That's 'cause he smells like one of them," Donna said.

Kirby rolled the Vernors can across his forehead, ignoring her.

"Hey, Kirb, I almost forgot," Donna said, rooting around in the side pocket of her cargo shorts. "I found something." She held up a stack of small foil envelopes and let them unfold like an accordion to the floor.

"Condoms!" Kirby said, reaching for them. "I knew you fancied me."

She snatched them back. "Back off, lizard man. I pulled them out of Goldwyn's enclosure yesterday. They're for your *collection*."

"Perfectamundo!" Kirby grinned, showing the gap between his front teeth.

Donna slid them down the table. "Goldwyn pawed them pretty good."

Kirby turned the packets over to examine them. "What a waste. A good brand, too. Bad Goldwyn. Good thing they weren't bacon flavored. He'd have eaten them, foil and all."

"What? Bacon-flavored condoms?" Caroline said, regretting this immediately.

Donna gave Kirby a look that implied there were children present. Caroline felt her face heat up.

"Don't go trying to *use* those, Kirb," Donna said. "This town doesn't need a clutch of little Kirbettes slithering around. We shudder at the thought, don't we, Caroline?" She winked, inviting Caroline back to the grown-up table.

"So, you have a condom collection?" Caroline asked, hoping she wasn't about to embarrass herself further.

"No, but I have an extensive detritus collection."

"Detritus?"

"Stuff we fish out of the enclosures," Donna translated.

Kirby got up, wiped his face with the dishtowel and left it in a wad by the sink.

"Geez, Kirb!" Donna protested. "Use a paper towel, for Pete's sake!"

"You wouldn't believe the weird stuff we find," he said.

"Like what?" Caroline asked.

"Let's see. I got a bowler hat, an old brass skeleton key, a pink boa—the feathery kind, not the reptile—a 1914 penny... 'course, we had to fish out about a million ordinary pennies to find it... a teddy bear—that was sad—and, oh, a $50 bill, but that didn't make it into the permanent collection." His impish look was almost endearing.

"Mostly, we find plastic bags, cups and water bottles—anything people carry around," Donna added. "Zoo animals are way too trusting. They think whatever they find in their space is food or an enrichment."

Kirby tapped his pop can on the table. "Plastics are worst. A giraffe in an Asian zoo died and they found a ton of plastic junk blocking her intestines."

"A lot of stuff gets dropped in by accident, but some of it gets thrown in," Donna said.

"Yeah, reptiles sleep a lot, and it makes some visitors mad, so they start pelting them with whatever. I even heard of a case where an alligator was stoned to death."

Donna drummed on the table in annoyance. "These new, open habitats are popular with visitors, but they make me nervous. Personally, I like a big, thick pane of glass between the public and my guys."

"Then they just hammer on the glass," Kirby pointed out.

Donna shrugged in resignation.

Caroline sniffed the coffee before pouring it into the sink. "Disgusting! Did somebody drain the hippo pond again?"

"Hey! I was just going to have some of that," Kirby whined. "And we don't have hippos."

His radio crackled with Peter's voice. "Your turtle is ready. Can you come by?"

"Sure thing. As soon as Caroline brews a fresh pot of coffee," Kirby said, grinning. "Can I bring you some?"

Later that summer, Caroline would write a blog post called, "Zoo Etiquette: Don't Wake the Sleeping Bear" in the *Zoo Nooz*. It would include photos of a hat, a feather boa, coins, combs, glasses, but no condoms, although Kirby protested the omission.

At the farmhouse that afternoon, Rafael followed Iris up and down the row of beans with a colander while Caroline stood at the gate, fidgeting with her cell phone, her hat and her ponytail.

"If you need to be somewhere, Rafa can walk himself home," Iris said, finally.

"No. No, I'm looking forward to it. Um, would you mind if I brought Zelda back a bit later than usual?"

"I guess not." Iris waited for an explanation that was not forthcoming.

Just before 6:00, Caroline, Rafael and Zelda set off down the path, leaving Iris to her own imaginings.

6:05. Zelda tugged gently at the leash to remind Caroline of the way home. They had been standing at the fence corner for exactly two minutes since Rafael had disappeared into his house. Zelda yawned patiently and sat down.

Caroline didn't notice this. In fact, she hadn't heard a word of Rafael's blow-by-blow account of his day, either. She had let Rafael and Zelda dawdle along the path, instead of hurrying them as she sometimes did. Her plan was to be there just after Neil—reasonably punctual, but not over-eager.

But Neil wasn't there when they arrived—and he wasn't there now.

6:06. She pulled Zelda behind a honeysuckle bush so Mrs. Rojas couldn't see them from the kitchen window. Salvadoran women who rendezvoused in the woods with men they hardly knew were probably bundled off to the Convent of Perpetual Regret.

6:08. She shrugged. He wasn't coming. He had fallen into a sinkhole, saving her from the same fate. All this was speculative, but one thing was clear: The man was less-than punctual, ergo, less-than perfect. Good. It was never healthy to idealize someone, particularly a man, because then it was all down hill. She exhaled loudly enough that Zelda stood up again, expecting forward movement. It was lucky, really, to find out now how unreliable and probably self-absorbed Neil was. She certainly didn't need another man who put her at the bottom of his priorities. Yes, that was the healthiest way of looking at BEING STOOD THE FUCK UP! She kicked a pine cone into the ravine, causing Zelda to jump.

6:09:30. She rocked from one foot to the other with a hand on her hip. Why did waiting always make her have to pee? If she squatted behind a bush, he'd be sure to show up. She sighed. How could a man she hardly knew take her from quivering anticipation to wretched humiliation in three and a half minutes?

6:10:33. "That's it," she said. She yanked on the leash, making Zelda jump again. "Sorry, girl. It's not *your* fault men are dicks. Let's go."

They started back toward Iris' at a brisk pace. After the first bend in the path, Neil wouldn't see her, even if he were just running late with an innocent explanation. So be it. She wasn't desperate for a man.

She would stop at Osaka Sushi on the way home—although right next door was Burger King, which was *really* tempting. She might still get in a run with Bella if she texted her—or, she could just pick up one of those little cartons of Mackinac Island Fudge ice cream and watch reruns of *Veronica Mars*. It was too hot to run, anyway.

Her sigh turned into a pathetic moan. *Damn him and all members of his gender!* She would not let anyone misuse her again—no matter how gorgeous he happened to be. *(When had Neil Stoddard gone from nice-looking to gorgeous?)*

6:12. A commotion behind her made her spin around. Magoo was bounding toward them, looking for all the world like Goldwyn with his mane flying back from his wide, blond face. He crashed through the underbrush, ignoring the path, and skidded to a halt in front of Zelda, who cringed in fear. Magoo dropped into a sit, his tail wagging hard. A reusable shopping bag hung around his neck.

Caroline gave both dogs a pat. "It's okay, Zel. It's Magoo. What are you doing here, boy?" Neil was nowhere in sight. In addition to time management issues, the man had zero control over his dog.

Zelda finally recognized her friend, and was circling him excitedly, tangling him in her leash, an interesting strategy, Caroline thought. She patted Magoo's head again and felt the bag. "What have you got around your neck? Hold still."

She reached inside and felt two glass bottles. Cold. She pulled one out. Bell's Two Hearted Ale.

"Caroline!" She looked up to see Neil running toward her, waving. "Hold up!"

She put her hand on her hip. "Lose your dog again, mister?"

He stopped before her, bending at the waist and gasping for breath, squinting up at her. "I'm . . . really . . . sorry. I was . . . running late . . . so I sent Magoo . . . under the fence."

"Like a St. Bernard with a cask of brandy? Clever."

"Well, brandy . . . or an engraved apology . . . would have been classier, but yeah." He stood up, his chest still heaving. "You gave up on me?" He had a very convincing hangdog look.

Caroline shrugged. "I figured you were at the bottom of a sinkhole."

"And you were going for help, right?" He eyed her, grinning. "Really, this was very poor behavior on my part." He untied the bag from Magoo's neck and gave him a good scratching. "Thanks, buddy. He would have been very disappointed if he missed his hike with Zelda." He grasped both of Zelda's ears and gave her the same affectionate treatment. Zelda leaned against his thigh and looked up at him, love struck. "Do you like beer, Ms. Finch?"

"I thought this was a hike."

"A happy-hour hike. Top of the line tour. Refreshments included."

"Lead on."

They walked back toward the fence corner.

"I see you've worn sensible walking shoes," he said. "A wise choice."

She ignored the barb. "I have to have Zelda back in an hour."

"Then we better get moving."

The gate to the mine property was unlocked. It creaked as Neil pushed it open. He was locking it behind them when Rafael came running toward them with a half-eaten hotdog in one hand.

"Where are you going?"

"Just a hike," Caroline said.

His eyes widened, she thought in fear, but then he asked, "Can *I* come?"

Neil said, "If it's okay with your mom."

Caroline walked Rafael to the house, feeling three-parts relieved to one-part disappointed that Neil didn't want her to himself. As Rafael translated, she told Mrs. Rojas the plan and promised to be back in forty-five minutes.

Mrs. Rojas looked doubtful. She pointed toward the sign and said, "*Peligro!*" Neil approached and introduced himself with Rafael translating. Finally, Mrs. Rojas nodded and they returned to the gate.

The rusty hinges squeaked as he padlocked the gate behind them. Inside, they followed the scar of a disused two-track.

"They had to bring equipment here when they filled in part of an old shaft years ago. It makes a nice jogging trail now." Magoo galumphed off behind Rafael but came back when he realized Zelda hadn't followed. Caroline let Zelda off the leash and watched as she catapulted down the hill.

"Stay where we can see you," Caroline called after Rafael.

Dozens of beech trees towered above them, as smooth and gray as Greek columns.

"You're right," Caroline said. "This is breathtaking. It makes you realize how much damage people do to forests. It's remarkable that your family has preserved it like this."

"It's just neglect, really. That, and the fact that everyone believes the ground is unstable."

"Man-eating, according to some," she said.

Rafael and the dogs came back up the hill and ran ahead down the path.

"Well, isn't it?" Caroline demanded. "Man-eating?"

"No, but don't tell."

She scowled. "Tell me the whole truth right now, and don't sugar coat it."

"Okay. There were one or two tiny sinkholes—cave-ins, really—waaaay before I was born." He pointed down the hill toward Willow Creek. "My dad had them filled in. The rest of the mine is all within the gypsum layer. Rock solid, as they say. Before digital imaging, the location and depth of the shafts were just guesses, so the idea of sinkholes scared everybody. My family let the myth sort of snowball because it kept trespassers out."

"If the land is stable, why hasn't it been developed?"

Neil shrugged. "For a long time, the mine made enough money to support the family, and it was considered too hilly. It could be developed now." He picked a beechnut off the ground. "Did you know that passenger pigeons used to feed on beechnuts and hemlock seeds in this woods?"

"Passenger pigeons? Here?"

"Sure. My great-grandfather hunted them and shipped them to New York City after they became scarce on the East Coast. My great-grandma used to make pickled pigeon breast. They said the flocks were so big they blocked out the sun and their wings sounded like thunder."

"I suppose no one imagined they could ever become extinct." She looked up into the green canopy. The oppressive heat of the day was gone. "It's surprisingly cool in here."

"It's the beeches. Their leaves let in light, but shade out the heat. I think they're my favorite trees."

"And they don't have carving all over them," Caroline said. "That's rare to see."

Neil frowned. "I wish that were true. I'll show you something shameful, but interesting." He started down the hill toward a massive beech that seemed to be keeping the entire hill from sliding into Willow Creek. Rafael and Caroline followed.

Neil patted the tree. "It's almost as big as the state record tree near Manistee that's sixteen feet around. That one takes almost three adults to reach around. It's a three-hug tree."

"But how do they know it's bigger than this one?" Rafael wanted to know.

"The state keeps records and I measured this one once."

Rafael's eyes popped. "But maybe it grew! We should measure it." He grabbed Caroline's left hand and Neil's right and leaned against the tree. "Come on. Let's hug it."

Caroline leaned against the smooth gray bark and stretched her hand until she felt Neil's fingers. "I can barely reach," she said.

"I guess it's time to take another measurement," Neil declared.

"So where's the shameful-but-interesting thing you promised?" she asked.

When he offered his hand and pulled her up to his side, she could smell his aftershave.

He was pointing at letters cut crudely into the surface. "My cousin and I used our Boy Scout knives to carve our initials when we were about your age, Rafael." He pointed to each letter, "C.J.S. 4. That's for Cornelius J. Stoddard, the Fourth."

"Cornelius? That's a funny name. What's the J for?" Rafael asked.

Neil cleared his throat. "Jan," he said, "Spelled J-a-n but pronounced 'Yon.'"

"Jan's a girl's name," Rafael said, looking horrified.

"Rafa," Caroline said, suppressing a smile, "it's not polite to make fun of people's names."

"Jan is Dutch for John. Like Juan in Spanish," Neil said, a tad defensively.

"Oh, I get it! Cor-*neil*-ius?" Rafael said. "Do they call you Corny?"

"Not if they want to keep their front teeth." Neil grabbed Rafael from behind and flipped him upside down.

"COR-nee! COR-nee! COR-nee!" Rafa chanted as Magoo began to bark.

Neil set him gently on his head and let him somersault into the crisp leaves.

"So, who carved these?" Caroline asked, fingering wider scars.

"Those are my great-grandfather's—Corny the First and his brother Harold. These are my grandfather's and his two brothers'. And *this* one, D.J.S. '80, is my cousin David. We own the business together, but I'm really just his useless lackey. We grew up playing in these woods. Our fort was over there somewhere." He looked expectantly at Caroline. "So, what about you, Ms. Finch? I hope your middle name is Mergatroyd or Lilybelle or something peculiar and embarrassing."

"Louisa. My mother was a fan of *Little Women*. Finch is my ex's name. It was too much bother to change it back to Scott. That's my whole, boring story."

Rafael had righted himself and was tracing Neil's initials with his finger. "Does it hurt the tree?"

"Sure it does," Neil said. "But I wasn't smart enough to ask that when I was your age. Promise me you won't carve your initials into any living tree, okay?"

"'Kay."

Neil squeezed his shoulder. "Good man."

They hiked back up to the valley rim, staying on the old road until it was time to turn back.

"How do you get into the mine?" Caroline asked.

He pointed east, away from the farm. "There's an entrance below that hill with a gate off a side street. I should show you the mine sometime. Gypsum has a certain beauty."

Was that an invitation?

"I'd love to see the mine," she said.

"Alabaster is gypsum that has a translucent quality, in case you were wondering," he continued. "It can be beautiful when it's polished."

"I would love to see the mine and the alabaster," she said, steering the conversation back.

"Great," was all he said.

They walked along the fence at the top of the ridge. Rafael and the dogs ran ahead, fell behind, then ran ahead again.

"I admire your strong interests," Caroline said.

"There are a lot of things, besides rocks, that interest me," he said, cryptically. The trail turned back toward the fence now. They would be at the gate in less than a minute.

"Really? I'd love to hear more." Could she be any more obvious?

Neil stopped. "Oh, no! We forgot to have our beer. I'm a bad tour guide."

"It's probably best, with Rafael. And I forgot to bring your tee shirt."

"Well, another time, then."

Another time? He was either blowing her off, or as hopeless as she was in the art of mid-life dating. She could see Rafael and the dogs already waiting for Neil to open the gate.

Once upon a time, there were clear rules about who did the asking. Heck, there were probably millions of potentially happy relationships that never happened because the boy never called the girl. But for heaven's sakes, this was a new millennium!

She stopped in the middle of the trail until he turned around.

"What?" he asked.

"When?" she asked, her hands were on her hips.

"When?" The surprise on his face softened to amusement. "You *really* want to see the mine?"

"Yes, I really would."

"Okay. How about Thursday? Grown-ups only this time. I'll pick you up at the farmhouse after you walk Rafael home a little after 6:00."

29

BLESSING OR BURDEN?

Wednesday, June 29

Iris leaned on her broom to admire her handiwork. Zelda was sniffing around the barn, making footprints on the freshly swept dirt floor. It had been a week since the flood. One thing had led to another and now, the place was cleaner than it had been since her parents were alive.

The Goodwill truck had picked up stuff that had been cluttering up the barn and her life for decades, and the two young men had even helped her rearrange some of the heavier items. She tried not to think about what she'd let go of. No looking back. No regrets. It was just stuff Annie and Cindy enjoyed rummaging through when they visited, but never managed to take home.

Last spring, Cindy had found a blue and white striped crock behind the tractor.

"Look! They had one like this on *Antiques Road Show*. It was worth, like, ten grand."

"Don't be silly. It's just an old pickle crock," Iris said. "But it might make a nice planter. Take it." But here it was, still in the barn, now rinsed out and on a shelf.

The size of the job had depressed her at first. How did she end up with so much stuff? She found her mother's Sunday-best tablecloths in a plastic bin. There were at least eight of them, all white linen, some embroidered with matching napkins. They were beautifully ironed, lovingly folded—and forgotten.

"Who uses these anymore?" she asked Zelda. She couldn't count the number of Sunday dinners she'd spent trying not to spill on them and incur her mother's wrath. For years, they'd taken up all three drawers in the sideboard, until one day she brought them all out to the barn—Walker-VanWingen family limbo.

Zelda had staked out a square of sun on the barn floor, where she whined occasionally, making it clear she was tired of barn cleaning.

"So, I ask you, Zel," Iris said with a sigh, "are these lovely old tablecloths a blessing or just a burden?"

The dog came closer to lean against Iris' leg.

Blessing or burden? That was the question. She stroked Zelda's ear absently.

In the end, she let four go to Goodwill. Two went back in the sideboard, and her girls, like it our not, were each getting one for Christmas as payback for *Knitting for Dummies.*

She applied the blessing/burden test to the old ping-pong table (burden), the girls' ice skates with cracked leather (burden), a yellow wicker baby bassinet (burden), a piano bench full of old sheet music (blessing), a box of Franciscan dishes with an apple pattern (blessing, maybe) and the old apple crate. That was an unexpected blessing when she needed a monkey trap. One never knows. In the end, her father's Flexible Flyer sled with his name scrawled on the back (blessing) got hung on a nail behind her mother's Eastlake dresser (blessing). The rest would remain in the barn until it became a burden to her daughters.

She looked around the tidy barn and smiled. It had been a terrible mess. She still wondered if Rafa had forgotten to turn off the hose after he filled Zelda's water bowl, but he looked so hurt when she accused him that she let it drop. Besides, it was just as likely that *she'd* forgotten to turn it off after she watered the geraniums on the barn windowsills. Maybe her cell rang or a bird caught her attention. She was so scattered these days. Just the other day she'd left soup simmering so long it turned to a charred black crust.

She scratched her forehead. Getting distracted wasn't like her. Accusing children wasn't like her. Confusing salt with fertilizer wasn't, either. But lately, well, she hardly knew *what* she was capable of.

Iris sat down on the apple crate and wiggled her behind. The box was as solid as ever. One year, Bill had hauled all the broken ones out into the field and built a huge bonfire. The girls invited their friends for a hotdog and marshmallow roast under a full harvest moon.

She was glad she'd kept one

crate. Her father had filled dozens like it every fall until they were stacked three high. He was a small, wiry man whose mind had stayed sharp until the day he died, although his body couldn't keep up. He walked with a cane, then a walker, before surrendering to a wheelchair.

Her parents remained in the tract house at the end of the driveway until the end. Her dad, Joe Walker, read several newspapers a day and wrote regularly to his congressmen or President Johnson, giving them advice about public education, the crisis of the family farm or that "unholy war" in Vietnam.

Eventually, his eyesight failed. She bought a tape recorder and her girls transcribed his letters and stories. When his hearing started to go, she'd find him staring into space, completely defeated.

One afternoon, when he was eighty-six, her mother called. "Your father won't get out of bed," she said. "I'm worried about him, Iris."

She walked down to the house and sat on the edge of his bed. "It's a lovely day, Dad. Let's go sit on the porch with Mom."

"Oh, honey, I've lost m'starch today," he said, his chin trembling.

Iris took his hand between hers. "Okay, Dad. Maybe tomorrow."

Her father looked at her with watery, useless eyes and expelled a great, pent-up breath. "You know, I always thought when I got this way—blind, deaf and no good to anyone, least of all myself—I'd be ready, you know, to *go*."

When she started to speak—to spout some useless platitude—he raised his hand. "But here I am, exactly at that point, but you know what? I keep thinking, maybe tomorrow . . . maybe tomorrow . . ." His voice trailed off.

"That's because you still have your mind, Dad," she said, leaning close. "You have all your good thoughts and memories."

"Yes. I'm grateful for that," he said, struggling to sit up. "I'll tell you a secret if you don't tell your mother."

"Cross my heart."

He sighed. "I've never understood why people are so certain there's an afterlife."

She arranged the pillows behind him and whispered, "Me neither."

"But I'm beginning to."

"Really? You? Born again, at your age?" Iris smiled, but didn't like this defection.

"Not born again, but I sure wouldn't mind trading this rust-bucket body for something lighter. Wings would be heavenly. God!" he said, raising his voice.

Iris thought her father was swearing, which wasn't like him, but then he called out: "God, You know I've never believed in You or Your Pearly Gates, I won't lie, but feel free to prove me wrong. A-men."

From deep in his chest came a long, hearty chuckle.

"A-men," Iris repeated softly and kissed his forehead.

He died a month later.

On the day of the funeral, Iris found her mother in the kitchen, fumbling with the wall phone.

"What are you doing, Mom?"

"I'm calling Mama. I didn't see her at the service today."

Iris took her mother's hands. "Mom, Grandma died years ago."

Her mother pulled her hands away as if she'd touched a hot burner. "You don't know," she hissed.

Until the end of her days, Nella Walker bustled around the farm like a wind-up toy, forever looking for something she'd lost, then forgetting what she was looking for. Old age and a lifetime of farm work had filled in the curves of her body until she was as sturdy as a Hereford heifer—and with about as much sense. The clock of her life began running backwards, and soon, better judgment, inhibition and even toilet training were forgotten.

She forgot what it was she once loved. She started complaining that Reverend DeWinkle's sermons at the New Netherlands Christian Reformed Church made no sense, which would have amused Iris' father, who called him Rip VanWinkle.

Annie and Cindy became their grandma's guardian angels. When she left a roast in the oven until the smoke alarm went off, they ran down the driveway to the house. When she went berry picking in the woods, one of the girls followed along to lead her home.

Mind and body rarely age in sync, and Iris didn't know which was worse—painful awareness or blissful ignorance. Either way, she herself would soon be downgraded from blessing to burden.

Not once in her life had Iris Walker VanWingen longed for immortality. She wasn't expecting to be issued a pair of gossamer wings and a halo in the Hereafter. She didn't expect old age to be painless, either. Her only request was to leave this world walking straight and thinking straight. At one time, that didn't seem like too much to ask.

A breeze kicked up, sending a handful of maple sailors twirling through the hole in the roof. How long had she been sitting here, feeling so old and a bit blue? She was ashamed.

What needed feeling sorry for was this old barn. It had served the Walker and VanWingen families well, sheltering ox teams, horses, milk cows, her own girls' 4H goats and rabbits and, of course, tons and tons of apples—Golden Russets, Ribston Pippins and Sweet Boughs. This barn deserved better—a new roof and a coat of red paint, for starters. On days like this, when the heat made the siding pop and the timbers creak, it seemed like a living, breathing thing.

"Blessing," she said, looking around her. "Definitely a blessing."

30

DEVOLUTION

Thursday, June 30

Caroline and Rafael met Iris coming out of the barn. She'd made oatmeal cookies, she announced, which Caroline took to be a peace offering for the hose incident.

"What happened to all the old barn stuff?" Rafael asked.

"Gone. But I saved the bike." She draped her arm around his shoulder and led him toward the house. "Wasn't I a knucklehead for leaving that hose running?"

Rafael squinted up at her and a broad smile broke across his face. "At least the barn got clean. You deserve an extra cookie for all that work." He ran ahead to the porch.

"Goodness," she said to Caroline. "I never let my girls have cookies this close to dinner. It's a wonder his mother lets him come here at all."

Caroline took a seat on the glider. Zelda lay down on her corner bed, but kept a watchful eye on things. There would be no games until her people had finished their treats.

Rafael appeared from the kitchen with the cookies. Iris followed with a tray of drinks. She lifted the pitcher to pour, then set it down, shaking out her wrist.

Caroline leaned forward. "Here, let me."

Iris sat down heavily. "It's my arthritis. All that work in the barn. I'm paying for it."

"It looks painful."

She attempted a laugh. "I'm devolving."

"Devolving?"

"It's just an hypothesis I've been thinking about. I used to make my students create them all the time." She took a long drink of lemonade.

"Ut uz ee-ul-in een?" Rafael asked through a mouthful of cookie.

Caroline handed him a napkin and laughed. "Wait until your

mouth is empty."

He swallowed and repeated, "What does 'devolving' mean?"

"Excellent question, Mr. Rojas," Iris said with a puckish grin. "You see, we humans have spent millions of years *e*-volving—that means, graaaadually, graaaadually becoming different from our humanoid ancestors. We started walking upright and using tools." She squinted into the distance, gathering her thoughts. "Since then, we've figured out a thousand ways to dominate the planet and make trouble for our fellow earthlings, like those endangered animals at your zoo. You can blame *these*." She held up her thumbs and wiggled them. "So handy—when they work properly. Oh!" She winced again.

Rafael dropped to his knees to examine Zelda's paws. "Zelda doesn't have thumbs."

"It's a good thing, too," Iris said. "She'd be in the kitchen right now, ripping open her bag of kibble and helping herself to what's in the refrigerator." Iris seemed amused by this.

"We could play catch, though," he said, looking disappointed.

Caroline stroked Zelda's ears. "Poor, thumbless Zelda."

Iris pointed to the spot where her thumb met her wrist, calling her unruly students back to the lesson of the day. "This most useful joint—the carp metacarpal—is often the first to malfunction as we age."

"That's not fair." Rafael possessed a highly sensitive fairness detector.

"If it's not our thumbs, it's our knees and hips. And do you know what these joints have in common?"

Rafael and Caroline looked at each other and shook their heads.

"They make us *human*. The carp metacarpal allows the thumb to swivel around so our hands can grasp pencils, steering wheels, hammers and cell phones. Our knee and hip joints allow us to walk upright and keep our hands free. These physical traits make us different from even our closest ape cousins."

"I have cousins in El Salvador, but they're not apes," Rafael offered.

Caroline laid her hand on his head and whispered, "Not that kind of cousin."

"Houdini has thumbs," Rafael offered, trying again. "Yup. He can peel fruit really good."

"Yes, but he couldn't hold a pencil. And he can't do this." Iris held up her good hand and touched her thumb to the tip of each finger. "That's a uniquely human skill. In a just and logical world," she said, addressing Caroline now, "these old-age afflictions would be some cosmic punishment for throwing spears, dropping bombs and generally making a mess of things. Pride before the fall."

"Divine retribution?" Caroline asked.

"Only if you think the cosmos has consciousness enough to punish us, which I don't believe it does."

"So, why else would these particular joints fail first?" Caroline asked, hoping to steer away from religion.

"Because they are add-ons—evolutionary retrofits, you could say. Our hands used to be front paws for crawling on all fours or hooks for hanging in trees. Ape thumbs—with the exception of baboons who live on the ground like us—are much less flexible than ours. Our tiny, complex thumb joints are so useful we simply wear them out."

Iris lifted one leg onto the wicker coffee table and massaged her knee. "Now, the human knee joint is a joke. Any first-year medical student could design a better one. Basically, we're just knock-kneed, upright apes with second-rate joints and big, dangerously over-sized brains."

"I hurt my knee when I fell off the bike," Rafael said, pulling up his pant leg to show a brown scab and a bluish bruise. He moved closer to Caroline to give her a better look.

Iris went on. "Anthropologists still don't agree whether humans walked upright because we were so busy using our thumbs, or if we began using our thumbs because we walked upright."

Caroline pictured humanoid Lucy stumbling along, twiddling her pair of brand-new thumbs. "Devolving, huh? You may be onto something, Iris. Our head zookeeper, Chappy, would love to hear this."

"This is my thumb, way down here?" Rafael got up to show Iris.

"That's where it starts—way down by your wrist."

"Your fingers have bumps," he said, petting her hand as if it were an injured animal. "Do they hurt?"

"My knuckles get sore sometimes, yes."

"Because you were a knucklehead?" he asked.

Iris gave a low, sardonic chortle. "You mean, for leaving the hose on all night? Yes, well, maybe that's why they hurt—because I'm a knucklehead. Serves me right."

"Because, *I* didn't leave the hose on," he said, just to be clear.

Iris slid one arm around his waist and squeezed. "I know, honey. It's just that while you're growing up, *I* seem to be going in the other direction."

"Rafa." Caroline patted the seat next to her. He came over to sit beside her. "Getting sore joints isn't a punishment." Mrs. Rojas was probably a devout Catholic and Caroline didn't want him thinking his mother's sore feet were divine retribution. "Miss Iris used her hands for *good* things, like taking care of her daughters, keeping this farm, teaching children and writing for the newspaper. Her thumbs are just a little worn out." She poked her finger through a hole in his jeans and laughed. "Like your jeans."

Iris seemed preoccupied. "Of course, our brains devolve, too," she was saying, "the crowning glory of *homo sapiens*. But when we age, we start to lose our cognitive abilities in the reverse order we acquired them. Our capacity to judge, predict outcomes, solve problems, make decisions, remember things—those go first." Her voice trailed off.

Her fatalism was startling, Caroline thought. "My grandmother was completely lucid until the day she died. She was nearly ninety."

Iris rose slowly from her chair and reached for the tray of empty glasses. "Rafa, would you get the door for me, please?" She disappeared into the kitchen. Rafael called Zelda into the yard. Caroline sat alone, working her thumb joint and feeling unsettled.

Iris came back onto the porch and sat down. A tennis ball bumped the porch floor and rolled under the table with Zelda and Rafael right behind it.

"I forgot to check the time. Rafa, look at the kitchen clock, please," Iris said.

He got up and cupped his eyes to look through the screen. "Um, the short stick is on six and the long stick is on the nine."

"You can't tell time?"

"Sure, I can, but not on old-timey, round clocks."

"Well, sir, old-timey, round clock time-telling will be on our agenda next week. But right now, you two need to get a move on. Your mom will be home when the long stick is on the twelve." She winked at Caroline.

"No, she comes home at *six*."

Iris and Caroline both laughed.

Caroline said, "After I walk Rafael home, a friend is picking me up here. I hope that's okay."

"As long as she isn't expecting dinner," Iris said, still chuckling.

"Before I forget, I asked our head keeper about the zoo's water treatment system."

"And?"

"All our waste water goes into the city system. Only surface run-off and rain goes into Willow Creek, but we're very careful to pick up any animal waste."

"Then how do you account for the cat smell?"

Caroline shrugged. "I can't. I think I smelled it, too, but it was stronger over by Rafael's house—which makes me think it's not coming from the zoo."

Rafael was creeping along the porch railing toward the phoebe nest. The gray and white bird flew into the lilac bush and bobbed its tail.

"You aren't keeping tigers at your house, are you, Rafa?" Iris asked.

"Tigers?" He twisted around, almost losing his balance.

"Come down from there, and leave that poor mother in peace," Iris said.

He landed on the porch with a thud. "Tigers?" His face clouded as he responded to Iris' newest accusation.

Caroline said, "Rafa, Miss Iris is teasing."

"Oh." Rafael flung himself across the porch and barrel rolled into the glider, pitching it wildly.

Caroline grabbed the porch rail to steady herself. "We're just wondering if there's ever a bad smell by your house. Like a stinky cat litter box."

"Yup, but my mom closes the windows."

Iris nodded at Caroline and crossed her arms. "I'm not ready to let the zoo off the hook just yet."

Rafael was upside-down now, pushing against the porch railing with his foot. Caroline put a hand across his legs. "You're making me seasick, mister." She looked squarely at Iris. "Fair enough. But next time we smell it, let's notice which way the wind is blowing."

Rafael sat up. "I know! Let's ask Mr. Neil if *he* ever smelled it."

"Who's Mr. Neil?"

"Miss Caroline's boyfriend in the woods."

Iris' eyebrows struck an inquisitive angle. "You have a boyfriend? In the woods? Well, I'll be."

"He's not my *boyfriend!*" Caroline protested, realizing immediately how juvenile that sounded. "He was just jogging by a couple of times when I was walking Rafael home and he asked me—us—to hike on the mine property. He owns the mine, apparently."

"We hugged a big tree," Rafael spread his arms wide. "And Zelda has a boyfriend, too. Magoo."

"Who's Magoo?"

"Neil's dog," Caroline said, "A gigantic golden retriever."

"So, that walk you and Zelda took the other day was a double date?" Iris snapped her fingers and Zelda looked up from her bed. "Do you want to tell me anything, missy?"

To her dog's ears, this sounded like, *Do you want your toenails clipped?* But since she didn't see the sharp, shiny instrument, she closed her eyes and pretended to be asleep.

"It wasn't a date," Caroline said evenly. "And, not that it's any of *any*body's business, but Zelda and I were perfect ladies, weren't we, Zel?" She patted Zelda's head and had a sudden thought. "Oh my goodness! Zelda's fixed, isn't she?"

Iris threw her head back and laughed. "You're asking this *now?*"

Their laughter faded into warm silence and Caroline's rhythmic gliding caused Rafael to slump against her shoulder. She pushed his black hair from his forehead. *At what point had this dreaded work assignment become something else entirely?* Caroline wondered. Next to her, Zelda snored softly, and the phoebe returned to her nest.

Iris cupped her ear and pointed to the nest. "Hear that?" One tiny peep, then another.

Rafael sat up. "Babies?"

Together, they listened to the sounds of new life.

Tires crunched on gravel. A red pickup with a white SCS logo on the door rolled to a stop in front of the porch steps. A blue tarp covered something in the back. Neil got out and shut the door.

Caroline rose to her feet, tugging on the front of her shirt. "He's early," she said.

Neil approached the porch, looking handsome in khaki shorts and a light blue polo shirt. Rafael and Zelda had already run to greet him.

"Hey there, Rafael, Zelda." He petted both their heads at once and smiled up at Caroline, who met him on the bottom step.

"Neil, this is Iris VanWingen. Iris, this is Neil Stoddard." She didn't expect to be so nervous, but her mouth felt chalky.

Neil reached his hand upward toward Iris. With one foot on the bottom step, he said, "You probably don't remember me, but my cousin and I used to play in your woods. It's been a long time."

Neil's open palm hung there in the void above the second and third steps for an agonizing half-second too long. Caroline watched as a flicker of confusion crossed his face. His empty fingers curled into a fist and disappeared into his pocket. He took a hesitant step backward.

Caroline looked to Iris for clarification, but her back was already turned. The screen door snapped shut with an angry report.

Caroline gave Neil a look of dismay as she pushed her hair off her forehead. "I, um, I just need to walk Rafa home, then I'll be ready. You can come with us."

From somewhere inside, Iris called out, "Rafael can see himself home. You go on."

She left no room for argument.

31

WHAT MAKES THE HEART SING

In the cab of Neil's truck Caroline stared straight ahead.

"I'm so sorry, Neil. I have no idea what that was about. Iris can be unpredictable."

He shrugged. "Maybe she's holding a grudge from that strawberry heist of thirty years ago." He glanced at her. "But I'm not going to let it ruin my evening."

She leaned her head against the window. "I just don't *get* her, you know? Maybe she's bipolar or something. We were having a perfectly wonderful conversation until you arrived."

He laughed. "I don't usually have that effect on people."

"Sorry. That didn't come out right. I mean, maybe she's getting Alzheimer's or something. I don't know. She can be very rude."

"Don't worry. I've got the hide of a rhino."

Caroline looked at his smoothly shaved cheek and thought to differ. How nice it would be to trace that dimpled crease with her finger and see for herself.

Neil shrugged again. "She probably recognized me from *America's Most Wanted*. That puts some people off."

Caroline laughed as he steered the pickup under the highway overpass to the valley below the Ridge.

He turned onto a side street, scattering a group of children kicking a soccer ball in the street. The locked gate between houses was the twin of the one by Rafael's house. A metal sign read Stoddard Cold Storage Entrance. It had the same SCS logo as the truck door. Neil got out and unlocked the gate.

Ahead was the steep hillside that was as close to a cliff as can be found in West Michigan's sandy terrain. Caroline leaned into the dashboard to see the top. Somewhere up there was where they had hiked. Beyond was the farm, and beyond that, the zoo.

Neil got back in, and the truck rolled through the gate into a gravel parking area. The lot was pitted and potholed and surrounded by low industrial buildings and old machinery. The ground was gray and powdery.

"It looks like someone spilled a few thousand buckets of white paint," Caroline said.

"A few million buckets of plaster, more like."

Three semi-trailers were parked to one side. Judging by the tall weeds growing in front of them, they hadn't been on the road in a while. Beyond them, a vine-covered neck of rusted machine stuck out of the undergrowth.

"What's that?" she asked.

"That's Dino—at least that's what we called him when we were kids. It's the conveyor that was used to bring loose gypsum out of the mine. A decade ago, you would have seen a mountain of the stuff over there." He pointed to another weedy field beyond a low building. "It would get loaded onto trucks and made into plaster board and a lot of other things. The wallboard plant was on Paris Street—as in plaster of Paris."

"Really? And Gypsum Lake?"

"That was near another gypsum mine. If you get me started, I'll put you to sleep with local gypsum lore."

"Lore? I love lore!" Caroline caught him looking at her skeptically. "Really."

"Okay. Well, back in 1666—"

"1666? Maybe not *that* much lore."

"Trust me, this is just the Cliffs Notes." He opened his window, draped one golden arm over the back of the seat and turned to face her.

"In 1666, London was destroyed by fire. The King of France knew the same thing could happen to his capital city, so he decreed that all the wood buildings be covered with plaster—which, being a mineral, makes an excellent fire retardant. It was a smart economic move, too, since gypsum was all over the place. Plaster mines sprung up, or I should say, tunneled under Paris. *Et voila! Plâtre d' Paris!*"

Caroline gasped, "*C'est incroyable!*"

"Ah. *Est-ce que tu parle le françaois, mademoiselle?*" he asked, speaking with fish lips.

"*Un petit peu.*"

"*Ah, trés bon. Tu—*"

She held up her hands. "Okay. Stop. That's the extent of my French, monsieur."

"*Hau, hau, hau!*" he honked. "*C'est domage!*" Then without pausing for breath, he continued. "So, in front of the Moulin Rouge is Place Blanc, so-called because of all the plaster spilled from wagons on their way to boats in the Seine."

"That would be an apt name for this parking lot."

"You know White Lake, the lagoon down by the river? That was where my great-grandfather stored the plaster before it was shipped to Chicago. It made quite a mess of the lake, I'm afraid."

"Cornelius the First, King of Plaster?"

"The very one."

"But also Cornelius the Terrible, for polluting the lake."

"Not like me. I'm known throughout the realm as Cornelius the Good."

She gave him a sidelong glance and laughed. "Or, Cornelius the Corny."

Neil opened the truck door, looking satisfied with himself as he produced a backpack from behind the seat. Caroline followed him toward a modest, one-story office building attached to a large pole barn built into the hill behind it. It had two over-sized garage doors and a small pedestrian door.

"So, how long has the mine been here?"

"Since 1905."

"When did it stop operating?"

"Five years ago, but we should have closed it sooner. We kept thinking business would pick up. It was a tough time. That's when my ex, uh, exited."

"I'm sorry," she said.

Neil gave a shrug that said, *What's done is done.* Then he said aloud, "My cousin Davy had the idea for a cold storage facility. The conversion was more expensive than we anticipated, but we're finally seeing light at the end of the tunnel."

"A good thing, for a mine. So, things were kind of rocky, eh?"

Neil smiled. "Yup. We were buried in debt."

"Because you were in over your heads?"

"Yes, but we dug ourselves out."

Caroline laughed. "You've probably heard all these before."

"Mining puns? Naw, miners are way too deep for puns." He stopped in front of the pedestrian door, adding, "We like *dirty* jokes, though."

He entered a code into a keypad, pushed open the door and

switched on the light. There was a hi-lo with the same white SCS logo on the side and a golf cart. Several stacks of wooden pallets, various tools and shelves were pushed against the walls.

"I got a geology degree so I could help run the mine. Not great timing, but I never considered doing anything else. Not that I love mining, but I do love rocks."

"Why did you close the mine?"

"Competition. From China, for one. And from power plants."

"Power plants?"

"When they put scrubbers in their smoke stacks, a funny thing happened. It turns out gypsum is a by-product of burning. They put it on the market and undersold us."

"That's too bad."

"I can't complain. We struggled while we got the storage facility underway. To be honest, we almost went under last year again—no pun intended—but we have some new clients now. We're finally turning a small profit."

Caroline turned in a slow circle. "So, what kind of stuff gets stored underground? Pirate treasure? Squirrel nuts? Dog bones?"

Neil laughed. "And the odd hatchet. Wait—you'll see." At the back of the garage was another overhead door. "Most mines have shafts that go down, but here they follow the shallow gypsum layer laterally, into the hill."

"Because we're at the edge of a primordial sea."

"Excellent. You weren't in my Geology 101 class, were you? I think I'd remember you." He shook his finger at her. "Actually, Michigan's deposits are some of the richest in the world."

He slid into the golf cart and patted the seat next to him. He reached behind and handed her a sweatshirt and a stadium blanket. "You'll want these."

He pressed a remote control on the visor and the door began to rise. A wall of cold air rushed past them as the cart lurched forward.

"Whoa! Is it always this cold?"

"Fifty-two year-round. Mother Nature's refrigerator."

Ahead, a dim passageway seemed to stretch into infinity. It was lit with a string of ceiling lights in wire cages. It looked more like a basement hallway than a mine, but since it was wider than it was tall, it made her want to duck. Also, there were no timbers holding up the ceiling, which seemed like a serious omission. She checked the ceiling for cracks, fault lines or oozing lava, but the walls were seamless, smooth and white-gray.

Neil noticed her fidgeting. "You're not claustrophobic, are you?"

"No, but cave-ins make me break out."

"I thought you craved excitement." He eyed her again. "Seriously. Are you okay?"

She arranged the blanket over her knees and pointed forward. "Eyes on the road, driver!"

As the cart hummed along, she reached out to touch the cool, smooth wall. "I thought it would be more, uh, dirty in here."

"I'll take that as a compliment. Back when pack horses worked the mines, there was so much manure my grandfather grew mushrooms commercially in here."

"Mushrooms, manure, plaster, cold storage. That's a pretty eclectic business plan."

"For the storage business, we poured this concrete floor and sealed the walls to keep the dust down."

"It looks nice."

"Thanks, I think so, too." He reached under the seat and brought out a flashlight. He stopped the cart where the shaft forked into two narrower tunnels. "I want to show you something." Where the shafts formed a V of rock, he touched the flashlight to the rock. The rock lit up with a cool white glow.

"This is micro-crystalline gypsum aggregate—alabaster. It can come in shades of pink or amber, too."

"It's beautiful, Neil. You're a good professor. Do you enjoy teaching?"

"Yeah, I do. I bring my students here at least once a semester. When most people think of geology, they think of the West where rocks are more exposed. Michigan's surface rock got pretty well pulverized by the glaciers, but there's a lot to study if you know where to look."

"I'm impressed, Doctor Stoddard."

"Let's not be formal. You can just call me Good King Cornelius the Fourth. Your Highness, for short."

Caroline smiled. "What was your dissertation about?"

"Everything You Never Wanted To Know About Gypsum and Were Sorry You Asked."

"Tell me more fascinating things about gypsum."

"Ah, that could take a month."

"I'll give you five minutes. If you exceed your time, I'll tell you everything you never wanted to know about charitable remainder trusts and gift annuities."

"Such pressure!" He inched the cart forward, gesturing left and right with the beam of light. "Let's see. The walls of the Pharaohs' tombs are lined with plaster that's lasted for fifty centuries. Yeah? Yeah? Fascinating?"

"Indeed. What are those shiny flecks?"

"That's selenite, another type of gypsum that's almost transparent. The Greeks used it for temple windows. They named it after Selene, the goddess of the moon." He stopped the cart and handed her the flashlight. "Shine it right here." He took a pocketknife and worked the blade between paper-thin layers of what looked like glass. He pulled out a thin shard and handed it to her. "You're never too old to be a rock hound."

He made a tight, three-point turn and drove back toward the entrance, then stopped in front of an ancient wooden door recessed into a sidewall.

"This old shaft hasn't been used in almost a hundred years."

"It looks more like a dungeon—or that lair you said didn't exist."

He produced a set of keys, but before he turned the lock, the door swung inward on rusty hinges with an ominous creak.

"Huh," he said, looking puzzled.

"What?"

"This door is supposed to be locked." He put the key in the lock and turned it several times, examining it with the flashlight. "We don't want customers going exploring." He turned to look at her. "Come on. We can walk from here."

Caroline looked into the pitch-black rectangle. "In *there*?"

"I want to show you what it looks like above the gypsum layer."

"Is this going to be on the test? Because, if it's all the same to you—"

"Come on, there's a story."

He reached for her hand and pulled her reluctantly into the tunnel. The beam of the flashlight was little comfort. The floor rose upward, becoming softer and more gravely with every step. The walls were white at first, but soon turned sandy-brown. Timbers held up the ceiling.

"Up ahead is where we had the cave-ins."

Caroline pulled him to a stop. "*What?*"

"Sorry. I should explain. The cave-ins occurred because the top of this shaft ran too close to the surface, but we're totally safe down here."

His hand felt warm and distracting around hers.

"Now for the story: Back in the 1920s, my great-grandfather hired a Cornishman named Digory Gwynn, who claimed to be a mining engineer. Turned out, he didn't know a pickax from a pickle. He ordered this shaft dug at an upward angle and managed to keep it a secret from my great-grandfather. He apparently convinced some of the workers they'd all get rich."

"What was he looking for?"

"The legend goes he thought there was copper or gold."

"Gold?"

He laughed. "I'm kidding about the gold. Even old Digory wasn't *that* crazy, but it always gets a rise out of girls." He led her further into the shaft and continued, "Digory was in trouble as soon as he got above the gypsum layer."

Caroline had stopped listening at "girls."

"So you bring a lot of 'girls' in here?" she asked, feeling a mix of jealousy, surprise and shame, in that order.

"Just Lisa and Jennifer and Katie—my high school girlfriends, but only one at a time."

She laughed. "Did their parents know?"

"Of course not."

"So tell me more about this Cornishman," she said, feeling nicely recovered. "Did Digory ever find copper?"

"No. Just a lot of loose sand and tree roots. When the top of the tunnel caved in and my grandfather found out about Digory's little enterprise, he fired him on the spot. It's lucky no one was killed." He turned around slowly, holding the flashlight under his chin, growling like a demented pirate. "An' no-un evar sor hide ner haaair of ol' Digory Gwynn. But sum say, 'e canna' rest 'til 'e finds the trez'r 'e wuz lookin' fur."

Caroline laughed giddily.

"Aye. The ghost o' Digory Gwynn kina stell be haard on a summer's eve amoog deeze hells."

He led her further up the incline. "A couple decades later erosion caused a second cave-in known far and wide as The Dreaded Sinkhole."

Caroline stopped, pulling her hand away. "*Here?* My God, Neil! We're standing *under* a sinkhole?"

"No. No. *Way* up there." He pointed into the inky darkness.

"This better be Neil the geologist talking, not Neil the adolescent playboy. Either way, this is as far as I go."

"There's not much more to see, anyway. My dad filled in the crater years ago and installed that heavy door in the main shaft."

"Just the same, I've seen enough," she said with a shiver.

"Wait. Would you mind holding the flashlight up that way for a second? You can stay here." He handed her the flashlight and began trotting up the incline.

"Where are you going?"

"Shine the beam ahead of me. I'll be right back." His voice became fainter.

And with that, she was alone.

The silence was more oppressive than the darkness. She heard rustling above her. Were there bats in here? She wanted to shine the beam up there, but she didn't dare move the light. She backed up until she felt the wall behind her. Dirt sifted into her hand and something dropped into the neck of her shirt—probably a rabid bat.

"Neil?" she said, whining like a six-year-old.

She heard footsteps.

"Coming!"

She gathered her wits when she saw him jogging toward her holding an empty, two-liter Pepsi bottle. "Sorry. I saw this up there and wondered what it was."

"It's an empty, two-liter Pepsi bottle," she said dryly.

"I see that *now*." He shrugged a bit sheepishly. "Sorry. I guess some of our workers did some unauthorized exploring."

They headed back down the incline with the beam bouncing in front of them. The main tunnel, with its string of electric lights looked positively festive in comparison. Neil locked the wooden door behind them and rattled the door to be sure it was locked.

Caroline shuddered. "You don't have to lock that door to keep *me* out. I think I heard a bat."

"Naw. There's no way for them to get in." He put the keys in his pocket. "Bears, though—"

"Oh, stop!"

He was smiling when they got back into the cart. "I didn't mean to freak you out."

Caroline looked straight ahead. "I'm *not* freaked out," she fibbed.

"Good. Well. Next on our tour, ladies and gentlemen, we move forward to the present time and our state-of-the-art, world-class, cold storage facility. Fasten your seat belts, please, and keep your hands inside the cart. Ready?"

"Only if it's sinkhole- and bat-free."

"I hope you're not going to give my tour a bad review."

She met his eyes and smiled. "This really is a pretty, uh, *unique* attraction you've got here."

Back near the entrance, he stopped in front of a set of ordinary glass office doors Caroline hadn't noticed before.

"We're converting two side shafts into storage facilities, although we can use the whole mine if there's enough demand." He unlocked the doors and the corridor was instantly flooded with fluorescent light.

"This doesn't look like a mine at all," she said.

"Thank you. That's the idea."

Against the walls were floor-to-ceiling shelves. Some were filled with boxes marked Heinz Ketchup, Newman's Own Ranch Salad Dressing and A1 Steak Sauce.

"Anything that keeps longer at fifty degrees can be stored here. Wholesale grocers buy in bulk and store it here. It's way less expensive than a refrigerated warehouse."

At a door marked Data Storage, Neil said, "This area has to be super clean and dry. Banks, municipalities, manufacturers—anyone who has to keep a lot of microfilm or digital records for a long time, could use this facility. Most of the renovation costs went here." He pointed toward a long row of file cabinets against one wall. "The Village of Appeldoorn keeps their archives here."

"I love archives. Can I peek?"

The first big file drawer opened easily. It was empty.

"Okay, well maybe not that one," Neil said, frowning. He looked around the mostly empty room and opened two other drawers. Both were empty. Then he smiled at her again. "Vacant so far, but knowing Davy, it won't be for long."

"This would make an awesome wine cellar."

"We're looking into that, too."

He ran his hand over the top of a cabinet and brushed off the dust on his shorts. An unreadable look flickered then vanished. He led her to the entrance and secured the doors behind them.

❧

Caroline blinked in the strong evening light as they crossed the parking area to Neil's red pickup.

"What's under the tarp, if you don't mind me asking?"

He vaulted gracefully into the truck bed and loosened the ropes to reveal a wooden crate about three feet square. Inside, something was packed in bubble wrap. One board had been pried back to reveal stone the color of a ripe peach. "It's a block of alabaster, or fine grained gypsum." He stepped back, watching her reaction.

"The color is lovely. Is it from the mine?"

"I wish. No, I had it shipped from Utah."

"What's it for?"

He jumped down, landing next to her. He hesitated, then came to some kind of decision. "I'll show you, but only because you asked. This isn't part of the official tour." He led her toward a low, nondescript building hidden by honeysuckle and gnarled junipers. "This is my studio."

"As in, *art* studio?"

"We don't have to go in. I mean, it's getting late—"

Caroline pointed at the door. "Lead on."

Inside, Magoo greeted them with a lazy stretch. Caroline scratched under his collar. "Aw, did we wake you up?"

Neil let Magoo out and propped the door open.

Inside, the walls were covered in pegboard holding dozens of odd-shaped hammers, brushes, small axes, chisels and tools she had no names for. Above, a row of clerestory windows ran the length of the roof peak, letting in angled rays of sun. At each end, huge exhaust fans sat idle. A heavy layer of white dust covered everything.

"This is an old processing building I saved from the wrecking ball." He watched her as she took it in. "I didn't get a chance to dust," he said self-consciously.

She made her way slowly around the room. In front of a row of windows were more blue tarps hiding various shapes. Rubber hoses with attachments that looked like dental instruments were coiled at the end of the workbench. She lifted a small pickax and felt its smooth handle.

"Saving this for the kids?"

He cocked his head.

"You said if you had kids you'd give them tiny little pickaxes to keep them out of trouble."

"Oh, *those* kids." He smiled, remembering. "Yup. This could *all* be theirs one day."

Caroline continued around the room, testing the sharp edge of a chisel and lifting an odd, squared-off hammer to feel its weight. She felt his eyes on her. "Are you going to show me what's under those tarps, or do I have to beg?" She read the hesitation on his face.

"I'm sensitive about my art. So, yes, you'll have to beg."

"Pleeeease?"

As he approached one, she considered what she'd do if it was a bust of Elvis or Daffy Duck, or something brazenly phallic. She fixed her expression into her most winning, on-air smile.

He lifted up whatever heavy object was under the tarp and set it in a square of sunlight. "Okay," he wiped his hand on the front of his shorts. "Come stand over here where the light's most favorable." He took a breath and watched her as she walked toward him.

"Ready." She held on to the smile—she would not judge.

The tarp fell to the floor.

Her smile faded as she examined a fragile twist of amber-orange light balanced on a black plinth. She reached out, then drew her hand back.

"It won't bite," he said, gauging her reaction.

She ran her hand over the silky contours. It seemed to absorb the sunlight and throw it back into the room like a small moon.

"It's just—I don't know—elegant. And the *color*. How long have you been sculpting?"

"Well, there were always little chunks of gypsum lying around, and when I wasn't carving up beech trees I made spear points and little race cars. I tried making a bong once, but that was later. A few years ago, after my divorce, I started working with some bigger pieces."

"May I see these others?"

He lifted each tarp in turn as she walked slowly among them, taking in the varied shapes. There was a free-form oval bowl in translucent pink, a suggestion of a bird in several orange and cinnamon tones and a twisted ribbon of pure white.

Caroline ran her hand lightly over each one and said, "Some traditional carvers believe each stone knows what it wants to be."

He pulled the covering off of a stone in rosy tones the size of a footstool and stepped back. "If this one knows what it wants to be, it's not telling me."

Caroline put her ear to the stone. "Have you asked her?"

"Her?"

She put her finger to her lips, calling for silence and leaned closer. "She's an Ojibwa maiden—with a—wait." She listened intently and nodded. "Yes? I *see*. She wants a flowing headdress." Her hand hovered over one side where the stone darkened to reddish brown. "Right . . . about . . . here. Yes." She shrugged. "She says, 'Thanks for asking.'"

Neil laughed. "I've never met a stone whisperer before."

Caroline smiled. "So, is this a hobby or a business?"

"Both. The alabaster in my truck is a commission for an airport terminal out west. It's going to be an eagle's wing—whether it *wants* to be, or not. It's my summer project. I'm going to start on it this weekend."

She sighed. "I love them all, Neil. I really do."

Neil rubbed his chin to hide a wide grin. "Thanks. Would you like to be my muse? The position happens to be vacant at the moment."

Magoo came back in, angling for attention. Sunlight had moved higher on the wall, changing the light in the studio.

"How about some dinner?" Neil asked.

"Is that part of the tour package?"

He bowed slightly. "Of course. I know a place with a view. Plus, I know the owner."

She followed him to the truck, but instead of getting in, he lifted a red cooler and a stadium blanket out of the back.

"It's just a short walk."

"Lovely," Caroline said as she followed him onto a narrow path. They passed the silent hulk of Dino at the bottom of the hill, then turned upward and followed several tight switchbacks up the hill.

"This is where Magoo and I start our run," he said, stopping to let her catch up. "Always gets my heart pumping."

"I hope you've got a double cheeseburger in there," she said, eying the cooler.

"Almost there. Don't look back yet. There's a view from the top you should wait for."

By the time they reached the top, Caroline was panting.

"Okay, now turn around."

Below them, all of Saskawan was laid out in a neat, undulating grid that stretched downward to the river. Green hills met the sky on the eastern horizon.

"Wow, Neil. You can see *everything* from here!"

"Keep turning."

In the other direction, where she expected to see a wooded plateau, was a deep cleft in the hill. On the valley floor, the waters of Willow Creek ran like liquid silver.

"See how the current has cut through the old dune down to the limestone layer?"

"And to think it all starts under our slimy flamingo pond." She turned in a full circle again. "I don't know which way to look. This is *spectacular*, Neil."

"My family always called it 'the overlook.' We used to picnic here."

Behind the hill, hemlocks and cascades of tall ferns waved in the warm breeze.

"I love hemlocks, don't you? They look like lace. So do ferns. They should call this Lacey Valley."

"They? Magoo and I are the only ones who come here now."

Caroline stroked Magoo's head. "Lucky dog."

Neil dropped his backpack and cooler to the ground, unfolded the stadium blanket and sat down, patting the spot beside him. "Come. Sit." Magoo trotted over expectantly. "Not you, ya big lout." He threw a stick into the brush and Magoo ran after it.

This was beginning to look more like a real date, she noted, sizing up the blanket situation. She sat down and hugged her knees, feeling as nervous as a chipmunk.

He was pulling jars and plastic tubs out of the cooler and setting them on the blanket between them. The two bottles of beer seemed to be the same ones she'd last seen dangling from Magoo's neck. She smiled at the memory. He opened one and handed it to her, opened the other for himself and clinked his against hers.

"Here's to—what? Getting acquainted?"

"I'll drink to that." She tried to look relaxed, stretching her legs out flat, crossing them and leaning back on one hand. "So, let me see: you're a miner, a geologist, a professor, a sculptor and a gourmet cook. Quite a resume."

He shook his head. "Lazy *shopper*, maybe—but not much of a cook."

"What else should I know about you?"

He thought for a moment. "That's it. I guess I should have saved something for later. Not a Nobel or a MacArthur grant to my name. Oh wait! I was Student-of-the-Week. Twice. Third grade."

Caroline sighed. "It sounds like you always knew what you wanted to do with your life. I envy that."

"Well, geology was a way to do my bit for the family biz but avoid the business side, frankly. I only started to teach when the mine began losing money."

"And the sculpting?"

"That came later. My grandmother made sure I knew my Michelangelos from my Mondrians. But for the longest time, I ignored the call."

"To be an artist?"

He shrugged. "I couldn't rationalize it. I was raised to think if it didn't make money, it had no value. And my wife—my ex—wanted a certain lifestyle which I felt obliged to provide." His gaze dropped before he took another drink of beer. "I kept asking myself—she kept asking—if the world really needed more sculptors. That sort of squashed my inner artist for a long time."

She reached for a strawberry. "What made you decide to go for it?"

"The mine closed and my wife left the same summer. Four years ago now. I set up the studio to get my mind off things, and it worked. I got completely absorbed. My first sculptures—" He shook his head and laughed. "Let's just say, I've seen better looking wallboard. But then I realized that when I'm sculpting, I don't feel I should be doing anything else. That's my definition of—I'm not sure what to call it."

"—of what makes your heart sing?"

"Yeah," he nodded thoughtfully. "That's right."

She thought of Iris with her garden, her nature column and her birds. The zoo staff with their total dedication to animals. And Rob, *damn him*, with his career obsession. And Bella, who didn't seem to need anything more than life itself to make her happy.

Caroline, on the other hand, wasn't sure her own heart could even carry a tune anymore.

Neil dug into the cooler once more. "Anyway, that was sort of an epiphany for me." He popped open two more plastic tubs and held them out for inspection. "Spicy lime-chili sauce and shrimp. Best with a beer chaser."

She dipped a shrimp and took a bite. "Mmm." After a pause, she said, "So, will you take up sculpting full time someday?"

"Oh, I don't know. I love teaching and it pays the bills. I need to help Davy at the mine, too."

"What do you do there?"

"Mostly, I just put on a tie and show up at meetings when he calls. I've offered to step aside, but Davy insists on paying me. But even with teaching full time, I always find time to sculpt."

"Do you sell in galleries?"

"Some, but mostly I sell turned wine goblets. I didn't show you those, did I?"

She shook her head.

"Monday is goblet day. I have to finish five before I can work on my large pieces. That's my rule."

"Why?"

"Because that's what people buy. The Saskawan Historical Museum has a permanent exhibit on the local gypsum industry that we underwrote in better times. I donated some of my larger pieces for the exhibit and display a few in the gift shop. Visitors admire the big stuff and go home with a fifty-dollar alabaster goblet." He shrugged. "It supports my addiction, so to speak."

He reached into the cooler again and pulled out a wedge of hard white cheese, rye crackers and asparagus spears wrapped in thin slices of prosciutto.

She looked inside. "What? No candelabra in here? When does the chamber quartet arrive?"

He grinned self-consciously. "I've overdone it, haven't I? It's been a while since I made a picnic for a woman. Like, since forever."

She suppressed the urge to giggle. "It's been even longer since a guy made me a picnic, like, since forever. Thank you, Neil."

When he turned to toss a cracker to Magoo, Caroline reached out and pinched the tanned flesh above his elbow.

"Ow!" he yelped. "Did you just *pinch* me?"

She brushed a crumb off the blanket and turned away. "Maybe. I had to make sure you were real."

He rubbed his arm and laughed. "Perhaps I have oversold the goods. Did I mention I'm pretty absent minded, sort of—or incredibly—messy, depending on who's judging, and that any six-year-old could beat me at Scrabble?"

Nice try, she thought. Truthfully, he—*this*—did feel a bit much. His world made hers feel puny and one-dimensional. Her own pitiful résumé consisted of "fundraiser and former potter." She was boring. Sooner or later, he'd figure that out.

"So, what makes *your* heart sing, Caroline?"

And there it was.

She drew her knees up until she was sitting in the fetal position. "I did ceramics back in college. I planned to open a studio in Chicago, but three meals and a roof over my head won out. Then, for about ten years, I supported my ex while he went to med school."

"Sometimes life gets in the way of, I don't know—"

"Of *living*?" Caroline looked between her knees at the blanket, already regretting that she'd revealed so much. Silence settled between them. Finally, she said, "I guess I'm still waiting for my post-divorce epiphany. I'm not sure what's next for me."

He sat up and leaned in her direction, with one elbow crooked over his knee and the beer bottle dangling from his finger tips. He was either genuinely interested or faking it nicely. "Must be fun being a local celebrity," he offered.

"Me? I'm not. Not anymore." She tossed a shrimp tail into the underbrush. "Anyway, that got old fast. Communications has always come naturally to me and fundraising is where the money is—unless, of course, you work at a small, under-funded zoo with AWOL monkeys and a dodgy future."

"What do you do for fun?"

She faced the city skyline, but her attention was on the warmth radiating from his left leg, which was almost touching hers now. Had he moved closer, or had she?

"I run with my friend Bella sometimes" she said, which sounded lame. "Honestly, I don't have time for much besides work."

"I can imagine," he said absently, touching a ripe strawberry to his lips and offering her one. "Maybe you can show me your ceramics sometime."

"I'd like that."

He tossed the green top over his shoulder and turned toward her looking utterly nonchalant, which was fine, since she had enough chalance for the both of them. It had been well over a year since she'd let a man get this close—and even longer since she'd wanted any kind of intimacy.

"These trees are impressive!" she heard herself declaring at a volume that startled her. "There are trees at the zoo almost this big, though," she babbled on, apropos of nothing. "There's a huge oak that shades the lion enclosure that was there when Lincoln's campaign train came through Saskawan in 1856. Did you know that?" She crossed and uncrossed her legs. She sort of had to pee, but couldn't imagine excusing herself to step behind a tree.

"I haven't been to the zoo in years," he said, absently. "Except for that neighborhood meeting."

"I'll give you a private tour," she said, which came out sounding sort of suggestive. Caroline took another sip of beer and felt a wave of giddiness that was only partly alcohol-induced.

Magoo moved closer to the blanket to sniff the shrimp.

"Leave it," Neil warned. He reached into his backpack and pulled out an enormous dog biscuit. "Did you think I'd forgotten you?"

Magoo dropped to his haunches to attack his treat.

Neil popped an olive into his mouth, rolled onto his back and put his hands behind his head. She envied this composure of his. She sat erect, hoping she didn't look as nervous as she felt. *Or prim. Oh God*! She *really* didn't want to look prim! She stretched out her legs again and leaned back on her hands. That was a start. *What would Bella do in this situation? No*, she didn't even want to *think* about what Bella would do. The silence felt awkward again and she fought the urge to fill it with more stress-induced non-sequitur.

Off in the distance, a mountain of clouds streaked with pink had drifted over the city. The tallest buildings across the river reflected the magenta sunset in their glass facades. The view calmed her.

"This place speaks to me," she said, finally. Her mind was only half on what she was saying. The other half was on Neil's straight jaw, mellifluous voice, the curve of his leg and most everything in between.

"I'm glad."

"And your sculptures. They speak to me, too."

He sat up and leaned toward her. His eyes settled on her mouth. "Don't move."

"What? Do I have food on my face?" She reached for her balled up napkin.

He pulled a leaf out of her hair, tilting his face to one side.

She licked her lips. "Oh, God. You're going to kiss me!"

"Would that be so wrong?"

"No. It's just—It's just that *first* kisses are so, um, fraught."

"Fraught?" He seemed to find this amusing. "*First* kisses, you say? So, you're pretty confident there'd be a *second*?"

She closed her eyes. "No! I mean—. Oh, never mind."

"Why don't we try *one*, then discuss seconds." His dimples were having the effect of kryptonite. "But, if you'd rather not, just say so."

"That isn't exactly what I meant." She could not blame the weather for the sudden heat she was feeling.

He leaned in again.

She stiffened a little. "What I meant was, kissing changes everything."

"Ah," he nodded, "so you *have* been kissed before. When you said, 'first kiss,' I wondered."

She rolled her eyes.

"I prefer experienced kissers." His lips were curved into a crooked smile. His eyes were searching every inch of her face.

"I'm not *that* experienced," she said. *Okay, that did sound prim.* "What I mean is, I'm just . . . I could be, um, a little rusty." It had been *twelve years* since she'd kissed a man other than Rob.

"Ah. I see the problem." He wagged a knowing finger at her. "PTKD."

"What's that?"

"Post Traumatic Kissing Disorder. A mild case, though. Very treatable with the proper therapy, by a *doctor*." He wiggled his eyebrows comically.

She looked straight ahead, frowning and smiling all at once. "I'm just going to shut up now."

"About time." He moved in quickly then. His lips barely grazed her mouth before he pulled back, looking triumphant and absolutely adorable.

She grinned.

"See? It's like pulling off a Band-Aid. Do it quickly and it hurts less." His eyelids were drooping now as he traced the contour of her cheek with the back of his fingers. His hand felt cool as it slipped to the nape of her neck.

"It didn't hurt at all." She licked the corner of her mouth where he had kissed her, finding the salty taste of olives, or perhaps Neil himself.

He whispered into a spot just below her ear, "Would you like a second, for comparison?"

"Yes," she breathed, "please." She could not move.

He pressed his forehead to hers and ran his fingertips the full length of her bare arm. He lifted her hand, put it to his lips and kissed the moist bowl of her palm. Her eyelids fluttered as he let the length of her hair trail through his fingers. She felt his warm breath on her neck and the pressure of his hand on her waist. She arched her back and gasped lightly as his lips touched her cheek, her earlobe, and finally her mouth. She sank back under his gentle pressure until his dark silhouette blocked out the green canopy above.

A wet tongue entered her ear canal, sending her bolt upright.

"Ew! Magoo!"

The dog pushed between them on the blanket, his tail swatting her face.

"Somebody's jealous," Caroline said laughing and picking dog hair out of her mouth.

Neil grabbed Magoo around the middle and flipped him over so his legs paddled the air and his tongue dangled from the side of his mouth. "Some wingman you are! Try that again, my friend, and I'll leave you at home."

Magoo jumped to his feet and barked.

"He's hungry," Neil said, gathering up the picnic.

Caroline slapped a mosquito that had found the same ear. "Ow! Everybody wants a piece of my ear."

It was nearly nine. The sun had sunk behind the beeches and hemlocks, behind Iris' red barn and behind Ridge Park Zoo. The heat of the day had dissipated and a breeze riffled the treetops. The clouds glowed orange now against a darkening eastern sky. Caroline felt a euphoria she hadn't felt in years.

"Thank you so much for this, Neil. The tour, your artwork, this picnic, the beer, the ferns, this woods—"

"—our first kiss, etcetera, etcetera," he said, getting to his feet.

Caroline shook her head. "Not that *first* kiss. The jury will disregard *that* kiss. But the *second* and third," she took a deep breath of the cool evening air, "and the 'etcetera, etcetera'—that was pretty great."

He offered his hand and pulled her up and into his arms again.

32

MORNING AFTER

Friday, July 1

It wasn't even noon, but the euphoria Caroline had felt the night before was dissipating like a warm puddle on hot pavement.

First of all, new yard signs—Vote NOO for a Zoo Moov!—had sprouted like mushrooms in manure all over the city. On her drive to work, the tally was twenty-three against to only eleven in favor—and that included the two she'd stuck in the Rojas' front yard.

Then, Victor had stormed into her office to tell her that he had pulled out a whole row of Vote NOO signs that "vandals" had planted in the grass by the zoo entrance. He was not amused.

Next, her mother called to say that the Schefflers had invited them all out on their boat tomorrow with their "recently single" son. Caroline was already dreading the Sunday pool party—and now this.

The final straw was Iris' strange rebuff of Neil last night, which she had successfully put out of her mind until this morning.

Come to think of it, there was a final, *final* straw: Neil, who kept intruding into her thoughts. Her stomach cartwheeled, or she felt like *doing* a cartwheel—both of which were embarrassing, immature and out of character. Was she so lonely and desperate that a little necking with a cute guy could reduce her to a quivering mess?

Neil had driven her back to her car in the zoo parking lot just after dark. By way of polite, post-make-out small talk—and to make it clear she wouldn't be sitting by the phone all weekend—she mentioned her three-day trip to Chicago. He, in turn, said he was anxious to get started on his new commission and would be in his studio all weekend. Were they playing hard-to-get already? Second dates were apparently as fraught as first kisses. If she had ever known how to date properly, which was doubtful, she had forgotten. She felt as rusty as old Dino.

They exchanged phone numbers in the truck before he walked her to her car. In the twilight, he had kissed her again, pressing her hard against the warm car door until she wanted to pull him into the back seat. Fortunately, he'd only asked for a nice, civilized dinner on Tuesday after the long holiday weekend. Breathlessly, she'd agreed. (Truth be told, she would have hopped a midnight flight to Vegas if he'd asked.)

She couldn't remember ever feeling this way with Rob, but last night she had possessed all the self-control of an orphaned puppy. She wasn't sure she liked these runaway emotions.

The short drive to her apartment was a blur. Lucky for her, there weren't breathalyzers for libidinously-impaired driving, she thought. The memory of his touch kept her tossing and turning. Later, there were dreams she couldn't repeat. She awoke still in a haze of—of what? Feverish infatuation? Inflamed ardor? Witless longing? Wanton horniness? It was all too much.

At noon, Caroline was having a small salad in the Bat Cave in anticipation of her father's candy-coated ribs and mother's creamy potato salad, when Chappy came in. He slid a plastic bag across the table toward Kirby, who had just finished two cheeseburgers and a double order of curly fries.

"For your collection, but I wouldn't open it in here," Chappy said.

Kirby scooted back, propped his size-thirteen boots on the tabletop and reached inside the bag.

Donna pushed through the doors next. "What are your Godzilla paws doing on the lunch table, Kirb?" She swatted at his boots on her way to the refrigerator.

Kirby pulled out a tangle of wet, black string.

Donna recoiled. "Jeez! It's dripping all over the floor."

Kirby let his long legs drop to the floor and stood up, letting the thing unravel to the floor. "Wow! Fishnet stockings? Way cool."

Chappy grabbed a handful of paper towel and began wiping the floor. "Remember I said the drain at Caratasca Island was slow? Well, that's why. They were caught in the grill at the bottom of the moat. You should have heard me trying to explain them to Rafael. I'm just glad it wasn't more condoms."

"I haven't seen a pair of these since—" Kirby shot a glance Caroline's way. "—never mind."

Caroline remembered the bacon-flavored condoms and kept silent.

Kirby held the stockings at arm's length and made them dance—spattering the table. Donna glared at him and moved to the next table. The stockings were stuck all over with bits of litter and what looked like the severed arm of a Barbie doll.

"What shall I call her? She's leggy. Betty Grable?" He winked at Donna who rolled her eyes right on cue. "She's going to be a star attraction in my summer collection. Thanks, Chap."

"The belle of the Detritus Ball," Donna said, shoveling a forkful of pasta into her mouth. "The girl of Kirby's dreams."

Kirby stuffed the stockings back into the bag, clapped Chappy on the shoulder and grinned. "This rare find puts me in a celebratory mood." He raised his voice and announced to the entire Bat Cave, "I'm making a run to Dairy Queen, anybody want anything?"

There were no takers.

Thirty minutes later, Caroline knocked lightly on Victor's door. "You wanted to see me?"

Victor looked at her over a pile of notebooks and files on his desk and gestured toward a chair. Caroline sat on the edge, hoping this wouldn't take long.

"How far along are you on the public announcement of the black-footed ferret acquisition?"

"I'm arranging a remote broadcast from Louisville for mid-August and some shots of a wild colony. We'll have an interview with the curator, including live shots of their ferrets. Gwen is helping me —"

Victor held up his hand. "Let me stop you there." He laid both hands, palms down, on his desk. "Louisville called yesterday. They know about the monkey escape and are concerned that it hasn't been 'resolved.' Their word. They want to make sure we're actually going to *have* a new zoo before they commit. I can't blame them." He sat back in his chair. "So, they have rescinded their offer, at least for now."

Caroline slumped in her chair. "But, the ferrets were going to be an incentive for yes voters. Can't they wait to see if the vote goes our way before they back out?"

"They have other zoos who are ready now." He ran his fingers through his bushy mane. "Keep this between us. Gwen knows, of course, but the rest of the staff only needs to know we're delaying the public announcement and media coverage. I don't want them getting discouraged—and I sure don't want the media getting wind of this."

So much for transparency, Caroline thought. She shuffled back to her office and looked at the phone. She wished Neil would call just to say hi, or that a florist would deliver a dozen roses—something to let her know she hadn't misread him. She wondered if he was in his studio right now, covered with alabaster dust, coaxing a translucent wing out of raw stone. She pictured their dinner on Tuesday—four whole days away—and was starting to imagine much more before she stopped herself. She got up and paced around her desk. All this thinking about Neil brought back Iris' rebuff.

Did Iris know something about Neil? Was she, Caroline, so desperate for Iris' approval that she imagined a snub when none was intended? Or, was she blind to some horrible flaw Iris saw in him?

What did any of this have to do with ferrets? She was pathetic.

She stared out the window at her Fiesta in the parking lot. At this time tomorrow, she'd be stuck on a sailboat making small talk with the "recently-single" Mr. Scheffler, Junior. She'd have to come up with a reason why she didn't want to "hook up" later at the nearest yuppie wine bar or at his apartment. Who was she kidding? He was probably going to show up with a bikinied blonde half his age and wouldn't give her a second glance, unless it was a patronizing smile reserved for divorced losers. Then, at the pool party, she'd have to face her parents' friends with their probing questions and sympathetic looks.

She watched Kirby pull in on his Harley with a Dairy Queen bag. Now there was a character. She'd never seen anyone so irrepressible, except Bella maybe. The loss of two ferrets wouldn't slow him down. Not Kirby. And the guy seemed totally unfazed by the staff's constant teasing. His crazy detritus collection was the perfect metaphor for Kirby's outlook on life. Most keepers carped about all the stuff that got dumped into the enclosures, but to Kirby, it was a treasure trove. A pair of stinking fishnet stockings made him delirious.

She turned back to her desk and tried to find some task she could finish with so little time and such flagging enthusiasm. Her screen saver shuffled through her photos—the capybara nuzzling its mate; a kid's drawing of Houdini being sprung by Spiderman; Paddy and the bimbo mugging for the camera.

She gave up and picked up the phone. "Iris? Hi, this is Caroline... um... If you aren't too busy, could I come over?... No, Rafa's not here today. Just me."

33

AN IMPERFECT, LOVABLE MAN

Caroline leaned into Victor's office to say she was leaving early to deliver some yard signs and to remind him she wouldn't be back until Tuesday. He mumbled a few niceties before taking a phone call.

She drove out of the zoo lot, dropped off two signs in the area and circled back to Iris'.

"I was just going to get myself some iced tea," Iris said, coming out of the garden with Zelda. She looked tired as she crossed the driveway and pulled herself up the porch steps.

"Let me get it. You sit."

Iris lowered herself gingerly into the metal porch chair and took a deep breath. "There's a pitcher in the fridge."

Caroline found a tray propped against the refrigerator and took two tumblers from the cupboard. Zelda watched through the screen door, backing up as Caroline elbowed through and set the tray on the side table.

Iris pressed the glass to her forehead. "It's hot in that garden, let me tell you."

"Do you have plans for the weekend?" Caroline asked.

"Just some writing. You?"

"I'm going to my parents' in Evanston. I haven't seen them since Easter." She sat on the edge of the glider and pushed her hair back. "Iris, I need to ask you something."

"The answer is, yes, I was rude to your boyfriend."

She decided to ignored the boyfriend barb, but asked, "Why? Do you know him?"

"Not really. I used to sell apples to his mother." She looked down at her hands and opened and closed her fingers. "Remember I told you I recognized Paddy Malone in your newsletter?"

Caroline nodded.

"Well, the last time I saw Mr. Malone in person he was a passenger in that red pickup your Mr. Stoddard was driving yesterday. Same logo. What is it?"

"SCS, for Stoddard Cold Storage. I think it's a new business name."

"No wonder I didn't associate it with the mine then. Anyway, he was driving."

"Who? Neil?" Caroline set down her glass on the table and went slack. She lifted a hand to her mouth and shook her head. "No. No, that—that can't be!"

"I'm so sorry, Caroline, if you like this man."

"Are you sure it was Neil?"

The silence answered.

Caroline rested her head on the back of the glider and shut her eyes. Iris' accusation ricocheted in the air between them. Everything suddenly felt upside down. She looked around the yard. She wanted to be anywhere but here, any time but now. In the corner of the porch ceiling, a spider crossed her elaborate web toward an entangled fly struggling listlessly.

Images of the pickup, the mine, the studio, the picnic and Neil himself popped up like thought balloons over her head. Others tumbled and replayed themselves. Neil pulling her to him, rows and rows of Vote NOO signs, Paddy's stuffed grizzly, Neil's smooth skin and probing tongue, black-footed ferrets, an inky black mineshaft, a half-empty storage facility, rows and rows of empty file drawers.

It could be developed, Neil had said of that beautiful, unspoiled woods. Was that an innocent comment or had he tipped his hand?

She stood up. "I need to make a call." She walked numbly down the steps and into the yard. She Googled "Village of Appeldoorn" on her phone. It was nearly five on a holiday weekend. She dialed quickly. She heard the screen door slam behind her.

"Village of Appeldoorn. Office of the Clerk," said a woman's voice.

"Oh! You're open! I'm doing some research on Appeldoorn. I would like to access the village archives. Old property and birth records, mostly. Is that possible?"

"Well, yes, but the records aren't here."

Yes! Caroline thought.

"They're all at our branch library. Do you need the number?"

"But—but I was told the old records had been moved to Stoddard Cold Storage?"

"What? Noooo," she said slowly. "Everything has been at the library for years."

"Thank you." Caroline hung up and stared at her phone. She walked back to the porch and lowered herself to the top step, covering her mouth with her palm.

"Is everything all right?" Iris said through the screen door.

"She said, um, Neil said, um—." She half-turned toward Iris. She wanted to explain, but first someone needed to explain it to her.

There were no archives at the mine. In fact, there wasn't much of *anything* stored there. And did Neil think Iris was too blind or senile to remember him and Paddy in his red pickup with its big white logo—the day Paddy threatened Iris? He wasn't as smart or perfect as he appeared—men never were. His interest in her was a ruse, a set-up. Seduce the lonely, naive divorcée to get close to an elderly widow sitting on a goldmine. It all fit too neatly.

Neil had lied.

She wanted to find that lying bastard and tell him she wasn't fooled, but she couldn't even find her breath. She slumped against the porch post.

Then without warning she cried. It didn't start with a lady-like sniff or a trickling tear or a lip quiver. No, *this* cry went from zero to sixty in just under three seconds. Her mouth twisted into a grotesque grimace. Strangled sounds came out of her that the world had never heard. Hot tears merged with mascara and the molten contents of her sinuses and ran onto her upper lip, into her mouth and down her chin until her face was coated in a slurry of liquid misery.

Caroline felt Iris' eyes on her back—taking in the curious spectacle of this young woman melting into her porch.

She made barking monkey noises, "*Arrawh! Arrawh!*" She was beyond mortified. She wanted to dash for her car, but she couldn't move. She gulped air like a drowning person. She pressed both hands to her face and wailed.

She heard water running in the kitchen. At least Iris had the good sense to leave her alone.

She'd quit her job and go live in her parents' attic. She'd get a cat—two cats, a houseful of cats! Maybe she'd even sail off with Mr. Scheffler, Junior, if he would have her. But none of this appealed to her nearly as much as sitting on Iris' porch until the spiders covered her like Miss Havisham's wedding cake.

She jumped when Iris touched her shoulder. She felt herself being pulled up, pushed through the kitchen door and into one of the chairs at the little drop-leaf table. She dropped her head and sobbed into the daffodil placemat. She felt a damp washcloth being tucked into her hand. She covered her face with it and exhaled a long, quivering moan. When she opened her eyes, Iris was moving around the kitchen with her back turned.

In front of her was a glass of water and a box of Kleenex. Finally, Iris sat down across the table. "So, what is this is all about, my dear?"

Caroline inhaled three times without exhaling. She wiped her face and squeaked, "I thought h-he was this gr-great g-guy. But he was just u-u-*using* me!"

Iris covered Caroline's hand with her own. "Start at the beginning."

In fits and starts, she explained Paddy's big donation to the referendum campaign, his bizarre collection of animal trophies, the public's growing opposition to a new zoo, Victor's sighting of Neil at Tom's office and Chappy's doubts about the move. Then, with her heart lying naked on her wet sleeve, she confessed her complete and utter infatuation with Neil Stoddard.

"He showed me around the mine last night. He said Appeldoorn's archives were there, but he was *lying*. The drawers were empty. What's he trying to hide?"

Iris frowned and sighed. "Well, it sure looks like he's connected to this Paddy character." She winced. "*Trophy* heads, you say? My word!"

Caroline blew her nose into one Kleenex after another until there was a disgusting, damp pile on the table. She scooped them up and put them in a waste can next to the door. "I think Neil asked me out to get near you," she sniffed, sitting down again hard, which made her head throb. "He and Paddy had it all planned."

"Yes. It would seem so. You said Paddy is heavily invested in the referendum campaign, right?"

"He's made the largest single donation."

"His behavior would suggest he's pretty confident he'll get the zoo property after you vacate."

"Yes, but I don't see how," Caroline said, pressing her temples. "The city owns the land. He must know something we don't."

"Or, some*one*. Someone inside City Hall," Iris said, cocking one eyebrow. "And if he's in cahoots with the Stoddards, that means they already have fifty acres of mine property."

"So, if they somehow get the zoo's twenty acres, all they need to connect the two—"

"—is my farm," Iris said, pursing her lips. "If they put the three parcels together, they'd have *ninety* prime acres inside the city."

"Worth a *fortune*."

"I'm the fly in the ointment. No wonder Paddy kept pestering me." Iris shook her head and scowled. "But Paddy's calls and letters stopped about a month ago. How do you explain that?"

"I think they realized intimidation wasn't working. So when I showed up at the fence, Neil figured he'd try seduction."

"Seduction?" Iris shot Caroline a look of alarm. "You didn't—"

"No. Of course not!" Caroline reached for another Kleenex and sighed. "But eventually." Caroline covered her face with her hands.

After a moment Iris said, "And your board president, Tom Engelsma? You say he's a developer. Could he be involved, too?"

"It would explain why someone with no previous interest in zoos shows up out of the blue with a hundred acres of free land and an offer to lead our board. I wonder how many of his so-called 'donors' are really investors in his scheme to move the zoo out of the way." She went limp at the thought. "Oh, Iris, I've been *such* a stupid fool! I don't know *who* to trust anymore!"

Another shudder overcame Caroline. Finally, she said, "I'm so sorry to unload on you like this."

Iris pushed back her chair and stood up. "Come on. Let's take a walk."

Caroline sighed. "I can't. I have to drive to Chicago tonight. I'll be gone all weekend."

"In *this* traffic? Wait an hour and you'll make the time up later. Trust me; I've made a study of it." Iris stood at the kitchen door, her elbow crooked out like a wedding groomsman. "Get up. I want to show you something."

Caroline let herself be led into the yard and around the barn. Where she expected to see orchards sloping toward the creek bed, there was a large, sun-filled meadow with a neatly mowed path winding through it.

"A secret garden. How beautiful."

"I call it Bill's Meadow, for my late husband. My girls had it seeded for me the year after he died. By mid-summer this will all be covered with coreopsis, coneflower, beebalm, bellflower and milkweed."

"How long has your husband been gone?"

"Seven years this August."

Zelda trotted ahead and disappeared into the waist-high grass with only the white tip of her tail visible.

"You must miss him."

Iris lifted her chin and led on. The path stopped in front of a large pond. Two crescent-shaped benches faced each other across a small clearing. Here and there, blue flag iris shot up like little fountains along the bank. Zelda waded in for a drink, causing two turtles to drop from a log into the water. Two green damselflies landed on a lily pad island.

Iris pointed out a sunny spot next to one of the benches.

"This is my petting garden. I made it for my grandchildren. *Stachys byzantine*, lamb's ears," she said, running a velvety, gray-green leaf between her thumb and first finger. "*This* is basil and that's lavender. Mmmm. Smell." She touched the leaves and laid her hands lightly on Caroline's flushed cheeks.

Caroline blinked back the tears that threatened to come again.

Iris lowered herself down on one of the benches and patted the space next to her.

"Bill's ashes are here, so he's in these flowers. He was good at nurturing things." She ran her fingers along a set of letters carved into the wooden seat: William Robert VanWingen 1928-2007. "My Bill." She squinted at Caroline. "So, you're ashamed of shedding a few tears over a man? The tears shed by women over men are what keep our oceans full, don't you know? No shame in that. I'm a world-class crier myself. A gold medalist in Olympic Crying." She traced the grooves of the W with her finger. "This is my wailing bench. This is my wailing meadow, and those are my wailing damselflies. Just look at all my wailing lily pads. Aren't they pretty?"

"You? I can't imagine. But thank you, Iris. You've been so kind."

"No, I haven't. I've treated you horribly."

"No. No. Don't say that. I haven't been exactly forthright either." She looked down at her hands. "You know, my boss sent me over here."

"To schmooze me. Right?"

"'Charm' was the verb he used. He just wants me to tell you about the zoo because he respects you and knows you have influence in the community. The zoo needs allies like you." Caroline shook her head.

"Anyway, somewhere along the line, with Rafael and walking him home and stopping off at your porch, I—I started looking *forward* to coming here—even if we never see eye-to-eye on zoos."

"I've enjoyed our porch sits, too. And isn't that boy a wonder?" She twirled a sprig of grass between her fingers. A robin landed on a rock next to the pond and scooped water into its beak. "I found the coffee pot in the refrigerator yesterday."

"The refrigerator?" Caroline repeated, wondering where this was going.

"Instead of putting the cream back, I put the coffee pot in instead."

Caroline laughed. "I do stuff like that *all* the t—"

"My watering can disappeared a few weeks ago—or I thought it did, and then I found it days later, right next to the kitchen door. I must have walked past it a dozen times. I let the car run out of gas, too."

"You have a lot to keep track of here."

"But I had just filled it—at least I think I did. Did you notice a big, dead area in the garden? Apparently, I got water softener salt mixed up with organic fertilizer."

Caroline didn't know what to say.

A breeze blew through the meadow, making the buds nod.

Iris sighed. "What I'm trying to say is, *I* left that hose running in the barn. I didn't think so at first—so I accused Rafa. Poor kid. But, you see, I still don't *remember* doing it." Iris bit her lip. "I don't remember a lot of things lately." She brightened then. "But at least it proves my theory."

"Oh, no! Not another theory," Caroline said, making an attempt at levity.

"No, the same one. I'm devolving. Re-entering the ape-like state," she whispered. "Also known as losing one's marbles."

"Oh, *Iris*. No, you're not! I poured orange juice on my cereal last week. And once I got all the way to work before I realized I was wearing one navy shoe and one brown one."

Iris pushed a pebble aside with the toe of her tennis shoe. "I said the same things to my mother, just as she was sinking into her own private hell."

"Iris, if you were . . . losing your marbles, I'd have noticed. But I learn so *much* from you. And your columns are full of wisdom."

"Maybe. Sometimes my mind feels like an overstuffed suitcase," she said, sighing. "I've been a child once. I don't care to be one twice."

Caroline turned to face Iris, hoping to change the subject. "Tell me about Bill."

Iris sat up straighter. "You're humoring me."

"I'm not. I'm humoring *me*. I need to hear something uplifting. Tell me how you met."

"Oh, let's see. I was a know-it-all, first-year science teacher at Central High. Bill had taught English there for four years, which made him seem very experienced and wise. I worshiped him from the day I met him. I think he found me spunky and entertaining more than anything. One rainy day, he saw me waiting at the bus stop after school and offered me a ride." Her mouth twitched into the faintest smile. "We were each other's matching piece. We weren't the same, but we *fit*, you know? He was a great teacher, father and husband, but, God, he was a poor excuse for a farmer." She brought her hands to her cheeks. "He was patient and warm, which, I don't have to tell you, I am not. Bill always managed to come a little over to my side when I couldn't budge."

"You were 'lucky in love,' as they say," Caroline said. She thought of all the years she had tried to fit her life into Rob's and felt a stab of bitterness.

"Did you know that after mating the female meadow vole rips her mate to shreds?"

Caroline laughed. "I did *not*, but I understand the impulse."

"But their close cousins, the *prairie* vole, mate for life. It's probably the same chemical trigger that makes baby animals imprint on their mothers, but for some reason the pair bond continues their whole lives. Perhaps it's the same for swans and turtle doves."

"And gibbons," Caroline added. "So, it's true. Love comes down to chemistry." The smell of Neil's lucky tee shirt came to her, but she pushed it aside.

"When it happens it's a lucky thing for the pair—until one dies, of course. Great pain is the final payment due for great love. Then, oh, well *then* . . . *Breathing* hurts. *Being* hurts."

"But it's worth it, isn't it?"

"Oh yes." Iris whispered, fingered the collar of Bill's shirt. "By the way, faithful little prairie vole couples are endangered in Michigan."

"Figures. I think marriage is what's endangered. Maybe someday there'll be a love vaccine and couples will just get booster shots."

Iris laughed. "Chemistry might be the only way to explain how a cranky, old article such as myself got a mate as sweet as Bill. Not that we didn't fuss and bicker with the best of them, but I don't think we ever considered not being a pair."

"That is rare. And you're not *cranky*. At least not when it counts. Not when an uninvited guest falls apart on your porch."

Two crows flew overhead, heading toward the house.

"Crows mate for life, too," Iris said. "They have my respect."

Caroline watched them land in the white pine by the porch. "We have a disabled barn owl at Ridge Park. A rehabber brought her to us when her broken wing didn't mend. Sometimes we find mice or small birds pushed through the wire of her enclosure. We think her mate lives in the area and is bringing her gifts. It breaks my heart."

"Yes, that is sad. Some women I know are *relieved* when their husbands die," Iris said. "Widowhood is a kind of liberation. Sometimes I envy them."

"Why?"

Iris blinked, choosing her words carefully. "It was a complete shock to lose Bill. I know that sounds dumb coming from an old person. Death is a run-of-the-mill occurrence for old people, except when it happens to *your* old person." Iris seemed preoccupied with rubbing at a stain on her denim skirt. "No one else was shocked, not even my daughters. They *adored* their father, but they accept his death in a way I just *can't*."

Caroline considered this. She had always held out hope that her own mortality would start making sense when she got older. "I'm sad for you, Iris, but you had a long, happy marriage. I'd trade a lot for that. Or at least I would have, once."

"Once?"

"Before my vow of celibacy."

"When was that?"

"About twenty minutes ago."

Iris threw back her head and laughed.

Zelda returned from her explorations and began nosing the hem of Iris' skirt, ready to move on. Iris took her freckled muzzle in one hand and traced its white blaze with her finger.

"The worst thing now," she said, giving Zelda a kiss on the top of her head, "would be to forget Bill. To be that *alone*." Her voice broke. Then she straightened her back, and found her composure in a way Caroline admired. "Memories are all I have of him." She fingered the collar of her plaid shirt and smiled. "That, and a closet full of old shirts."

Iris rubbed her arms as if she felt a chill. "Time you got on the road." She stood, offered her arm again and led Caroline toward the house.

"I wish I had known Bill," Caroline said.

"He would have liked you—which isn't saying much."

Caroline drew back, surprised.

Iris chuckled. "Bill liked *everybody*. Like I said, he was nothing like me."

"You don't like me?"

"Not at first. Goodness no! I thought you were too, too—"

"—prim? A prim little kiss-ass? Miss Congeniality? Take your pick."

Iris laughed. "I was going to say 'sunny.' I remember you from the TV, you know." She patted Caroline's hand which was wound around her forearm. "But, you've grown on me—like that moss on the barn roof."

"So, I'm a fungus?" Caroline said, laughing now.

Iris shook her head. "Mosses are bryophytes."

Caroline rolled her eyes as they walked on in silence. Finally she said, "I've never given old age much thought. I'm too worried about surviving middle age."

"When I was a girl, our church was full of crippled old widows who wore their lipstick catawampus and their hair in bluish pin curls. They had mink stoles with the heads still on, which scared me. The thing is, I didn't realize these grotesque creatures had once been *children*. Then one day, my grandmother showed me a tight, blonde curl tied with a pink ribbon that had been hers. The color matched mine perfectly. I suppose she thought I'd be pleased, but I was horrified. I realized then what aging was."

"That would be a shock."

"Well, I was a bit dim, I guess. Still am. I stink at being old. I just can't get the hang of it." She held out her hand in front of her and turned it over. "Look at this old claw! Where did it *come* from?"

Caroline smiled. "A couple of weeks ago, I was chatting with a cute guy behind the counter at my little coffee place. I was telling him about this coffee cooperative I visited in Costa Rica back in college. I thought we were sort of flirting, you know? But then he hands me my coffee and says, 'So wow, they had fair trade coffee *way back then*?'"

Iris laughed again. "Trust me, it only gets worse."

Caroline picked up a stick from the path and flung the stick over

Zelda's head. . "I don't know, Iris. At the rate I'm going, I'm never going to find someone like Bill. Did you know I was divorced last year?"

"I'm not surprised."

"Am I that pathetic?"

"No. You just seem like the marrying kind. Most young people can't commit to anything more than a tattoo these days. But you're more traditional. Trusting. Romantic. Am I right?"

"Less today than yesterday."

"Your tears say otherwise."

Zelda brought the stick back.

"Those were cleansing tears," Caroline said, heaving the stick again. "That bud, as they say, has been nipped. I've got great friends, a supportive family and an interesting job. I don't need a man. Besides, Iris, every relationship I've ever had has ended in failure."

She felt Iris shrug. "All courting relationships—according to Western cultural norms—end in failure, until you find the right mate. It's called 'dating,' by the way."

"I suppose you've made a scientific study of this?"

"Before we found each other, Bill and I had plenty of failed relationships. He once dated a girl with twelve toes."

"*Twelve?*"

"He invited her to the beach, and when she took her shoes off she had six complete toes on each foot! He said she was a lovely girl—pretty, smart and a good conversationalist, but he couldn't pry his eyes off her feet all day and he couldn't bring himself to ask her out again. He was so ashamed of himself, but he loved telling the story. Attraction—or lack of it—isn't always rational."

They came into the yard again, still giggling, and stopped at Caroline's Fiesta.

Iris released Caroline's arm and laid a hand on her flushed cheek. "Don't look for the perfect man, honey. He's not out there. Look for a man you can love enough to forgive his imperfections. *That* man you'll find."

Caroline pulled Iris into a long hug. "Thank you. Thank you, Iris." Then reluctantly she lowered herself into the front seat. "You are right, of course. I need a man like your Bill—not a career-obsessed, narcissistic doctor or a miner-artist-professor-lying bastard plotting to bulldoze your farm and my zoo!"

"*Your* zoo? Does that mean you'd like the zoo to stay where it is?"

Caroline considered this. "Honestly, I don't know anymore. It's just that we have a problem that isn't going to be solved with a referendum. I don't know what will happen, but I know the zoo can't move out and leave a mess in its wake. I'll fight that."

"And you can count me in. Maybe I—*we*—can't stop Paddy and the rest of those vultures, but we can go down fighting."

She met Iris' blue-gray eyes and laughed. "I can't think of anyone I'd rather have next to me on the front lines."

~

Two hours later, Caroline pulled off I-94 at New Buffalo near the Indiana line. Her eyes looked like purple puffballs and she had a raging headache. Aspirin and truck stop coffee was what she needed. From the second stall of the bathroom, she phoned her mother. She'd be there in a couple of hours, she said, barring holiday traffic jams or construction delays.

Her stomach leapt into her chest when she saw a text from Neil. "Drive safe. See u Tues." She hesitated, hit delete and stuffed the phone into her purse.

Back in the car, she considered one of her favorite classical CDs, but then switched to U2, fearing Barber's "Adagio for Strings" would send her into the median.

She was doing seventy-five behind a silver minivan with a big, yellow dog panting at her through the back window. She hit the gas, changed lanes and passed them. She didn't want anything to remind her of Magoo, Neil, her job and her train-wreck of a life. As she passed Michigan City, she tried tossing all of them into her mental junk drawer to be sorted out later, but by the Indiana Dunes exit, they were banging around in there—demanding her attention.

Time to de-clutter. She slowed down to concentrate.

For months Paddy and maybe—probably—Neil had tried to pressure Iris into selling her farm, but now they seemed to be using her, Caroline, to lead them to Iris. Victor saw Neil leaving Tom's office, but Neil hadn't made any contributions to the zoo or the referendum—which he would have if he wanted the zoo to vacate, but not if he wanted to avoid suspicion. Besides, he had land to contribute to Paddy's development and she believed him when he said he didn't have any money.

Had Neil known where she worked *before* he showed up at the neighborhood forum last week and just pretended he didn't? And what about Tom? Was he an unwitting victim, or in on a development scheme with Paddy and Neil? Could Neil be an unwitting victim? Where did Neil's cousin fit into all of this? Neil had appeared truly surprised to find the file drawers in the mine empty, but why had Iris seen him with Paddy?

A merging tanker blared its horn before forcing her into the passing lane. She had completely zoned out. She needed to lay out the facts, like a forensic anthropologist arranging bones on a table. She needed paper and pen, graph paper, sticky notes, color-coded markers and a white board. She needed a situation room with space to pace in circles. How could she do any of that in a speeding car or a pitching sailboat? None of this could wait until Tuesday.

She exited at Burns Harbor, slowed down and hit speed dial.

"Mom. It's me again. Listen. We've got a crisis at work and I just can't get away this weekend after all... No, not another escape... No, I'm fine. It's just that I have work that can't wait ... I know. I know, Mom. I'll come home soon, I promise. I *really* want to, you know that. ... Give Dad a hug for me. I'll call again soon ... Have a great weekend. .. I love you, Mom."

She crossed the overpass and headed down the eastbound ramp toward Saskawan.

34

BOUNDARIES

By early evening, Caroline was back in her apartment in a pair of boxers and a baggy tee shirt. She made herself a salad and was looking forward to a quiet evening of uninterrupted, heavy-duty thinking.

She set up her laptop on her dining table and was making a list of what she knew, what she suspected and what she needed to find out. In the morning, she planned to go straight to the office and tell Victor her suspicions. There was an odor hanging over the zoo, but it wasn't coming from anything four-legged.

THUD! Something banged against her door. THUD! She tiptoed to the peephole, ready to run the chain lock into its track and dial 911.

"-aro! Un-uh UH!"

Caroline laughed and opened the door. Bella, with keys dangling from her mouth, stumbled forward with four bags of groceries hanging from her skinny, tattooed arms.

Caroline picked the keys out of Bella's teeth.

"I saw your car outside," Bella said. "I thought you were in Chicago eating ribs. What happened?"

"I changed my mind. That guy had a bad heart despite the rich coat after all. Besides, I have stuff to figure out."

Bella shrugged. "Grandmama Canelli knows her stuff, eh?"

"I thought you were up north."

"Another case of a bad heart. Saw him at the Third Base with the missus. I'm no prude, but I have *some* standards."

A can of off-brand tomato soup hit the floor and headed for the sofa. Caroline picked it up.

Bella pushed past her and dumped the whole lot on the kitchen counter. Then she ran to the bathroom and left the door open while she peed. "So, how are Mama and Papa Bear taking the news of Baby Bear not sleeping in her itty-bitty bed this weekend?"

"Disappointed, but they understand."

"Ouch. See, mine would just refuse to speak to me until Christmas," she shouted above the flush. "That's so much kinder, really." Bella came out of the bathroom rolling down the top of her yoga pants. "Hey, are you up for dinner? I bought lots of stuff, eh?"

From the looks of it, 'dinner' and 'stuff' meant ersatz tomato soup, Ritz crackers, white bread and Jif.

"Okay. That would be nice." Actually, dinner with Bella *did* sound nice. She had all night to work.

Bella went across the hall to put away her fish sticks, Pop-tarts and ice cream and came back with the bread, a box of red wine and the can of soup. She began slamming cupboard doors.

Caroline watched from the doorway.

"What are you grinning at?" Bella demanded.

"You, Bell. You feed my soul."

Bella grunted. "You mocking my food choices? Where's your can opener?"

"That drawer. You should learn to take compliments, eh?"

Caroline pushed her laptop to one side of the table to make room for a bowl of salad, two steaming bowls of soup, a bag of bread, the Jif jar, grape jelly, crackers and two glasses of wine.

"Oh, goody—a slide show," Bella said, spooning soup into her mouth as she watched random shots of zoo animals. "What's that one?" she asked, pointing to a bristly, pig-sized animal with an over-sized head.

"That's a capybara." Caroline froze the photo.

"A what?"

"Her name is Maritza. She's the largest member of the rodent family."

"Well now, there's something to be proud of, eh?" Bella laughed.

"She's related to guinea pigs."

Bella pointed with her spoon. "I had a black and white guinea pig named Oreo once. Much cuter."

"Well, I like Maritza. She's related to beavers and porcupines, too."

"Where do capybaras live?"

"South America."

"Hmm." She crumbled a handful of crackers into her soup. "She looks like a hippo, eh?"

"She wallows like one, too, but she's very gentle."

Bella shuddered. "Give me a dog any time." A drop of soup splashed onto her white tee shirt. "Shit." She went into the bathroom and came back wearing her white sports bra. Caroline covered her mouth to hide a smile. There were ironing boards better endowed than Bella. She admired her friend's complete lack of modesty.

"It just needs to soak," she said, sitting back down and resuming her meal, with her eyes fixed on the screen. Caroline watched another drop of soup splash onto Bella's sports bra, but she did not point this out.

Bella was full of questions: Why were the otters swimming with rocks? (To open clam shells.) Why do flamingos stand on one leg? (Probably to dry the other one and warm themselves.) Bella was the perfect distraction from a terrible-horrible-no-good-very-bad day. But Caroline still had a lot of thinking to do before morning.

Bella pointed at the screen with her spoon. "What's that?"

"That's the ribbon-cutting for the new monkey island."

"Hey! Is that the bimbo?" She pointed to Sarah standing next to Paddy.

Caroline frowned. "Did I tell you about her?"

"Yeah. A couple of weeks ago."

"I shouldn't have called her that. Her name is *Sarah*. She's sweet and sad. She showed up that night dressed like a hooker with a man old enough to be her father. Now she's a joke."

Bella leaned closer. "Fishnets. I see what you mean."

"*What?*" Caroline turned the screen to examine a shot of Sarah's long legs thrust forward in a Vegas showgirl pose. She was wearing black fishnet stockings. Caroline pushed her wine glass away and tried to fit this information into her disorderly collection of thoughts.

Bella stopped chewing. "You look like you've seen a ghost."

"Yeah. Maybe. I don't know." She shook her head. "It's just that one of the keepers found a pair of fishnets in the drain of the monkey island."

"Really? What does that mean?"

Caroline slumped in her chair. "I'm not sure. She took them off and threw them at the monkeys? I have no idea."

"What if she did?"

"A monkey escaped twelve hours after that photo was taken. Maybe there's a connection. But why would she take them off in the middle of a party?"

Bella snorted. "Have you ever *worn* those things? They make your feet all waffly. Besides, a girl wouldn't wear them on a date if she wanted to *keep* them on."

Caroline drew back in disgust. "At the zoo?"

Bella raised her dark eyebrows, "Stranger things have happened in stranger places. Maybe they're in the One Hundred Zoos Club."

"Is there such a thing?"

"I wouldn't doubt it." Bella dragged her chair around the table to sit next to Caroline. They both leaned closer to the screen. "Do you have more pictures of her?"

Caroline opened her file of event photos. She knew them by heart, but she was always looking at the monkeys, not at Sarah's legs. She called up several shots of Paddy and Sarah late in the evening.

Bella tapped a bright green fingernail on the screen. "There. That's her. And there. She's kind of a diva, eh?"

Caroline zoomed in on Sarah's legs and enhanced the brightness. "It's too dark to tell if she's still wearing them."

"There. Zoom in."

Sarah had her back to the camera and was leaning on the railing watching the flamingos, showing more thigh than Caroline cared to see under normal circumstances. The lights from the parking lot flooded the area with light. Caroline zoomed in and brightened the image. "Look! She's not wearing them. That's clear."

"And look at that." Bella pointed at something black hanging out of Paddy's coat pocket. "Why, that old lech! What kind of parties do you throw at that zoo of yours?"

Caroline got up, still staring at the photo. "Thanks for dinner, Bell. You've been more help than you know, but I have work to do."

"What work?"

"Work work," Caroline said, cryptically.

"Come on, Sherlock!" Bella whined. "Let me be your Watson."

"Sorry." She hugged Bella and hustled her out the door. Before it closed, she dialed Paddy's number.

"Malone residence," said a girlish voice.

"Sarah? It's Caroline, from the zoo."

❧

Sarah looked completely different. Her long, highlighted hair was cut into a chin-length bob. She wore loose jeans and a gray and white striped tee shirt. No earrings, jewelry or makeup.

A pile of boxes, several suitcases and a couple of garment bags were piled on top of each other in the foyer under the lifeless gaze of a dozen dead animals.

"Are you taking a trip?" Caroline asked.

"Sort of. Come on in. I made us drinks." The Southern drawl was gone.

She padded down the dark, central hallway with Caroline following. They passed a still life of dead pheasants and a powder horn, then a ornately carved cabinet filled with Italian or Spanish dishes and leather-bound books with gold lettering.

"I thought we could sit by the pool. It's nice out tonight."

On the phone, Sarah had said Paddy had returned from Africa, but was away for the weekend.

The back of the house opened onto a flagstone patio overlooking a tiled pool with a hot tub at the other end. The yard was cloistered by an ivy-covered wall. On its sunny side, climbing roses in several shades of pink filled the air with perfume. A life-sized statue of a woman holding a basket of flowers stood in a niche in the back wall.

"I should have told you to bring a bathing suit," Sarah said, pointing Caroline toward one of two wrought-iron chairs. "You could borrow one of mine."

Caroline eyed Sarah's D-plus endowment and imagined the suit in question. "Thanks, Sarah, but I can't stay long."

Two tumblers with ice and a small pitcher of tea sat on the glass-topped table between them. Sarah filled both and handed one to Caroline. She sat down and curled one long leg under her, turning to face Caroline. "On the phone you said you have something to ask me?"

"Yes, it may sound odd and kind of personal, but I need to ask."

"I got no secrets." She pushed her hair back and raised her chin defiantly.

"It's about the night of our ribbon cutting."

She nodded, fixing her blue eyes on Caroline. "Okay."

Caroline took a sip of her tea and coughed. "What kind of iced tea is this?"

"Long Island."

Caroline thumped her chest and coughed again. "What's in it?"

Sarah held up her hand and touched each finger in turn. "Let's see. Vodka, gin, tequila, rum and a splash of triple sec. Oh, and a tiny bit of Pepsi to make it look right."

"No tea?"

"Sure," Sarah blinked, "the Long Island kind." Irony was, apparently, lost on this woman.

Caroline cleared her throat. "I remember that you wore fishnet stockings that night."

Sarah wrinkled her nose like a child caught stealing a cookie. "Paddy bought 'em for me in Vegas. He really wanted me to wear 'em. I didn't know we'd be walkin' so much. I had blisters for a week."

"Is that why you took them off?" She took another sip of her drink. The concoction was surprisingly smooth.

"Like I said, they gave me blisters." Her voice rose defensively.

"Do you still have them?"

"The stockings?" Sarah looked as if she were trying to do long division in her head. She pulled both legs up on the cushion and hugged her knees. "I'm leaving first thing tomorrow morning."

Caroline guessed Sarah was either trying to remember or stalling while she thought of a plausible lie.

"So those are your bags in the foyer?" Caroline asked, casually enough.

"Yup. He's gonna walk in here Monday night, and I'll be looooong gone. No forwarding address. Nothin'!"

"Where are you going?"

"Home. To Dearborn," she said, which explained the missing Southern accent.

"Why?"

"That big jerk is off with his buddies *again* for the *whole* weekend. They're fishin' on the big lake. I wasn't even *invited*." She looked away and pulled on a lock of hair. "He never takes me with him anymore. We used to have a lot of fun. Now, he just wants me to clean this creepy ol' house, cook his meals and warm his bed, as my mom would say."

Caroline looked into her glass.

"So, anyways," Sarah heaved a huge sigh. "I don't give a shinin' shit if the whole world knows wha' that man did." The tea was taking a toll on Sarah's speech. She leaned in and whispered, "I know this is 'bout that monkey gettin' out."

"You do?"

"I ain't—I'm not dumb, ya know." She shot Caroline an admonishing glance.

"I know that, Sarah." Caroline set her glass on the table. "We found a pair of fishnet stockings at the bottom of the monkey pond this week. If they got in there the night of the party—the night before the monkey escaped—there might be a connection."

Sarah laughed. "Oh, there's a connection all right! Paddy would be so pissed if he knew I was tellin' you this." She held up one hand. "Not that the escape is funny, or anything. I was so glad Little Houdini wasn't hurt or anything. My gosh, he's so cute! The *monkey*, not Paddy. Paddy thinks 'cause he gave the zoo a wad of cash he *owns* it. But, it ain't right, what he did."

"What did he do?"

Sarah got up and moved to the edge of the pool to dangle her legs into the water. "We were both pretty plowed that night. After a while, I took 'em off—the fishnets—cause they were killin' me. He put 'em in his pocket. He didn't wanna go back to the party tent. Called you a buncha tree-huggin' faggots that could kiss his ass. Sorry, but that's what he said. After a while, we were alone at the monkey island and he started danglin' my stockings over the side, tryin' to get the monkeys to grab 'em—'fishin' for monkeys,' he called it."

"Dangling them? You mean, *into* the enclosure?"

"Yeah. Over the water. He kinda tossed em over and hung on to one toe. They went down pretty far, you know. I have long legs." She straightened one leg to show its length. "The other toe went almost to the water. He even put a piece of banana from the banana splits in the toe. Then he asked if I wanted one for a pet or just have it stuffed." She wrapped her arms around herself and shivered. "I shoulda walked away right then."

"What were the monkeys doing then?"

"Most of them ran away. I mean, there was this crazy man wavin' those stockings around. But a couple of the littler ones thought it was a game. They were hoppin' and jumpin' around, and tryin' to grab aholt, but they couldn't reach em without gettin' wet. Finally, the stockings caught on a bush. Hanging way down into the water. We saw somebody coming, so we hightailed it outta there real fast. The next day when we heard about the escape, Paddy thought it was hilarious. Ha, ha, ha!"

Sarah bit off one of her long nails and spit it out. "What a jerk! I wish I could be here to see the fit he'll throw when he sees I'm gone."

While she was listening to Sarah's account, Caroline had taken more sips of her tea than she intended to. Now, the garden walls were rippling like the surface of the pool. This new information would take more sober analysis than she was capable of at the moment. She set her glass on the table.

"Thank you for being honest, Sarah. I'm sorry about you and Paddy."

"I'm not. Not at *all*. He's nothing but a big, fat liar!" She kicked water onto the pool deck. "He doesn't give two hoots about me, or the zoo, neither."

"Then why did he give us so much money?"

"Because Tom *asked* him to. He does *whatever* Tom tells 'im."

"Why?"

"Tom's cookin' up some big business deal about the zoo property—the *old* property, not new land he wants to give you. And I'll tell you one thing—Tom *really* wants that land. Paddy's in on it, too. He practically *pees* himself every time he looks at Tom. Thinks this deal'll make him some big ty*coon*. Anyway, that's who Paddy's with now. Tom and another guy—the three of them are tight."

"What other guy?"

"I don't know, but he owns property by the zoo. A mine, I think? No, that can't be right. Are there mines around here? His name is Shepherd, or something."

"Stoddard?"

"Yeah, that's it."

The breeze blew a leaf across the pool. Caroline gripped the arm of her chair. Her ears were ringing. *If there is a hell, it will be a place where the people you care about turn on you.* She felt as if she might be sick.

"Are you okay?" Sarah asked, getting up. "You don't look so good."

Caroline tried to moisten her dry lips. "I'm—I'm fine."

"I'm getting you some water. Stay here."

The whole earth tilted on its axis. Caroline wouldn't have been able to move if her hair caught fire.

Sarah returned with a tumbler of water. "Here you go, hon."

"Sarah, please don't tell Paddy that you've told me any of this."

She threw back her head and laughed. "Are you *kidding*? He'd *kill* me if he knew I told you *any* of this. Besides, I don't plan to ever *see* the old perv again."

Caroline took a drink of the water.

"Paddy is *not* a good man," Sarah said. "And I wouldn't trust any of those guys he hangs out with neither. That's why I'm on the first bus outta town in the morning."

"I hope you find something better in Dearborn."

Sarah shrugged. "My mom owns a burger place she got from my third step-dad. I was totally bored waiting tables there, but believe me, I'm looking forward to it now." She looked around the manicured backyard and lifted her chin. "I'll be fine."

"I should go." Caroline stood up slowly, steadying herself on the back of the chair. "Thank you, again, Sarah. You've helped more than you know."

On the way out, Sarah poured the rest of their drinks into the kitchen sink.

The Fiesta crawled home through the back streets of Saskawan, well below the posted speed limit. She could hear the distant pops of firecrackers in a dozen backyards as the holiday weekend got off to a noisy start.

She tiptoed past Bella's door, hoping to avoid a late night conversation. She heard Mumford and Sons singing, "*I really fucked it up this time . . .*" Years from now—unless they perfected selective memory lobotomies—she would associate that song with this particular summer.

She didn't bother with lights. Her laptop glowed eerily on the dining room table, still shuffling through photos of smiling, conniving zoo donors. She slammed it shut and went to bed.

35

SAVED BY THE BELL

Saturday, July 2

Victor squinted in the bright morning sunlight as he approached Caratasca Island. "Aren't you supposed to be in Chicago?" he asked Caroline. He was looking peeved at being summoned on a busy Saturday morning and his look said, *This better be good.*

"Thanks for meeting me here," she said.

Chappy came from the opposite direction. "Hey, Caroline, Boss. What's up?" His eyes darted between the two of them.

Caroline glanced behind her to make sure they were alone. "I have news." She walked to an area of the railing where a juniper bush grew over the top of the wall.

She recounted Sarah's story of the ribbon-cutting and Paddy's drunken antics, ending with, "So, our Little Houdini apparently climbed up a pair of fishnet stockings that Paddy Malone left hanging on this bush."

Caroline watched the two men's faces change from surprise, to relief, to confusion.

Victor ran a hand through his hair and let out a low, rumbling sigh. Chappy gave a long whistle. They walked along the wall to look at the bush from every angle.

"But why didn't they *all* climb out?" Chappy asked.

"After Houdini climbed out, the stockings must have fallen into the water," Caroline said.

Chappy said, "And once he was out, he wouldn't have been able to get back in."

Victor didn't look convinced. "But wouldn't you have seen the stockings the night before?" he asked Chappy.

Caroline sprang to his defense. "Sunset was about 8:20 that night, so by 9:00, when Chappy brought them in for the night, black stockings would've been hard to see."

"But if Houdini got out in the morning," Victor said to Chappy, "and the stockings were still hanging there, you'd have seen them, right?"

Chappy continued studying the bush.

Caroline said, "On a sunny morning like that one, the whole side of the overhang would have been shaded—like it is now." Caroline pointed to the huge oak that was shading part of the island. "By the time Chappy came out onto the island with their breakfast, the stockings were probably at the bottom of the moat and Houdini was on his way to Iris' barn."

Victor nodded and Chappy let go of a breath he'd been holding for more than three weeks. "I need to call my wife."

Caroline gave Victor a pained look and said, "We can't go public with this and embarrass a major donor."

"You mean we have to just *sit* on this?"

Victor put a hand on Chappy's shoulder. "At least you're in the clear."

"But if no one *knows*—" Chappy squeezed the bridge of his nose.

Caroline said, "Think what the media would do with this information, Chappy. Paddy would probably deny it. Then where would we be? We'd lose his support and create a bigger scandal."

Chappy whistled again. "Fishnet stockings? I can't believe it." He turned to Victor. "Okay. I get it, but I hate living under this dark cloud of suspicion."

Victor nodded. "I'll let the AZA know. They'll understand our need for discretion."

They stood in silence and watched several monkeys charge a flock of house sparrows drinking at the edge of the water.

"If it'll make you feel any better," Victor said finally, "the cloud of suspicion over my head is a lot darker than yours."

"Yeah, but you're better paid," Chappy said, smiling weakly. "One thing. Don't make me keep this from my wife. We've been keeping each other's secrets for thirty-eight years."

Victor nodded. "Go call her. And take her someplace nice tomorrow. I'll cover for you here."

Caroline and Victor walked back toward the admin building.

"Damn it, Caroline! We'll lose financial support if we go public, and yes votes if we don't. *Entre la espada y la pared.*"

"Between—what?"

"Between the sword and the wall."

"Yup. That sums it up nicely."

Sarah's "iced tea" still roiled in Caroline's stomach. She reached into her pocket for an antacid and offered the roll to Victor. He took two.

Somewhere in the distance, firecrackers popped and a church bell rang. Inside the admin building it was quiet. The air conditioning hummed to little effect.

As they walked to their offices, Victor said, "I'm not sure how I'll handle this with the city and county."

"Maybe they'll be satisfied if you tell them a donor is at fault, not us."

He looked doubtful. "The politicians want to look tough." He walked past her toward his office, then stopped. "Maybe Szczesny can run interference. He's been loyal."

"Um, Vic. I have more to tell you." She beckoned him into her office and waited for him to sit down before she closed the door.

He looked up at the ceiling, seeking strength. "What now?"

"It's Paddy." She described his trophy collection, his hunting trip to Africa, his repeated attempts to buy Iris' farm and his veiled threats to her. Then, she told him about Sarah's fear of Paddy and her description of his "big business deal" with Tom Engelsma.

By the time she'd finished, Victor was pacing in a tight circle in front of her desk with his hands shoved deep into his pockets. "Why is it so hot in here?" he demanded. "Useless air conditioning."

"Also, I'm pretty sure Neil Stoddard is involved. You saw him at Tom's office and Iris says he came to the farm with Paddy last spring. Paddy's girlfriend—ex-girlfriend—says Neil and Paddy are on Tom's boat this weekend. Think of the money they'd make! They already have the mine. If they get this property and the farm—"

"You're talking conspiracy—you know that, don't you?" He threw up his hands and dropped them. "Unbelievable!"

"It fits, though. Tom donated the land, Paddy gave big money when neither of them had showed the slightest interest in us before. Neil has the mine property. It's a lucrative partnership."

Victor stopped pacing. "Okay, but what about the park the city's promising to build here?"

Caroline shrugged. "Maybe the CAUZ picketers are right—maybe the city won't ever build a new park here. Tom's a developer who probably has lots of useful connections at City Hall."

He looked past her into the parking lot and the tops of Iris' apple trees. He walked around her desk and slid open the window with a bang. "Jesus! It must be eighty-five in here!"

Caroline turned her chair to follow him. "The way I figure it, the only obstacle to a big, lucrative land development—"

"—is getting Iris VanWingen off her land. Yeah, I get it."

More fireworks popped and the church bell continued clanging.

"What's all that racket? It's annoying." Victor pushed his hair back and propped himself against the windowsill with his arms crossed tightly over his chest and his shoulders pulled up to his ears. "But the mine property isn't stable enough to build on."

Caroline lifted a finger. "Actually, that's not exactly true."

He sniffed. "Your boyfriend tell you that?"

Caroline pulled herself up, taking umbrage, and continued, "Neil showed me the spot where there were cave-ins decades ago. The area was filled in and the whole mine has been digitally mapped."

"And you *believe* this guy?"

"Why would he lie about *that*?" It may have been the only thing he told her that was true.

The clanging continued. It *was* annoying. She got up and stood next to Victor, hoping to catch a breeze.

"You aren't still seeing this Stoddard guy, are you?"

She didn't trust her voice. She shook her head.

"Good," he said.

There's something about that bell, she thought. She tried to separate that one noise from the traffic, a chatty flamingo, the wind in the trees and the distant buzz of a lawn mower.

Victor was saying, "—must have somebody on the Commission in their camp—some way to get the city to sell to them." He paused, then said, "Szczesny's been pushing hard for the move."

The wind died down just as a traffic light created a break in the noise. Three quick—*clang, clang, clang*—followed by three slow, *clang . . . clang . . . clang!*

Caroline gasped.

"What? You think Szczesny's involved?"

"No. No, that bell. I know it! It's on Iris' porch!" She reached for her phone and dialed Iris', asking Victor, "How long has it been ringing like that?"

Victor shrugged. "Since before we came in. Five minutes, maybe."

The call went to voice mail.

"Something's wrong. I need to go." She ran out of her office, down the hall and into the parking lot. She dialed Iris again, but there was still no answer. *Clang, clang, clang! Clang . . . clang . . . clang!* Three short, three long—the VanWingen distress call! She ran to the sidewalk.

The bell stopped.

She slowed down, remembering Iris' rule about the bell and the baby birds. Maybe Iris was away and Rafa was fooling around. She felt silly now. After the revelations of the last day, she saw danger lurking behind every bush.

Still, just to be safe. She set off at a brisk pace toward Iris', conjuring up excuses along the way. *I needed some air, so thought I'd pop over. Or, I was just delivering yard signs in the neighborhood . . .*

Ahead, she saw Rafael tear out of Iris' driveway at a sprint. When he saw Caroline he stopped, cupped his hands around his mouth and yelled something, but the words were drowned out by a passing truck. He jumped up and down, flailing his arms wildly. Then he tore back up the driveway.

She began running. When she reached the gravel, he was already out of sight. She sprinted to the top of the rise. Iris' station wagon was backed up to the porch steps with the tailgate down. Iris was on her knees on the ground.

"Iris!" Caroline screamed.

Iris rose to her knees. "Caroline! It's Zelda!"

Now she could see Zelda lying at the bottom of the porch steps on her side. Her legs pawed the air uselessly and her mouth was covered in white foam. Iris was trying to lift her into the car.

"I—I can't!" she cried, looking up at Caroline helplessly.

Caroline put a hand on Iris' shoulder. "Wait! Just wait. Let me get help." She knelt beside Iris and dialed her phone.

"Peter. It's Caroline. We need you at Willow Creek Farm! Iris' dog is having a seizure or something. Can you come? Oh, Peter! She's *really* sick!"

Zelda's eyes rolled back in her head and she vomited something orange into the grass.

Caroline nodded into the phone. "We won't . . . Okay. *Thank you, Peter!*" She locked eyes with Iris. "Our vet is coming. He says not to move her."

Iris nodded, her chin quivering. Rafael crouched next to Zelda with both hands on her flank.

"Rafa, sweetheart," Iris said, cradling Zelda's head in her lap, "run inside and get the blanket from the couch. Quick now!"

He was off like a shot.

"She got into something, Caroline. I don't know what! She was fine a while ago."

Rafael leaped off the porch with a crocheted bundle in his arms. He knelt beside Zelda and tucked it around her. His face was bright pink. Zelda gave a deep groan.

"Oh, honey girl," Iris moaned, stroking her head.

The zebra-striped van rolled to a stop a few feet from the station wagon. Peter jumped out. Caroline stood up and pulled Rafael back, hugging him tightly from behind.

Peter dropped to one knee. "How long has she been like this?"

"She started staggering around the yard about fifteen minutes ago," Iris said. "She couldn't get her balance. I was trying to get her into the car when she just collapsed. I c—couldn't lift her!" She covered her mouth with her hand. "I—I tried to call my vet, but my cell phone is dead. Then Rafa thought to ring the bell, hoping someone would come. So he decided to run to the zoo for help." She reached for Caroline's hand. "We thought you were in Chicago, *but you came*! Thank goodness, *you came!*" Her eyes were brimming with tears.

Peter was examining Zelda's mouth and opening her eyelids. He leaned close to smell the orange foam on the ground.

"What's her name?"

"Zelda."

"Okay, Miss Zelda, I'm taking you to the clinic now. Mrs. VanWingen, you can ride with me." He lifted Zelda into his arms. Caroline ran ahead to open the back of the van as Iris got into the passenger side.

Rafael stood alone, hugging the porch post, his face streaked with tears. Peter called out from the driver's seat, "I could sure use a junior zookeeper to assist me." Rafael leaped off the top step and scrambled in next to Iris.

Peter motioned to Caroline. "It looks like she ingested some kind of poison. I need you to look around for anything she might have gotten into. Think alcohol, cleaning products or suspicious garbage, especially antifreeze. Look for a jug with liquid the color of Kool-Aid—bright orange, by the looks of it. It will smell sweet. Call me with anything suspicious and bring me the container if you find it." He lowered his voice. "We need to work fast."

As the van sped toward the zoo, Caroline spun in a tight circle. Where to begin? *The house? The barn? The garden? The meadow? Antifreeze?* She remembered her parents' car dripping purple antifreeze onto the garage floor. She ran to the spot where Iris parked the station wagon. *Nothing.*

She ran into the barn. There were bags of undisturbed topsoil, cow manure and organic fertilizer. There were shelves with jars and bottles and cans of paint, all upright and out of reach. She ran into the house and searched frantically under the sinks in the kitchen and bathroom. Sponges, vinegar, unopened soap. Nothing suspicious or lying open. She searched a broom closet in a corner of the kitchen—nothing.

She raised a hand to her forehead. What was she even looking for? *Something with a skull and crossbones?*

She bolted into the yard and zigzagged around the back of the barn. She skirted the garden fence. She knelt at the compost heap and pawed through coffee grounds, melon rinds, egg shells and grass clippings.

She sat back on her heels and begged, "Oh, God! Oh God, *please*!" Her vision blurred with tears—that wouldn't help. *Okay. Stop! Just stop, Caroline. Keep it together!*

She stood up. *Iris would never leave toxic chemicals around.* But there in front of her, in Iris' garden, was the patch of dead, salt-contaminated earth. Caroline shook her head, disallowing the thought. *Iris is NOT losing her mind. She isn't!*

What was she missing? The situation called for a rational, systematic approach. She made a quarter turn and faced the street. Any of the houses there might be poison warehouses. She couldn't search them all, and besides, Zelda didn't wander. She turned again, facing away from the house toward the woods. That didn't seem a likely place for poisons. She turned again, facing the barn and caught a glimpse of something white in the tall grass. She ran toward it. Hidden by tall weeds was a slab of broken concrete that had probably been the floor of an old shed. A clear jug lay on its side with an inch of orange liquid in the bottom. The cement was still wet and tinged orange.

She picked up the jug and dialed Peter.

∽

Peter, Iris, Julie and Rafael were standing in a tight circle around a metal examining table when Caroline arrived. Zelda lay on her side on the crocheted afghan. Julie was shaving a spot on her paw while Peter prepared an IV.

"Antifreeze is a serious poison," Peter was explaining, "but you all acted quickly, so she has a good chance. You need to let Julie and me work on her now. We'll call you in a couple of hours."

"What are you going to *do* to her?" Rafael asked, his voice rising in panic.

Julie took him by the shoulders. "Rafa, Zelda needs to throw up the antifreeze in her stomach."

"Will it hurt?"

"It isn't fun, no, but she'll feel lots better after."

"Will she be hungry then?"

"Not for a while. She'll just want to sleep. We'll give her a nice soft bed. Don't worry."

Peter turned to Iris. "I'd like to keep her for a day or two. Her kidneys are my main concern. Of course, you could take her to your own vet."

"No, no, please go ahead, if it's not too much trouble."

"Trouble?" Julie chimed in. "Compared to the wild beasties we usually handle? We had to give an enema to a python this morning." She leaned close to Zelda's face and whispered. "Zelda's a cupcake."

Peter smiled. "It's no trouble."

Iris bit her lip, unable to speak. Caroline and Rafael led her to the Bat Cave to wait.

Two hours later, Julie called. "A very sweet doggy is asking to see you guys. She's weak, but awake."

Zelda was curled up in an open crate with the afghan tucked around her. She raised her head and beat her tail against the side of the crate, but didn't try to get up.

Caroline rolled a desk chair next to the crate and Iris sat down to stroke Zelda's ears and rub her belly. "S'okay, girl."

Peter appeared in the door leading to the clinic's backyard, pulling off a pair of surgical gloves. "She's comfortable now. You can stay with her until she's asleep, but then she needs to rest. Julie or I will call you if anything changes, but I really think she's through the worst of it."

Iris sighed, "I am so grateful, Doctor."

"It's Peter," he said.

"When can she come home?" Rafael asked.

"We'll see," he said.

"That means you don't want to make a promise you can't keep, right?" he said, eying Caroline.

"You are wise beyond your years, young man," Peter said.

Zelda had closed her eyes and was asleep again.

"If you're ready, Iris," Caroline said, "I'll drive you and Rafael home."

"Oh, my goodness, no," she said. "We've been sitting all day. The walk'll do us good, won't it, Rafa?"

They left with their arms around each other. Before the door closed, Caroline heard Iris say, "It's a good thing you thought to ring that bell, Rafa. You are just about the best neighbor I've ever had."

36

NOISY NEIGHBORS

Sunday, July 3

Natural Curiosity: Notes from Willow Creek Farm
Iris Van, *Saskawan Evening Star*

For the third summer, an Eastern phoebe is raising her family in a nest she built under the eaves of my porch. This little gray flycatcher isn't the least bit bothered by my slamming screen door or cars coming up my driveway. My young neighbor and I fed a pair of chickadees out of our hands a few weeks ago. Both species have little fear of humans. The same can be said for the great blue heron. These stately shore birds were a rare sight in West Michigan when I was a girl, but now we see them flying over parking lots and wading in park ponds. They seem to have made peace with the sound of planes overhead and sirens on our streets.

But most animals aren't so comfortable with our noisy ways—especially the kind of uproar we make on the Fourth of July. Our fireworks make the holiday a stressful, even dangerous, time for many animals that share our community.

Deer, rabbits, raccoons, woodchucks, foxes and many kinds of birds panic at our celebratory booms. Some run into streets in front of cars. Startled birds can even fly into the sides of buildings.

Early July is the height of the summer nesting season. Fireworks can scare birds off their nests. Foxes and raccoons may abandon their dens, leaving their babies vulnerable to predators or exposed to the elements.

Waterfowl near Riverbend Park—where the city's annual fireworks display will be held at sundown tomorrow—are at even greater risk. Ducklings can easily become separated from their parents, which is often fatal for them.

Even house pets can be sensitive to excessive noise. If you have a dog who is fearful of loud noises, for Heaven's sake, don't set off firecrackers in the yard. Keep Fido crated, if that makes him feel safer, or at the very least, keep him indoors.

Veterinarians and animal shelters dread the Fourth of July. Each year, they witness the consequences of pets who run away and are hit by cars or become lost. (Be sure your dog has tags or a microchip.) If your pet cowers at the first cherry bomb, ask your vet to prescribe a short course of anti-anxiety medication.

And remember, my fellow Saskawanians, there's a new noise ordinance in town. The use of fireworks is limited to today and tomorrow, and only between 10:00 a.m. and 10:00 p.m. This ordinance is for everyone's benefit. Police tell me they will be ticketing violators this year.

So, if you need fireworks to show your patriotism, do it safely, legally and *briefly*. Better yet, wave the flag and sing the "Star Spangled Banner" at the top of your lungs. Your animal neighbors will appreciate it.

37

THE SOURCE OF THE NILE

Iris and Rafael were waiting in the staff parking lot when Caroline arrived just before eight that Sunday morning. In the clinic, Zelda was waiting patiently in her crate.

"Good morning, my dear girl!" Iris called out from the doorway.

Zelda sat up, but the movement of her tail caused her to lose her balance and she lay down again.

"Aw, Zel. I know just how you feel," Iris said, easing into the chair next to the crate and opening the latch. Zelda leaned forward to lick Iris' hand.

Peter came out of his office and reported that Zelda had slept well. Then he asked Rafael to take Zelda on a slow walk around the fenced yard behind the clinic while Iris and Caroline watched through the window. Nose to ground, Zelda investigated the exotic scents in the yard.

"She must recognize some of the scents that come out of this place," Iris said, "but she's never gotten this close to the source. It must be like discovering the headwaters of the Nile."

But soon, the excitement was too much for her still-fragile system and she was back in her crate again, curled in her afghan and snoring softly.

Caroline walked Rafael up to Caratasca Island to help Victor complete his duties as substitute zookeeper, while Iris sat with Zelda and watched Peter and Julie at work.

Along one wall were cages and tanks of all sizes, most of them empty, but some were draped in blue fabric. A glass-front cabinet was filled with bottles and small boxes of medicines. The opposite wall had a long counter with intriguing instruments, a laptop and rows of notebooks and files. A stethoscope dangled from a cabinet handle. In the center of the room was the stainless steel table with a large lamp over it.

Peter checked clipboards, stroked his white beard and jotted notes.

Julie opened and closed cages, changing water bowls and filling food dishes with chopped fruit, vegetables or meat, depending on the occupant. Finally, Iris got up and walked slowly around the large room with her hands clasped behind her, peering into the cages and tanks. Chirping came from a cage draped with a blue sheet.

"Rocky's coming around," Julie announced. She lifted the drape slightly and motioned to Iris. "Have a look."

"Why, forever more, a flying squirrel!" A small gray squirrel with huge black eyes peered at them momentarily from inside in a wooden box filled with leaves. He was rearranging the leaves in the box.

Julie laughed. "I guess he doesn't like the nest I built for him. Sorry, dude."

"What's wrong with him?"

"Some Girl Scouts found him caught on a barbed-wire fence near Newaygo. He was really weak, but Peter stitched him up. He just needs to rehydrate and fatten up a bit."

"Then what?"

"The Scouts will release him where they found him." She made a note on a clipboard, then opened the drape. Then she lifted the cage, set it closer to the window and draped three sides. "He's nocturnal, so he'll rest better if he can see it's daytime. We keep this side of the cage draped so he can't see us and lose his fear of humans. Sweet dreams, Rocky."

Peter came in from the yard. "Would you like to meet an ornery oryx, Mrs. VanWingen?"

Iris followed Peter to a stall in the clinic yard where a large, black and tan antelope was working on a pile of fresh hay. When he saw Peter, he stomped a bandaged hoof and lowered his straight, three-foot horns.

"Ornery is right," Iris said.

"I can't blame him," Peter said. "He cracked his hoof and it got infected. We had to restrain him last week to treat him and he's holding a grudge." Peter reached over the railing and patted a flank. "I saw you stomping on that foot, old boy. Would you like to go back with your mates?"

Iris asked, "Where did he come from?"

"He was born here and thinks he owns the place, which I suppose he does. People sure don't come to the zoo to see *me*." Peter scratched the butterfly-shaped patch of white on the oryx's face. The oryx shook his equine head and backed up.

"Are oryx endangered?"

"Not his kind, but the Arabian oryx became extinct in the wild in the 1970s. Zoos around the world were able to breed a healthy herd for wild release. Several Middle Eastern countries now have protected wild herds again."

"Zoo animals released into the wild?" Iris sounded skeptical.

Peter nodded. "For me, that's the most exciting part of zoo work today."

"How often does that happen?"

"Since the eighties, more and more."

Iris wasn't sure what to make of this or of this charming Santa look-alike. She watched the antelope pull hay from the pile.

"Don't zoo bred animals become inbred?"

"They would if we didn't keep studbooks."

"Studbooks? Like, for racehorses?"

"Sort of. But for racehorses, the goal is to improve the breed and create a faster horse. Zoos use studbooks to preserve what nature created. Come on, I'll show you."

In a small office off the main room, he pulled a thick, leather-bound book off the shelf and set it on the desk.

"This is the international studbook for snow leopards. Nowadays, studbooks are kept online, but this'll give you the idea."

Iris opened the book to a photo of a spotted feline with an unusually thick tail, and feet so big they looked like fluffy bedroom slippers. "'Snow leopards,'" she read out loud, "'have been kept under human care since 1851, when the first specimen was exhibited in Antwerp.'"

Peter sat on the edge of his desk. "All the relevant data on snow leopards in accredited zoos is maintained by a guy named—" He flipped to the title page. "—Leif Blomqvist at the Helsinki Zoo. If Ridge Park tried to breed our snow leopard, we'd be in a heap of trouble with Leif." He flipped to a page of data and pointed. "This number represents our snow leopard, Dotty. It shows her sex, age, other physical characteristics and her lineage. She's got great genes, I'm proud to say."

"Have you bred her?"

"We don't have room for cubs here. She'd have to go to another zoo on loan. Of course, if we rebuild in Nord Haven, that could change. Either way, it would be up to Mr. Blomqvist."

"Would the goal be to release her cubs in the wild or increase the zoo population?"

"That depends. Breeding programs are highly controlled. If numbers in zoos are stable, breeding of a species can be stopped entirely. If an individual animal is inbred or hybridized in some way, it might be sterilized or even euthanized. Good management helps us avoid that. Someday, if there's a wild reserve that needs repopulation, Dotty's descendants might be good candidates for release. I hope so."

"What about the giraffe that was euthanized in Copenhagen in 2014? That was unfortunate."

Peter winced. "Yes and no. The Copenhagen Zoo allows its herd to reproduce at will, as they would in the wild. That's really important for social animals like giraffes, but in zoos, inbreeding can happen. Zoos trade animals to decrease the likelihood, but it still occurs sometimes. Today's zoos, like Copenhagen, give the health and viability of the species higher priority than an individual animal. So when no other zoo could take an inbred giraffe, they had little choice but to put it down. It would have put the entire herd at risk." Peter crossed his arms and sighed. "It's a harsh reality, but so is culling wild deer or Canada geese to control their numbers."

"But feeding the giraffe's carcass to the lion while the public watched? That was a poor decision."

"Agreed." After a pause, his face softened into a smile. "Our Caroline would never have allowed that."

Iris laughed. "No, I don't believe she would." She bent over the chart showing captive snow leopards. "So, when captive populations become inbred, don't zoos just go out and capture a wild specimen?"

"Very rarely, and only if it's for an individual animal's protection or for the protection of the species. In the case of the black rhino, some have been removed from the wild and taken to Australia and Florida where they can be protected from poachers. Today, it's more likely that zoos are asked to help repopulate wild populations with captive-born animals."

"Like the Arabian oryx."

"Yes. That's why we need to preserve every gene God gave them."

"But zoos have crossed lions with tigers." Iris said, still unconvinced.

"No *legitimate* zoo would do that," Peter said without defensiveness. "Genes are what make a tiger solitary and a lion social. A tiger with a social lion gene would be in big trouble in the wilds of Asia. Unfortunately, we don't have adequate laws to regulate zoos, menageries, circuses, test labs or private collectors. That's why zoos police ourselves through organizations like the AZA. Right here in Michigan, I get calls from people who want us to take their wolf-dog after it's eaten the family cat. Most end up euthanized, but some probably get dumped in the wild, which jeopardizes the entire wolf population."

Iris paused to think. "I suppose a wolf needs to be the real McCoy, not part poodle. The things we do to animals in the name of love and entertainment." Iris closed the book. "Dr. Peter. Did you know the circus used to camp right here when this land was still part of my parents' farm? My sister and I used to sit in those apple trees, or ones like them, to watch." She pointed out the window to the treetops visible above the privacy fence behind the clinic. "A family of elephants came one summer."

Peter was putting the studbook back on the shelf. "Actually, I do know that. Our elephant came from that circus."

"No, no. That was before you were even born."

Peter sat down across from her. "The way I heard it, a circus came through Saskawan just after the war with a baby elephant for sale. She went to the Detroit Zoo."

"Yes, that's right. To Detroit."

"Then, a few years later, Ridge Park bought her. Her name was Judy. She lived here until she died in the early 1960s. We have all the old rec—," Peter stopped when he saw Iris cover her mouth. "Are you all right, Mrs. VanWingen?"

"Princess." Iris whispered. "That was her name. Penelope was her mother. We were just kids, my sister Lillian and I. The night they took Princess, Penelope was inconsolable. She wouldn't get into the truck. The men. They b-beat her. My father—" Iris turned away. "It was like watching a lynching."

Peter paused for a long moment, then said gently, "Judy's life— Princesses' life— is a cautionary tale for this zoo. My predecessors here, and zoos and circuses in general—did a terrible injustice to her kind. But, I can tell you, Mrs. VanWingen, Ridge Park will *never* have another elephant, no matter where we end up."

Iris looked up at Peter and felt her chin tremble. The weight of the last twenty-four hours had made her vulnerable. She nodded, but knew better than to try to speak.

Caroline knocked on the open door. "*Here* you are! I see Zelda is still sleeping, so I was wondering, Iris, if you'd like to see a bit of the zoo? Rafa says Houdini has been asking for you."

On the highest rock of the lion exhibit, a cardboard giraffe with blue polka dots sat on its haunches. Below it, a red, white and blue striped zebra—formerly an appliance box—was grinning in the tall grass. Two very real lions, Goldwyn and Daisy, had reduced a third beast to a pile of confetti.

Donna turned away from a crowd of delighted visitors when she saw Caroline and Iris.

"Iris VanWingen, this is Donna, our large mammal keeper."

Donna extended her hand. "Nice to meet you, Mrs. VanWingen. I'm so sorry about your dog, but I hear she's going to be just fine. Peter's the best."

"Yes, he is," Iris nodded. "I'm very grateful."

A small girl in a yellow sundress and flip-flops tugged on Donna's shirt with a look of disdain, "That zebra doesn't even *look* real."

"You're right," Donna said. "It doesn't fool the lions, either, but it's a fun game for them. They're pretending to hunt and they like finding the meat hidden inside."

"Oh," she said, considering this. Then she pushed through the crowd for a better look.

A pre-teen in a Ridge Park Zoo Camp tee shirt pointed out the cardboard prey to someone in the crowd. "Me and my friend Megan painted the zebra. He's Sir Loin. We put, like, ten pounds of raw meat inside of him. Gross!"

At the outer edge of the enclosure, the newcomer, the lioness Kenya, had locked onto the meaty scent of Sir Loin. She circled her prey, then crouched in the tall grass, digging her back claws into the dirt, gaining traction. Suddenly, she shot forward, rose on her hind legs and slapped Sir Loin's square back, ripping his body from neck to flank in one fluid motion.

"Whoa!" someone said. "That cat means business!"

The crowd clapped and whistled as Kenya settled in to enjoy her boxed lunch.

Donna turned to Iris and Caroline again. "Are you taking a tour?"

"Just hitting the highlights while Zelda sleeps it off," Caroline said, casually.

Iris was still watching the lioness. "What's the purpose of hiding meat in cardboard?"

"We call this an enrichment. It provides stimulation," Donna said. "I call these Cracker Jack enrichments—a prize in every box."

Iris nodded thoughtfully.

"By the way," Donna said, "I liked your piece about fireworks and animals, Mrs. VanWingen. I hope people listen."

"Thank you. When I was writing it I wondered how zoo animals react to fireworks and other noises."

"It depends, of course. Almost all of our animals will be inside by sundown, but I heard of a giraffe once that bolted at a firecracker and broke its neck. But I also read about an orangutan who would crawl to the top of a tree to watch fireworks." Donna looked around the crowded viewing area with her hands in her pockets. "So, what do you think of Ridge Park so far?" This innocent-sounding question made Caroline squirm.

"Well, I see what you are trying to do to educate the public," Iris said, choosing her words, "but I still prefer conservation work that's done in the animal's native habitat."

Donna nodded. "I agree, that's vital. But it's not always enough."

Iris raised her chin. "How so?"

Donna frowned. "Wild habitats are being destroyed so quickly that some species literally have no safe place to live *except* in zoos and animal sanctuaries." She noticed Caroline's pained look and softened her tone. "At the risk of sounding preachy, may I give you one example?"

Iris nodded curtly.

"When the Javan tiger became endangered, the government of Java took your approach. They set aside a huge reserve in its native range, but they were never able to stop poaching and deforestation by loggers and farmers."

"So, what happened?" Iris asked.

Donna shrugged. "The Javan tiger is extinct."

"So," Iris said slowly, "you think that outcome could have been avoided if a select number of tigers—representing a diverse gene group—had been sent to zoos or sanctuaries for captive breeding. Do I have that right?" Iris met Donna's startled look with a wry smile. "That nice vet of yours has already done a bit of preaching this morning."

Donna's face broke into a wide grin. "Watch out for that Peter. He has special powers."

"I noticed." Iris nodded, still deep in thought. "But what's the point of keeping *lions* in zoos? They aren't endangered."

"Right, but that could soon change—probably in my lifetime. Meanwhile, these guys are ambassadors for their species. They show visitors in 3D what could be lost." She nodded toward the delighted crowd. "Hopefully, these lion fans won't let that happen."

Iris watched Kenya gnaw on a large bone. "Well, you've given me lots to chew on, too."

Donna touched her hat. "That's my job."

Caroline introduced Iris to Victor, who was subbing for Chappy at Caratasca Island. He wore the heavy work boots, shorts and a battered safari hat of a keeper. There was straw caught in his black and silver hair.

"Victor gave Chappy the day off," Caroline explained.

Victor arched his back and frowned. "Which seemed like a good idea at the time. I don't remember zookeeping being this strenuous." He looked behind him. "Rafa is around here somewhere. He's been a big help this morning."

Rafael came tearing up the walk. "*Miss Iris*! Did you see Houdini?"

"No. I was waiting for you to show me," she said.

He pulled her over to the railing where Iris surveyed the enclosure.

"My goodness! What a nice, big island he has. And so many monkeys! Which one is he?"

"There! That's him—the one at the top of the rope ladder. He's a really good climber. You can tell it's him by the little spot of dark fur on his forehead."

"He's grown a little, don't you think?" Iris watched for a moment, then pointed to several monkeys combing through the grass. "What are they doing?"

"I tossed raisins and nuts on the ground this morning," Rafael said. "But they find bugs, too. I saw a monarch butterfly in there this morning, but they didn't catch it. Do you think it was the same one we saw at your house?"

"Could be."

He looked up at Victor. "Miss Iris has lots of butterflies at her house. Look, Miss Iris, there's butterfly milkweed." He pointed at a plant covered with clusters of bright orange flowers just inside the railing.

Victor said, "Our landscaping volunteers are replacing our old plantings with native grasses and wildflowers."

Iris nodded her approval.

Victor turned to Caroline. "Be sure you visit our turtle project."

Behind the giant tortoise exhibit, Peter unlocked a solid wooden gate marked Private. He let Caroline and Iris step into a cement yard enclosed by a tall privacy fence. At one end, several dozen turtles were sunning themselves at the edge of a shallow cement pool with a few aquatic plants growing in submerged pots. More turtles were perched on a floating log.

"This is the best we can offer right now," Peter said, sounding apologetic. "We're really just care-taking until we can find a better facility and safe release sites."

He picked up a shiny, black turtle the size of a cereal bowl. Its shell was flecked with yellow. It paddled the air, stretched its long neck and yellow chin and blinked up at Peter.

Iris touched the turtle's snout and it retracted its head. "You're breeding them for release?" she asked.

"Exactly. Our reptile expert, Kirby, is working with Sas-U students to identify potential sites." Peter flipped the turtle over. "This one lost part of her back leg, so she won't be released, but she can breed, and we'll protect her young until they can return to the wild."

Iris scanned the yard, looking perturbed. "But Blanding's turtles need ponds for feeding as well as upland woods for nesting sites. Their needs are very specific, pretty complex and hard to replicate in a zoo."

Peter seemed to be amused by this. "True," he agreed. "And they won't breed until they are in their teens and they don't lay as many eggs as most other native turtles." He smiled at Iris. "But I suspect you know that, too."

Iris walked slowly around the yard with the air of an inspector. "A female Blanding's," she said, her voice rising, "will travel a mile to find a nest site to her liking. She'll try to cross roads and parking lots—often getting run over in the process. Even if she finds a nest site, her offspring have to migrate back to the marsh—facing the same set of hazards." She turned back to Peter, seeing his satisfied look for the first time. She laughed. "Oh my, I suspect *you* already know all this, too."

She walked back toward Caroline. "I applaud your efforts, Peter, but it's probably just a matter of time before Blanding's turtles are gone from Michigan."

Peter cocked his head. "I'm more optimistic than that. We're not draining wetlands like we used to and we're creating new ones all the time. Blanding's turtles can live to be seventy, so if we can maintain safe habitats—."

"If . . ." Iris said, raising her eyebrows.

Caroline said, "If we build a new zoo, these turtles will have a more natural pond."

"That's right," Peter said. "They'll learn to identify and hunt for their own food. It'll be sort of a turtle academy. Then, we'll release them with all the skills they need to thrive." Peter handed the turtle to Iris. "I like these guys. I think we owe them that."

Iris examined the turtle's injured stump. "Her leg seems to have healed nicely." She set the turtle gently on the ground and watched it limp steadily toward the water.

"She's slow—even by turtle standards, but she's a survivor," said Peter.

Iris and Caroline looked in on Zelda, who was still sound asleep, then they visited the aviary, where they found Matt, a ruddy-cheeked intern from Sas-U, surrounded by visitors. Howl, the nearsighted owl, was perched on his gloved hand. Caroline introduced Iris to Matt.

"Matt will be representing Ridge Park in the piping plover project up at Sleeping Bear Dunes this year."

"Really? Say more," Iris said.

"Well, they're a critically endangered shore bird of the Great Lakes," Matt said. He pulled his smart phone out of his pocket without disturbing Howl, and scrolled the screen with his thumb. "Check this out," he said, showing them a video of white, robin-sized birds with black neck bands running along a beach on stiff, yellow legs.

"They look like wind-up toys," Caroline said.

"Exactly," he said. "This will be my second year there. Last year, I roped off nest sites on the beach to keep predators out. This year, I'll get to incubate eggs and raise abandoned chicks in the lab."

He tapped the screen and showed them a picture of a dozen chicks. "Cotton balls on toothpicks."

"How do hand-raised chicks survive in the wild?" Iris asked.

"We don't handle them and they can't even see us, so they never lose their natural fear of humans. We release them to a safe beach with other chicks when they're about a month old. They hook up with their foster siblings right away. A bunch of them made it to Florida last winter."

"It sounds like a worthwhile summer project," Iris said.

Matt frowned. "Well, *I* think so. But my buddies give me a lot of crap—excuse my language—about interning at a zoo. They, like, boycott all zoos but, at the same time, they support rehab centers and animal shelters like crazy. They have no idea that zoos do a lot of the same stuff." He put his phone back in his pocket and grinned. "So when they ask, I just say I'm hangin' out with chicks at the beach all summer."

After lunch, Iris and Caroline stopped to watch the flamingos dabble in the duckweed in their cement-bottomed pond.

"I haven't had a chance to ask. How are you today, Caroline?" Iris asked.

"Trying to keep busy," Caroline said, lifting her chin in a show of resolve. "Mostly, I'm trying to blot out what's-his-name. I still have to cancel our dinner on Tuesday. If I weren't such a wimp, I'd just stand him up or confront him. But I don't have the stomach for it."

Iris shot her a look that went through Caroline like an x-ray.

"Really. I'm fine." Caroline looked away, then down at the scummy green water. "This is arguably our worst exhibit, Iris. I hate to have you even see it."

Iris looked up at the pair of shagbark hickories that shaded part of the exhibit. "This pond was once full of turtles and frogs," she said. "There were marsh marigolds and a stand of Joe Pye weed over there on the other side." Iris raised her hand in a sign of surrender. "But you know what? Back then, my dad sprayed DDT on everything, and we let the circus bring their sorry collection of animals here. There's no point getting too nostalgic."

Caroline nodded. "And your mom planted invasive yellow iris in Willow Creek."

"Only because *I* dug it up from the riverbank and brought it home to her! Good grief, do you believe I did that?"

They were both laughing when Donna walked by and pointed at her walkie-talkie. "Peter says Zelda wants to go home."

"Praise be!" Iris said, slipping her arm through Caroline's.

38

ROCKETS' RED GLARE

Monday, July 4

Zelda pushed her nose under the sheet and huffed softly. The warm form of Iris VanWingen rose and fell. Zelda raised a paw to the sofa cushion and dug at the blanket.

Iris freed one hand and patted the air until she felt fur, then opened one eye just in time to see a pink tongue make contact with the bridge of her nose. She rolled herself up and felt around on the floor for her moccasins.

"Good morning to you, too, my sweet puppy," she said.

Iris stood up slowly and pushed the pad of her thumb into the sore spot deep in her right hip joint. She thought to pull the sheets off the sofa, but decided to leave them. She'd made up the sofa to save Zelda the trip upstairs, but truth be told she was glad to save herself the climb, which was feeling like an alpine expedition lately.

She looked at the dining room clock and subtracted twenty-two minutes. It was nearly nine. The old clock had been running fast without Bill around to fiddle with it. She should just let it run down, but the steadfast tick-tick felt like the house's comforting heartbeat.

Proper clock winding was just one of a thousand topics she hadn't thought to cover with Bill before he died. Did heart disease run in his family? What part of Holland had the VanWingens come from? Which uncle had made the walnut burl nightstand?

It was the clock that brought Bill back this morning. But sometimes, it was the smell of his old cardigan as she pulled it around her shoulders or the sound of a lawn mower revving up or the scrape of a coat hanger against the rod in their bedroom closet. So many things ignited a memory—reigniting the pain.

"Oh, Bill," she exhaled into the morning air.

Zelda whined from the kitchen, starting her sideways dance toward the porch. How long had she been standing there, lost in memories?

"Coming." She reached for Bill's blue seersucker robe on the sofa arm and scuffed into the kitchen, commencing their morning ritual. Dog and dog owner going their separate ways—apple tree and bathroom. Rendezvousing at the kitchen door.

Iris started the coffee and filled Zelda's bowl with kibble. She sat down at the table and watched Zelda pick at her food without her usual gusto.

The coffeemaker wheezed, then hissed to a stop. Iris filled a thick white mug and went onto the porch.

The phoebe flew in with a bug still wriggling in its beak. In the garden, rows of lacy carrot tops were just visible. The clumps of faded irises and peonies around the porch steps needed deadheading. Another rotted shingle had slid off the barn roof and lay on the driveway next to the station wagon. She cocked her head sideways and lined up the barn corner with the porch post. Was the barn starting to lean? She sighed. She couldn't even think about it.

Zelda came close to lean against Iris' thigh. Iris wiped the sleep from the dog's eyes with the hem of her bathrobe.

"Antifreeze, Zel? *Really*. What were you thinking? I could have lost you." She touched her forehead to Zelda's and felt the dog pull side to side in sync with her tail.

"Happy Fourth of July," she said without much enthusiasm. "How about a nice holiday bath?"

Zelda backed up and dropped to her haunches.

Iris laughed softly. "No? I didn't think so."

Antifreeze. She vaguely remembered putting a jug on the shelf in the barn after the flood. But it was way out of a dog's reach and had one of those impossible childproof screw caps.

She set her mug on the porch railing and crossed the yard to the barn. She stood with her hands on her hips and took a visual inventory of the shelves. There, on the top shelf was the jug in question. Its contents were purple.

She rubbed her cheek. *Were there two before—one of them orange?* She was sure not. And besides, Caroline found it in the yard. It made no sense, but neither did the salt in the garden, her wandering watering can or the flooded barn. If *she* didn't do those things, who did? *Who would?* Of all the things she *didn't* want to contemplate right now, her own mental decline was right there at the top of the list. Then again, denial was probably the first symptom.

She moved back into the sunlit yard. The spikes of blazing star by the garden gate were going to be stunning this year—the same blue as the cloudless sky above. And the first scarlet beebalm looked like bursts of holiday fireworks.

"Let's you and I just take it easy today," she said to Zelda who, not seeing the old metal washtub, had decided it was safe to come off the porch.

How many Fourth of Julys had she spent in this yard? Running through the sprinkler with Lillian. Spitting watermelon seeds into the grass. Eating at the old picnic table under the apple tree with her parents and later with Bill and her own two girls, and then the grandkids.

Back on the porch she topped off her coffee mug and sat down to rest. Zelda nuzzled her knee.

"You sure gave me a scare yesterday, girl."

When Zelda had staggered into the garden, the memories came back—Bill stumbling out of the barn clutching his chest. When Zelda lay helpless in the zoo clinic, she saw Bill, so weak and remorseful in his hospital bed, promising her he'd exercise more and learn to like fish—*promising* to get better.

Then the alarms. Nurses pushing her aside. Doctors snapping orders. Technicians running, pushing carts. Circling the carcass. Then . . . *then*, the awful silence and the apology. "We did all we could." And the acceptance that made her so *furious*.

"*Do* something! Make him *breathe*! Don't give up on him! I w-won't have him d-die! I can't let him—!"

"I'm so sorry, Mrs. VanWingen. We did everything we could. He's gone."

The death of the elderly cardiac patient in room 602A was a bad day at work for the staff of Saskawan General Hospital. But for her, well, there were just no words.

I thought we would have more time, Bill.

There were things—so many things—she still needed to tell him.

I wasn't done with you.

A red squirrel chased a flock of morning doves from under the feeder.

Iris smiled into the distance. *You should have seen it, Bill, a monkey in our barn! And the crows, carrying on so!* She needed to tell him about that and everything that came after: *Rafa, that joyful boy, and sweet*

Caroline. I tried my best not to like her, I did, but it's no use. And the zoo! You wouldn't believe the things they're doing over there these days.

Bill had thought her opinionated. "Iris knows her own mind," he'd say, "and everyone else's, too."

I'm not closed-minded. If credible evidence presents itself, I can change my position. She could see Bill, clear as day, with his dolphin smile and one bushy eyebrow cocked at an angle, sitting in the matching porch chair. She lifted her hands and dropped them again. *Okay. I was, apparently, unaware of some of the things modern zoos are doing. See? I can admit it.*

They laughed until the mother phoebe fled the nest, making her babies squawk in protest.

Zelda barked.

"Hey, Miss Iris!" Rafael called out from across the drive. "I came to see Zelda."

Caroline slept until nine, did two loads of laundry and sorted several days' mail. The day ahead—one she'd reserved for driving home from Chicago—felt like an eighth day added to her week. She planned to do some serious relaxing and give absolutely no thought to the week's events.

A flyer pushed under her door announced a tenants' barbecue on the roof at 2:00. The management was providing hot dogs. BYOB. *Could be fun. Probably not.* She might go if Bella was going.

She turned on the TV and dusted the living room as she watched part of an infomercial for "Mimi's Sizzling Summer Fashions." For only $19.99, plus shipping, a blue and green smocked mini-sundress that looked like it was designed for a five-year-old could be hers. But wait! If she ordered in the next fifteen minutes, she'd receive a pair of metallic gladiator sandals, plus a bottle of designer suntan lo—

She switched off the TV and took her cell from its charger. One more thing needed doing. She scrolled through her contacts and found Neil's number. Since he was on a boat in Lake Michigan conspiring with his cronies—not working on his sculpture as he'd tried to make her believe—she'd be able to end this thing by digital proxy. *Nice and clean and final.*

The phone rang. *Nip it in the bud.* It rang again. *Quick 'n easy.*

"Hello?" She waited for his recorded greeting.

"Caroline! Hi! Nice to hear from you."

"Um, hi." She shut her eyes and pictured him drinking martinis and smoking cigars in a marina bar with Paddy and Tom.

"How's Chicago?" he asked.

She shook her head and squeezed her eyes shut. "I—I'm calling to cancel our dinner tomorrow."

"Oh, no! I've been looking forward to it all weekend. But that's okay. We can reschedule."

"No. We can't. I'm sorry."

"Not *ever*?" he said, laughing.

Caroline exhaled slowly. "That's—that's right."

There was a long pause. "Okay. . ." There was half a question mark at the end of this.

She listened for the sounds of a boat motor, waves, real estate fraud or criminal conspiracy going on in the background, but heard nothing.

"Do I get an explanation?" he asked.

"It's just . . . um . . . not going to work out." She hung up the phone and was alone again.

She pulled her yoga mat from under the sofa and unrolled it in the last remaining spot of morning sun. She stood in mountain pose, emptying her lungs of ragged breath, emptying her mind of poison antifreeze and poison relationships.

Inhale . . . hands to heart . . . exhale . . . concentrate on the breath . . . inhale . . . swan dive down . . . exhale . . . forward fold . . . Neil in Iris' driveway . . . inhale . . . lunge . . . tree hugs . . . Neil hugs . . . exhale . . . plank . . . inhale . . . chaturanga . . . exhale . . . "Not ever?" . . . up-dog . . . inhale . . . down-dog . . . good dog . . . Magoo dog . . . "Do I get an explanation?" . . . Exhale . . . child's pose . . . "Do I get an explanation?" . . . "Do I get an explanation?"

Inhale, inhale, inhale . . .

She had no idea how long she sobbed into her yoga mat.

She got up and washed her face, fixed a bowl of oatmeal and tried to distract herself with the TV again. The Saskawan Fourth of July Patriots' Parade was on, but the sight of a red pickup hauling a giant chicken brought tears again.

Next, she tried Deep Cleaning Therapy—pulling everything out of the refrigerator and tossing the limp lettuce and cracked cheese. But even the blue-green ends of the French bread took her back to their picnic on the hill. *Who was this Neil Stoddard?*

She punished her disobedient mind with a half hour of Sudoku, but got nowhere.

She picked up the phone again. "Iris? Hi, it's Caroline. I was just wondering how Zelda is today?"

"Caroline, I'm so glad you called."

A flag billowed festively from a porch column as Caroline drove into Iris' driveway. Rafael ran alongside the car, directing her like an over zealous traffic cop.

"Thank you, Officer Rojas," Caroline said, getting out. "And Happy Fourth of July!"

"Hey! You look like a flag, Miss Caroline," Rafael said when he saw Caroline's blue shorts, red and white striped tee shirt and blue scarf on her ponytail.

Iris stood on the porch with one hand on Zelda's collar. She wore a white apron over a white skirt and a blue and yellow flowered blouse. She wore a bit of pink lipstick and her hair was loosely piled, making her look startlingly pretty. *A classic beauty,* Caroline thought.

Caroline set a bag on the top step and took Zelda's muzzle in her hands. "*Zelda daaaaling! You look maaaaavelous!*" she said, kissing a black freckle. Then, she reached into the bag and presented a rawhide chew the size of a turkey leg. "This should keep you quiet for a while." Zelda took it in her teeth and made a beeline for her bed beside the glider.

"It's not easy with *that* one around," Iris said, eying Rafael, who was upside-down and pumping the glider to its limits. "Let's get the ice cream in the freezer. I've been waiting for you to help me move the table to the porch."

Caroline followed Iris into the kitchen. "Thanks for letting me invite myself over."

"Don't be silly. We were just about to call you, weren't we Rafa?"

"It was *my* idea!" Rafael called from the porch.

Iris whispered. "He wanted me to call 'Mr. Neil,' too."

Caroline rolled her eyes.

"Did you canceled your date yet?"

Caroline leaned against the counter. "On the phone, he was all innocence and confusion. 'Do I get an explanation?'" she mimicked. "He sounded genuinely disappointed, actually."

Iris sniffed. "Disappointed he won't have you to help soften me up."

A volley of fireworks popped somewhere in the neighborhood and was answered from another direction.

"By the way, that was a nice column yesterday, Iris. I used to have a cat that threw up all over the house for weeks after the Fourth." Caroline backed up to look through the screen door at Zelda. "She seems pretty calm."

"Peter gave her something to keep her quiet—but she's no fan of fireworks."

Rafael called from the glider. "Miss Iris, are we going to do fireworks today?"

"Baby birds, remember?"

"Oh, right. My mom doesn't like 'em either—but I do."

Caroline said, "I brought some sparklers for later. Those are fun."

He came to the kitchen to examine the box and took them outside.

Iris folded down the drop leaves on the kitchen table and said in a low voice, "I was sitting on the porch—feeling at loose ends, to be honest—when Rafael showed up. He said his mom had the day off and was cleaning the house. I couldn't stand the idea of them having no place to go on the Fourth of July. It's un-American, don't you think? Anyway, I sent him home to invite her over. He is really glad you're here—I am, too."

"Thanks, Iris."

They slid the table through the door and onto the porch. Rafael was lying on the glider, waving an unlit sparkler. "I'm practicing writing my name," he said.

"Mrs. Rojas is bringing a dish. What's it called, Rafa?"

Rafael made a face. "*Curtido*."

"What's that?" Caroline asked.

He shrugged, stabbing the air like a fencer. "I don't know. Leaves. If you never ate it, you're lucky." Rafael rolled off the glider to the floor and crawled toward Zelda who had worked one end of the rawhide to a white gum.

"Well, I can't *wait* to try it," Caroline said.

"Hey, Snicklefritz," Iris said, "Why don't you run home and walk your mom over."

"She knows how to get here."

Iris looked down at Rafael with her hands on her hips. "Still, it would be *nice* if you would walk her. Skedaddle. Now, please."

Rafael hauled himself slowly to his feet.

"Thank you, kind sir," she said, giving his neck a squeeze.

Caroline arranged four chairs around the table. Iris handed her a tray with a red and white checked tablecloth, silverware and glasses and a pair of clippers.

"Maybe you can find some flowers for the table," Iris asked.

Caroline selected red beebalm, blue bellflowers and some early white daisies. She inhaled their scent but also smelled something less fragrant. That stink again. The flag on the porch was blowing inward—*toward* the zoo, not from it, she noted. She wanted to point this out to her hostess, but decided not to dampen the festive mood.

She put the flowers in a glass vase in the middle of the table. She stood at the open door and watched Iris bustle around the kitchen.

"You must have made a lot of picnics in this kitchen."

Iris was opening a package of hot dogs. "I wish I still had the old picnic table out under the apple tree." She disappeared into the dining room and raised her voice to compensate. "It rotted, and I haven't replaced it." She reappeared at the door with four navy and white bandanna handkerchiefs trimmed with white rickrack. She handed them to Caroline. "My mother and I made these years and years ago."

"Perfect," Caroline said, going back to the porch. She arranged them on the checked tablecloth and stepped back. "Eat your heart out, Martha Stewart."

Iris looked through the screen. "There'll be no room for the food, but who cares," she said lightly.

Caroline came into the kitchen again, smiling.

Iris caught the look. "What?"

"Oh, nothing. It's just that this is turning out to be a good day, after all."

Iris wiped her hands on her apron. "Let's go sit for a few minutes." They came out to the porch. Iris took her chair; Caroline, the glider.

"I've had a thought," she said.

"A *thought*? About what?"

"That Blanding's turtle project and that really god-awful enclosure you've got them in. What if you moved them here, to my pond? Just until you find something permanent. They could winter here, too, if need be. You could fence off an area along the back."

Caroline grinned at Iris just long enough to create awkwardness. This was a turning point—a victory that would be unwise to make too much of. (Turning cartwheels, she decided, was probably a bad idea.)

"That's a really generous offer, Iris. I'll talk to Victor tomorrow."

"Ah! Our guests have arrived."

Rafael and his mother were walking toward them from the footpath.

Mrs. Rojas carried a heavy bowl glazed in royal blue, yellow and orange, covered in foil. She wore a loose fitting white blouse with embroidered red flowers and a flowing blue skirt with red and yellow trim. Rafael was holding a fistful of sky-blue flowers and looking decidedly peeved. He had changed from his tee shirt and shorts into a white button-up shirt and pressed black pants. His long bangs were wet and combed to one side. Caroline imagined the wardrobe battle that must have raged just moments before.

"Bellflowers, how lovely!" Iris said, taking the bouquet. "Mrs. Rojas, you remember Caroline Finch from the zoo?" She put a hand on Rafael's shoulder. "It's your job to translate today, remember?"

Rafael rolled his eyes at the ignorance of these monoglot adults.

"Translators get seconds on ice cream," Caroline said with a wink.

Mrs. Rojas spoke. "Please, I am Josseline. I speak a little English. I bring *curtido*. Is from El Salvador."

Iris took the bowl and motioned for Josseline to sit on the glider while she and Rafael went into the kitchen. "You look very handsome today, Rafa," Caroline heard her say. Caroline added the flowers to the centerpiece and sat down next to Josseline.

"It's a beautiful day. Yes?" Caroline said.

"Very beautiful." Josseline motioned toward the yard. "All is beautiful here."

Staccato pops in the distance made Josseline cover her ears. "Oh, no! Very loud! No sleep."

Caroline nodded. "Yes, it will be loud all day and all night." She glanced down at Zelda who had fallen asleep with one paw protecting her rawhide. "How long have you lived here, in the United States?"

"Ten years and one half. When I come I was—," she patted her stomach, "Rafael?"

"Pregnant?"

"Jes. My husband, he live here, but he family is Salvadoran. He come to my village. We marry, but he die in fighting there."

"I'm so sorry," Caroline said softly, wishing she could say more.

Josseline lowered her dark eyes, but when she raised them again, she was smiling. "My mother say, 'Go! Go to America.'" She made a sweeping, theatrical gesture with her arms. "'Have *America* baby!'"

Rafael and Iris joined them on the porch. Josseline spoke quickly in Spanish, nodding at Rafael to translate.

"She said we lived with my dad's mother here in Saskawan," Rafael said, watching his mother, "but then my grandma, she died. My mom, she cleaned hotel rooms and saved all her money for our house. Sometimes, she didn't even eat."

Josseline touched his arm and shook her head.

"She didn't say the part about not eating," he said, "but it's true. I remember. She made *pupusas* to sell to the other ladies who cleaned. She made *lots* of money."

Josseline laughed and shook her head again. "No, just, how you say? Enough."

"What are *Pupusas*?" Caroline asked.

"Um, like, sandwiches," Rafael said, without prompting. "The other ladies at work bought them. My mom is the boss of all the cleaners now. It's her new job."

"What a nice American success story to hear on the Fourth of July," Caroline said. "Your mother is an *independent* woman, Rafa. Independent on Independence Day."

Before he could translate, Josseline nodded. "Yes. Thank you." Then she spoke to Rafael in Spanish.

"She wants to know if you'd like to see pictures of El Salvador. I can go home and get them."

"We'd love that," Iris said, pouring the iced tea at the table. "Let's eat first, then you can run home. Everybody grab a plate and come to the kitchen."

The food was arranged along the kitchen counter—hot dogs in toasted buns, corn on the cob, blueberries in honeyed yogurt, watermelon slices, potato salad, baked beans and the *curtido* dish. Rafael held his plate steady as his mother spooned food onto his plate and then hers. Caroline and Iris followed. They each found a place at the table.

"*Delicioso*," Josseline said, taking a second bite of her hot dog.

"Delicious," Rafael corrected.

"Don't be such a stickler," Iris said.

Rafael was about to ask what a stickler was when Iris cut him off. "This meal's nothing fancy. A real patriot would grill the hot dogs, but that was always my husband's job."

Caroline tasted a forkful of the *curtido*. "Oh my goodness. It's like coleslaw. Perfect for a Fourth of July picnic, *y muy delicioso!*"

As they ate, the phoebe babies could be heard demanding their dinner. Zelda woke up, brought her rawhide over and crawled under the table.

"Rafa, have you told your mother how you helped Zelda?" Caroline asked.

Rafael rolled his eyes, embarrassed by the attention.

"Did you tell her about the bell?" Iris asked.

Rafael mumbled something to his hot dog.

Josseline frowned, putting her hand under Rafael's chin, "Rafa?"

Rafael groaned.

Caroline looked at Iris, "I guess the grown-ups will get ice cream seconds."

"Yum," Iris said, winking at Caroline.

"O-kay," he said, trading pride for sweets.

He spoke quietly in Spanish, pointing to Zelda, the bell, the driveway and the zoo. Judging by her look of surprise, Josseline had not heard the entire story. She drew a deep worried breath, stroked Zelda's head and said something to her son that probably meant, "So, what, it never occurred to you to *tell* me about this?"

"We are very proud of your son," Caroline said slowly, making sure Rafael translated. "He's been a big help at the zoo, too."

He mumbled a Spanish translation. Josseline brightened and laid one hand over her heart and the other on Rafael's shoulder. "Thank you for tell me."

Rafael slid off his chair onto the porch floor, covering his ears. "ARRAGH! I'm tired of talking!"

"Rafa!" Josseline grabbed his ankle and yanked, making everyone laugh.

Finally, he stood up. "I told my mom about the baby phoebes. Can she see them? I don't know if we have phoebes in El Salvador, so I just called them phoebes."

Rafael dragged his chair to the corner where Josseline climbed up and stood tiptoe on the railing to see into the nest. She gasped in delight, "*Los bebés son lindos!*"

"She says the babies are cute." Rafael translated.

A string of firecrackers popped like machine guns behind one of the neighboring houses. Josseline yelped and dropped onto the porch floor in a crouch.

"Sorry," she whispered, covering her mouth with her hands. "I so nervous."

Rafael helped her back to the table.

"Loud noises make my mom remember the fighting at home when my dad got killed."

"Of course," Iris poured her another glass of iced tea. "We understand."

Caroline patted Josseline's shoulder. "We do." She felt embarrassed and frustrated by the inadequacy of her words.

Zelda had crawled closer to Iris' leg with her tail tucked between her legs.

"I think Zelda's a little nervous, too," Rafael said. "Can I throw her ball?"

Iris stroked Zelda's ear. "Not today, but you could take her for a nice stroll to your house to get those pictures."

"Okay." He leaped off the top step. "Come on, Zelda."

Iris called after him, "I said, a *stroll*."

He turned back to look at her. "What's a stroll?"

"A *slow* walk," Caroline said.

"Rafa, *la llave*," Josseline said, holding up a key.

Rafael walked toward them with exaggerated, stiff-legged slowness. "I . . . am . . . strol . . . ling . . . *Es . . . toy . . . camin . . . ando . . . lenta . . . mente.*"

The women broke into laughter.

When Zelda and Rafael disappeared into the arch of trees, the women began clearing the table, scraping plates and taking care of leftovers in the efficient, unspoken language of women.

Finally, Iris untied her apron and announced it was time for a walk. "Rafael and Zelda will find us."

In the vegetable garden, Josseline pointed at the rows and said slowly, "Tomatoes. Carrots. Squash. Right?" She asked for the English names of chard and kale.

In the barn, Josseline climbed the ladder to look into the loft, her colorful skirt billowing like holiday bunting in the breeze. *She's so young,* Caroline thought, *probably barely in her thirties and already a widow.*

When Iris took Josseline's arm to lead her into Bill's meadow Caroline felt a prick of jealousy, followed by deep shame. These women were both widows, while *she* was merely a poor judge of character.

At the pond, they shared a bench and watched a dragonfly cruise the lily pads. Josseline ran her hand over the lettering and sounded out, "Wee-lee-um Van Win-jen?"

Caroline pointed to Iris. "*Esposo.*"

KA-BOOOOM!

A thunderous clap shook the ground and ricocheted off every surface.

Josseline crumpled to the ground. "*Oh, Dios mio!*"

Caroline and Iris leapt to their feet.

"*What* was that?" Iris said, searching the sky.

Caroline expected to see a ball of fire or a mushroom cloud rising over the trees. "Sounds like somebody's stash of fireworks went up all at once."

Josseline was crouched in a tight ball, covered her ears.

Caroline wrapped an arm around her shoulder and pulled her up. "It's okay. Just big fireworks."

"Rafa!" Josseline cried out.

Iris motioned toward the house. "Let's go back. *Mi casa.* Such a loud holiday. Boom! Boom! Don't worry," she said, laughing lightly.

With Josseline between them, the three women walked back to the house. The yard was quiet. Caroline sat Josseline on the glider while Iris went to the kitchen. Josseline kept her eye on the footpath across the driveway. Iris returned with an uncorked bottle of pinot grigio and three stemmed glasses. Iris cocked her head toward the footpath and shot Caroline a look.

Caroline rubbed her bare arms and said, "I'm going to get my shirt out of the car. I'll just be a minute." She walked to the far side of her car, leaned into the back seat and dialed her phone. "Hey, Victor. Happy Fourth."

"You, too."

"Everything okay over there?" she asked.

"Packed in like sardines, but fine. Why?"

"Didn't you hear that blast just now? Like fireworks, but a lot louder."

"Maybe. The air conditioning is loud in here though. I heard some of the staff talking about hearing something on their walkie-talkies. Probably fireworks. Why? Are you *here*?"

"No, I'm at Iris'. It was *really* loud over here. I just wanted to make sure Caratasca Island didn't erupt or something." She laughed nonchalantly.

"It's not raining monkeys, if that's what you mean."

"Okay. Never mind. See you tomorrow. I have some *good* news, for a change," she said, thinking of the turtle project. "I'll explain then."

She grabbed a white, long-sleeved shirt from the back seat and walked toward the porch. There was that odor again, and it was really strong. Iris must have noticed it, too, but was on her best behavior.

At the bottom of the steps, Caroline gestured over her shoulder. "I think I'll just go meet Rafa and Zelda. I'll be right back." She smiled reassuringly at Josseline, who was perched on the edge of the glider.

Caroline tied her shirt around her waist and started down the path at a brisk, but casual, pace. When she glanced over her shoulder, Josseline was watching her.

39

WHERE THERE'S SMOKE

As soon as she was out of sight, Caroline broke into a run, scanning the woods and backyards as she passed. A small dog yelped from somewhere nearby, a chainsaw revved, a lawn mower hummed, but the woods were quiet.

The smell was strong. *Ammonia?* Caroline thought as she ran. Ahead, a gray haze was visible now, appearing and dissipating in the shifting breeze. She tore around the last curtain of vegetation and saw the Rojas' house standing peacefully, exactly as it should be.

"Rafa? Zelda?" she called out. She crossed the backyard, expecting to see him watching TV or playing a video game in the living room. She knocked on the sliding door and cupped her hands to peer in, but the house was locked. A dog barked somewhere. It could have been Zelda, but she wasn't sure.

She called their names again, louder. It was not time to panic. She ran to the front of the house and scanned the street for Rafa, evidence of an explosion, a crowd of onlookers or fire trucks. Nothing. The air reeked, but she couldn't see an obvious source. She ran into the backyard again. The wind died down and she saw that the haze was heavier inside the mine fence. Pushing aside the undergrowth, she made her way along the outside of fence toward the gate, thinking, *Please, dear God, don't let it be unlocked.*

But it *was* unlocked. Unlocked and standing open. Her chest tightened painfully. She heard barking again.

"Zelda!" she called. She rushed through the gate, bolted to the top of the valley rim and came to a dead stop. Below, a cloud of ugly, yellow-gray smoke hung over the forest floor. She moved downhill until she could see where smoke was billowing out of the ground.

Caroline's throat and eyes began to sting. She untied her shirt from her waist and covered her nose and mouth as she made her way past the big beech tree toward the source of the smoke, screaming for Rafael, over and over. The only reply was her heart hammering against her ribcage.

The wind shifted then and pushed the smoke away from her. She wiped her smarting eyes and saw that the leaf litter had given way to bare ground. She was standing on the edge of a blast crater.

Suddenly, Zelda was there, whirling in circles and barking frantically. Caroline grabbed her collar as smoke re-enveloped them. She stumbled back up the hill, still shouting for Rafael.

Just above the big beech tree, she dropped to her knees and dialed her phone.

A woman's voice answered, "911. What's your emergency?"

"There's been an explosion! At—at the gypsum, um, Stoddard Cold Storage—the old gypsum mine by the Ridge! A little boy—" her voice broke, "I can't find him! He m-might be inside the mine. It's burning! I think he's hurt!"

"There's a boy *inside* the mine and it's burning?"

"I—I think he fell in. Oh please, just send somebody. Please, hurry!"

"Okay. I'm sending someone now. I see your location, but I don't see an access road. Can you direct the fire department there?"

"I—I don't know." Caroline put a hand to her forehead and looked around. She didn't know the address of the Rojas' house or how to direct the rescuers to the gate hidden by thick undergrowth. "Um. They should—they should come to the mine entrance, I think, past some old equipment. There's a trail up the hill. I'm sorry. I don't know this area very well."

"Okay. Now, you need to move to a safe place. Can you stay on the line?"

"No. Sorry. I need to call someone." She hung up. What if she'd given all the wrong information? She wasn't even sure where the overlook with its switchback trail was from here. She got to her feet and found her call log. She heard it ring three times . . . four . . . five. *Pick up! Pick up, please. Damn you!*

"Caroline?"

"Neil! There's been an explosion in the mine! I think Rafael might be in there. I called 911, but I don't know if they can find us, or how they can even get in the gate at the entrance. I didn't know what to tell them!"

"Wait. An explosion? Rafael? *Where?*"

"The old sinkhole, I think. Below the big beech tree. *What should*

I do?"

"Okay. Stay there. I'll open the gate and come to you."

"You're *here*? *At the mine*? *Now*? I thought..." Her voice was shrill. "Thank God! Come quick! I don't see Rafa *anywhere*!" She felt her teeth begin to chatter. "Hurry, Neil!"

She could hear him running, panting into the phone. "I'm opening the gate. I hear sirens. I'm on my way to you."

She hung up, clasped the phone to her chest and fell to her knees again.

"RAFA! RAFA!" she screamed until her voice cracked. Zelda panted, looking ready to collapse.

She dialed her phone again. "Victor. It's me. Don't talk. J-just listen. There's been an explosion at the mine with a lot of smoke and fumes. Rafa is m-missing and might be hurt. I've already called 911, but I need you to go to I-Iris' house." She struggled to get the words out. "Rafa's mother is there. She speaks very little English, so tell her help is coming. Bring her to the mine gate behind her house—she knows where it is—but don't let her anywhere near the crater."

"On my way," he said.

Her mouth was completely dry. She imagined Rafael buried alive, or worse, somewhere below her. She buried her face in Zelda's fur and prayed.

She pulled the scarf from her ponytail and tied it to Zelda's collar, making a short leash. They traced a circle around the crater, stopping and starting to stay upwind of the fumes. Dirt and exposed roots were strewn with broken glass, shredded or melted plastic and blackened containers. A charred frying pan and the leg of a table or chair were tossed to one side. A propane tank, like ones she'd seen on barbecue grills, lay on its side with a ragged hole blasted through it.

Zelda tugged on the scarf, leading Caroline toward several charred two-by-fours sticking out of the ground at odd angles and half hidden by a pile of brush below the crater. When she got closer, she saw a gaping, black void about two feet across which looked to be a crude tunnel. The hole belched gray smoke intermittently. All around it were fresh footprints, including Zelda's. She couldn't tell if any were Rafael's. She dropped to her knees and crawled toward the opening. Zelda barked excitedly. Caroline covered her nose with her shirt and squinted into the abyss.

"Rafael? *Rafael*!" She saw nothing but blackness. She heard nothing but silence.

Zelda barked again, but this time, she was looking behind them, toward the overlook. Neil was sprinting toward them. He was covered in white dust and wore safety glasses. A dust mask and set of ear protectors flopped loosely at his neck.

"Neil!" she yelled. "Here! Hurry!"

At the edge of the debris field, Neil scrambled toward her.

"Is Rafael *in* there?" he asked.

"I don't know! I found Zelda here. He *has* to be, Neil! What should we do?"

His chest heaved as he crawled closer to the hole. "Move back, Caroline! This whole area could cave!" Then, he pulled the dust mask over his face and tossed a set of keys at Caroline's feet. "I need you to go into the mine and unlock the wood door at the bottom of this shaft. Remember where I found that pop bottle?"

She nodded.

"Go back down the hill and find the door off the parking lot. Remember? It has a touchpad lock. The combination is 57273. 5-7-2-7-3," he repeated more slowly. He pivoted feet-first toward the hole. "Once you're inside, go in a few hundred feet to the wooden door on-the right in the main shaft. Use the skeleton key to open that door. Do you understand?" He crawled backwards toward the hole.

She nodded again. "5-7-2-7-3! 57273! *Okay.* Be careful, Neil."

Caroline watched in horror as he dropped into the void and disappeared.

"*Neil*!" she screamed as she crawled forward on her elbows and knees, still holding Zelda with her scarf. "Neil! Can you hear me? *Answer me*!"

She heard a muffled, "I'm fine. *Go!*"

The sirens were close now. She started toward the overlook, but heard a scream above her.

"RAFA!"

Just inside the gate, Josseline was doubled over, struggling against Victor's firm grip. "*Mi hijo! Rafael!*"

More figures appeared behind Victor, one by one, silhouetted against the afternoon sky. Chappy, Donna, Julie, Kirby, Gwen and Peter. The instant they spotted her, they began stampeding down the hill.

Her people had come, she thought. They had come for Rafael and for her! They had *all* come.

Kirby stared into the crater as the color drained from his face. "Is Rafael *in* there?"

"I don't know!" Caroline was fighting tears now.

Peter reached for Zelda and led her away from the fumes.

Chappy shouted to be heard above the sirens on the street below. "Tell us what to do, Caroline."

"Neil—the mine owner, went in there to look for Rafa. Go down and meet the firefighters and bring them here. I'm going in to open the door to this shaft." She held up the keys.

Julie caught Caroline by the wrist. "NO! You *can't* go in there!"

"Julie. I *have* to get them out."

Donna drew Julie back. "Go, Caroline! We got this."

Caroline sprinted through the woods toward the overlook, chanting *57273, 57273* in rhythm with her footsteps.

The first firefighters reached the overlook and were fanning out, looking for the source of the smoke.

"There!" Caroline shouted, pointing toward the crater. Behind her, she saw Kirby hoist a coil of rope onto his shoulder. Julie, Peter and Donna were taking shovels and axes from the firefighters and leading them back toward the crater. She heard Gwen bark, "Of course I can carry that, you idiot!"

At the overlook, Caroline began an awkward, sideways gallop down the steep grade, cutting across the tight switchbacks, grabbing at trees and branches to remain upright.

"5-7-2-7-3," she repeated.

When she reached the bottom, there were so many rescue vehicles that she had to push through brambles and climb over the bones of Dino to get to the parking lot. Next to a hook and ladder truck, a female firefighter in full gear was unloading more shovels and axes.

Caroline called to her without breaking stride, "I'm going to open the mineshaft. Follow me in." *5-7-2-7-3*. She came to a stop at the door with the keypad. *5-7-2-7-3*.

"Ma'am?" the firefighter called out. "Ma'am, stop! You can't go in there!"

Caroline's right index finger jerked uncontrollably over the first key. She grabbed her wrist and cursed. Finally, she made contact with the five, then pressed *7273* in quick succession. She heard a click. She was in!

The garage was dark and strangely quiet. The air was clear. She felt the wall for a light switch. Nothing. In the dimness she saw the golf cart parked where Neil had left it. She calculated the speed of driving versus running, then pictured Rafael and Neil overcome with fumes or burned. She slid into the cart.

The firefighter stood in the doorway now. "Did you hear me? Stop right there!"

Caroline felt for a key on the steering column. *Damn!* She felt along the dashboard and found it. She turned the key as she called over her shoulder, "I know where they are! Follow me!" She pressed the accelerator and lurched forward to the second garage door blocking the way into the main shaft. How had Neil opened it? She closed her eyes and pictured him driving, stopping, reaching—up. *The visor!*

"Ma'am! Stop!"

She found the opener and pushed the button hard. *Open! Open, damn it!* Metal clanked against metal as the door inched up. *Come on!*

"Stop right there," a male voice said behind her. "There are fumes in there."

Caroline hit the accelerator and plunged through the opening. "Follow me!" she yelled, hoping firefighters didn't carry handcuffs.

The sound of hurried footsteps and unintelligible shouts receded as she drove into a wall of cold air. Miraculously, the air was still clear. Her relief evaporated when she realized that the long string of ceiling lights were off—and she had no idea how to turn them on. The light from the open doorway illuminated the shaft for a few yards, but soon the darkness was so dense it felt solid. She patted the dashboard searching for headlights but found none. She felt under the seat for the flashlight she remembered Neil using, but couldn't find that, either. She felt a sharp jolt as the cart bumped the wall on the left side. She corrected and hit the right side. Her heart sank. *I can't do this!*

She knew the entrance to the old shaft was in the right wall, but she couldn't remember how far in—"a few hundred feet," Neil had said, or did he say 'yards?' Without light, she'd have to inch along and find it by feel, but she couldn't reach the right wall from the driver's seat.

She glanced back toward the receding, pale gray rectangle of light coming from the open door. Why weren't the firefighters following her?

She shouted into the darkness. "Neil! Rafael!"

Silence. She felt blindfolded and claustrophobic. The front fender scraped the right wall again. She corrected until she scraped the left wall. She heard the cart hum, but had no idea how fast she was going or where she was. She heard herself whimper.

"*Neil! Rafa!*" Her shrill voice bounced back, mocking her. Desperation was turning to hysteria. They were probably dead by now, and it was *her* fault!

She braked and got out of the cart, moving by feel until she touched the right-hand wall. Then, with one hand on the gypsum and her other gripping the keys, she began running blindly in the direction of the old door. She heard the slap-slap of her shoes hitting concrete, but she had no sensation of forward movement.

Her shin hit something hard, pitching her forward onto her elbows and stomach. She heard the keys skid away from her across the floor. She was sprawled across a pile of loose lumber. She came to her knees and crawled forward, sweeping the floor for the keys. Pain overtook fear and she was suddenly terribly, horribly angry.

Shouts came from behind—faint, but getting stronger.

"Here! Hurry up!" she barked. A spot of light danced on the ceiling. *Flashlights!*

Light flashed off the keys. She pounced on them and got to her feet. Metal clanked against metal in sync with approaching footsteps. Four firefighters in gas masks and bouncing headlamps approached, carrying shovels, bolt cutters, axes, oxygen tanks and other equipment she couldn't name.

The smallest, she guessed, was the woman she'd seen in the parking lot. She thrust a gas mask at Caroline and said in a muffled voice, "Put this on and leave, *now!*"

"No!" Caroline said. "A man and a boy are in there and I know where they are and I have a key."

The firefighter reached for the keys with her gloved hand, but Caroline pulled them back. "Shine your lights that way," she ordered. "Look for a wooden door on this side."

Firm hands spun her around. The gas mask came down over her head and straps cinched it tight. The shrunken world of the mineshaft shrank even further. She heard her own smothered, Darth Vader breathing. Her first rational instinct—to take a deep breath—filled her lungs with the stench of rubber. Panic hit like a tsunami. She clawed at the straps, but as she struggled, she imagined Rafael and Neil on the other side of the locked door, gasping for air, waiting for her to rescue them.

Her fingers clamped down on the keys. She would *not* lose it! *Not here, not now.*

The crew was searching the shaft in both directions. Caroline got back into the cart and moved it forward. Ahead about twenty yards, a light beam caught the timber above the door.

"There!" she shouted as loud as she could. She sped toward it.

From the other side she heard a muffled, "Caroline!"

"Neil! I'm here!"

The firefighters stepped back to let her through.

She pushed the skeleton key into the lock. This time, her hands were rock steady. She turned the key, heard the bolt give way, and pushed the door hard. Gray smoke drifted into the main shaft. Neil was on the floor, slumped against the wall, breathing into his tee shirt. Rafael was on his lap wearing Neil's dust mask.

Caroline dropped to her knees. "Are you okay? Is Rafa okay?"

Two firefighters pushed past and ran up the sandy incline. One asked, "Is anyone else in there?"

Neil shook his head and pointed up the shaft. "There's an escape tunnel. The boy fell into it." He listed to one side, and began coughing.

Several more firefighters had reached the door. "How far in?" one of them asked.

"Fif-fifty yards," Neil said, almost choking. "Drug lab. Careful."

Caroline felt Rafael's cheeks and searched Neil's face for clues.

Neil rolled his head against the wall and closed his eyes. Rafa was conscious, but barely. Even in the dim light, she could see Neil's lips were gray. His eyelids fluttered as he fought to stay conscious. "His ankle is broken, I think."

"Can you turn the cart around?" a firefighter asked.

Caroline got back into the cart and managed a three-point turn that took way too long. Neil was on his feet, leaning on the female firefighter. She helped him into the cart and put Rafael on his lap. Then she hooked both of them to oxygen tanks. She spoke into her radio but only static came back. She turned to Caroline. "Find ambulances outside and get them both to the ER. Tell them we may be dealing with a meth lab. *Go!*"

Rafael moaned, "Zel-da," but didn't open his eyes.

Caroline patted his knee and said through her gas mask, "Zelda's fine, Rafa. She's with Mr. Chappy and your mom. You're going to be okay, kiddo."

"My leg. *Hurts*," he groaned.

"I know. We're going to get you help." Caroline drove at top speed toward the blessed, shimmering beacon ahead—the light at the end of the tunnel.

The parking lot was ablaze with sunshine, shouting firefighters and flashing lights. She sped forward until a tangle of fire hoses blocked their way.

"Help! Over here!" Her shouts were muffled by her gas mask. She waved her arms over her head, "Help! Over here!"

Several uniformed paramedics and firefighters stopped what they were doing and turned, not knowing what to make of a golf cart, a woman in a gas mask, a sleeping man covered in white dust and small boy rolling into the middle of their emergency.

Two paramedics ran forward. "Were you in the mine?" one asked Caroline, lifting Rafael off Neil's lap.

"*They* were—Neil Stoddard and Rafael Rojas," Caroline said, clawing at the strap of her mask. "Get this off me!" The EMT removed the mask and Caroline wolfed several large gulps of sweet air before saying, "He may have a broken ankle and they both inhaled fumes. There may be a drug lab in there, too!"

A firefighter spoke into his radio. "We got the boy, and a man and a woman, too. Looks like we got ourselves a meth lab. Careful up there. Out."

A paramedic whose badge read Renee leaned over Neil. "Can you walk, sir?"

Neil rose slowly to his feet, staggered to one side and caught himself on the golf cart.

Renee lowered Neil to a stretcher. "Can you tell me how long you were in the mine?"

He didn't answer.

"Ten, maybe fifteen minutes," Caroline called out.

Renee knelt in the gravel. "Can you hear me, Neil?" His eyelids fluttered open and closed again.

Renee adjusted Neil's oxygen mask and laid the tank between his knees.

"Will he be all right?"

"If I have anything to say about it." Renee smiled reassuringly and popped the stretcher to its full height. "Don't worry." Then she pushed him quickly toward the gaping rear doors of an awaiting ambulance.

Caroline dialed her phone as she stepped over hoses, around puddles and dodged firefighters and paramedics. "Victor, we've got Rafa! He's okay. He's okay! He may have inhaled fumes and hurt his ankle, but he was asking about Zelda. That's a good sign. They're taking him to the hospital now. Take Josseline there."

A second paramedic was bending over Rafael inside a second ambulance. "If you want to ride along, get in now," he said looking up. Caroline climbed in and sat facing him, with Rafael in between. His badge read Steve.

She pushed Rafael's bangs off his forehead and his eyes opened. "We're taking you to the hospital now, sweetie. Your mom will be there."

He pushed out his lower lip and started to cry. "She'll—she'll be so *mad* at me!" he sobbed. "She t-told me not to go into those woods, but I heard a boom and the gate was open and I—I thought Mr. N-Neil might be h-hurt. Then I f-fell and couldn't get *out*."

She squeezed his hand. "Shh. Shh. Your mom is going to be *so* happy to see you, Rafa. She'll forget all about being mad."

Steve was putting a pressure cuff on Rafael's other arm. "I'm just going to squeeze your arm, kiddo. This won't hurt." He smiled as he pumped the bulb. "So, tell me, was it really smoky and stinky where you fell in?"

Rafael's eyes were enormous now. He nodded. "At first. But the floor was, like, a hill," Rafael said, showing the steep incline with his free hand. "I went away from the smoke. I had to crawl because my ankle was hurting me."

"That was a pretty smart thing to do," Steve said, writing on his clipboard and nodding at Caroline.

When Rafael closed his eyes again, Caroline slid to the back of the compartment to look out the rear door. They were just loading Neil into the other ambulance. His eyes were closed. She had never longed to be in two places at once more than she did at that moment, but someone slammed the rear doors shut and both ambulances rolled forward.

"Can you spell your names for me?" Steve asked, eying her closely.

She spelled them slowly, feeling all her emotions catching up and threatening to overtake her.

"And how are *you* feeling, Caroline Finch?" he asked.

"Fine." She bit her lip and blinked hard.

"Were you inside the mine?"

"No. I mean, yes, but not near the fumes really. Well hardly."

"Are your eyes smarting?"

"A little." She looked from Steve to Rafael and back to Steve and felt her chin quiver. "How is he?"

Steve nodded. "Pretty good, considering." He handed her a Kleenex. "There'll be a lot of questions at the hospital. If you need to, now would be a good time to let 'er rip."

Caroline shook her head. "I'm fine, but can you call the other ambulance? I want to know how Neil Stoddard is doing."

"Sure," he said, "after we take care of you." He reached for a red oxygen tank, lifted it over Rafael and set it between Caroline's knees. He handed her the clear plastic face mask. "Put this on."

"I'm fine. I don't need it."

"Ms. Finch. In this rig they call me King Steve, Emperor Steve or the Big Steve. Take your pick. If you don't do what I say, things could get ugly." He was smiling, holding out the mask to her.

"But I—I just need to know how, um, the other patient is doing!" Her voice rose.

"Sure. So how about *you* put this on, while *I* check on your friend. Deal?"

She stretched the elastic band over her head and inhaled. Was Neil her friend? That was the question.

"Wilson!" Steve called to the driver. "Radio Renee. Find out for Caroline how her guy is doing over there."

Caroline wondered whether "her guy" meant Renee's or hers.

The radio crackled. Wilson called over his shoulder. "Coming around, but nauseous."

Steve smiled. "Looks like you can ask him yourself in a few minutes."

Caroline smiled weakly and looked down at Rafael who was watching Steve with red-rimmed eyes. "Close your eyes, sweetie," she said. "I'll wake you when we get there."

Five minutes later, the two ambulances arrived at the ER.

She squeezed Rafael's hand. "Your mom is on her way. I'm going to check on Mr. Neil, but I'll be *right* back, promise." Caroline ran to the other vehicle and watched the legs of Neil's gurney snap into place on the pavement.

"Neil!" she called out. She reached for his shoulder and ran alongside as they pushed him toward the doors. "Thank you, Neil. It was so brave what you did."

He shook his head and squeezed his eyes shut. "No. I'm—sorry," he said under the mask. The wide doors of the ER slid shut behind him.

She caught up with Rafael's gurney, which was now surrounded by nurses and doctors in pastel scrubs. Steve was reciting Rafael's vitals to a zaftig nurse with black, penciled-on eyebrows who was shaking her head. "*Another* meth lab?" When she saw Caroline, she swung around."You the mother of this kid?"

Caroline's eyes widened. "No! He fell into the meth lab *after* it exploded!" She knew immediately how ludicrous that sounded.

The nurse jerked her head toward the waiting area. "Wait out there."

Caroline snapped back, "I'm *not* leaving until his mother gets here!"

"Miss Caroline?" Rafael's hand waved limply.

"I'm *here*, sweetie." She took his hand as he tried to sit up.

"Take it easy, champ," one of the doctors said.

The two gurneys with full entourages rolled along the corridor like macabre parade floats. At a desk marked Intake, Pencil Brows summoned a security guard. "We need SPD and protective services on this as soon as the mom arrives." Then she mouthed, "Meth lab," and waddled off.

Caroline followed Rafael into a trauma bay and stood with her back to a blue curtain to watch the spectacle in disbelief.

"Are you the one who brought him in, miss?" the doctor asked.

"Yes," Caroline answered, stepping forward.

A nurse started to cut through the leg of Rafael's pants.

"No! These are my Sunday pants!" Rafael wailed. "My mom's gonna be mad at you!"

"It's okay, Rafa," Caroline said. "They don't want to hurt your ankle. Your mom *won't* be mad."

They wrapped him in a sheet as he coughed and cried out in pain.

"Were you in the lab with him?" someone asked. Pencil Brows was back.

"No!" she said, too defensively. "He lives nearby and I was there, visiting a friend. We all heard the blast. He was just being a curious little boy when the ground gave way. I went to look for him." She glared at the nurse in disbelief, feeling like Alice who had just walked through the looking glass. "None of us knew there was a meth lab."

The doctor probed Rafael's ankle, causing him to yelp in pain.

"Rafa!" Josseline ran toward the sound of her son's voice. Her face was streaked with tears. Victor and Iris were right behind her.

"Mamá!" Rafael cried out.

She reached his side and kissed his cheeks and forehead, touching his face and chest. Examining every inch of him with her eyes. *"¿Estás herido?"*

"¡Me duele el tobillo!" he said, looking at his leg.

Iris stood to the side with her hands crossed on her chest. When she saw Caroline, she spread her arms and Caroline fell into them.

"Thank God you went looking for him!" Iris said. "He could've—oh! Thank God!"

"I think he's going to be fine now." Caroline held Iris tightly.

Victor addressed the doctor. "Doctor, this is Rafael's mother, Mrs. Josseline Rojas. She speaks Spanish. Please tell her how her son is doing. I will translate."

The doctor nodded. "Mrs. Rojas, your son may have a broken ankle." He spoke slowly, leaving time for Victor to interpret. "If he was exposed to chemical fumes, he also needs to decontaminate, which is basically a nice, long shower." The doctor's manner was calm and reassuring. He smiled down at Rafael. "You're lucky they didn't give you a cold shower with the fire hose. Now, do you think you can put up with that ankle for a few minutes more? I'll put an air cast on it, but I'd like you to have that shower before we take you for an x-ray."

Rafael looked at his mom, who listened to Victor's translation and nodded.

Caroline watched Pencil Brows march off to sit in judgment on other patients.

A much more pleasant white-haired nurse—Patricia, according to her badge—lowered Rafael into a wheelchair and pushed him toward a back hallway, beckoning Josseline to follow.

Victor blew out a long breath and gave Caroline a haggard look. "So *this* is how you spend your days off." Then, he wrapped one arm around her and squeezed. "Nice work, Finch."

Somehow, Caroline managed not to dissolve into tears.

Iris nudged her gently. "Come on, let's get *you* looked at."

"Me?" Caroline asked. "I'm *fine*."

Both of them were looking at her shin, which she realized for the first time, was crusted with blood from her knee to her ankle.

"Oh, I guess I fell," she said with a shrug. Her belly flop in the mineshaft seemed to have happened in a galaxy far, far away. "I can't even feel it." She touched the purple and black gash and winced. "Ow!"

Nurse Patricia appeared with a bowl of water and a bottle of antiseptic and, after washing the wound and wrapping it in a bandage, she sent Caroline to the waiting area.

Caroline collapsed into a chair between Iris and Victor.

"A *meth* lab?" she said. "Can you *believe* it, Iris? *That* was what we kept smelling."

Iris nodded. "Anhydrous ammonia. Nasty stuff. Very hydroscopic."

Caroline looked at her sideways, "'Hydro'— what?"

"It pulls water from wherever it can get it—eyes, lungs, and skin. Meth cooks use it to extract methamphetamine from ephedrine. They probably stored it in a propane tank, which corroded the fittings and caused it to explode."

Caroline remembered the burst tank. "*How* did you know that?"

Iris rolled her eyes. "Forty years of teaching chemistry."

"Caroline Finch?"

They looked up to see a police officer towering above them.

"Yes?"

"I'm Officer Flood, SPD. I'd like to get a statement from you about the explosion. Follow me, please."

40

A PERSON OF INTEREST

Officer Michael Flood escorted Caroline to a windowless room with a long table and several chairs, probably reserved for interrogating child abusers and wife beaters, or informing people that their loved one was DOA.

He gestured toward a plastic chair and adjusted his heavy equipment belt before sitting down across from her. He looked to be no more than thirty—tall, handsome and African-American. He took out a small recording device and set it in the middle of the table.

He asked for her name, contact information and why she was on the mine property at approximately 6:10 p.m. on July the fourth.

She told him everything she could think of about the explosion. He jotted notes with a stubby, orange pencil on a pocket-sized notepad. She told him about Rafael's role at the zoo, how he must have heard the blast, found the gate open, got too close to the crater and fell in.

"How did you come to have keys to the mine?"

She explained her brief acquaintance with the mine's owner, Neil Stoddard, their tour of the mine four days before and Neil's mad dash up the hill to rescue Rafael.

As she talked, Officer Flood had no visible reaction. The recorder seemed to be doing most of the listening.

When she finished, she folded her hands in her lap and waited for him to dismiss her. This was probably just a formality. Any minute now, he would thank her for her quick thinking and escort her back to the waiting room.

Instead he said, "When did you learn about the meth lab?"

"When Mr. Stoddard told the firefighters, after he rescued Rafael."

"How long has the lab been in the mine?"

She cocked her head. "I have no idea. Like I said, I just learned about it, maybe an hour ago."

"But you mentioned a tour of the mine last—" he looked down at his notes and continued, "—Thursday evening. Did you enter the lab then?" He was looking at her like a cat looks at a chipmunk cornered in the garage.

Caroline recalled the inky darkness of the old side shaft and Neil leaving her there to retrieve the empty Pepsi bottle. "The meth lab was at the end of the abandoned shaft. We didn't go that far in." For some reason she left out the part about Neil going further up the incline.

"Then how did you know to go there today?"

Caroline shifted in the hard chair and reassessed her situation. When had her "statement" become an interrogation? She felt something uncomfortable happening in the vicinity of her stomach.

"As I said before, he gave me a tour of the mine last Thursday. I saw where the old mineshaft was, but the meth lab wasn't on the tour." She realized that sounded snippy and added, "We didn't go near the meth lab."

"How long have you known Mr. Stoddard?"

"Just a couple of weeks."

"How well would you say you know him?"

She thought about their picnic, their long kisses, his lies and then, just now, his cryptic but incriminating apology. She looked down at her hands and felt her eyes well up.

"Not very well at all."

"How did you come to have a key to the meth lab?"

The officer wasn't looking at her.

Caroline pushed her hair off her face. Her ponytail was a dirty tangle and she could feel foreign objects projecting from it. She sighed in frustration. "It wasn't a key to the *meth lab*! It was a key to an old mineshaft which I found out *just today* contained a meth lab which, as I *keep saying*, I didn't know was even *there*!" She tried swallowing, but her mouth felt stuffed with sawdust.

"Why did Mr. Stoddard have a key to the meth lab?"

"Because he *owns* it! I mean, the keys were to the *mine* he owns." Her voice rose until she sounded like she'd been inhaling helium.

"But *you* didn't know about the lab. Is that your statement?" The way he said it made it sound implausible.

She searched his face. He was putting together the facts she'd given him into a completely distorted picture. Did he *honestly* think she and Neil were making meth in the gypsum mine? She would kill for a glass of water. Wasn't hydration a right of the accused—like a phone call or an attorney? *An attorney!* Should she shut up and call her lawyer? *Did he handle drug cases or just divorces?*

The whole thing felt like a scene from some cheesy TV crime show. It was impossible to believe this was real and happening to *her*, Sunny Finch, prim little kiss-ass Miss Congeniality, of Evanston, Illinois. The room was shimmering. She could hear the blood forcing its way through her temples. She wanted to fling something.

Her arms began to itch and she realized they were covered with scratches from her run down the hill. Her face was probably bloody, too. She must look like one of those meth-head mug shots.

She thought of Iris and Bella and how indignant and forceful they'd be in her situation. *They wouldn't allow this overgrown kid to intimidate them.* She cleared her throat and sat up straighter. She leaned forward, eyeballing her nemesis.

"Officer Flood, once again, I did *not* know there was a meth lab in the mine. I simply went to investigate an explosion and the disappearance of a very sweet little boy. I knew there was an abandoned section of the mine because the owner gave me a tour last Thursday and showed me the old mineshaft. But it was dark and we went out again in about three minutes. I had *no* idea there was a meth lab at the far end."

"Three minutes." He wrote that down and looked up again. "What happened during that three minutes?" He touched the pencil to his mouth and sat back.

The guy was unbelievable! She half-turned away from him and crossed her legs and arms. He was trying to trip her up. Now, she was going to have to account for exactly three minutes—one hundred and eighty seconds.

She took the offensive. She was no patsy. She spoke directly to him as if he were a child who had not been paying attention. "On Thursday evening, the door to the shaft had been left unlocked. Neil seemed concerned."

"Concerned? How so?"

She shrugged. "The way you would be if someone had been in a section of your mine that was supposed to be locked." She felt her forehead bead up with guilty sweat. She should have said "surprised," not "concerned."

"Perhaps his 'concern,' as you put it, Ms. Finch, was that the meth cookers had been careless about locking up after themselves? Could that be what 'concerned' Mr. Stoddard?"

"No, that wasn't it. It's just that he saw an empty pop bottle a little ways up in the shaft. I got the impression he was surprised, or thought it was odd to find it in a shaft that had been abandoned and locked for years. They'd been having work done to convert the mine into a storage facility. He said it was probably some of the workers nosing around."

He wrote something down again. The air seemed to have been sucked from the room.

"Wouldn't he also be 'concerned' if one of his meth cookers had gotten careless, leaving equipment—like pop containers—lying around and leaving the doors unlocked?"

She looked at the ceiling, trying not to gasp for air like a beached fish. She felt like she was inside her gas mask again. Was she hyperventilating? She'd never hyperventilated before. The room was sweltering. She glared at Officer Flood. He was very muscular. She tried picturing him naked, but it didn't help.

"Did you know two-liter bottles are often used to store chemicals used for cooking meth, Ms. Finch?"

"Why would I know that?" she snapped.

"You mentioned 'they.' Are there other people who work at the mine?"

"I'm not sure. Just a cousin—David—David Stoddard. That's all I know."

"Do you know why Neil Stoddard was at the mine today, on a holiday?"

"He told me he planned to work on a piece of art in his studio all weekend." That was technically true. There was no reason to bring up Tom's boat and their fishing weekend. Had Neil returned early? Had he gone at all?

Officer Flood said, "If he was in his art studio, as you say, when the explosion occurred—why didn't he call 911? He must have heard the blast."

Caroline thought about this. "I don't know. Maybe he just thought it was fireworks. Maybe he was working with power tools—He's a sculptor—and didn't hear. He is covered in white dust. You can see for yourself."

Yes, that was it! Neil was also wearing a dust mask and goggles when she saw him. *He couldn't have been out fishing with Paddy and Tom. He's innocent!* Caroline sat up straighter. *But Iris saw him with Paddy and*

Victor saw him at Tom's office. Maybe Neil wasn't a meth cooker, but he still could be conspiring with Tom and Paddy. She slumped back into her chair again and rubbed her eyes.

"—Ms. Finch?" He was waiting for her to speak.

"Sorry? What was the question?"

"Are you sure the white powder you saw on him was dust from his studio?"

She cocked her head quizzically. "I—I don't understand."

"Have you ever seen someone after a meth lab explodes, Ms. Finch? They're often covered in ash."

The subject was unresponsive.

"So, is it possible that Neil, the sculptor—the one you say you hardly know—runs a meth lab out of his mine? Do you think that's possible?"

If her lawyer were in the room, he would have said, "You are badgering my client. This interview is over."

She gripped the table and leaned forward to show she wasn't afraid of young, up-start Officer Flood, but also because she was shaking so violently that she needed the support.

"It's possible," she said slowly, angrily, "that 'on the side' Neil is undercover for the CIA or part of a terrorist cell—but I very much doubt it, Officer Flood. You wanted to know my opinion, and I'm *telling* you, I don't think he knew about the meth lab before today—when he went in and risked his *life* to rescue a little boy who could have died! If I were you, I'd be focusing on that tunnel coming out of the lab. The real meth cookers probably used it to escape after the explosion. They're probably just some *random* drug dealers who found the old shaft and figured it would be the perfect place to hide a meth lab. They probably cut through the fence somewhere and Neil never even knew about it."

She sat back and crossed her arms. He obviously hadn't thought of *that* scenario. She waited for him write it down. She was quite sure, in fact, that she'd just cracked the case wide open with powers of deduction superior to those of Officer Smugface.

She tapped the tabletop with her index finger. "That escape tunnel is how Neil got in to rescue Rafael. He didn't even know it was there until *I* showed it to him. That man deserves a medal!"

Officer Flood looked at her without the proper deference or gratitude.

She nodded toward his pad of paper. "You should be writing this down!"

He set his pencil on the table with a look that said, *Make me.*

"Thank you for your time, Ms. Finch. We're done for the time being, unless you have anything else to add."

"Yes. I would like to restate my belief that Neil Stoddard is not a meth lab... operator or cooker or whatever you call those people." But of all the things she had said in this interview, that was the one thing she wasn't absolutely sure of.

Flood looked unmoved—the way, she supposed, you would look when you're lied to on a daily basis.

He clicked off his recorder and rose to his feet, hiking up his heavy belt that had dragged his pants down. She wondered if he had had plumber's butt the whole time they'd been talking. The mental picture (and possibly some residual fume exposure) made her unaccountably giddy. His belt held a gun and holster, a flashlight-slash-skull-crusher, a can that was probably pepper spray and a radio or maybe a Taser—she wasn't sure which. *Inspector Gadget.* A leather pouch was the perfect size for a donut, but she thought better of asking. He hiked up his pants a second time. That was one advantage female officers had—hips to hold their pants up—although it was never a good look, fashionwise.

She felt lightheaded.

He was looking at her oddly. "I said, you can go now, Ms. Finch."

"Oh."

"But I wouldn't leave town any time soon."

Suddenly, her green and pink bedroom in Evanston, with its heated backyard pool and leftover barbecue and potato salad tugged like a powerful magnet. She was supposed to be there now, fending off the unwanted-but-flattering advances of the horny Mr. Scheffler Jr. But, then Rafael might still be lying at the bottom of an exploded mineshaft. The thought sickened her.

He pushed his card across the table. "Call me if you think of anything later."

Officer Michael Flood, Saskawan Police Department, she read. She reached for her non-existent purse to offer her non-existent business card—a nice, civilized gesture between well-respected members of the community. Instead, she sat there looking for all the world like just another poor sod brought down by addiction. Her fall from grace had taken just under two hours. When she stood up, her kneecaps were twitching.

She made it to a bathroom just in time to vomit into one of the toilets. At the mirror, she discovered what guilt incarnate looked like. Her face was crosshatched with raised scratches and purple welts. Dirt smudged her chin and forehead. Stick-tights clung to her shirtfront. Somehow she'd smeared blood from her leg onto her upper lip and under her eye. She worked on the burrs in her hair but gave up. She washed her face with dispenser soap and paper towels before going back to the waiting area.

Chappy had joined Victor and Iris. Caroline described her police "statement" and somehow managed not to burst into tears of outraged humiliation.

Chappy gave her a bear hug and Iris looked ready to turn Officer Flood over her knee. Victor did everything short of beating his chest, but ended up giving her the name of a defense attorney.

"Thanks, guys, but I don't think he seriously thinks I knew about the lab. He was just trying to scare the truth out of me. And by golly, it worked. Have you heard anything new about Rafael or Neil?"

Iris said Rafael had a broken ankle and they were keeping him overnight for observation.

"And Neil?"

Iris dropped her eyes. Victor shot Chappy a meaningful look.

"What?" she asked.

"The police have been talking to him," Chappy said.

Iris bit her lip. "It looks like he was involved. I'm so sorry, Caroline."

Later, when Chappy and Victor got up to stretch their legs, Caroline turned to Iris. "You don't know how much I want that *not* to be true."

"Yes," Iris said, reaching for her hand. "Yes, honey, I think I do."

Over the next several hours, Chappy and Caroline convinced Victor to go home. It had been a long, exhausting weekend without a break for him.

Caroline tried several times to see Neil, but officers said they were still "taking his statement." Did they think she and Neil might compare stories?

Caroline tracked down Nurse Patricia and made sure she knew of Neil's bravery before she asked, "Can you tell me how he's doing?"

"Mr. Stoddard will be fine. We're keeping him on oxygen for now. He's conscious and sitting up. Try back tomorrow." Then she added, "I might be able to give him a message, but I can't promise."

"Thank you. Please, tell him . . . " *Tell him what? I hope you're not a meth dealer or a corrupt land developer?* "Um, just tell him that Caroline sends her gratitude."

By ten o'clock, Rafael had a cast on his ankle and had settled in on the pediatric floor. After the painkillers kicked in, he wolfed down a hamburger, fries, red Jell-O and chocolate pudding as if it were five-star room service. Josseline plumped his pillows and rubbed his back when he coughed. Caroline and Iris promised him a double ice cream cone and sparklers as soon as he got out of the hospital. Chappy brought him balloons, a book of word puzzles and a pencil with a plastic lizard on the end.

"They didn't have any monkey pencils in the hospital gift shop," he said. "Can you *believe* that?"

A nursed rolled in a cot for Josseline, and Chappy announced he was taking Caroline and Iris home.

In Iris' driveway, Caroline went from Chappy's car to her own as Iris trudged up the steps to let Zelda out.

There may have been fireworks that night in Saskawan, Michigan, but they were not seen or heard by Caroline Finch, Iris VanWingen, Rafael or Josseline Rojas or any number of Ridge Park Zoo employees.

41

AFTERMATH

Tuesday, July 5

When Caroline opened her eyes again it was light out, but it took several seconds to sort her nightmares from a reality that was more horrifying. Her whole body resisted movement. She quite literally stumbled into the shower.

Still wrapped in a towel, she checked her messages. Victor ordered her to stay home. Bella said she "saw the news," and "What-the-hell? Call me, eh?" Derrick from WSAS-TV wanted a statement. Her parents had heard the news, too.

She called her parents to tell them she was all right. She apologized again for canceling her visit and promised to come home soon. (She didn't mention Officer Flood's warning about not leaving town.)

She woke up her laptop and played the evening newscast from the night before.

"*Good evening, West Michigan. Happy Fourth of July to you. At the top of the news, a ten-year-old boy is lucky to be alive this evening after tumbling into a burning mineshaft late this afternoon at the old Stoddard Gypsum Mine in the city's Ridge neighborhood. The explosion and fire started in an illegal methamphetamine lab operating in the mine. Though the blast was heard miles away, most people dismissed it as holiday fireworks. The boy, Rafael Rojas, told police he went to investigate the explosion behind his home on Russet Ridge Drive when the ground gave way. The mine's owner, Cornelius Jan Stoddard, is being hailed by some as a hero for rescuing the boy, but Saskawan police say he is a person of interest in the case.*

"*Stoddard and young Rafael are being treated for smoke inhalation and chemical exposure at Saskawan General Hospital. The boy also suffered a broken ankle. Both are in good condition this evening. Some viewers may remember Rafael as the boy who helped capture a monkey, now known as Little Houdini, who escaped from Ridge Park Zoo just last month. Police are still investigating the meth lab and plan to formally charge Stoddard as soon as he is released from the hospital."*

Her first thought was how much Neil would hate that they'd mispronounced his middle name. Her second was to call Derrick at WSAS. She got his voice mail.

"Derrick? Caroline Finch. Cornelius Stoddard isn't the only owner of that mine. You should check up on the cousin, David Stoddard. He's the one in charge. And one more thing, his middle name is pronounced 'Yon.'" She hung up.

She found her navy shorts on the floor by her bed and dug Officer Flood's card out of the pocket. She left him a similar message.

She unwrapped her bandaged shin, which had become a many-colored thing overnight—and hurt like hell. No Sizzling Summer Sundresses for her. Painfully, she pulled on a pair of loose-fitting khakis and a long-sleeved linen blouse that covered the welts on her arms. She dabbed foundation over the scratches on her cheek, then she called Bella and left a message promising gallons of juicy details—*later.*

A few minutes later she parked in the garage under the hospital. Upstairs, she found Rafael and Josseline in the physical therapy room, where Rafael was test-driving a pair of crutches on a set of wooden steps. His ankle was in a white plaster cast—*hydrated calcium sulfate*—she couldn't help thinking.

"Miss Caroline, look what I can do!" he said, pitching forward.

"Slow down," said the therapist. "Let's not break the other ankle."

"*Stroll.* Remember?" Caroline laughed. "May I sign your cast?"

The therapist called for a break and found a felt-tipped marker. Caroline drew a cartoon of a frowning Little Houdini with a thought balloon saying, "Boo-hoo! Miss yoo at the zoo!"

Rafael clapped his hand over his forehead. "Oh no! I'm missing my zoo day, but I'll be there Thursday."

Josseline shook her head. "No, Rafa."

Caroline patted his knee. "You stay home and let that bone heal for a while."

Josseline walked Caroline toward the elevator. "I cannot speak what is here," she said, pressing her hand to her heart. "Thank you is not—enough big."

Caroline knew how alone Josseline was in this world. "I'm happy Rafa is okay. When can he go home?"

"Today! Iris come. She drive us home."

"Wonderful. I'll come to see him soon."

Caroline turned to leave when she felt Josseline's hand on her wrist.

"The man? Your friend. He is okay?"

Caroline shook her head. "I don't know."

"You like him, yes?"

"I don't know."

Josseline searched Caroline's face. "We say, *Mejor solo que mal acompañado*. Better—How you say? —alone—

"—than with the wrong person." This time she nodded. "I'll keep that in mind." She hugged Josseline and continued down the hall.

At a desk labeled Information, she asked for the room number of Neil Stoddard. The nurse behind the desk was wearing V-neck scrubs printed with dozens of spouting blue whales. She tapped her computer keys, paused, frowned and then with unnecessary coldness, informed Caroline that she had no information.

"But he came in through the ER last night," Caroline protested. "Has he been released?"

"As I said, I don't have any information."

Caroline leaned closer. "Is that because you don't *have* any, or because you won't tell me what you see there on your screen?"

The nurse folded her hands on the desk. "I can't help you."

Caroline wanted to grab her by the whales and shake her. "Thanks a lot!" she said, dripping sarcasm. "And by the way, that's a *whale* of an ensemble you're wearing."

In the elevator, she assaulted the innocent down button with her index finger. The doors started to close, then opened again.

Nurse Patricia stepped in. "Good morning. How's our boy?"

"Going home. Thanks for asking." Then, she sighed. "Um, I know I shouldn't ask, but I'm looking for the man who rescued him. They won't even tell me if he's still *here*."

The nurse wrestled with some decision, then said, "It's because he's under police guard. I'm sorry."

Caroline backed up, leaning against the back of the elevator, feeling utterly defeated. "I need to thank him. It would just take a minute."

The elevator stopped on the second floor and the doors opened. Patricia stepped out, catching the door just before it closed.

"Act like you know where you're going and don't make eye contact with the nurses. Look for a police officer outside the room, but be careful." Then, she reached in, pressed the button for the third floor and let the doors slide shut.

The corpulent copper guarding room 357 appeared exceedingly bored. Caroline wondered how many innocent bystanders he had shot to land such a plum assignment. She walked casually past him and ducked into an empty room. She watched until he got up to study a diabetes poster on the bulletin board. Then she walked silently down the hall and slipped into Neil's room.

His eyes were closed and he had an oxygen tube in his nose. One wrist was handcuffed to the bed rail.

"Neil?" she whispered.

His eyes blinked open.

She reached for him, but pulled her hand back. "It's me," she said.

His eyes closed again.

"Oh, Neil, are you okay?"

He rolled his head away.

"The meth lab—" she said. She couldn't make her voice form the question.

He swallowed with difficulty and pushed the words out in a husky whisper, "I—I didn't—"

"Hey! How'd you get in here?" The officer grabbed her upper arm and began pulling her backwards.

"Okay. Okay. I'm leaving!" She watched Neil struggle to sit up before starting to cough uncontrollably. His shoulders shook, but his eyes followed her as the officer propelled her out of the room.

Neil's pleading expression matched her own exactly.

By the time she reached the underground parking garage, she felt sick again. *What was Neil about to say? That he didn't know about the lab, or he didn't mean for Rafa to get hurt in the meth lab he was running?*

She longed for the good old days, when Neil was merely a white-collar conspirator on a dodgy land deal. What was she supposed to think of a guy who quite possibly cooked meth in the morning then risked his own life to save a child the same afternoon? Anyway, she was over him. At least, she *wanted* to be over him. She was *ready* to be over him.

But what if she had everything wrong?

He was in his art studio when she called, not on Tom's boat. What if he was there all weekend, just like he said he would be? And if he was, how could he be involved with Paddy? What if he was innocent?

But why hadn't he called 911 after the explosion? Was he hiding something?

How could a man handcuffed to a bed for a drug offense be so utterly lovable? Imperfection was one thing, but *this*?

She dropped her forehead to the steering wheel and wept.

Most of the zoo staff was in the Bat Cave when Caroline arrived. The TV was on with the sound turned down, just as it had been the day almost a month ago when Little Houdini escaped.

A huge, half-eaten box of donuts sat in the middle of the table.

"Hey look! Caroline's here!" Julie jumped to her feet starting applause that was quickly picked up by everyone in the room.

Caroline beamed. "Thanks, you guys."

"We didn't expect to see you today," Kirby said, one cheek puffed out with donut—powered sugar, judging by the front of his shirt. He pulled her into a tight hug and kissed the top of her head.

Peter pulled out a chair for her. Julie set a hot mug of zoo brew and a donut in front of her and touched her hand to a welt on Caroline's cheek. "Are you okay? Those scratches look nasty. Did you breathe in any of the meth fumes? You didn't get high did you?"

Caroline laughed. "I'm fine. I took a shortcut through flesh-eating brambles at the bottom of the hill."

Donna slid a bright blue envelope and a pen across the table. "We got a card for Rafa." When Caroline reached for it, Donna grabbed her wrist. "We're all *so* relieved you and Rafael are okay."

The room was silent as everyone imagined a very different outcome to yesterday's drama.

Caroline felt yet another flush of emotion. "You were all *amazing* yesterday. Charging down that hill. You looked like the cavalry coming to the rescue." She bit her lip. "I've never seen a more welcome or heroic sight."

Kirby slapped the table. "Weel, shit! When they make the movie, Clint Eastwood can play me."

Chappy laughed, "I don't think *I* was much help, really. After running all that way, I was so winded I had nothing left to offer the firemen."

Kirby said, "Gwen looked like Little Houdini, standin' next to those Amazonian firewomen."

Gwen tipped back her chair and scowled. "You shoulda seen Kirb wrestling with that coil of rope. If it'd been Monty, the python, he'd a been *lunch*."

Caroline laughed. "I mean it. You guys are the best!"

"Back at cha, Caro," Kirby said, lifting his mug in a toast.

Peter nodded. "Going into that mine took some guts."

Caroline shook her head. "Neil Stoddard's the real hero."

She saw Julie shoot a look at Peter as an awkward silence fell over the room.

Finally, Gwen said, "The news is on. Everybody pipe down." She turned up the volume.

The WSAS Morning Report opened with a shot of the mine parking lot full of emergency vehicles.

"Good morning, West Michigan. I'm Lauren DeHaan. We have new developments to report in yesterday's explosion in a meth lab at the Stoddard Gypsum Mine. Derrick Wolcott is live at police headquarters. Derrick?"

"Thanks, Lauren. We've just learned that two men have been arrested in connection with that explosion at the old plaster mine. One of the suspects, who has not been named, sought treatment for burns to his hands and arms at a Muskegon med center. Authorities had asked the medical community to report any suspicious burn injuries. Of course, the frequency of fireworks-related burns during the holiday made this more difficult.

"SPD is also holding one of the mine owners, Cornelius 'Neil' Stoddard, who they say was in the meth lab when it exploded."

Caroline shot to her feet. "That's not true!"

"Stoddard, who is also a professor at Saskawan State University, was treated for respiratory distress. Firefighters said Stoddard risked his own life by rescuing young Rafael Rojas. The ten-year-old, who lives near the mine, apparently fell into a hole at the blast site. By the way, Lauren, the boy is fine and suffered only a broken ankle.

"Stoddard will be released from the hospital into police custody later today. In a statement from his attorney, Stoddard said he had no prior knowledge of the meth lab and was elsewhere on the property when the explosion occurred. However, firefighters say he was in the lab when they found him. A spokesperson for Saskawan University says the school has

put the popular geology professor on administrative leave pending a full investigation.

"Just as background, Lauren, the mine ceased operations several years ago, then reopened last year as a cold storage facility. Police speculate that this business venture was failing and Stoddard was shoring it up with profits from the illegal drug lab—"

Caroline ran to her office and shut the door. *Where was Neil when the meth lab exploded? That was the question. Could he have escaped the explosion only to reappear just in time to play the hero?*

She had always been a trusting person, but she knew there were coaches, priests, doctors and kindergarten teachers who cheated on their taxes, robbed banks, molested children and cooked meth in their garages. It wasn't impossible that Neil was leading a desperate double life to save the family business. *Not impossible at all.*

Had she conjured up this miner-runner-geologist-professor-sculptor to be the man she wanted him to be—just as she'd done with her promising doctor-husband for far too long? She spun in her chair to look out her window.

When Neil ran toward her up the hill, was he covered with plaster dust or meth ash? She was the only one who saw him before he dropped into that god-awful hole. He hadn't hesitated or thought of his own safety. Was that because he knew exactly what was in that shaft? If he wasn't on Tom's boat, what *was* he doing all weekend?

She heard a soft knock on her door.

"Come in," she said.

It was Chappy.

"You have feelings for this guy they've arrested, Neil Stoddard?" He searched her face for clues. She turned away. "Because if you do, it sure sounds like he could use a friend right now."

Any response was stuck behind the lump in her throat.

Caroline reached into the back seat of her Fiesta and shook the shirt she'd worn yesterday. Neil's keys jingled in the breast pocket. She drove to Iris'. The station wagon was gone. Iris was probably picking up Rafael and Josseline at the hospital.

She parked under the apple tree and walked briskly down the footpath. When she got to the mine fence, she pushed through the undergrowth behind Rafael's house until she came to the mine gate. She tried one key, then another and another, until she found one that fit the padlock. She pushed the gate open and locked it behind her.

She had not intended to stop at the crater. She wanted to hurry by. Not even look. But now, she stood in the path, paralyzed by the sight of a bowl of churned up, brown earth with its gaping, black vortex.

On a childhood trip to the Indiana Dunes, she had watched a hungry ant lion at work. It dug a pit in the loose sand and buried itself at the bottom. An unsuspecting ant walked into the crater, but when it tried to climb out, the sand gave way. As the ant became more and more frantic, clawing the sides, it only sank deeper into the pit. Finally it was pulled under—into the ant lion's waiting jaws.

She felt strangely winded. She grabbed the nearest tree. Sweat ran into her eyes seconds before her brain identified her *stone cold fear*. This place would be the setting of her nightmares for years to come, but at this moment she could not take her eyes from it.

Yellow police tape ringed the crater. The whole area had been trampled by the firefighters. Charred debris was piled to one side. She wondered if any of it would end up as "Exhibit A" at Neil's trial.

One thing caught her eye because it wasn't black or melted—a pair of bright blue ear protectors that Neil had been wearing around his neck as he ran toward her from the overlook. *That's why he didn't hear the blast or called 911*, she thought.

She heaved a sigh as she hurried along the old service road where she and Neil had hiked with Rafael, putting a tick mark in her mental "Innocent" column. She continued on toward the overlook and the valley of ferns where they had kissed. The city was laid out below, static and unaltered.

At her feet, the ferns lay torn and trampled. She started down the hill, trying to shake off feelings of violation.

At the bottom, she skirted the brambles and the rusty hulk of Dino. The parking lot was empty now. From this vantage point, she could see that the garage doors into the mine wore matching, accusatory yellow Xs of more police tape. The studio, too, had its own yellow tape. The SPD apparently hoped to discover a stash of meth or a bag of unlaundered drug money under mounds of alabaster dust.

She fingered the keys in her pocket. This was an official crime scene, strictly off-limits, and yet here she was, creeping around like Nancy Drew. She scouted the street for squad cars before hurrying past the gate and around the back of the studio. She rubbed the gritty glass with her palm and cupped her hands to see inside.

Morning sun flooded the interior. The workbench was even dustier than it had been that night with Neil. This was encouraging.

And there, in the middle of the workbench, was what she had hoped to find—the block of peach alabaster last seen in Neil's truck, which had taken on the unmistakable curve of an eagle's wing.

She leaned heavily against the sun-warmed cement blocks and slid slowly to the ground, offering up a small prayer of thanks toward the morning sun. *Neil couldn't have been on a fishing boat with Tom and Paddy or cooking meth in the mine and make such wondrous, incredible, undeniable progress on his new commission.* She stood up again and was looking in at the sculpture when pair of great, furry paws thudded the inside of the glass, making her jump.

"*Wooof!*"

"Magoo, you poor thing!" She ran around the building and peeled back the yellow tape, ignoring CRIME SCENE DO NOT CROSS as Magoo whined and scratched at the door.

"Hold on, boy."

She selected a likely key and unlocked the door. Magoo rushed past her to lift his leg on the nearest bush, then he made a U-turn and bounded around her. His leash hung just inside the door. She stepped inside, not sure what other evidence of Neil's innocence she might find. The exhaust fan churned in the roof peak.

She heard a familiar sound—*ping*—she couldn't quite identify. She waited. *Ping.* The coffee maker. She crossed the room, leaving a trail of incriminating footprints behind her. The hot carafe had a crust of burned residue in the bottom. She turned it of, walked back out and shut the door behind her. She clipped the leash to Magoo's collar.

"Come on, boy. You must be starving."

When they reached the overlook she dialed Officer Flood.

"This is Caroline Finch. You interviewed me yesterday about the explosion in the gypsum mine?" She didn't know how many meth lab explosions he might be investigating.

"Yes?"

"On the news this morning, WSAS reported that Neil Stoddard was *in* the mine when it exploded. But he wasn't." She described his studio, the fan and the coffee pot left on, ending with, "Besides, the sculpture he was working on shows *days* of work since I saw it last Thursday. And that dust on his clothes was *alabaster*, not ash. Your crime lab will confirm that. Like I tried to tell you, Neil went into the mine *after* the explosion to save the life of an injured boy. And by the way, I forgot to tell you, he was wearing blue ear protectors when he ran up to the crater. He had been using power tools in his studio. That's why he didn't hear the blast or call 911."

"But he heard his phone when you called."

She considered this. "He'd have his phone on vibrate, don't you think? *And,* he left his dog in his studio which indicates he was there, not in the mine. Didn't you find the dog when you searched?"

"We haven't been inside yet. Mr. Stoddard told us about the dog this morning. Animal Control picked him up."

"No. I have him."

"The dog? *You* have the dog?"

"Hum-mum, uhm, er," Caroline mumbled something inaudible and evasive.

There was a long silence on the other end of the line, then a sigh. "Okay, Ms. Finch, I have your information. Anything else?"

"Yes, please let Mr. Stoddard know that I have his dog."

"I can't promise—"

"Imagine being locked up, knowing your dog is without food or water, then thinking he's at the *pound?* Haven't you ever had a dog?"

Officer Flood was silent.

"He's Magoo."

"Magoo?"

"The dog's name, Magoo."

Another sigh. "Okay, ma'am, I'll tell him his dog, Magoo, broke out of a *sealed* crime scene and somehow ended up in your custody. Do I have that right?"

She was ready to plead the fifth when she heard a low chuckle and, "Is that all?"

"No, one more thing. Did you get my voice message? Neil owns the mine with his cousin, David Stoddard. Are you investigating him?"

"We're following multiple leads."

She was getting cop-speak again. "Okay, but you *need* to follow *that* one," she said, "and don't forget to tell him about the dog."

"Magoo. Yes, ma'am."

42

DO-OVER

Iris and Zelda were on the porch when Caroline and Magoo reached the driveway.

"I wondered where you were," Iris called out. "Come. Sit."

"I brought a friend." Magoo yanked the leash out of Caroline's hand and took the porch steps in a single bound, skidding to a halt at Zelda's nose.

"And who is your gentleman friend?" Iris asked, letting Magoo sniff her hand.

"This is Magoo, Neil's dog."

"Neil's?"

"*Long* story. Can we borrow some dog food first? He's starving."

Magoo sniffed Zelda's empty bowl and lapped up her water. Iris went into the kitchen and came out with a big mixing bowl of kibble. "He must eat like a horse." She stroked his wide back as he plunged his muzzle into the bowl, scattering kibble across the porch.

When he was finished, Caroline pulled him toward the glider where he flopped down next to Zelda, panting contentedly.

Iris sat down and sighed. "Zel and I are two bumps on a log today. We've both had enough excitement to last us a long, long time."

Caroline sank lower in the glider and covered her eyes with her forearm. "I know. I tried to go to work today, but I can't concentrate."

"It's no wonder. You must be exhausted. Zelda and I accomplished one thing today, though. We brought Rafael home from the hospital."

"I saw him this morning. He's a resilient kid."

"I don't envy Josseline with him on those crutches."

Caroline tucked one leg under her. "Was Zelda glad to see him?"

"Oh my, yes! I thought she'd turn inside out when he got in the car. All night long she probably thought he was still down that hole. Poor thing."

Caroline sank her fingers into Zelda's black fir. "It's hard being a dog sometimes, isn't it, Zel? Limited English. No thumbs. You were so worried, weren't you?"

"Must be a little like being deaf, being a dog," Iris mused. "They see and sense so much, but without oral language they miss a lot."

Caroline took a deep breath and caught the fresh, spicy scent of newly-opened roses twining themselves around the porch column. Above them, impatiens drooped in their hanging baskets.

"Iris, where's your watering can?"

"By the hose, if it hasn't sprouted legs again. Why?"

Caroline pointed at the wilting flowers and got up. She filled the can at the hose and soaked the baskets until they dripped onto the porch floor.

"Thank you," Iris sighed. "So, are you going to tell me where you've been and how you ended up in possession of Neil's dog?"

"Yup, and other stuff, too," Caroline said, sitting down again, smiling.

"What stuff?"

"Well, for starters, I've committed two, maybe three, crimes so far today. I'm losing count."

"Do tell!" said Iris, perking up.

"I sneaked past the guard outside of Neil's hospital room, broke into the mine property and then into a sealed crime scene. And it feels *wonderful!*" She laughed giddily. "Should that scare me? Anyway, that's not even what I really came to tell you."

She described the evidence she'd found at the crater and in the studio, ending with, "Paddy's ex-girlfriend Sarah told me Neil was on Tom's boat with Paddy all weekend, but he *had* to have been in his studio. That big chunk of rock didn't carve itself."

Iris didn't look convinced. "But that doesn't prove the three of them aren't in cahoots on the land deal."

"I know, but at least Neil didn't lie to me about where he'd be. Oh, Iris, you should have *seen* him yesterday! He dropped into that horrible, smoldering hole without any thought to his own safety." She felt her eyes fill up again. "I'm not sure about any of the rest, though. Either I've fallen for the worst kind of scumbag, or an innocent man is going to jail."

"Neither of those are great options," Iris said.

"I know. I *hate* this!" Caroline rubbed her eyes until she saw stars. "I know it *looks* bad, but I just can't make myself believe he's involved in making *meth*. Am I being naive?"

Iris's face was a mix of unreadable emotions. "Don't forget, he was in that red truck with Paddy, right there in my driveway."

"I *know*," Caroline groaned. "I know."

"Well," Iris said, "until you know for sure, you'll just have to trust your instincts, not a bunch of unsubstantiated rumors or an old lady's poor eyesight."

Caroline sat up, looking hopeful. "You have poor eyesight?"

Iris laughed. "No, but anybody's eyes—or memory—can play tricks."

"Sorry. I didn't mean—"

Iris smiled, "I know."

They were quiet again. Somewhere, a woodpecker drummed on a hollow tree. Two crows called to each other from the white pine above the porch. Off in the distance, the zoo's cockatoos were arguing loudly.

"Caroline," Iris said finally, "a lot of people have put a great deal of faith in those instincts of yours—your 'way' with people. What you dismiss as ass-kissing. I mean, you won over an old sourpuss like me, didn't you?" She chuckled softly. "It's time you gave yourself the same respect. Where is that gut of yours leading you?"

"Into a life of crime?" Caroline laughed weakly and thought about this. "You're very kind, Iris. But, I don't know *how* I feel anymore—about a lot of things. I used to be so *sure*—of myself, mostly. I was so *confident*. I knew what I wanted. But lately—I don't know."

"So, when you were younger, say, in your twenties, you were decisive. Brash, even. You knew *exactly* what you wanted. You never hesitated. You just *plunged* right in. Do I have that right?"

Caroline smiled. "You've been spying on me?"

"Oh, honey girl," Iris laughed. "You're not *twenty* anymore. You've lived long enough to make mistakes. Welcome to the club. You know too much to be so reckless. You know there are potholes ahead because you've been down that road before. That's not lack of confidence—or second-guessing—that's maturity."

Caroline closed her eyes and pondered. It certainly put a better spin on her own indecisiveness. At last, she said, "But what if my instincts are being led by something else?"

"Such as?"

"Loneliness . . . libido, a little of both?" She felt her cheeks redden. "Oooh! That man can *kiss*!"

Iris' eyes twinkled. "Well then, by *all* means, you must give him the benefit of the doubt!"

They were still laughing when a maroon minivan rolled up the driveway.

"My *Star* delivery lady," Iris announced, starting to her feet.

Caroline jumped up. "I'll get it."

An Asian woman with a broad smile handed the newspaper through the window and exchanged waves with Iris.

Caroline unfolded the paper on the table between them and let out a gasp. Neil Stoddard's haggard face was staring at her from above the fold. She had never seen a mug shot of someone she knew. He leaned toward the camera with his chin low and his eyes half shut, holding up a number as if it were as heavy as a boat anchor. His hair was matted. He had several days' stubble—more evidence of working alone in his studio all weekend.

"This is *awful*," Caroline whispered. "They made him look like a criminal."

Next to Neil was, presumably, his cousin David, who looked angelic with his short-cropped, gelled hair and white polo shirt. He looked as if he had dropped in for headshots on his way to the country club. A third photo subject was half-man, half-skeleton, with hollow cheeks pocked with ugly, black lesions. There was a tattoo of Asian characters on his thin neck which probably meant, "Insert needle here."

"This *is* awful," Iris agreed.

Caroline read the article aloud. There was nothing new.

"So, that's Neil?" Iris said, tapping David's photo.

"No. That's *David*, Neil's cousin."

Iris pointed to the caption. "But, look, it says, 'Cousins David Stoddard (left) and Cornelius 'Neil' Stoddard (right) were arrested on suspicion of operating an illegal drug lab in the Stoddard Gypsum Mine.'"

"Hmm. They got the names reversed."

"I see why. There's more than a passing resemblance."

"Maybe," Caroline conceded, "But Neil looks like the *evil* twin. He sure didn't look like this when I saw him last week."

Iris sat back in her chair, slack-jawed. "Oh Caroline. What have I done?"

"What do you mean?"

"What if it was *David* I saw driving the mine truck, not Neil?" Iris leaned forward to study the picture. "The driver never got out of the cab. Of course, it was that red truck and the logo that stayed with me, so I guess, I thought—Oh dear."

Caroline sat up straighter. "So, maybe it was *David* with Paddy? Do you think Victor could have made the same mistake? I mean, focusing on the truck and assuming the driver was Neil? So it was David he saw outside of Tom's office?"

"Yes, but they could *both* be involved," Iris said.

There was another crunch on the gravel, but this time it was a police cruiser rolling slowly up the driveway. Magoo and Zelda sprang to their feet, huffing and growling.

Caroline drew her knees to her chest. "Oh Iris! They're here to arrest me!" The thought hit her with concussive force. She felt the blood drain from her face.

"Now, just hold on," Iris said. "We're going to sit here calmly and let them come to us." She folded her hands in her lap.

Zelda started down the steps, growling. "No, Zel. Come here—" Iris commanded, "—not that I blame you."

Caroline unfolded just in time to grab the leash before Magoo tore down the steps, too. Then, taking a cue from Iris, she rearranged herself in a pose that would project virtue and unimpeachable moral rectitude. Legs crossed at the ankle, arms folded in her lap. Saint Caroline of Saskawan.

The cruiser rolled to a stop. Officer Flood and his even younger sidekick got out slowly, hiked up their pants, adjusted their hats and looked deliberately around the yard.

Caroline whispered, "That's the same cop who interrogated me at the hospital. He's probably been tailing me. Oh God!" She slumped lower in the glider hoping to make herself invisible. In a stage whisper, she said, "If my instincts are so trustworthy, why are they telling me to vault this railing and hop a plane to Argentina?"

"Shush," Iris said in her commanding dog handler/school teacher voice. "I'll handle this."

The two officers sauntered over. "G'day, ma'am," Officer Flood said, touching his hat. "I'm Officer Flood. This is Officer Baker. Are you Iris VanWingen?"

"I am."

"May we speak with you privately, Mrs. VanWingen?" He must

have noticed Caroline sitting there, but he was looking at Iris. The glider under her began to shake.

"It will have to be right here," Iris said. "Bum hip. And my friend needs to stay, for the dogs," she added, nonsensically. "Have a seat officers, won't you?"

Officer Flood turned his attention to the glider and registered surprise. "Ms. Finch?"

Apparently, her arrest, trial and life behind bars were not the purpose of this house call. Caroline wanted to fall to her knees in limp relief. Instead she nodded with passable poise, "Officer Flood."

He touched his hat again.

Does the police academy offer a course in hat tipping, she wondered. *Scare the bejebers out of perfectly innocent people, but do it with a "yes, ma'am" and a tip o' the hat?*

Officer Baker took the metal chair next to Iris, leaving Officer Flood the other end of the glider. Caroline watched him bend awkwardly onto the low cushion until his knees nearly touched his chin. When he reached into his belt for his little notebook, Caroline gave the glider a stiff push. He dropped his orange pencil and bent to pick it up, sending a quizzical look in her direction.

Saint Caroline returned a beatific smile.

Finally settled, he said, "Mrs. VanWingen, we have a suspect in custody, a Gregory Michael Lafevre, who we believe has a connection to the mine explosion. Do you know this man?"

Office Baker showed Iris the same mug shot of the scrawny man they'd just seen in the paper. Iris shook her head.

Officer Flood continued. "We apprehended him after he sought treatment for burns related to the production of crystal methamphetamine in the mine next door. His attorney is seeking a plea agreement, so that Mr. Lafevre can provide evidence about others who may have been involved in the drug operation and the explosion."

Iris nodded.

Caroline stopped breathing. They were going to reward this meth head for pointing the finger at Neil?

"Mr. Lafevre told us that he and his partner, who is still at large, set up the drug lab in the mine about a year ago, on the condition that they share the proceeds with the mine. As far as we can tell, it was a profitable arrangement."

Caroline pulled Magoo closer. She would adopt him when Neil

went to prison. She would have to get a house with a yard though, and quit her job to take care of him. But she couldn't afford a house if she didn't have a job. *None of this would work—Oh dear God!* She buried her face in Magoo's neck. She felt like a shaken can of pop. She wanted to throw back her head and let out a heart-stopping scream.

Officer Flood was still talking. "Mr. Lafevre says he was occasionally paid for other services." He cleared his throat and flipped a page in his notebook. "He was asked to vandalize your property—to frighten you, he said—so you would sell your land."

"Frighten *me?* I don't know what you mean."

He read from his notebook. "Mr. Lafevre said he moved items around—a watering can, a garbage pail? He siphoned gas out of your car."

Caroline stood up suddenly and moved to stand behind Iris.

"Did he—he put salt in my garden?" Iris asked, her voice rising. "Did he flood my barn?"

He studied his notes and nodded. "Yes, ma'am."

Iris reached for Caroline's hand.

Flood nodded toward Magoo. "And the dogs? Have they been okay?"

Caroline pointed to Zelda and gasped. "No! She nearly *died* a few days ago!"

"Yes. I'm afraid our suspect left antifreeze out to poison her."

Iris brought her hand to her mouth. "I—I don't *believe* this!"

"Mr. Lafevre also admits to forgetting to lock the gate to the mine after putting out the poison. We believe this allowed the boy, Rafael Rojas, access to the mine property after the explosion. Lafevre may get a suspended sentence for his cooperation, but he's got no beef with you, Mrs. VanWingen. He won't bother you anymore."

"But what about the owners of the mine?" Caroline asked.

"One of them is going away for a while."

Caroline flapped her hands and shouted, "*Which* one?"

Officer Flood paged back though his notes again, licking his thumb.

"*David* or *Neil?*" she demanded, stomping her foot. "*Which* one?" She wanted to grab him by the neck and shake him like a chew toy.

"Hold on. I want to get this right." He consulted his notes. "Lafevre and one of the owners—" He paged forward and back again and finally looked up. "Lafevre says his arrangement was with *David* Stoddard. David confirms this, and says his cousin, Cornelius Stoddard, was apparently, um, not involved in the day-to-day operations of the business and had no knowledge of the drug operation."

Caroline fell to her knees, keeping a firm grip on Iris' hand.

"Caroline," Iris said. "You were right. You were *right!*"

Caroline looked up at Officer Flood, her cheeks already wet. "Where is he? Where is Neil now?"

"We're processing his release downtown at the jail."

She felt Iris push her away. "You should go to him."

Caroline raised her eyes to meet Iris'—thinking of all that would mean—to "go to him."

She nodded, breaking into a surprised smile. "I will! I'll *go to him!*" She sprang to her feet and began pulling Magoo down the steps toward her car. "Flood!" she called over her shoulder, "Move your cruiser. I need to get downtown!"

On his third try, Officer Flood was able to leave the glider. "We're going there now. You can follow us," he said.

Caroline and Magoo got into the Fiesta and were waiting for the cruiser to turn around when she flung the car door open again.

"Wait, Flood! Wait a minute," she shouted, taking the porch steps in two leaps and seizing Iris' hands. "I *knew* you weren't losing your marbles. I knew it!" she said, giving Iris a kiss on the cheek. "I was right about *that*, too!"

Iris wiped her eyes and laughed. "Oh go on. Get out of here!"

An SPD cruiser and a tailgating lime green Fiesta sped through three yellow lights and two iffy, reddish ones, arriving at the underground police garage in just under six minutes. Officer Flood led Caroline up a back stairway and opened a door marked Processing.

Seated alone on a metal bench at the far end of a windowless room was Neil, his head in his hands. He looked up as she rushed toward him.

"Neil!" She wanted to fling herself into his arms, but froze.

She had doubted his innocence.

He rose wearily, his face completely unreadable. His clothes hung limp and he looked somehow thinner.

She reached out. "Neil. I—I—" Her eyes pleaded, but neither of them moved. She felt the pull of his gravitational field. She whispered, "Can you ever, *ever* forgive me?"

She listened to his breathing and to his silence. She took a step closer. "I tried not to believe you were involved. I should never—"

"Caroline," he said softly. "We *barely* know each other."

She let her arms drop to her sides. There was no defense. She had ruined everything. She'd second-guessed what she felt to be true. Now he was pushing her away. She couldn't blame him.

She took a step backward. "I just wanted to apologize," she whispered. She turned to leave.

"I mean, we need to work on that. The getting-to-know-you part," he said, closing the space until she heard his rushing breath and felt his heat.

"We could?" she squeaked, searching his face.

He touched her shoulders and pressed her against the steady thump of his heart.

"This is *my* fault, Caroline." He released a long, ragged breath. "If I had been paying more attention, Davy would *never* have done this—and Rafael wouldn't have—" His voice broke. "—almost—."

"Shhh," she said. "Shhh."

They would debate this point later. She would tell him she understood the crushing burden of family and career, the limits of one's power over others and the irrelevance of salvation to those willing to sell their souls—but not now, not when words just wouldn't come.

She didn't know she had started to cry until he wiped a tear with his thumb. She reach up and wiped away one of his.

Behind them, Officer Flood cleared his throat. "I told him about the dog."

"That's right, he did," Neil said, smiling. "Thank you, Officer Flood."

She reached for Neil's hand. "Come on. I'm taking you home."

In the garage, Caroline let Magoo out of the car so he didn't shred the upholstery when he saw Neil. When the dog finally calmed down, the three of them piled in and pulled into downtown traffic. For the first time, she noticed that Neil's pants were three inches too short and so baggy they needed cinching. His gray-white tee shirt was torn at the neckband.

"New outfit, eh?"

"They took my clothes to the crime lab," he said. "It was this or a jumpsuit, but orange has never been my color."

She drove through the bright July afternoon.

"Take a left at the river," he said, starting to cough.

Caroline turned right.

He looked at her quizzically.

"I said, I'm taking you *home*." She beamed at the road ahead.

He flashed a toothy grin, tilted his head back and closed his eyes.

In her parking space she touched his shoulder. He shook himself awake and looked around. "Your place?"

She nodded. "I'm not letting you out of my sight until I know you're okay."

He coughed pitifully, but smiled. "That could take a while."

She led Magoo and Neil up the stairs, stopping on each landing to let Neil catch his breath.

"Now I know what it feels like to be a hundred."

She unlocked her door and let man and dog sniff around her apartment.

"I just *happen* to have a lucky tee shirt in your size," she said brightly. She showed him into the bathroom and handed him a towel, his MSU tee shirt and a pair of her boxers. While he showered, she put clean sheets on her bed.

She heated some pesto ravioli, made a green salad and was setting the table when Neil appeared barefoot in the doorway, releasing fresh pheromones into his lucky tee shirt and her lucky apartment.

"Do I dare ask who owns these boxers? He's not going to show up and kick my ass, is he?"

"They're mine," she said, reining in some fairly provocative mental images involving use of the kitchen counter. There was a *man* in *boxers* in her *kitchen!*

Over dinner, they talked of Rafael's quick recovery, her clandestine visit to the studio and David's shocking confessions. But soon, Neil became so exhausted he could barely hold his fork. It was still light out when she ordered him into her bed and went off to make him a cup of chamomile tea.

When she returned, he pulled her to the edge of the bed. He ran his hand under her hair and pulled her into a long kiss, which ended in a spasm of coughing.

"Sorry," he said, rolling his eyes.

"Over," she commanded, patting his shoulder. "Flip."

He rolled onto his stomach and balled the pillow under his chest. She ran her hands over his back and gently worked the knots in his shoulders. Moans and grunts soon turned to even breathing. She lay her hand on his tangled, damp hair and let the curls wrap around her fingers.

She showered and looked in on Neil obsessively all evening, but he didn't move. She took Magoo for a short walk along the river, then gave him the leftover ravioli mixed with a can of tuna.

"Don't get used to this," she warned him. "It's back to proper kibble tomorrow."

She made up the sofa for herself, but lay awake for a long time, ticking off all the bright new things in her life.

Sometime in the cool, blue hours before sunrise, Neil's hand found the curve of her back. His lips found the fold behind her ear.

She rolled onto her back. "Hey."

He sat next to her and whispered, "Where'd you go?"

She pressed her hand to his cheek. "Not far," she murmured, feeling drowsy and susceptible. *Never far.*

His arm reached under her shoulders, the other behind her knees. He drew her up and she clung to him as if he were a life ring—and perhaps, he was.

She awoke to the sound of a man making breakfast in her kitchen. He stood at the stove with his back to her—his boxers were crumpled at the seat and his hair sprang out in every direction. She threaded her arms through his until he stopped scrambling the eggs.

"How's my patient this morning?" she asked.

He turned, holding the spatula and oven mitt over his head, and kissed her forehead, her ear, her neck and her mouth. "Patient? I haven't felt *this* good in a very long time." Then he began to cough.

"Mmm. You need to spend the day in bed." She propped her chin on his chest, looking up.

"I like the sound of *that*," he said.

She sighed. "I need to show up at work today or they'll stop missing me, but stay, *please*? I'll try to come home early."

"Well, since I don't have a job, a car or any clothes I'd wear in public, I guess I'm your captive."

Caroline curled her lips into a maniacal grin. "At laaaast, I have you in my grasp."

"So, you *were* stalking me."

In the doorway, under a hail of soft kisses, Caroline nearly forgot all about her impressive work ethic. Fleetwood Mac sang out from Bella's apartment. She owed her friend a call, but it would have to wait.

As soon as she reached her office, she dialed Officer Flood.

"Ms. Finch," he said with the inflection of, *You* again. "What can the SPD do for you *today*?"

"Actually, maybe *I* can do something for *you*."

"Okay."

"I have some facts that just don't add up."

She summarized the triangular relationship between David Stoddard, Paddy Malone and Tom Engelsma. She described their sudden interest in the zoo and their attempts to buy Willow Creek Farm. "I think they're planning some sort of mega-development on the combined mine, farm and zoo properties."

"Huh," he said, which didn't sound very cop-like. She had his attention. "But the city owns the zoo land. It's not for sale, last I knew," he said.

"Right. So, that's why I figure they might have someone inside City Hall."

He paused. "That's a *serious* allegation, Ms. Finch."

"I know. Maybe you can make it add up some other way. I can't."

"Okay, Ms. Finch—"

"You can call me Caroline. May I call you Mike?"

"No."

"Ooo-kay."

"It's *Mick*."

She laughed. "Okay, Mick. Call me if you learn anything new."

43

THE BEST AND WORST OF TIMES

The rest of July and August were the best and worst of times for Neil and Caroline. New love enveloped them in a sweet, pink haze just as storm clouds gathered on every horizon.

Neil recovered his strength and made half-hearted offers to move back to his own apartment, but Caroline ignored every one of them. Yet true to her nature, she fretted about appearances.

"We only had one *real* date before you moved in." She was curled around the back of him with one hand resting lightly on his sternum.

"Are you worried about that?" he asked.

"Maybe. A little."

He rolled to face her. "How about the time I pulled you out of the mud?"

"That wasn't a *date*."

"Well, we can grandfather it in—retroactively. And what about that time we had drinks and dessert in the Bat Cave?"

"Zoo brew and animal crackers?"

"That's two." He shifted to his back and laced his hands behind his head, concentrating on the ceiling. "Tree hugging with Rafael on our walk with the dogs, that's three."

She brightened. "That makes our first kiss on the overlook date number *four*."

"That one should count double or triple—considering the mine tour, my studio, the picnic *and* making out."

"Okay, I'll give you four and five." She sat up. "This is *good*. Go on."

"What about the time we dropped in at that burning meth lab? A smokin' hot date!"

She ran two fingers down his chest and stopped just short of his boxers. "*Six!*"

"And the rendezvous in my hospital room? Brief, but pivotal."

"Seven. Plus, our meet-up at the police station. That's eight. Wow! We've been dating, like, for*ever*."

"In *all* the trendiest places."

She threw one leg over him, pinning his wrists to the pillow. "I'm *not* a slut, after all. So, don't go thinking that, mister."

"Too late," he grunted, flipping her onto her back.

When the euphoria after Rafael's rescue subsided, the staff of Ridge Park Zoo realized the magnitude of Tom and Paddy's betrayal. There would be no land in Nord Haven, no public referendum, no new zoo. They could forget about black-footed ferrets or any kind of expansion. Ridge Park was stuck in limbo.

Victor stayed in his office for the rest of the summer. Auditors arrived and stayed for days. Board members came and went silently. Several resigned.

Julie and Gwen invented cruel and unusual punishments for Tom and Paddy, including turning them into live enrichments for Goldwyn and mounting what was left of their heads on the Bat Cave wall. Chappy talked of retirement. Peter and Donna remained stoic, but Caroline suspected Donna was looking for a new job. Only Kirby—dear, weird Kirby—maintained his equilibrium, handing out gummy worms when his baby massasauga rattlesnakes hatched. But even he couldn't dispel the pall that hung over the zoo.

The media wanted to know the zoo's plans, and no one, least of all Caroline, knew what to tell them. Gate receipts went flat. Sponsorships for the fall fundraiser were getting a lackluster response. She continued her zookeeper's blog, but wondered if she should rename it "Requiem for a Zoo."

"We need *something* to bring in visitors," she mused over lunch one day, to no one in particular.

"Another escape?" Julie said. "I think a meerkat or a wallaby, this time."

"Paddy could help," Gwen sniffed. "Anybody have his number?"

"County jail," Donna said bitterly.

"An escape involving lingerie," Kirby said through a mouth full of fries. "That was a nice touch last time."

If the staff was disheartened, the public seemed split between anger and confusion. Caroline reminded them that the zoo was the victim, but conspiracy theorists still insisted, beyond all logic, that the zoo was somehow complicit.

When SPD arrested Commissioner Szczesny, it only confirmed many people's mistrust of the city. Anti-zoo activists said the scandal proved that "wildlife is always the biggest loser." Some even demanded that the zoo close down entirely. Only Missy and her CAUZ group of neighbors seemed happy to keep Ridge Park in the city.

Caroline announced a new Ridge Park Zoo Renovation Fund and called on every major donor to contribute. A few agreed, but many said they'd "think about it"—donor-speak for "No, thanks." Although she couldn't prove it, Caroline suspected that more than a few had been silent investors in Tom and Paddy's development scheme.

One humid afternoon in August, Caroline and Chappy were alone in the Bat Cave.

"I've been meaning to tell you something, Caroline."

"Sure, what?"

"You know I wasn't entirely behind the move to Nord Haven, but I hope you know this wasn't the way I wanted things to end."

Caroline sighed. "I know, Chappy. Of *course*, I know that."

He looked into his coffee cup. "I still think this could be a fine zoo."

A week later, the Ridge Park Zoo Renovation Fund received a five thousand dollar contribution from Chappy and his wife.

For Neil, witnessing his cousin's downfall was excruciating. He was interviewed, subpoenaed and deposed. He sat through David's preliminary and bail hearings.

"I've never believed in conspiracy theories. Do you know why?" he asked Caroline one evening over dinner.

"No, why?"

"People can't keep secrets. The urge to confess is even stronger than the urge for self-preservation. I mean, Davy seems *relieved* to have been caught. I think he would have turned himself in eventually." Neil let his fork drop to his plate and sat back. "But I guess we'll never know for sure. He says the whole thing started when Lafevre and his partner wanted to store a little pot in the old shaft. When Davy realized they were cooking meth and tried to kick them out, Lafevre threatened to turn Davy in and skip town."

"But why did Davy take the drug money in the first place?" Caroline asked.

"He sank everything into the renovations for the cold storage operation. He even took out a second mortgage on his house, which he failed to tell me. The cold storage venture was a failure from the start. Davy was desperate. When he saw a way to make money, he took the risk."

"Were Tom and Paddy part of the drug business?" Caroline asked.

"Not at first. They approached Davy about a year ago to buy the mine. At first, Davy saw selling the mine as a way out of the drug business—pay Lafevre off and close for good. Paddy promised to 'take care of Lafevre,' but then secretly hired him to harass Iris. What a nasty business."

"How did he keep all this from you?"

Neil blew out a long breath. "That was the easy part. I had no interest in the business. I did whatever he asked—show up when he called me. I thought I was doing him a favor by staying out of his way, instead I threw him to the wolves."

All summer, forensic accountants picked through the bones of the business and found little to confiscate, other than the property itself. Neil continued to blame himself, and his cousin's remorse only made it worse.

Rafael spent two weeks in July recovering at home and at Iris'. (She called him "my little impatient.") By August, he returned to the zoo on crutches and presided over everything from a stool in the kitchen, where he chopped and weighed vegetables and pestered the staff with endless questions. Chappy chauffeured him around in the golf cart, while Kirby or Donna brought him pop and chips from the vending machines and gave him piggyback rides. At the clinic, he helped Julie give bottles to a preemie kid goat. By mid-August, he graduated to an air cast that barely slowed him down.

Just before Labor Day, Rafael and Caroline found Neil's truck backed up to Iris' garden gate. Neil was turning a load of gypsum into the salt-contaminated earth while Iris supervised. After that, Caroline and Rafael often found Neil on Iris' porch, deep in geek-to-geek debates about all things geological and environmental.

"Iris is going to speak to my Wetlands Geology class this fall," Neil announced one afternoon.

Iris nodded. "In return, his students are going to replant the pond on campus as a Blanding's turtle release site."

Rafael began arriving at the zoo kitchen pulling Iris' Radio Flyer loaded down with chard, spinach, broccoli, tomatoes and carrots from her garden. Grocery bags of fresh produce also went to Josseline's kitchen or home with Caroline.

Sometimes, in the middle of a workday, Caroline would slip away to surprise Neil in his studio. The peach-colored stone was slowly becoming an airy, translucent thing, poised to lift off in the slightest breeze.

One day, Neil surprised her with a potter's wheel and a small kiln he had installed in the corner. "I hear it's like riding a bicycle," he said, with a grin. "Wanna take it for a spin?"

Meanwhile, Bella wondered when Caroline would come to her senses.

"Is that guy *ever* going home?" she asked on one of their Saturday morning runs. "He looks perfectly healthy to me, eh?"

"He is—perfectly."

"You know, you don't owe him anything."

"*Owe* him? First of all, 'that guy' has a name. Second, Neil hasn't gone home because I don't *want* him to. And third, I love . . . having him around—a lot. Would it make you happier if I told you we had a huge fight last weekend?"

"You *did*?" Bella asked, brightening.

Caroline laughed. "No. But, if it'll make you feel better, he leaves the seat up, cheats at Scrabble and can't fold laundry worth beans."

Bella gagged as if she had a hairball. "You two are nauseating."

For Iris, the mine explosion changed everything. Both her daughters flew in, despite her protests.

"My God, Mom, those meth heads could have *killed* you!" Annie said, as she dried dishes at the sink.

"And that poor boy!" Cindy said, joining them from the dining room. "He's probably traumatized for life. And poor Zelda." She leaned down to kiss Zelda's forehead.

"Don't be melodramatic, girls. The bad guys are behind bars, Zelda's fine and Rafa is as resilient as a rubber ball."

"But what still gets me is that you didn't *tell* us what was happening, Mom," Annie said.

Iris squirted more detergent into the roasting pan she was scrubbing and sighed. "That's because I thought *I* did all of it. I thought I was going as batty as Grandma."

"Oh, *please*," Annie said, rolling her eyes. "You could be down a couple of quarts and *still* run circles around the rest of us." She hung her towel over the oven door handle and touched her mother's arm. "Let that soak, Mom. I want to visit Dad before the mosquitoes come out."

Iris hung her apron on a peg and led her daughters into the meadow. Ahead of them, Zelda chased goldfinches off the ripening coreopsis.

"You know, girls," Iris said, "it's always been my goal to hold on to the farm until my last breath, but now that I realize that could be next Tuesday, it's just not long enough anymore."

She saw Annie shoot a look at her sister. Her daughters hated her end-of-life talks even more than they had hated her birds-and-bees talks when they were eleven.

"Mom," Cindy began, "you know we wish we could keep the farm in the family, but it's just not practical when we live so far away."

"I know that. I don't know how some parents manage to keep their kids and grandkids close by. Where did I go wrong?"

Annie smiled. "You sent us to camp and let us do foreign study. You've got no one to blame but yourself—and Dad."

Iris slipped her arms around her daughters' waists and squeezed them close. "I have no regrets, really. But, one way or another, I don't plan to take death lying down."

"Shall we bury you standing up?" Cindy asked, laughing.

The three VanWingen women sat down side-by-side on the curved bench to watch the glassy pool darken to the same navy blue as the night sky. Annie ran her hand over the carved letters and whispered, "Hey, Daddy. "

Cindy said, "Annie, do you remember how he used to say, 'Iris, if you stomp your feet at the weather—"

"—all you'll get is sore feet,'" Annie added in a manly register.

Iris said, "And *I* would say, '*Bill*, there are things in this world worth getting sore feet over.'"

44

MISSING THINGS

Sunday, August 28

Natural Curiosity: Notes from Willow Creek Farm
Iris Van, *Saskawan Evening Star*

I've been missing things lately. I don't mean things I've misplaced, like my favorite kitchen shears or my spare car key. I mean things that are gone forever, leaving me feeling wistful and the world a bit empty. I mean the big oak in front of my house that blew over in a storm last summer and the night song of the whip-poor-will.

Do any of you, my good readers, recall the meadow of sunflowers, sky blue asters, orange milkweed and purple coneflower that used to burst into bloom where the Wal-Mart now sits? Do you remember the frog pond behind the hospital? (It's buried under the cancer wing now.) Do you remember finding box turtles in the woods when you were a kid? I do.

If you're too young to remember, you may wonder what I'm fussing about. It's hard to miss the call of a whip-poor-will if you've never heard one. Can any of us honestly say we mourn the passenger pigeon the way we would the robin or the oriole if they didn't show up next spring?

I've been thinking about this all summer and I've come to the conclusion that the human desire to protect and preserve is fed by memory and personal experience.

Only recently—when a little South American monkey showed up in my barn—did I think to apply this logic to zoos. Instead, I used this bully pulpit to tell all of Saskawan about the evils of keeping animals behind bars. I was, of course, recalling the truly horrific zoos of my childhood. But shame on me for not walking next door to Ridge Park Zoo to see how things have changed.

Well, I finally made that visit a few weeks ago, and I was stunned.

The staff there is doing important conservation, as well as vital education. Zoos around the world can take credit not only for saving the American black-footed ferret, the Arabian oryx, the California condor and the last wild horses, but also for releasing new populations back into the wild. Our own Ridge Park is keeping Panamanian frogs out of harm's way while an epidemic ravages the wild population. Descendants of the healthy zoo-raised animals we see today may one day be the second Adams and Eves of their species in the wild.

Just as seed banks safeguard plants from extinction, zoos are one way to protect animal species. I've seen for myself that zoos are working on the forefront of nutritional and reproductive research that is benefiting both zoo animals and their wild cousins.

A few weeks ago, I proclaimed that habitat conservation deserves our support, but not zoos. I now realize *both* are urgently needed. If you think wild animals are better off in "wild" ranges that are being burned, logged or paved over, think again. I know I have.

I now firmly believe that if zoos didn't exist, PETA, the Humane Society and the Sierra Club would demand that we create them. It's sad to say, but well-run zoos are becoming the safest place on earth for critically endangered species like tigers, rhinos, pandas and gorillas.

In my own personal version of heaven-on-earth—and perhaps yours—all animals would roam at will. But until we control our species' own explosive breeding, which now tops 7,000,000,000 individuals, this won't be possible. Compare this number to other mega fauna—polar bears: 25,000, tigers: 4,000, giant pandas: 2,000, Northern white rhinos: 3—and you see the magnitude of the problem.

Our species is on a collision course with nearly all others on the planet. Climate change and habitat loss of *our own making* threaten a mass extinction not seen since dinosaurs disappeared 66 million years ago.

Some very smart scientists are predicting that twenty to fifty percent of *all* living species, both plant and animal, will cease to exist by the end of *this* century. This is a *very, very* sobering reality, my good readers. We all need to step to the front lines in this battle to save our planet home.

So, if you prefer Earth with butterflies, leopards, wolves, bats, turtles and rhinos, then please, support worldwide conservation. Our own little Ridge Park Zoo would be a great place to start.

45

TURTLE HEAVEN

Tuesday, September 14

Iris stood at her kitchen window listening to the sounds of a late summer morning. A crow called out as it flew over the barn, looking single-minded and late for an appointment. A flock of robins on the dogwood jostled each other to get at the bright red berries. They'd have the branches picked clean by supper time. In the distance, she heard Goldwyn making his morning declaration. She glanced at the clock and smiled. 10:14. The old guy had overslept.

Raucous shouts came from behind the barn. Since nine this morning, biology students from Sas-U had been fencing off the back half of the pond for a new Blanding's turtle habitat. Zelda had given them a royal welcome when they drove up packed into several beat-up cars. They were followed by that tall drink-of-water, Kirby, in the zebra van.

Willow Creek Farm would host several dozen turtles this year, getting the healthiest ones ready for release and allowing those with permanent injuries to find mates.

She was filling a thermos with coffee and putting cream, sugar and fresh scones on a tray when Caroline appeared at the kitchen door.

"What's cookin'? Am I too late for a sample?"

"Apricot-ginger scones, and you're just in time," Iris said. "I'm on my way to the pond, I mean, the 'Ridge Park Turtle Research Station.' Pretty fancy, eh? Can you grab the coffee?"

"Put everything on the tray. I'll carry it," Caroline said. "I came to take pictures and was hoping for a coffee break with you. I have news."

"Oh?" said Iris. "Good news?"

Caroline picked up the tray and smiled over her shoulder. "Coffee and scones first."

Kirby and half a dozen students dropped what they were doing and swarmed the coffee and baked goods Caroline set on the bench.

A student in hip waders emerged from the pond holding a jar of water up to the light.

"Wow," he said. "This place is turtle heaven."

Kirby took a closer look and nodded. "Cool. We'll supplement their food for a while, but eventually they should be able to find what they need here." He looked around the circle of students. "How will we monitor that?"

A tall blonde raised her hand and mumbled through a mouthful of scone, "Weigh them?"

"Bingo," said Kirby. "They need to learn to hunt and forage before they're released." He nodded at Iris. "This place is awesomatious. What do you think, Mrs. V? The fence won't spoil the view?"

"Not at all," Iris said. "As long as you're *sure* it's awesomatious."

"Totally!"

The students got back to work pounding fence posts into the pond bottom. Caroline took a few pictures before sitting down next to Iris.

"So, what's your news?" Iris asked.

"We had an emergency board meeting this morning. Officer Flood was there to go over the charges against Tom Engelsma, Paddy Malone, David Stoddard and Commissioner Szczesny. Lafevre, the meth dealer, will testify against David and Paddy. Neil is hoping he won't have to. Officer Flood showed blueprints of the development—get this—an *eighteen-hole* golf course with over one hundred and fifty condos and thirty home sites."

"Blueprints? I'm surprised they didn't shred them."

"They probably did, but a set came in the mail a few days ago addressed to me. No return address. I suspect they rode the bus out of town with Sweet Sarah-of-the-Fishnets. Bless her brave heart."

"Hmm," Iris said absently. "So how were they planning to acquire the zoo property from the city?"

"That was the Commissioner's job. His plan was to stall the park project and drive up the cost so the city would sell—to Tom, of course."

"And those arrogant sons-of-bitches almost got away with it!"

"Yup. Paddy and Tom were willing to give us land and put thousands of dollars into the referendum campaign because they stood to make *millions* on the development."

"What will happen to the mine property now?"

"The police are threatening to confiscate it as ill-gotten gains from drug trafficking, but with Neil as half owner, we're hopeful that won't happen. He doesn't want to run the cold storage business and he can't afford the taxes, but he doesn't want the land to be developed, either. It seems inevitable, though."

Two students were struggling to attach fencing to a post in the water when one of them fell backwards and came up sputtering. The whole project threatened to become a joyous mud fight before Kirby intervened.

"Go up to the house," Iris called out. "There's a hose at the corner of the porch." She turned to Caroline again, smiling now. "Kirby and Peter want me to work with students here this fall."

"So I heard. That's wonderful."

"I *have* missed teaching, but it's been ages."

"Pish posh. You've never *stopped* teaching, Iris. And we could sure use your help." She touched Iris' wrist. "I have more news. Remember I swore you to secrecy about those fishnet stockings? Well, this morning Victor told the board and the whole staff about Paddy's role in Houdini's escape. I called WSAS-TV and broke the story, so that's *one* mystery solved."

"One? What's the other?"

"The future of Ridge Park Zoo."

EPILOGUE

Late September - Four Years Later

Chappy stood on a stepladder tying an eight-foot banner between light posts in front of the flamingo pond. Caroline stood on the pavement below, shading her eyes from the late afternoon sun.

"Higher on the left, Chappy, and a little tighter, if you can." She stood back to admire the sign. The Living Pond - A Restored Habitat. "That's perfect. Thanks."

He climbed down and swung the ladder into the truck bed.

"So, what do you think?" she asked, taking in the scene.

He pushed out his lower lip and nodded. "Looks straight to me."

"No, I mean the *pond*, the *exhibit*. Peter says some of the flamingos seem to be pairing off already. This was *your* idea. Remember?"

Months ago, the cement at the bottom of the pond had been removed. Under Iris and Chappy's careful supervision, the pond was replanted with water lilies, pickerelweed, marsh marigolds and other native plants, some brought over from Iris' pond.

Chappy seemed to be giving Caroline's question some serious thought. "Well, Iris said it's the way she remembered it. I'm hoping the cardinal flowers over-winter." He pointed to a tall plant across the pond that had been covered with bright red flower spikes. "I won't call it finished until then."

"It's already beautiful, Chap." She slid into a golf cart—the same one she'd used to rescue Neil and Rafael from the mine four years ago. Neil had donated it to the zoo when the mine closed. In the cargo space behind her, there were pots of sky blue asters and the same pair of oversized, gold scissors that had cut the ribbon on Caratasca Island. She looked at her watch and released the brake. "See you in about ten minutes," she called out.

The cart hummed up the walk past the old fieldstone wall. Overhead, two capuchins chased each other through a giant, Slinky-like coil wrapped in wire netting. The tube stretched over the walk and through the trees from Caratasca Island to where the maned wolf enclosure used to be. She wondered if the monkey scampering above her was Houdini. He certainly wasn't so little anymore, but at least he had managed to stay within the zoo boundaries since his great escape. In the distance, she heard Chappy whistle for the troop to come in for the night.

Where the path had curved left toward Uncle Ed's Barnyard, it now forked right, behind the clinic. And where the old perimeter fence once stood, a post displayed directional signs:

Willow Creek Farm / Walker Farmhouse .1 mi

Monarch Meadow / Turtle Pond / South American Pampas .2 mi

Grandpa Bill's Meadow .3 mi

Coming Soon! American Black-Footed Ferrets

A couple walking by waved her to a stop. "Excuse me," the man said. "But those are the new ferrets, right?" He gestured toward an exhibit with mounds of exposed dirt and several rabbit-sized animals peeking out of the holes.

Caroline idled the cart. "No. Those are prairie dogs."

"Told you," said the woman, elbowing her companion.

Caroline said, "They're digging the tunnels where our ferrets will live when they arrive next spring."

"Then, they'll live with the prairie dogs?" the man asked.

"Well, no," Caroline said, holding back a smile. "Black-footed ferrets *eat* prairie dogs. We'll give the prairie dogs a new enclosure."

"In that case, I bet they won't mind moving," the woman said, laughing.

Ahead, Kirby and Donna were walking through the orchard toward the farmhouse. Kirby held out his thumb. "How 'bout a lift?"

Caroline stopped the cart and got out. "You can take the cart. I could use the walk."

Donna gave Caroline a serious appraisal. "You okay?"

She nodded without meeting Donna's eyes. "Would you mind taking these asters to the pond? Arrange them around the flagstones. I'll meet you at the house."

Kirby winked as he got into the passenger side. "Sure thing."

Donna slid into the driver's seat and headed toward Grandpa Bill's Meadow.

Caroline stepped off the trail into the long orchard grass—the same grass Iris said she had once fed to Princess, the circus elephant who became Judy. Slanting sun rays caught the glistening wings of honeybees returning to their white hive boxes set like gravestones beneath the apple trees. She reached for a ripening apple. Two years ago, Iris had recruited volunteers from area fruit farms all up and down the Ridge to prune some life back into the gnarled old trees. Iris had been so pleased to see them bloom again last spring.

At the far end of the orchard, Caroline could just make out the back of the farmhouse and barn. The house was a lemon yellow now, with white gingerbread trim and smart gray shutters. Iris had picked the colors herself. But she seemed even more pleased with the barn's new coat of fire engine red paint and green shingles. Over the door, a hand-painted sign read "Willow Creek Farm, Marita and Thomas Walker, Est. 1875."

The driveway had a fresh layer of gravel now, too. The copper bird feeder still hung from the apple tree by the garden gate, but a small amphitheater of benches had been added there. Just a month ago, Iris had talked to a group of day campers about butterflies, turtles and crows—three of her favorite subjects. Her garden was several times its former size with a long plastic covered hoop houses at the back which produced fresh vegetables for zoo residents almost year-around.

Three young volunteers pushing wheelbarrows full of carrots and squash greeted Caroline on their way to the zoo's kitchen. Next to the walk, a blackboard propped on a wooden easel announced the day's farm demonstrations:

Rewilding Your Yard, 10:00

Food Preservation: What Grandma Knew, 1:00

Insect Friends and Garden Partners, 3:00

Two years earlier, Iris and Zelda had moved into a small, one-story house on Russet Ridge Drive. The back wall of the farmhouse's kitchen was bumped out to make room for a cooking island and ten stools. Cooking and gardening classes were held there nearly every weekend. Under Iris' watchful eye, the rest of the house had been restored to its nineteenth-century glory.

As Caroline approached the corner of the house, she caught sight of Victor and Gwen in the driveway chatting with the VanWingen family. She ducked quickly behind the white pine before anyone noticed her.

She needed a minute. Just one more minute.

She wrapped her sweater tighter against the cool fall breeze and looked up. The crow family was gathered around their stick platform, perhaps discussing the angle of a twig, the best strategy for its expansion, or, very possibly, philosophy, religion and world domination.

She laughed at herself. She was having another "Iris moment." Her brain was stuffed full of weird thoughts and observations put there by her friend. Her "Iris eyes" noticed red-bellies, red admirals or great blue lobelias that were once all but invisible to her. Her "Iris ears" enjoyed frog choruses, wren chatter and the warning calls of chickadees.

The world is never quiet if you're listening, Iris liked to say.

This memory buoyed her, even as the weight of others threatened to flatten her.

Because even now, when the farm was this quiet, when she was tired or distracted and hurrying toward her office—she could almost see Iris waiting for her on the porch with Zelda at her feet, Rafa on the glider and a pitcher of lemonade on the table.

Things were different now. Better in almost every way.

But still.

She pressed her hands to her cheeks, blew out three cleansing breaths and stepped into the open.

"Hello!" she called out, wading into the circle. Both of Iris' daughters, she noticed, had their mother's thick blond-gray hair and intelligent good looks. "How was your tour?"

"Wonderful and exhausting!" Annie said, taking her sister's hand. "We covered every *inch* of this place! Ninety acres. My goodness!"

"It's quite a transformation," Cynthia said. "It isn't like any zoo I remember."

"Not that we'd know," Annie said. "Mom never took us to zoos."

"Well, she supervised every detail of the farm restoration," Caroline said, "And nearly wore out the golf cart."

Cynthia grimaced. "So, was Mom a *complete* pain?"

"Of course not!" Caroline said, then she laughed. "Okay. Well. *Occasionally*, but she was usually right."

Chappy and Julie approached from the path and Caroline introduced them to the family.

"So, is the farm like you remember it?" Julie asked the sisters.

"Gosh, no," Cynthia said, looking at her children. "It never looked *this* good, did it?"

A grandson, who appeared to be in his twenties, said, "Grammy Van was always trying to get Grandpa Bill to paint the house or fix the barn roof."

Annie said, a touch defensively, "Dad was more of a poet than a handyman."

A granddaughter asked, "Does anyone remember what Grandpa used to call this place?"

"Wither Crank Fart!" they said in unison, breaking into laughter.

Kirby and Donna rolled up in the golf cart and joined the gathering. Caroline checked her watch again. 6:02. The zoo was officially closed.

She chatted with Annie while keeping one eye on the path that led toward Rafael's house. Next to the trailhead, another signpost read:

Mine Loop Trail 1.5 mi

Michigan's Second Largest Beech Tree .2 mi

Raptor Aviary .5 mi

Lacey Valley / City Overlook .7 mi

Black Bear Cave / Gray Fox Hollow .8 mi

Moose Fen / Otter Pond / Porcupine Den .5 mi

Coming Soon! Animals of the Night & Stoddard Geology Center.

In protracted negotiations with prosecutors, Neil had agreed to donate the mine property to the city in exchange for a reduced sentence for David. David served two years in prison, then moved to Georgia to manage a granite quarry.

The old path to Rafael's house had been widened and covered in wood chips. Three overlooks with benches, railings and interpretive signs jutted out at dramatic heights over the ravine. The exact spot where Caroline had skidded on her backside into the creek was now Willow Creek Vista. (Neil had lobbied for Lover's Leap, but was overruled.)

Where the rusty fence between the farm and the mine once stood the trail continued along the old service road all the way to the City Overlook and what was now officially called Lacy Valley. Someday, with additional fundraising, a funicular railway would ferry visitors from the hilltop down to the Stoddard Geology Center and exhibit space inside the old mine. With any luck, a wild bat colony might someday redeem ol' Digory Gwynn's ill-fated mineshaft.

Kirby nodded toward the Mine Loop Trail. "Uh-oh. Here comes trouble."

A toddler in red leggings, a purple and pink striped shirt and a purple, zippered jacket emerged from the trail with Neil in hot pursuit.

"Mummy! Mummy! Mummy!"

Caroline dropped to one knee. "Iris! Iris! Iris!" she mimicked, as the little girl tumbled into her arms.

"Daddy taked me to see bears and rocks."

Caroline kissed her red-gold curls and stood up.

"Sorry we're late," Neil panted. "*Major* potty incident and no bathrooms between here and the Overlook. We had to dig into the emergency pants collection, which sort of ruined the outfit you laid out. Sorry about that, too." He sighed loudly.

Caroline laughed. "I'm just glad you made it."

Iris patted the knees of her leggings. "My 'mergency pants are red."

"I see that." Caroline brushed pine needles off them and scooped her up. "I missed you, snicklefritz." She smiled up at Neil. "You, too, Daddy-o."

Cynthia squeezed Iris' shoe. "So *this* is Mom's little namesake. Hello there, little Iris. Aren't you as cute as they come!" Iris buried her face in Caroline's shoulder and popped a thumb in her mouth.

A Harley roared up the driveway piloted by a leather-clad elf. Kirby's face broke into a goofy, lovesick grin.

"Auntie Bella! Auntie Bella!" Iris kicked to get down.

Bella took off her helmet and gave Iris a hug. "Hey there, Junior."

Kirby reached Bella in three long strides. He wrapped his spindly arms around her and kissed her spiked, blue hair.

Caroline whispered to Neil, "It's a wonder he hasn't poked an eye out."

Bella and Kirby had been inseparable ever since Caroline had roped Bella into helping at a fundraiser last fall. Afterward, Bella was indignant. "I thought you said there were no cute guys at the zoo."

Then, last April, a bed of purple crocuses poked through the frozen lawn below Bella's balcony forming the words, "Mary me, Bell" —misspelled, and the M looked more like a B, but Bella got the message.

She didn't speak to Kirby for three days. Finally, she showed up in the Bat Cave and stood over Kirby with both hands on her hips.

"This your idea of a sick joke?" she demanded to know.

Kirby dropped to one knee in front of half the zoo staff and whimpered, "Baby. I *need* to marry you *baaaad*!"

Bella blushed a color rivaling her then-magenta hair and said, "Kirby, you are one weird piece of shit. You know that, eh?" They wept in each other's arms.

The wedding was held a month later under the full bloom of Iris' apple trees. Kirby gave Bella a Harley Street 759 as a wedding gift, because she had declared: "I'm not ridin' on the back of any 'hog,' and I'm nobody's ol' lady."

Caroline and Neil gave them matching leather jackets for their honeymoon ride around Lake Michigan. By all accounts, Kirby and his Harley were embraced by the Canellis of Ishpeming, Michigan.

At the sound of barking, the whole group turned to see Zelda prancing up the driveway between Rafael and Josseline. Rafael was a head taller than his mother now. His most recent passion—aside from another zoo intern named Adrienne—was veterinary medicine. He volunteered at the clinic with Peter after school.

Iris squealed when she saw Zelda and began flapping her arms so wildly she looked ready to lift off, but when Zelda came in for a sniff, she dove between Neil's legs.

Then, Zelda pulled Rafael onto the porch, where she pawed at the kitchen door and whined to be let in.

Caroline dropped her head onto Neil's shoulder and whispered, "I can't do this."

He pressed his lips to her temple. "Yes, you can."

She drew a deep breath and blinked. Then, she caught Victor's eye and nodded.

Victor clapped his hands together. "Well, welcome, everyone. I think everyone is here. Please follow me." He led the group around the barn and into the meadow. Annie and Cynthia walked behind him, followed by their husbands and children. Caroline followed with Neil carrying Iris, then Rafael, Zelda, Josseline, Chappy, Peter, Gwen, Donna, Julie, Kirby and Bella.

At the edge of the meadow, four maned wolves stood belly deep in little blue-stem grass, eying Zelda with curiosity. A monarch butterfly fluttered on orange and black wings above the grass.

Iris sang out, "Daddy, a bubberfly!"

"I see," he whispered, putting a finger to her lips, "but remember, it's quiet time."

"I DON'T WA-ANT KIET TIME!" She threw back her head and stiffened, gearing up for a tantrum.

Neil whispered, "Quiet girls get *ice cream* before bed, remember?"

Caroline jabbed him with her elbow. "We're stooping to bribery now?"

"All's fair in love, war and parenting a two-year-old."

Ahead, at the edge of the pond, stood a one-story building almost completely concealed by an earthen berm. Its roof was ablaze with goldenrod and deep blue asters. Wide, glass doors opening toward the pond were festooned with a wide, red ribbon tied in a festive bow. Potted blue asters surrounded the patio.

Several Blanding's turtles plopped into the water from their floating log, rippling the glassy surface. Annie and Cynthia took their seats on one bench with their husbands. Caroline and Neil faced them on the other. Neil opened a small tub of Cheerios and offered them to Iris who popped one into her mouth, tipped her face up to Caroline and whispered, "*Shhh, Mummy!* Kiet time girls get ice cream."

Victor stood with his back to the pond and waited for the rest of the group to arrange themselves in a loose semi-circle. Finally, he said, "This is an historic day for Ridge Park, for the VanWingen family and for the entire Saskawan community. But to honor Iris' wishes, we have made this a private gathering."

He paused before speaking again. "I've been thinking recently about the frailty of dreams. Years ago, as a young zoologist, I dreamed of running a first-class zoo that would focus on preserving threatened American species. But with limited resources, limited space, limited time, and perhaps my own limited imagination—my dreams gradually faded. I made do, worked with what I had and settled for less.

"Four years ago there were tantalizing glimpses of the dream—the promise of new land with more space—but it was only a cruel hoax. My dream, I thought, was shattered.

"I didn't know that one small monkey's visit to this farm was going to change everything. Back then, Iris VanWingen didn't like us very much and didn't mind saying so. She was a formidable adversary, but in the end she didn't stand a chance. You see, I had a pair of aces up my sleeve—Caroline Finch and Rafael Rojas. It was their patient diplomacy that convinced Iris to become Ridge Park's greatest champion and benefactor. Her gift of this farm three years ago changed my life and everyone else's here, most especially the animals you see around you. Ridge Park will continue to be a place to display, breed and rehabilitate exotic and endangered animals from around the world, but our focus will be on native wildlife, both animals and plants, who live among us again, as they have for thousands of years—Blanding's turtles, red-shouldered hawks, bald eagles, gray foxes, nine species of Michigan frogs, crows and chickadees. That's why we now call ourselves the Ridge

Park Zoo and Conservation Center.

"I should add here that Iris wasn't the only one to come under Caroline's spell that summer. She also managed to sweet talk Neil Stoddard out of his family's pristine woods, so we now cover ninety acres. Even my wildest dreams never came *close* to the reality we enjoy today."

Victor nodded at Iris' daughters. "So, today we celebrate your mother's remarkable life and dedicate the Walker/VanWingen Family Homestead and the new Iris Walker VanWingen Amphibian and Reptile Research Center in her memory. She worked long and hard to make it happen—supervising the work from the driver's seat of our golf cart. And, as you know, Iris was *very* comfortable in the driver's seat.

"Dreams are one thing, but expectations can be just as fragile. I *expected* Iris would be with us for this dedication. I heard the rumor that she was eighty-nine, but I refused to believe it. I saw only a woman bursting with energy and new ideas.

"Ann, Cynthia, you have said what great fun it was growing up on Willow Creek Farm. I know I speak for *all* of Saskawan when I say we are so very grateful that you are willing to share it with the rest of us."

Victor took a slow breath before continuing.

"Iris VanWingen was a scientist, a teacher, a writer and a lover of life in all its forms. Some called her a tree-hugger, a curmudgeon, an alarmist, but in the end, she proved to be a true optimist and the biggest dreamer of us all."

Victor stepped to one side and nodded at Caroline.

Caroline stood to take his place and let her gaze take in the group. Julie had slipped her arm through Peter's. Kirby's long limbs were wrapped around both Bella and Donna. Rafael stood rigid and stoic between his mother and Chappy, holding tightly to Zelda's leash. His eyes were fixed on some distant point.

Caroline began. "Little Houdini could not have picked a better place to take refuge on that summer morning almost four-and-a-half years ago. And, he could not have appreciated the impact his little escapade would have on all of us. That day, Iris VanWingen became a towering presence in my life. At first, she scared the *heck* out of me! Her wit was sharp and her tongue could be sharper. She was a fierce adversary, who became an even fiercer ally and, finally, the dearest of friends." Caroline looked up into the trees across the meadow and blew out a long breath. "Oh boy, do I miss her! When I'm struggling with some decision, I find myself reaching for the phone. 'Hey Iris, got a minute? Hey Iris, can I stop by?'"

Iris looked up at her mother with her mouth full of Cheerios. "Mummy?"

There were quiet chuckles as Neil pulled her onto his lap and whispered in her ear.

"We came dangerously close to losing this zoo, this farm, this meadow, these frogs and turtles—along with the beautiful mine property—to people who claimed to be our friends. If they had their way, this very spot would be the water hazard on the sixteenth hole. So, thank you, Iris VanWingen, Little Houdini, Rafael Rojas and, of course, my sensational husband, Neil Stoddard, for securing a very different future for this wild patch of West Michig—" She blinked up at the racing clouds and waited for calm to return.

"Iris would understand my tears—she always did—but I know she'd rather I—we—put our energy into the great work ahead of us. I'm sure that somewhere she's saying, 'Now that I'm gone, you'll all just have to work harder.'

"Iris wasn't religious in the traditional sense, but she was deeply *reverent*. 'Smell this?' she'd say, 'It's a spice bush.' 'Taste this; it's a wintergreen berry.' 'Hear that? That's the wood thrush, the troubadour of the north woods.' She held the whole world in awe, and that has had a profound influence on me.

"Iris didn't dwell on her declining health, but she did confide that she wanted to cross the finish line under her own power. Just a month ago, she and her Sas-U students released fourteen baby turtles born in this very pond into their new pond on the campus. Iris finished her race a winner.

"To you, Annie, Cynthia, your mother felt tremendous gratitude. Her gift of this farm to Ridge Park Zoo and Conservation Center is as much *your* gift to her. She loved you very, very much for that.

"And to my Ridge Park colleagues, I will say just this: Respect that is earned is the best kind. Iris recognized in you what she liked best about herself—a willingness to work against all odds and without any superpowers to make the world a better place for all God's creatures. She told me more than once what a great honor it was to work at your side."

Caroline paused for the lump in her throat to dissolve before continuing. "Five years ago, when I came to this zoo, I was alone, adrift and in grave doubt of my abilities. Iris opened my eyes and my ears. Most of all, she helped me discover the people and the work that makes my heart sing. I will never, never stop missing her. Thank you."

She took her seat and leaned into the warmth of Neil's embrace.

Annie stood then, hugging a blue and white pickle crock she'd found the barn. Then, she and Cynthia walked to the edge of the meadow and tipped their mother's ashes into the tall grass. An evening breeze lifted them up before releasing them back to the earth.

Caroline closed her eyes and let her fingers trace the newly-carved lettering on the bench.

Iris Walker VanWingen, 1930-2018

Then, she thanked the great flowing river of life for everything good and verdant in this world.

When she opened her eyes, Rafael was standing before her looking stiff and miserable.

"My mom wants me to tell you she brought *pupusas* for everyone," he said, avoiding her gaze.

Caroline rose to her feet and led him to the edge of the clearing. "Rafa, look at this place! Isn't it amazing? The turtles, the bees, the maned wolves in their grassy meadow. Miss Iris is *here*. She'll *always* be here." She took his hands in hers. "And she's in *us*, too. You and me. Always."

He sank into her then, and she held him gently until his shoulders stopped shaking.

"Wafa. Look! *Wafa*! " Iris was tugging at Rafael's pant leg, hoping for a playmate. "Look, Wafa, I got a *tone*." She held up a pebble she'd found between the flagstones.

Rafael dried his face on his shirtsleeve and knelt beside her.

"What have you found, Junior?" he asked, rolling the pebble between his thumb and index finger. "Ah-ha! This one's a keeper. It's a little piece of the moon."

Iris lifted her face and searched the darkening September sky. "The moon?"

"That's right, Iris. If you know what to look for, there's a story in every pebble."

NOTES & ACKNOWLEDGMENTS

Raised in Captivity is a work of fiction, but like many novels it has some basis in fact. In 2000, Fred Meijer, owner of the Meijer retail chain, offered a large tract of land just outside Grand Rapids, Michigan to John Ball Zoo. Unlike my nefarious duo, Tom and Paddy, Mr. Meijer's motives were purely philanthropic. Nevertheless, his offer led to a spirited debate about the merits of zoos and a public referendum. As with all meaty controversies, good people disagreed vehemently. In the end, voters turned down Mr. Meijer's offer, but in the meantime, we all learned a thing or two about zoos. Today, John Ball Zoo remains in the city and has expanded up and over a wooded hilltop with spectacular views of the city.

My fictional narrative was also inspired by local tales of a traveling circus that camped on a farm near the city's western edge. In 1978 "Big Sid," a 16-foot python, escaped, terrorizing the neighborhood before being recaptured several weeks later.

My characters are purely fictional, though Baba Dioum, a real Senegalese environmentalist, actually said, "In the end, we will conserve only what we love; we will love only what we understand; and we will understand only what we are taught." (I couldn't say it better, so I didn't try.) And, as far as I know, Lief Blomqvist, is still matchmaker to the world's captive population of snow leopards.

Comeback stories of critically endangered species—the black-footed ferret, the Mongolian wild horse, the Arabian oryx—are true and accurate to the best of my understanding, as are Caroline's stories of zoo escapes—except, of course, Little Houdini's.

Some of the animal characters are not quite fictional. Howl, the near-sighted barred owl, is much like a feathered resident of Blandford Nature Center in Grand Rapids. Magoo was the official Golden greeter at Fountain Street Church for many years. The real Zelda, complete with three white socks and crooked blaze, held an honored place in the Arnold household for fourteen happy years. I still miss her.

The city of Saskawan exists only in my imagination, but it reminds me of several West Michigan communities that have my full affection. Some of Iris' pioneer stories reflect the experiences of my New England and Dutch ancestors who settled in and around Kalamazoo and Grand Rapids. In Grand Rapids, gypsum mines left tunnels and sinkholes that are the stuff of legend (and children's nightmares). As this book went to press, a new mine sinkhole had just opened up near the banks of the Grand River in downtown Grand Rapids. Several old mines have been converted to cold storage facilities—though none to my knowledge has ever harbored a meth lab.

The real Fruit Ridge (or "the Ridge") has its center near the village of Sparta, Michigan and spreads over parts of Kent, Ottawa, Newaygo and Muskegon counties. Third Base, Last Stop Before Home, is a small grocery near Plainwell, Michigan with a name fit for borrowing. Finally, West Michigan's quirky weather, pioneer history, unique geology and diverse ecosystems are as factually accurate as an English major could make them.

Although I am a passionate gardener and outdoorsy type, I am neither a zoologist nor a degreed naturalist. I've done my best to present an accurate picture of the complex and vital work of modern zoos, which is too often sadly misunderstood.

So many people helped with this book for so long that I fear I may have forgotten some. Extra-special thanks and big bear hugs are due my wonderful and patient proofreader/editors, Lisa Annette Prentice and Shirley Thompson. Beyond their awesome technical contributions, their enthusiastic critiques always came just when I needed them most. I'm deep in debt to both of them. (Any lingering typos or grammatical bloopers are my own late additions.)

For their thoughtful comments on an unfinished manuscript, I thank my kids, Leah Arnold and Sam Arnold and Laura DeGrush, as well as Ruth Block and Joan Kullgren. They somehow saw beyond the awkward bits to understand my intent. Their insights, questions and opinions are more important than they know. I love them *all*.

I'm also grateful to Mary Jane Dockery, the founder of the Blandford Nature Center, Brenda Springer at John Ball Zoo and Ashley Wick at the Kalamazoo Nature Center who shared their considerable knowledge of geology, zoology and lepidoptera, respectively.

Several environmental groups have influenced my understanding of the natural world and my place in it. I am grateful to the Kalamazoo Nature Center, the Garfield Nature Center, the Kent/MSU Extension Master Naturalist Program, Blandford Nature Center and River City Wild Ones. They are all truly forces of nature.

This book could never have been written without two consummate storytellers—my parents, Betty and Ed Thompson. Mom captivated me with stories of her pioneer ancestors, while Dad's bedtime stories were remarkable works of improv fiction. They were also the first to call me "a writer." They were both decades ahead in their understanding of environmental issues. Dad argued precedent-setting environmental and land use cases in the courts, while Mom was a "master naturalist" long before there was an official designation. I am still in awe of them.

No one is happier to see *Raised in Captivity* out of my head and into print than my husband, Paul Steiner Arnold. Once again, he was my labor coach—a calm, steady presence reminding me to breathe. I am enormously grateful for the endless flow of creative ideas—and his beautiful cover-to-cover book design is the *best gift ever!* Like the ever-faithful prairie vole, he is my mate for life.

CPSIA information can be obtained
at www.ICGtesting.com
Printed in the USA
BVHW07s0108020718
520453BV00005B/13/P